WIND OF WRATH

Andrew

WIND OF
WRATH

The Old man

SLOANE SPENCER

[signature]

TIGERLAND PUBLISHING

TIGERLAND PUBLISHING
90 Harrowgate Road, London E9 5ED

Published 2002 by Tigerland Publishing

Copyright Simon Sloane and John A. Spencer

The right of Sloane Spencer to be identified as author of this work
has been asserted in accordance with sections 77 and 78
of the Copyright Designs and Patents Act 1988.

A catalogue record for this book is available from the British
Library.

ISBN 0–9543952–0–4

Digitally printed in Great Britain
By Intype London Ltd
Units 3/4 Elm Grove Industrial Estate
Elm Grove, Wimbledon SW19 4HE

To Emily

The Arabian Peninsula, 2000

It was an old story often told, one the young man at the side of the Doha road knew well. The ancient people, the story went, held no value in the land. Wealth for these nomads went on four legs, *at Allah*, 'God's gift,' the intractable camel. That was the story, that was the myth. He pulled the woolen djallaba closer around him. The cold of the desert night bit deep. Dawn was still an hour away.

The man looked along the road once more, back towards the Saudi border. No movement, no lights. They would come though. He was sure of that.

The myth had served the Ruler well. That huge family, all those holy relatives who compounded themselves logarithmically by the day, by the hour. This breed had substituted Range Rovers and Hummers for the lowly beast, couldn't even walk across the street without four wheels.

He looked up at the black night again. Just stars. Like sand, millions of specks of shimmering sand. The Ruler had looted the young man's and his brothers' birthright. He had tossed his rights at the feet of the Americans who, knowing no better, had trampled them underfoot.

A faint scratching in the sand broke into the man's reverie. A tiny sand cricket deceived by the stillness above struggled to the desert's surface. The moon's orb, suspended brilliantly above, reflected a dull silver on the insect's wing-case. The cricket rested, its body coiled. The young man watched it for a moment then turned away, lifting the Russian-surplus nightscope he held to his eye. The sudden movement released a trigger in the tiny insect. Its accordioned legs sprung open and sent it flying into the center of the road where it rested once more.

The man pointed the nightscope down the valley as he had done a dozen times already that night, the ragged skyline of Doha showing pale in the circle of his vision. Tilting the barrel up, he raised the sight towards the monstrous shape out on the water, the vessel's myriad lights glittering like opals. The lights began to vibrate, shaking in spite of the firm grip he held on the device. I am cold, he told himself; that is all. Cold.

As if in answer his secret voice said: Do this. Do this for him. "Be loyal to thy tribe, to its spirit." Now was the time to begin. A survivor, he had become a leader of the men. Now he would lead. God is God, God is good.

Six new moons rose over the hump of the road, the headlights of three vehicles isolating the standing figure from the empty landscape. The lead vehicle of the convoy, a camouflaged box-shaped missile launcher, slowed to a halt. Pulling the djallaba tightly round his shoulders he opened the launcher's passenger door, his body obscuring the royal insignia painted on its side for a moment, then pulled himself into the heated cab. The door closed, the vehicle picked up speed, its two support vehicles following down the long slope to the city.

Silence returned to the desert, the cold hand of night settling again on its heart. The sand cricket so recently emerged from the safety of the sand lay crushed on the road, its black carcass indistinguishable from the asphalt to which it was now eternally joined. High above, a miniature planet, its metallic gleam quite visible to the naked eye, flashed through the deadly cold of space, its eye noting the movements below. In a tracking room at Langley, Virginia, eight and half thousand miles away, the central mainframe received the encrypted data from the orbiting satellite and added it to the summary that would be run out for analysts on the morning watch, the intelligence already history.

CHAPTER 1

The Hindu Kush

The wheel-less pickup sat at the side of the road, the familiar Toyota logo on the tailgate just visible through the grime. A man sat on the flat bed facing them, his head sunk in his chest, his back against the cab. Lis thought he would look up as they drove by. She assumed their passing would be an event in these desolate ranges of brown hills. Then, in the same instant, she realised that he wouldn't, ever. A piece of electric cable wrapped round his chest held his body upright. The man's face was blackened, his mouth hanging grotesquely open, a weight attached to the lower jaw. His hands had been severed at the wrists, his feet at the ankles.

"A dealer of drugs," the driver yelled over the roar of the engine. Lis said nothing. She had spent the trip from Miram Shah staring straight ahead, not wanting to engage the driver. More than once she'd had to brace herself against the frame of the truck as they swung round one more perilous bend to avoid falling against him.

They had set off at six, the turbaned driver and Lis in front, a gun-toting bodyguard in the back. Neither man had given his name nor had asked hers. The vehicle a familiar "Hi-Lux" had stopped in front of the hostel as scheduled and she had climbed in.

"American?" the driver asked. Lis shook her head. Satisfied, the man had slipped a cassette into the truck's deck and for the last five hours they had listened to the endless whine of an Imam preaching against the West.

Tarred road had abruptly given way to impossibly rough track. The sun had risen hot behind them. She had not been able to sleep. Stomach-wrenching precipices had opened up to one side or the other as they climbed into the mountains. Once, a figure had appeared in the road ahead, waving them to a stop. There was no habitation visible, no reason for the checkpoint, just an invitation to pull over backed up by a brandished AK-47. The driver had ignored the man and his pointed gun, recklessly it seemed to Lis. These were the same people who had hung Mujadidi Najibullah and his brother, Shahpur Ahmadzai, by wire from a concrete post outside the presidential palace in Kabul. That was after they had dragged their former president by his heels through the streets of Kabul from the back of a jeep then shot him through the head. At some point the Taliban had also cut out the men's testicles, a butchering the militant peasants usually reserved for their livestock.

For the first time since they had left Miram Shah, watching the wreck's image recede in the wing mirror now, Lis Charnay allowed herself to think the unthinkable: she shouldn't be doing this, shouldn't be here alone. She craved the sense of detachment she got on these assignments, the feeling that she was lost without trace, beyond recall; but this time she was feeling something closer to panic. The cab of the truck smelled of unwashed body even with the windows rolled down. The constant rocking and turning was beginning to affect her. She had a desperate sense that sooner or later she was going to be found out. The sight of the blackened figure in the back of the truck left her in no doubt what her fate might be if her discoverers didn't like what they found. She pulled up the collar of her shirt and wrapped the black head-scarf more tightly round her face.

Lis, always Elise to her mother God rest her mean little spirit, was thirty, defiantly single and presently Near-Asian correspondent for Cable News Network. There had been a time when that last fact might have counted for something. Now, it only meant that since she was somewhere between Peshawar and Athens she might as well cover whatever had just come up or down on the Afghan border, too. Those were the economies that currently prevailed in electronic news gathering. Get the footage, get it cheap, get it fast, get out. Nobody cares that much anymore, anyway. It's just so much noise. We do it for ourselves, she encouraged her friend and soul-mate Tim Short, a newspaper journalist, when he had gloomily wondered over his second or third Guinness what the point of it all was. We do it for us, she repeated.

She wasn't doing it for the footage, that was for sure. She had left the cameraman and his expensive camera at the Pearl Continental Hotel in Peshawar, left him the new Global Star cell phone the network was handing out these days, then moved into Green's. Green's was where the hippies on the hashish trail used to hang out in the sixties. Now, it was a temporary, sometimes terminal home for street-dealers in cheap weapons and cheaper opium that washed over the Afghan border like a tidal wave.

It wasn't her choice but she was less visible here. She was a Westerner even though she'd been born to the sound of gunfire in Beirut as her Lebanese mother continually reminded her father, challenging him to do something about it. Her father had finally done just that, leaving their meagre apartment in Cyprus from which he monitored the Middle East for French Radio, taking only his Nagra tape-deck. She had never seen him again.

And she carried a US passport. She and her mother had gone to the States after Cyprus, her mother marrying again to ensure nationality for Elise and a comfortable retirement for herself in Florida, then, in a bitter irony, dying there of skin cancer soon after. Lis had gone on to Northwestern University, then Columbia, then back to the Middle East.

Most of all though, she was a woman. There were no women allowed here, no women who did what she did anyway. It was only her darkly boyish looks and almost passable Pashto that had let her get this far.

Lis had arrived in Peshawar five weeks before, joining the queue of foreign journalists who were needlessly risking their lives to get across the border and get an interview with whoever was currently claiming to hate Uncle Sam and had the wherewithal to do something about it. You could basically make up whatever you wanted in this trackless quarter. No one could ever verify the authenticity of your claim. It hadn't taken Lis long to figure out that most of the leads she and the others came up with were just locals gouging the Westerners for another roll of dollar bills.

She had hooked up with a Pakistani cameraman who had led her to Yusuf, a reporter on The Peshawar News. Visits to the paper's dingy offices two blocks from Green's, long conversations over countless little cups of strong, sweet tea had led to the arrangement of a meeting with a local warlord for an on-camera interview. Possibly. Be patient. Then she had got the call.

Yusuf had telephoned. It was on, he had said, but there were conditions.

"How much?" Lis asked, her own voice echoing back to her in the silence of the scruffy hotel lobby where she had taken the call.

"No, not money. No camera. Just you."

"But he'll give an interview? The commander?" It was still worth it.

There was a pause. Lis watched a line of dusty pickups go by the hotel. After the bombing of training camps at Khost – or whatever it was the CIA thought the meagre collection of huts in the hills represented – a price had supposedly been put on every Westerner's head in Peshawar. Everyone including Lis had been jumpy ever since though as far as she knew the story was just one more rumour. She still couldn't help pressing herself back against the wall.

Yusuf broke in. "That is his message"

Yusuf gave her the arrangements: where to stay in Miram Shah, when to expect a contact. She had made the journey to the border town that same day. The hostel Yusuf had picked out made Green's seem like a palace. She had ended up sleeping on the floor in spite of the bugs. Then, last night, a boy had shown up at her door and told her to be ready.

The hollow sound of an explosion echoing off the walls of the mountain pass they had crested brought her back to the present. She ducked involuntarily then looked up to see the white flag, its green letters spelling out the timeless message: There is no God but God.

The Toyota slid to a stop at the main gate of a compound, actually just a break in the wire. A barren mound of earth with the name of the camp spelled out in whitewashed stones – Darunta. Hundreds of dispossessed seventeen and eighteen-year old Pakistani youths arrived here by the busload and at other camps along the border to receive religious and small arms instruction. If they hung around long enough and survived the live-fire training, they were given instruction in the use of more advanced weapons: rocket-launchers, anti-aircraft guns, even fighter aircraft. For most of the unemployed young men, the camps promised regular food, a comfortable bed and immediate employment in the Taliban front-line.

A boy, fourteen at most, took the crumpled identity pass Yusuf had given Lis, studied it intently. His dark eyes lifted from the paper and scrutinised her face. There was no curiosity in the gaze, no malice. Lis realised he probably couldn't even read. The boy slung his Kalashnikov, its magazine held on by duct-tape, and waved their vehicle through.

As they drove across the plateau to a huddle of buildings on the other side, some of them little more than piles of rubble, Lis picked out the source of the recent explosion. The charred wreck of a car, flames still licking at the window frames, sat off to one side of the track. A little way beyond, a small group of men watched, lean hands shielding their eyes from the harsh noon sun. The spectators wore robes cut rigorously short above their ankles. The exception was a tall black man. He wore military fatigues. His outstretched arm, carrying what looked like a TV remote slowly dropped to his side.

His name, as Lis would learn, much, much later, was Elhassan and he was, as only a fellow-American could recognise, a "cowboy." Elhassan had been a "shooter" from the old days in Beirut. Born in Philadelphia as Washington Harvey he had drifted out of the U.S. Army and into the war in Lebanon in the '80s, on to the Afghanistan-Russian conflict in 1986, then to Bosnia and Chechnya along with many other graduates of the Afghani mujahedeen. In his long migration Elhassan had learned many useful lessons, among them rigging car bombs. He watched the truck and its passengers as it wove its way across the bomb-pitted plain and then stop at the first low building.

Lis waited for someone to make a move but neither the driver nor the bodyguard behind got out, the engine still running. Was it a test of some kind? She stayed put too, waiting for someone to give them a command. Then, a willowy figure in a loose white shirt appeared in the doorway of the building. He stood in the shadow, observing her for a moment, as if trying to decide. A desert wind blew across the dry plain picking up dust and wisps of acrid smoke from the demolished car. She put her hand up to her face for a second to shield her eyes. Then, the man was standing next to the window, slightly behind her so she had to turn awkwardly to see him properly.

"You are American?" the man asked.

Lis looked at the man's hand holding onto the door handle. It was slender, the nails manicured, a bureaucrat's hand. Then she caught his reflection in the wing mirror. It wasn't anyone she recognised.

"No," she said.

"But you are with an American news station."

The voice was liquid, slightly accented but not noticeably. Arab, yes. Maybe went to an American school. There was a hint of something.

"I work for myself," she said. "Freelance." It wasn't true but if this was a test, she had no intention of failing it. If he knew the truth already, she didn't really have anything to lose. "Can I get out?"

The man's hand stayed by the handle. It could have been yes or no. She waited.

"Is he here?" she ventured; "the man I have come to see? I was promised an interview."

There was a sound of small-arms fire from across the plain then the swoosh of a grenade-launcher or small rocket and the crump of an explosion. Lis looked for the origin of the sound. When she turned her head back the man had come round to the front of the window and was looking straight down on her.

Except for a livid scar across the right eye, it was an unremarkable face, the face of a man who would tell you the best way to the hotel in a Cairo street or bring you coffee at an outdoor café in Paris.

"The commander," she went on; "is he here?"

"He is not."

She reached for the door handle and yanked it impatiently. His hand slapped down hard on the panel, pushing the door closed again before she'd even got it half open. "He has a message that you will take with you." He reached into the waist pocket of his loose shirt and pulled out a videocassette, passing it through the window to her.

"What is it? I'm a journalist, not a messenger. Deliver it yourself."

"You have been chosen." The man said no more, his black eyes ranging over her half-hidden face. He seemed to be exploring her, feeling her out.

"It is a warning," he said at last. "Attacks on innocent people can not go unanswered. This is our answer. You will see. We are not animals. We give warnings, not like Americans."

The man slapped the panelling again and on cue the driver set the pickup in drive and swung the vehicle back up the track they had come down not ten minutes before.

"Wait," Lis said angrily. "I haven't finished here." But they were already travelling at speed. She twisted round in her seat to get a last look. The man was still there standing just beyond the doorway of the building, motionless.

She looked down at the cassette in her hands, looking for a clue. There was no label, no indication of the tape's contents. The driver plugged in his audiocassette again and the whine of the Imam resumed. Lis look back once more but the man had gone.

From the upstairs room, Ibrahim, the man who had talked with Lis, watched the pickup clear the rise and start back down towards the gate, watched the black man, Elhassan, towering over his students, walk away from the wreck of the smoking car towards the barracks.

"I," he said quietly. "I am the messenger."

CHAPTER 2

Washington D.C.

"We are talking to American people. We are talking to American mothers of soldiers, to American mothers."

The voice was quietly insistent, high in pitch and a little hoarse as if the advice the speaker was giving was as painful to him as it must be to his intended audience.

"We do not differentiate between Americans who are dressed in military uniforms and those who are not. All are targets in this fatwa. To kill Americans and their allies is an individual duty of every Muslim who is able, in any country where this is possible until American soldiers, shattered and broken-winged, depart from all the lands of Islam."

The man was perhaps forty. His wild beard was streaked with grey, the features in the long face beginning to droop. But the eyes were clear. They were the eyes of a believer, sure in the faith that what they saw was the true light, the path of righteousness. The man looked down at his hands, as if looking for guidance, then up again.

"We predict a black day for America." The subtitled warning lingered on the screen for a second, then the camera pulled back, revealing the makeshift library that served as a backdrop, the shelves filled with old encyclopaedias. The wrinkled map of the world taped to the whitewashed wall suddenly

took on an ominous significance. The battered AK-47 leaning against the wall was too close to his lean hand to be there only for decoration.

"That's the message that`s being sent to the West from Afghanistan tonight. There doesn't seem to be any question, given the mood here, that he means what he says. Whether his threat will prove to have any substance remains to be seen. This is Lis Charnay for CNN in Peshawar, Pakistan." The sound from the monitor went dead, the image cutting away.

Jay Peterson, sitting in his office in the "bull pen," put the remote down and picked up a copy of al-Hayat. This would cost them he knew that. This would cost them.

Jay was lead analyst on the recently minted FBI. Special Task Force, its sole mission to locate and apprehend the world's leading terrorists. A cop's job, Jay thought snapping open the paper, this whole thing. Jay knew cops, he'd grown up downtown in Baltimore. It had been a long roundabout journey to this smart new office at the Bureau certainly – scholarships, mentors – but he hadn't forgotten the way cops always worked.

He'd been out there, spent time in Islamabad, in Cairo. He'd tried to get into their shoes, tried to see it their way. When the US arbitrarily targeted a pharmaceutical plant in the Sudan then blew it off its foundations because it might be a manufacturing site for VX elements, Jay knew what the people in Khartoum were thinking. He'd been six when white cops had bust down the door of their row house and dragged his old man out by his heels, his head bumping on the steps; one, two, three. That sort of thing made a lasting impression.

"Hey there." It was Jeff Cohen, one of Jay's staffers in the group. Cohen's U-Penn T-shirt was black with sweat. He swung his backpack to the floor of the cubicle across from the open door to Jay's office, set a cup of coffee and a bagel on the desk. There were already three other staffers at their desks; the rest would be there within the hour.

"Running?" Jay asked pointlessly.

"Yup. Seven minutes!" Cohen said triumphantly, flopping in his chair, glad to be asked. "Just over seven."

"You start at home?"

"Yup."

"Nice going."

The bull pen could have been any corporate group in any headquarters. A perimeter of glass-walled offices around a central maze of cubicles separated by chest-high oatmeal-coloured partitions. It was material evidence of the administration's commitment to its anti-terrorism mission: a fraction of the billions allocated to protect America from its worst nightmare. Clean offices to fight a dirty war. Even this early, seven a.m., the bull pen's anxious heart beat softly. Its ear was very much to the ground. Fax machines received and stored station reports from around the globe, the insistent beep of e-mail alerts claimed immediate attention, telephones rang, voice-mail recorders kicked in. It was a trading floor of information with no opening or closing hours. The market was just about to get rocked.

"How the fuck did she get in there?"

The explosion from the corridor preceded the entry of Bob Lorenz, Assistant Director of the FBI's National Security Division and Jay's boss. A bullet of a man in his late fifties, he was the Bureau's single greatest asset. His attack-dog manner was tempered only by his fierce loyalty to the Bureau and his determination to see justice served. He brooked no opposition, and took no prisoners. He deferred only to his boss, the Director of the FBI, also a New Yorker. Lorenz's failing, one he willingly confessed to, was his political naïveté, a weakness Washington did not easily forgive. It was Lorenz's job to oversee all counterterrorism operations but he had made the apprehension of Osama bin Laden and the others his personal crusade. He took any militant's threats personally.

"How come little Miss CNN can skip into Central Asia with her camera and lights and we don't even know where they are from one day to the next?"

Lorenz was followed by his long-suffering assistant, Barbara Huber, and a few remaining task-force staffers he had swept up on his way to the bull pen. Bringing up the rear was a silver-haired, immaculately turned-out man Jay didn't recognise.

Lorenz barked an angry "In here" at the raised heads in the bull pen and led his entourage into Jay's office like an invasion force.

"Good Morning, Bob," Jay said.

"It isn't and it won't be until I get some answers," Lorenz snapped back. Barbara squeezed in behind her boss giving Jay a knowing smile. It was going to be one of those days.

"Jay," she said sweetly indicating Lorenz's suave companion. "This is John Enrico, your new counterpart at the CIA John, this is Jay Peterson. He heads up the analysis section here."

Jay stretched a hand across his desk. "Pleased to meet you," Enrico said. The voice was smooth, polite, but the blue eyes said: "Beginner."

Jay knew the dogs on Capitol Hill must be snapping at Lorenz's heels. This had happened before when ABC got its crew into Afghanistan for a face-to-face with Osama bin Laden. Now, they were out for him again. Enrico's presence made that very clear. Lis Charnay's report had run late last night, was repeating now on the early morning editions. It included coverage of the drug trade in and out of Afghanistan and commentary on the support of the warlords of the traffic. They needed the cash to finance their ongoing war against the insurgents in the north. As CNN's correspondent had pointed out, the one promise that had been made the Afghani people, a cessation of the war, had turned out to be false. That wasn't the part that was upsetting Lorenz though.

"It was a tape," Jay said.

"What do you mean?" Lorenz shot back.

"We already checked. It's a tape. She made the feed from Peshawar, did the stand-up afterwards. They delivered a cassette and she just worked it into her piece."

Lorenz's square face cleared, the thick eyebrows straightening. That was better news. "A tape." With no apologies and no explanations, Lorenz shifted gears and addressed the company. "This is John Enrico. He's at the CIA In case you didn't already know they are our strategic partners in this matter. What's theirs is ours. Right, John?"

"Pretty much," the silver-head nodded deferentially.

"John and his team have a strike-force on standby. What are they, John? A Delta team?"

Enrico let the question pass. "We're in the same business as you all." The delivery, in contrast to Lorenz's staccato, was polished, a father explaining a complex issue to his teenagers. "Whether it's our strike force or the millions your Director has put up for their apprehension that does the job is irrelevant. What matters is that we stop these very dangerous elements from continuing their operations."

Jay knew that wasn't really what mattered to Enrico. In spite of all the sweet talk, the rivalry that had existed for so long between the CIA and the FBI had not ended with the reconciliation crafted by the Justice Department. The reorganisation that had given the FBI oversight of foreign operations, once the exclusive preserve of the CIA, was considered an insult by many at the Agency. Enrico was clearly one of them. Beneath the veneer of co-operation there existed some deep-seated distrust and a deal of jealousy.

Jay looked round the cramped office at his assembled staff then back to Lorenz.

"Bob. We've been over this ground before. I'm not sure this latest broadcast changes anything."

Lorenz waited impatiently for the rest, his hand moving involuntarily to the picture of Jay's sister, Dana, on the desk. He picked it up, looked unseeingly at the uniformed figure pictured in the frame then set it down again.

"We only have circumstantial evidence to show that Al Qaida were behind the bombings in Sudan and Kenya," Jay went on; "and the testimony of the convicted foot soldiers. We've never substantiated a direct monetary link between them and Ramzi Yusef. For all we know, the last time they were active was in the '80s, financing shelters for the muja-hedeen in Pakistan. We don't even know if they've run out of funds."

Lorenz said nothing. Jay was right. It was old ground and they had fought over it long and hard many times before.

"Are you saying that Al Qaida should not be a target?" It was Enrico.

Jay studied the question for a moment then its author. "No. That's not what I'm saying," he answered quietly. "I'm saying that we have no hard evidence to show that they are anything more than what they appear to be: charismatic cheerleaders. All they have to do is sound the call and leave it to any one of a thousand groups anywhere, groups we don't have any hint of, to carry out the attack. It could be over there, it could be right here. Chemical or explosive, or both."

"But we know that a chemical or biological attack is beyond the capability of most of these groups, don't we Jay?" The question sounded condescending. Jay rose to the bait.

"How do we know? We've had strong indications that they may have outstayed their welcome in Afghanistan, may already have taken up residence in Baghdad. We know that Saddam has stockpiled constituents of VX and anthrax. That's a dangerous combination."

"So what are you saying?"

"An attack could come out of anywhere anytime. As long as we have assets in the Gulf, we're vulnerable. Look at Al Khobar. My own guess is that the next one will be here at home. They did it before with Ramzi Yousef, they'll do it again. It's a matter of pride."

"That kind of makes your job here a little beside the point, doesn't it Jay?" Again the smooth delivery covering a sharp edge.

"Our job is to identify individuals or groups who mean us harm, Mr. Enrico, whether that's overseas or right here at home. It may be bin Laden, it could be someone else. We have to understand them, understand their motives, their possible targets and provide that information to people best able to act on it. Like you, Mr. Enrico."

Lorenz beamed. His star pupil was going head-to-head with the CIA and winning points. The earlier embarrassment of the broadcast was completely forgotten. All that mattered now was that Lorenz and his beloved Bureau could hold their heads up. "Okay," he said abruptly. "Show's over. Let's get on with it." Lorenz shoved his way out of Jay's office, Barbara in tow. Enrico hesitated before following them out.

"Your wife?" he asked, indicating the picture of Dana.

"My sister," Jay said. "She's a plane captain on the Truman. They're in the Gulf."

"I can see why you'd be worried."

Jay studied Enrico's face for some clue of what he was really saying but saw none.

"She can look after herself," Jay said.

"I'm sure," Enrico said and followed Lorenz out into the hall.

CHAPTER 3

Qatar, the Persian Gulf. 05.00

The USS Harry S. Truman, CV75, flag ship of the US Navy's Twelfth Carrier Battle Group, was a floating city one third of a mile long, its population over 6,000. From the shore of Qatar three kilometres off, its superstructure ablaze, the Truman washed the eastern horizon with its own false dawn. Its panoply of armaments, eighty combat aircraft, rack on rack of missiles and bombs, nuclear and conventional, cast a sinister shadow for a thousand miles out.

Commander Bill Kobel, keeping the dawn watch on the starboard wing of the Flag bridge high above the blue-green waters of the Gulf, took no comfort in the thought. Kobel commanded one of the group's air wings, a squadron of Super-Tomcats. The Hawkeye was already aloft, the Combat Air Patrol making another sweep. Kobel scoured the horizon for his two jets but saw only the dirty ribbon of Doha's waterfront. Brown air hung over the cement and fertiliser plants that sprawled across the barren terrain behind the city. The bump of Aba al-Bawl, at three hundred and forty five feet, Qatar's highest point and not much above Kobel's sightline, poked through the haze. Between ship and shore, a flotilla of small craft trafficked the waters: sailing dhows, motor launches and oil barges. The Truman would be better off at sea where they could track any incoming threat with time to spare. In here, so close to Doha, she was a target. Not for sophisticated armaments but for something dumb; an oil barge rigged to explode on contact, an ambush against one of the carrier's launches ferrying the few crew members willing to squander precious shore leave into town. This was the Truman's third day on post and Kobel would be happy if it was her last.

Dana Peterson had been up since three but hadn't seen the daylight yet. Slight and serious she was one of the US Navy's "fast-burners," at twenty seven already a Plane Captain in an environment where competition for promotion was a contact sport and being a woman still a serious handicap. A small furrow creased her brow as she read.

"Hey, girl. Don't you ever quit?" Dee Kipling, the weapons specialist on her team, was standing in the mess-room door in cutaway T-shirt and shorts. Dana flipped the book shut and shifted down to let Dee in.

"Carlos! Where's those eggs at?" Dee yelled towards the galley as she squeezed onto the bench seat. Dee flipped over Dana's book to read the jacket. "'Qatar: Its Land, Its People?' Are you permanently damaged, girl, or is this something that you're going to get over real soon?" Dana smiled her shy smile, said nothing. Carlos appeared with a plate of eggs and ham for Dee in one hand, a pot of coffee in the other.

"More coffee there, Dana?" he asked filling Dee's cup at the same time.

"No thanks, Carlos; I'm fine."

Carlos gave Dee a sly wink that said he thought so, too.

Dee wasn't going to let that one go by. "Get back in your greasy kitchen, you pathetic little chilli pepper." Carlos retreated. Dee and her fellow crewmen, Jared, Iasi and the others were fiercely protective of their chief. Especially Iasi.

"That brother of yours remember your birthday?"

"He sure did," Dana smiled holding up the book.

"He sent you that?" Dee said incredulously. Dana nodded. There had been a cassette too, Jay's home-made video taped at his apartment on Capitol Hill. Birthday greetings, Jay singing the song alone, grinning wildly, then a serious lecture on the risks run by US personnel ashore. March was Haj month. Over two million Muslims from all over the world would be making their pilgrimage to the holy sites in Saudi Arabia. That raised another smile. Jay didn't want her going ashore so he sent her the guidebook instead. Just like Jay.

"Who'd want to go ashore in this armpit anyway?", Dee said. "Dubai yes, Bahrain anytime. But Doha? Please. So, what's on the menu today?" she asked, weighing in to the ham and eggs.

"They've got the local dignitaries coming to look at a plane prep on C Deck at 08:00. Me and Iasi can handle that. You work on that Tomcat topside."

The day was both Dana's birthday and the Ruler of Qatar's. This latter fact had given some sales-happy admiral at the Pentagon the bright idea that this would be a perfect opportunity to bring the Truman into Doha Harbour. There had been objections, of course. But, the Defence Security Assistance Agency, the Pentagon's thinly-disguised sales force, had given the thumbs up. The only weapon that could get under the Truman's skirt was a Hughes Sargasso missile and only the Saudis had those, they reassured the faint-hearted.

24

The DSA had sold the advance technology to King Fahd as a sweetener to secure a record order for combat aircraft in the face of fierce competition. All other resistance had been drowned out by contemplation of the potential upside: access to Qatar's vast gas reserves offshore and the future security of the brigade's-worth of equipment stored in the sheikhdom against a repeat of Desert Storm. A no-brainer.

Carlos came back carrying a single blueberry muffin on a plate. He set it before Dana. One lit candle flickered on top of the muffin. "Happy birthday Dana," Carlos said.

"Hey, thanks Carlos," Dana said blowing out the candle.

"Make a wish?"

"Already did," she said.

The Truman's morning intelligence report included a summary of satellite surveillance of the hinterland behind Doha as well as the east and west shorelines of the Gulf. It had turned up nothing out of the ordinary. On the Flag bridge, the ship's senior intelligence officer, Carole Choh, handed the faxed sheet over to the captain without comment. An earlier signal that a mobile missile launcher had gone missing from the notoriously poorly-guarded Saudi weapons-park at al Hufuf had been cancelled.

"Anything new on the local front, Carole?" Captain Durling asked.

"Nothing forthcoming, sir."

"Let's make another overfly then, just to be sure."

The Air Boss acknowledged the order and dispatched the two Tomcats already aloft to check the area behind the port one more time.

"We've got company," Kobel announced from the wing of the bridge. The officers watched the visitors stepping out of the Sea Stallion helicopter on to the flight deck far below. Black robes flapped wildly in the down-draft from the still-turning rotors revealing brilliant white thobes underneath. For a moment it seemed as if the men wearing them might take off, too.

Two rusted iron gates guarded the abandoned cement works out towards Umm Said, twelve kilometres to the south-east of Doha. The young man from the Doha Road sheltered in the cool wedge of shade thrown by the arch above and watched the dark silhouettes of the two US Navy jets fading down the wadi. A trickle of sweat ran down his face. The day was already stiflingly hot.

Saeed bin Sayyaf squeezed back through the gate into the courtyard behind. The compound was silent, abandoned months before by its bankrupt owners, but not empty. Against the far wall, hidden from the air by the deep shadow of the derelict cement-batcher and their own protective netting, three vehicles were parked in a rough triangle. Their dark grey bodywork was covered by fine white dust but the military insignia of the Royal House of Saud was still faintly visible. Forming the base of the triangle was a box-shaped missile-launcher, its bed levelled by hydraulic lifts at its corners and centre. The anxious face of the driver was just visible under the netting. Above the cab, three metallic missile tips painted Day-Glo orange gleamed like exotic fruits. Two other vehicles flanked the missile launcher, a generator truck and a command-and-control vehicle, a driver behind the wheel of each, two other men standing outside.

Saeed nodded to them, trying to hold down his growing apprehension, hoping it didn't show. The men began stripping the camouflage netting from the launcher.

In the body of the command-and-control vehicle a satellite technician, a Russian, was already seated at the console. He had figured that once the satellite guidance had been engaged and the target was "hot," they could expect a grace period of at best fifteen to twenty seconds before the electronic sweep of their target's surveillance would pick up the lock and trigger the vessel's automatic defence systems. Count a further five seconds, at the outside, for the Truman's Sea Sparrows to launch; that would give the team about forty seconds to aim, target, fire and evacuate the area before, as the technician gleefully emphasised, "di shit hits di fan." Assuming, of course, that the Americans were crazy enough to let loose over Qatari soil.

No escape plan had been discussed, no exit route given. Saeed had assured them all that Allah would provide. Only the Russian technician seemed unconvinced and had double-counted the wad of US dollars Saeed had handed him.

The Russian tilted the joystick on the console and the dish on the vehicle's roof swung obediently. He pulled a disk from a sweat-stained breast pocket and inserted it into the console's drive. The drive clunked metallically for a second then stopped. The codes had been accepted, the satellites engaged. Saeed waited patiently at his shoulder. The Russian looked back. "Bloody brilliant, ya?" he said, his enthusiasm for the moment overcoming his nervousness. Saeed said nothing, simply passed him a folded sheet of paper. The technician flattened the paper on the desktop then keyed the co-ordinates into the launcher's computer. The server crunched its equations, relaying the instructions to the Sargossos' telemetry and activating the warheads. The launcher was armed and aimed. Saeed took a last look at his watch: 8:30.

Dana and her team stood out in front of the Tomcats parked on the starboard side of the rear hangar deck. Over the last months, especially since Iasi's arrival, they had developed an understanding that went beyond camaraderie. Iasi Constanta, a bear of a man, red hair covering his barrel chest and trunk-like arms, rarely spoke. His skill as a mechanic was exceeded only by his loyalty to Dana. The visitors in front of them, the four Arabs and their advisors, paid little attention to Dana or her team, didn't even seem to care about the Tomcat towering over them.

The huge doors on each side of the hangar had been rolled back giving them all an open view of the Gulf to one side and the dusty skyline of Doha on the other. On an operational day the lifts from the flight deck would be functioning, the pistons of the catapults crashing, the engines of the planes readying for launch running up. Now, there was only the faint whistle of the huge ventilation fans. The black-robed guest-of-honour looked at his gold Rolex pointedly then whispered something to his companions. It appeared they wanted to leave before they had properly arrived.

In the darkened "watch" section of the Truman's tracking room, the Combat Information Centre, the Anti-Air Warfare officer's intent face was lit by a blue glow from the huge illuminated situations board and the greenish tint of the radar consoles. A low electric hum filled the air. At one side of the room, two of the Sonar Controllers were talking in low voices. The urgent ring of a phone interrupted the measured calm. An enlisted man picked it up and passed it to the officer.

"Booth," the man said into the phone. "Still negative? Thanks, Carole." As Booth passed the receiver back, another more strident bell began to chime.

"Lock! We have a lock," the sonar operator beside him yelled, his eyes fixed on the screen in disbelief. The double digital display above the console tumbled through an eight-figure series before coming to rest on the cross-co-ordinates that the ship's radar had determined as the source of the hostile radar lock. The Hawkeye's radar, their "eye-in-the-sky" 30,000 feet above the ship, confirmed instantaneously. The automatic defence system began locking on.

The sudden and simultaneous explosions from the transporter in the cement works, followed by the successive blasts of fiery heat from the launcher's exhausts, turned the enclosure in a second into an inferno, scorching the exposed skin of the men outside and coating them in a sticky layer of fine white dust. The three rockets burst one after another from their tubes at two-second intervals, rocking the launcher sideways and back on its suspension. The men in the compound covered their ears protectively, their bodies crouched and turned away from the blast, their ear-drums shattering. The projectiles accelerated violently into the desert sky, burning a trail of acrid smoke in the heated air then dropped, falling spectacularly over the low horizon to their programmed trajectory forty feet above the ground.

Three kilometres off the coast, Bill Kobel, still patiently keeping watch on the Truman's bridge, became the only member of the Truman's 6,054 complement to see the brilliant flash of the first missile as it skimmed the roof of the Al Wakrah Hotel and flattened out over the water at less than ten feet above the surface. It took five seconds, the longest Kobel had ever lived, for the sleek silver tube to cross the water, roaring by the oil barge and then dodging a returning launch. For an instant, as the missile disappeared below the level of the deck, Kobel thought it might somehow have passed miraculously through the ship. Then the sudden and huge impact as it hit the starboard side ten feet above the water line, threw him hard against the bridge housing, breaking his collarbone.

Dee Kipling, working on the artillery of a Tomcat on deck, was hurled forwards along the aircraft's wing then flattened by a second explosion as the charge in the missile's nose ignited one of the vessel's side aviation fuel compartments and threw a huge fireball up and over the side of the Truman's flight deck.

Instantaneously, the clattering howl of the Phalanxes, the six-barrelled close-in defences in the gun pits, drowned out the dull boom as the first Sea Sparrow connected with its target, the last of three missiles, 2,500 meters out. The machine-guns hurled a wall of lead at the remaining projectile headed for the Truman's side, the spray of unspent ammunition cutting a swathe through the scattered fleet of small boats sheltering between the Truman and the shore before destroying the speeding missile in a flash of high explosive directly over the lumbering oil barge. The air shook again and again as a column of burning crude erupted straight upwards, a flaming pillar in the sky raining fire for a hundred meters around.

In the seconds following the missile's impact secondary explosions cracked along the hangar deck as hydraulic lines popped and fuel lines burst. Their blasts transformed the huge space into a terrible furnace, the turning fans and cross draught whipping the flames into a great fireball that swept across the hangar floor. The families of Dana Peterson's Tomcat team on C Deck were assured that their loved ones would have felt nothing. The blast was too sudden, too deadly. But, in the instant between life and death, between this moment and eternity, Dana Peterson saw the body of Iasi Constanta, that instrument of precision and power that had always placed itself between her and danger, erupt towards her in a hurricane of torn flesh.

CHAPTER 4

Washington D.C.

Four days had gone by since the call came, Bob Lorenz waking Jay at home at three in the morning, the reporters close on his heels. Jay had had no comment then, was still not speaking about it now. Two days past, he and the families of the twenty eight other crew-members killed in the Harry Truman had huddled under the awning at Dover Airbase while the Marines and sailors executed their perfect and agonisingly slow shuttle through the light drizzle, carrying twenty nine flag-draped coffins down the ramp of the C-130, loading them gently into the waiting hearses. Coming home, they called it.

The crack of rifle fire started a covey of mallards from the riverbank below, the volley's crash ringing back across the hillside. They're very good at this, Jay thought: the hero's burial, the precisely folded flag handed reverently to the surviving family. Arlington Cemetery was full of duty done, orders obeyed, all laid out under neat white headstones, black and white, men and women in orderly rows. Just rewards.

Dark-coated figures fanned out across the lawn, heading

back to their cars, back to their families, their offices. Jay thought about that. Dana was his family, all of it. Now, she was just another little white marker like all the rest. He stood there silently, tears at last welling up behind the round horn-rims, the anger still burning deep down.

A figure detached itself from the group at the roadside and headed back towards him. It was Lorenz. Even at a distance, the charging walk was unmistakable. Behind him, Jay picked out the tall, courtly figure of John Enrico watching them both. "Time to go, son," Lorenz said when he reached him. "Come on. John's got a car waiting." He put a bearish arm round Jay's shoulder, half-embracing, half pulling him towards the roadway. When Jay didn't move, Lorenz let his arm drop not knowing what else to do.

His voice low and tight, as if he were talking only to himself, Jay said, "I was supposed to be the one taking care of her. The older brother who knew everything, the hot-shot analyst who knew which group was active, which one wasn't. Supposed to know where the next hit was coming from. And in the end I didn't know shit."

"You couldn't have known," Lorenz said, looking away. "None of us did."

Jay rounded on his boss, his anger drowning out the grief: "That's the whole point. The whole fucking point. We sit over here in our sanitised offices pushing little pins into the wall, pretending we know what the terrorists of the world had for breakfast, pretending we know what's going on and in fact we know shit. Shit."

"You're wrong, Jay," Lorenz said, on the defensive now.

"The Qataris already grabbed the perpetrators. Turned them over to the Saudis. They executed them this morning. All six."

"How do we know they got the right ones, Bob?" Jay spat back. "We're not even sure who bombed Riyadh or Al-Khobar. The Saudis just cut a few a heads off then tell us it's all taken care of. And we go back to sticking pins in the map waiting for the next hit."

Lorenz recovered his balance: "So, what do we do, Jay? Run down every Mohammed from here to Djakarta? Hang around the souk in Riyadh or Islamabad waiting for a hot tip? That's not the way we do it, Jay. You know that. It's one small step at a time. One little piece of evidence after another. Not very glamorous, I admit. Not like your buddy Connolly down the road there with his conspiracy claptrap. But it's our way." He indicated the folded flag in Jay's hands. "This is a tragedy, a tragedy, Jay. But we've got to keep going no matter what."

Jay imagined how the two of them must look from Enrico's viewpoint by the road; the squarish, animated Lorenz and Jay, taller, leaner; the outsider by temperament, background and by colour. Enrico would be sure to register that.

He started to speak but Lorenz cut him off. "Look, Jay. Take all the time you need. Okay? A vacation. Whatever." Lorenz wanted out now, Jay could tell. He wasn't good at personal tragedies, didn't know how to give comfort wanting none himself. "And if there's anything I can do, any of us can do, just say the word. Right?"

Jay nodded. "Right."

"Give you a ride?" Lorenz said, relieved to be back on solid ground.

"No. I'm fine. You go on."

Lorenz marched back to the waiting car, exchanged a few

words with Enrico then ducked into the back seat. Enrico raised a hand in farewell and followed. Jay watched the car start down the hill then laid the precisely folded triangle of flag that had draped Dana's coffin on her grave.

Balance. It was a runner's thing, Jay knew, the need for forward motion weighed against the body's protest. He'd been where Jeff Cohen was now at one time, measuring miles against the clock, measuring time. Then Jay had extended, running distances, twenty miles, thirty miles. Time didn't matter anymore, getting there didn't matter. All that mattered was balance. The body could bear it as long as the mind willed it. A girlfriend had asked him what he thought about while he was running. Running, he had answered. After that there wasn't any place for the conversation to go. Their relationship like their conversation had ground to a halt.

He stood in his apartment, two sparsely furnished rooms on Capitol Hill, looking at what was left of his life. He didn't usually see this place by day, leaving early to run, working late. The office, the tan-coloured fortress on Pennsylvania Avenue, had become his real home. There was nothing here. He surveyed the shelves of books, the stacks of newspaper clippings, articles torn from foreign-language magazines, faxes, e-mails, the abandoned packets of take-out he'd shared with various staffers after they had decamped from the office to continue discussions in a friendlier environment. And all for what? It seemed like a joke now. The one person he really cared for, his baby sister, had been torn apart while he and his so-smart colleagues had argued over which group had formed, which disintegrated, wrangled over who was active, who wasn't.

Jay kicked a pile of file-folders adding a "Goddamnit!" to the action. The papers scattered over the floor, reams of reports, memos and bios with photos attached skidding over the wooden parquet. "Goddamn you." He pulled books from the shelves, hurled a volume at the wall, another. It wasn't just Dana now; it was the years of being the "good black," keeping his place around people like Enrico, staying in line, soldiering on. A volume connected with the answering machine by the door, red message light blinking. The instrument fell to the floor, the impact activating its announcement. "Two fifteen p.m. Three calls, one message."

Jay slumped into the couch, his head in his hands, sobbing unashamedly. Here he was, the champion of American justice, all of thirty years old, crying like a little boy.

There was a light tap at the door. "Jay? You okay?" It was Lyndi, his downstairs neighbour. She was a writer or claimed to be. Jeff Cohen, some of the others, teased Jay that she had a thing for him. Maybe. Most likely she was just a poor, lonely little girl trying like all the rest of them to make sense of the life they'd been pitched.

"Yeah, Lyndi. I'm okay. Just moving a few things around, cleaning up a bit," Jay said. He pushed himself off the couch, nudging the piles he'd overturned together with his foot. None of it made sense any more, none of it mattered. By the time Lorenz and the rest had pieced together what had happened in Doha from whatever information the Qataris or the Saudis would let them have, another group would have come together, some bunch of angry, hot young men wanting to see their names, written large up on the wall for all their comrades to see. All the while, Jay and the rest of his team would be dutifully compiling more bios, matching noms-de-guerre with real faces in the hope that once, just once, they might be able to dismantle a group before it got enough momentum to be dangerous, before it just faded back into the surrounding noise of protest. And all the while, Lorenz and Enrico and the eager Senators on the Hill would be urging their troops on to bring whoever was responsible to justice. That's what they understood: cowboys and indians, us against them.

Jay picked the answering machine off the floor and set it back on the table, pushing the "Play" button at the same time.

"Jay, boy. It's me, Brian. Look, I know this is not the way to do this but you know where I am. If there's anything at all . . ." It was Brian Connolly, Jay's former mentor at Georgetown University Foreign Service School. Connolly's voice trailed off. Then, "You know where I am. Call me if you feel like it, okay?" and hung up.

He hadn't seen Brian for over a year, too long to be explained away by a casual apology, long enough to seem like a deliberate snub. Brian Connolly, dubbed the Pariah of the Gulf by Lorenz for his questionable loyalties; Connolly the conspiracist. What Connolly characterised as getting to know the subjects of their investigation better Lorenz saw as treason. To Lorenz they were all "Mohammeds," all potential enemies in a dangerous sea of possible threat. To Connolly they were individuals, each with his own story, each just waiting for the call.

The thought slowed Jay down, started him thinking. He

couldn't just leave it like this. Couldn't dutifully show up at the office and pretend nothing had happened, picking over the fragments of other people's lives looking for a pattern, a match. The loss of Dana, the loss of order in his life had tilted him off his base, reached into the core of his being and tripped some switch. He was going to have to do something, the same way all Lorenz's "Mohammeds" had to do something. Jay pitched the book he was holding onto the couch, slamming the door to the apartment behind as he went out.

CHAPTER 5

Turkey

Paradise was a country whose geography was unknown to Ibrahim, a territory whose name was familiar but whose language and customs were foreign. Ibrahim was a resident of all countries, crossed freely over all borders save that one.

He had crossed the border between Iraq and Turkey at Silopi, the Iraqi diplomatic plates and ministry pass causing no comment from the silent border guards. Turkey had enough trouble on its hands with its Kurdish neighbours to find time to record or question a legitimate entry even at this remote point. His journey from Peshawar to Baghdad had been circuitous but uneventful, the meeting with the man called Khuda Bax and the arrangements made quite satisfactory. He had left Bax in Baghdad and continued on alone. Ibrahim was familiar with conventional wisdoms that taught that crowds were the best screens from surveillance. So they were. But crowds came with cameras, with trained watchers, with records. Silopi was a town which didn't care who came and went, barely knew on whose border it lay. That served Ibrahim's purpose well. Perpetrators should have no histories, leave no memories, harbour no desires. Only their objectives should have value. From these nothing would turn them.

The Mercedes, a black E320, was stolen, had probably

been run across the same border with little more notice paid to it then than was offered it on its way back. If the insurance company was lucky it might even find its way to its original owner within a few weeks. On the other hand, if the police force at Van where he was headed had not been paid in several months as was usually the case in eastern Turkey, it might end up in the driveway of the Chief of Police or some other local official. It was of no matter to Ibrahim. His passage scarcely attracted any attention in the primitive hill villages he passed through, the children running beside the car for a few paces, a brave boy throwing a stone or two before the car accelerated away.

Ibrahim had travelled into Dahuk in the northern tip of Iraq the night before. The city was an ugly blight of crumbling concrete buildings, barely passable streets crammed with camels and run-down antique American cars, and a crossroads for dealers of arms and drugs from Turkey, Iraq, Syria. Ibrahim had found the Mercedes behind the hotel where the ministry had reserved him a room under his own name. He had collected the keys to the car from on top of the driver's-side front wheel where they had been secured with tape and without entering the hotel had crossed the street to another, less luxurious accommodation. The elderly manager there had taken the cash handed to him and shown Ibrahim his room. No words were spoken, no questions asked.

In the bare room overlooking the street, Ibrahim had busied himself in preparation for the next day's journey. He had removed his passport from his jacket pocket placing it in a grocery bag along with his driver's license and credit card. The rest of his effects he would take care of later. He took a second passport from the lining of his case and spread it open on the narrow bed. His own face, younger without a moustache, the hair shorter, looked back at him. The opposite page bore his name and nationality: Ali bin Fatta al Hussein, United Nations. It was satisfactory. Pulling a razor from his bag, he slowly shaved the moustache from his upper lip, working slowly so as not cut himself in the cold water. He was a careful man.

Ibrahim had lost his innocence at fourteen. He was a native of the Eastern Province of Saudi Arabia, a territory that boasted more of the kingdom's oil fields than any other and wealth beyond imagination. While the foreign executives of Aramco, the joint Saudi-American oil company, fuelled the tanks of their great cars with the petroleum from Saudi's sacred soil, flaunted their wealth and their wives, Ibrahim and his people, voiceless in the kingdom, sank like drowning men deeper into the soundless pit of poverty. Ibrahim and his family were Shia in a nation where ninety percent of the population was Sunni. The Shia were as devout, perhaps more devout Muslims than their Sunni neighbours. They kept the same beliefs, were children of the same Prophet. But the *muwahidin*, the stern keepers of the nation's faith and the strictest of the Wahhabis, had decreed that the beliefs of the Shia were anathema.

The Rulers had wasted little time in profiting from the decree. No matter that the Shia were largely responsible for development of the wealth upon which the royal family's power now rested, had managed the complex oil-refineries, had balanced the company books and counted the money for the infidel Americans. In Saudi Arabia to be Shia now was to be an outsider, no more a Saudi than the lowly Pakistanis who swept the streets for a few riyals to send home to their families.

Ibrahim, a native Saudi, could no longer serve in Saudi's armed forces; jobs his Shia brethren had created were taken away and given to Sunni; Shia lands were polluted, their villages razed, their water drained or poisoned. Ibrahim had seen this. He had heard the stories that blew through the province like so many dry winds. But he had not known it in his heart, not until he was fourteen. Then, in 1980, he had been arrested, a boy caught with a handful of stained political pamphlets that he could scarcely read.

Three policemen had thrown him into the back of the American jeep, one of them holding his face to the sour smelling surface of the vehicle's rear seat. His family he discovered afterwards were never told where he had gone, never dared ask. He could not have told them himself. He was blindfolded and taken from the jeep, led upstairs to a darkened room and told to stand. He had stood, first on one leg then on the other. When he could stand no more and one leg began to fall of its own will to the floor, one of the men beat him with a stick.

How long had he stood, tears rolling down his face, aching for sleep? Two days? Three? He could no longer trust his mind. It projected strange pictures on the wall, formed strange words his cracked lips could only mumble.

Finally they had released him and Ibrahim had stumbled home, his eyes staring but unseeing. They had taken the flyers from him when he entered the jeep. They had taken his innocence and youth from him in the jail. They had left him with nothing.

In 1985, aged nineteen, Ibrahim and hundreds of young men like him, had offered their lives on the battlefields of Afghanistan in a war that was not theirs for a land where they did not belong. There was no future for a young Shia in Saudi Arabia.

In Afghanistan then there had been one holy cause. Shia and Sunni were one faith, Islam. Here all were brothers in one struggle. Two years of living rough in the hills, two winters of deep snows and scarce food had hardened the young man. When the light plane Ibrahim had learned to fly for reconnaissance was shot down on a snow-covered plain in the foothills north-east of Kabul, he had dragged his co-pilot from the wreckage. They had huddled together as a T62 Russian tank with a flame-thrower attachment bore down on them, Ibrahim covering his friend. But his friend had run, terrified by the monster's fiery breath. The blaze had caught his back, the young man's thin, frost-bitten body flaming like a reed for a moment, bright orange against the grey winter skies, his screams smothered by the roar of the flame-thrower.

Ibrahim had not fired the grenade that had stopped the tank but he had been present for the ensuing execution. The four terrified Russian soldiers, no older than himself, had emerged from the turret, their hands stretched vainly upwards. Ibrahim knew then that no fight would ever be won, knew then the true meaning of jihad. It was a war without a beginning, without a middle or an end. There was no battlefield. All countries, all lands were battlefields. Jihad was a forward force; a way of life that strove as relentlessly towards the truth as a plant beneath a stone grows towards the light.

*

Ibrahim pointed the Mercedes north-west, the sun rising at his back, the road winding into the mountains that locked Turkey's eastern border. By noon he had crested their summit and could look down on the city of Van where he would abandon the car, stripping it of its plates before boarding a plane for Ankara and the onward flight to France. The man he had met in Baghdad, Khuda Bax, had not disappointed him. He had provided. He would be rewarded in the manner that was deserved.

He pulled the car over and in his own way and time performed his midday prayer. Afterwards, taking the grocery bag and a can of gasoline from the trunk, he walked through the scrub to a low outcropping of rocks. There he made a small mound of his possessions: the passport, the driver's license, the credit card. He poured a little of the gasoline onto the pile and with his lighter set fire to it, the bag igniting with a faint "whump." A convoy of trucks with German license plates roared by in the opposite direction, headed for the Iranian border, their ten-wheel trailers snaking behind the eighteen-wheel rigs like great ships of the road, their backdraft flattening the flames as they passed.

Clean-shaven, dressed now in white shirt and slacks, sunglasses shading his eyes, Ali Fatta Hussein climbed back into the Mercedes, indistinguishable from the thousands of other Middle Eastern men who thronged the streets and suburbs of cities and towns from Peshawar to Paris.

CHAPTER 6

Washington D.C.

"Good Christ, boy. You could at least knock!"

Professor Brian Connolly swung his feet off the desk and faced the intruder standing in the doorway to his room. It was Jay, drawn by some inexorable force to the campus overlooking the Potomac, sprinting the last blocks through Georgetown. Now, he stood in the doorway of Connolly's office in the basement of the Foreign Service Building not quite sure yet what he had come looking for.

The professor threw down the paper he was reading, suddenly recognising his former student. "Jay! It's you," he said, wrapping his arms round Jay and holding on hard. "You poor man," Connolly said, his mouth close to Jay's ear, the pain in his voice as much for himself as for Jay.

They'd spent evenings together, Dana and Jay, Brian and one of his notoriously short-lived romances, at Jay's apartment on Capitol Hill, afternoons fishing and drinking beer on the Potomac. Connolly had thrown one of his infamous barbecues when Dana's promotion came through, claiming that he'd wait for her always. The truth was that Connolly took more than a friendly interest in Dana but was too shy to admit what everyone else could see a mile off. Then Professor

Brian Connolly, in his own words, had been excommunicated and all the lines went down.

"God, I'm sorry man, awfully sorry," he said. "It was today, wasn't it. The funeral?" Jay nodded. "Here. Come in, come in." He ushered Jay into the cubicle-sized room, pushing a stack of Arab-language newspapers off a chair, then perched himself on the edge of his paper-strewn desk. They'd done this before so many times, the professor and the student, Connolly energised, never still, Jay listening, soaking up the other man's knowledge. Connolly regarded Jay closely. "She was doing what she chose to do, Jay. You know that."

"I know that," Jay said deliberately as if the topic was off limits. Connolly persisted.

"And she did it damn well. You should be bloody proud of her, just the way she was of you. She worshipped you."

Jay took a moment to collect himself. He hadn't planned on dealing with his loss in front of Connolly. "There was nothing, Brian. No warning. They came out of nowhere."

Connolly continued to scrutinise Jay, trying to read between the lines. "Now, Jay. We didn't sit here all those wasted hours so you could tell me that. They all come out of somewhere. Even bin Laden came out of somewhere."

"We'll never know," Jay said. "The Saudis took the perpetrators into their custody. Executed all of them, five Arabs, one Russian. Their investigator's report won't be worth the paper it's written on."

Connolly nodded thoughtfully. "And now, since the FBI doesn't know what to do next, you want to do something useful; find the real culprits; take your own revenge." Jay felt caught out again. He'd forgotten how quick Connolly could be, how he always stayed at least one step ahead.

"That's not it, Brian," he came back sharply.

"So you came to see the Pariah of the Gulf, Mr. Conspiracy himself to see if he could help out. Didn't have time to tell him there was a funeral though." There was an echo of a deeply buried bitterness in Connolly's voice. In his time at Georgetown, he had gained a formidable reputation for his fiery temper, the extraordinary range of his contacts and his questionable judgement. His sympathy and partisan support of the IRA made him *persona non grata* in England, much sought after in certain circles in Boston. In the world of militant Islamic groups, his area of special expertise and the subject he had taught Jay, his sympathies rested with the underdogs as they did in his native Ireland. His "reach" was legend; his penchant for far-fetched theories was another matter.

He had steered clear of handicapping suspects in the downing of TWA Flight 800 leaving the field open to other wilder Internet conspiracists. But his exhaustively-detailed memo to Jay's boss, Bob Lorenz, on the coming Islamic wave of terror in the US and the highly developed network of terrorist cells within the nation's borders beginning with certain college professors had caused the Deputy Director acute embarrassment. Lorenz, buying into his old and trusted friend's carefully plotted theory one hundred percent, pitched a wide-ranging pre-emptive strike to the White House's Co-ordinator Sub-Group on Terrorism. When news of the plan leaked out – even the White House's basement where the prestigious Sub-Group met was damp, one waggish commentator pointed out – Lorenz's reputation took a brief but dramatic nose-dive. He had no way of substantiating his suspicion that someone at the CIA had been responsible for the leak.

Connolly, on the other hand, the cause of Lorenz's very public pillorying by the one million African-American converts to Islam and the five million or more Islamic immigrants beginning to find a unified political voice in their adopted country, got it with both barrels.

The phone on Connolly's desk rang. Connolly hunted for it under the pile of paper, picked it up, said: "Yeah?" then "No." He jammed the receiver back down. "Let's get out of this shit-hole and get some air." He shepherded Jay up the stairs and out to the green campus. The pathways were filled with students dressed much like Connolly. The fifty-year-old Irishman in jeans and faded T-shirt under an unbuttoned red-plaid shirt looked almost young enough to pass for one of them. Jay, in his dark suit, was the outsider.

"I need a name," Jay said abruptly. Connolly's reply was drowned out by a jet on final approach to National Airport. Jay waited for the noise to subside then repeated his request: "A name."

"I heard you the first time," Connolly said roughly. "You know, you've got some sweet nerve busting in here after all these months and just pumping me for a lead like I was one of your precious staffers. I was a hell of a sight better friend to that sister of yours than you've ever been to me, Mr. Peterson. One hell of a sight better." Connolly lit a cigarette and blew the smoke decorously away from Peterson.

"You should stop that . . ." Jay began.

". . . before it stops me," Connolly completed. The Irishman slumped down on a bench seat beside the quadrangle's central lawn then laughed.

Jay sat next to him. "What?"

"Know who that was on the phone?" Jay shook his head.

48

"It was Bob Lorenz's office wondering if I'd seen you around. You must be in it up to your ears. What did you do? Go over the wall?" It was closer to the truth than Connolly knew. After the showdown between Connolly and Lorenz, Lorenz had become obsessed with politics and his own inability to understand them. He made up for it by second-guessing his subordinates at every turn. Section members were warned off any contact with Connolly on pain of immediate termination. If word got back to Lorenz of Jay's meeting today, there would be no quarter. Jay could be looking at federal prosecution, worse. Connolly dragged on his cigarette, his gaze drifting to a pretty red-haired girl entering the University's main building. "Your man there, Mr. Bob Lorenz; I'll bet he sees the hand of Al bloody Qaida at work. Am I right?" Jay nodded. "And since you're here and in such a state, I'm guessing you don't."

Jay eyed Connolly carefully. Brian was right. He was going over the wall. "We were intercepting their satellite phones till they got wise and started using runners," Jay said. "We're still watching their vehicle movements and tailing all known associates. We reckon they have cells, some active, some sleepers, in over sixty countries. The CIA have a strike force on permanent standby just waiting for the go. Nothing. We don't know if they have access to funds, if they have any left. We don't really know where they are."

Connolly ground the cigarette he was smoking out on the arm of the wooden bench, defiling what was probably the precious gift of some grateful alumnus. He blew a long stream of smoke into the air.

"You got any ideas?"

"Who knows? Who cares? Baghdad's a regular Casablanca these days. Abu Nidal, Abu Douad, all the usual suspects."

Another jet passed overhead, a USAir 737 winging its way down the river. When the jet's roar had dropped away Connolly said: "That's where your Mr. Lorenz has got it all wrong. He thinks he's dealing with another band of whacked-out locals bankrolled by some naïve Saudis and high as kites on the Koran. You and I, Jay, know that organising and setting up one of these attacks, especially something as sophisticated as the Truman, takes time and a bundle more than they've got left in their checking accounts. You'd need instant access to funds and freedom of distribution. This isn't just some embassy truck-bomb." Connolly regarded his former student, the idea briefly presenting itself that this might be some kind of set-up, one of Lorenz's stings. Jay said nothing.

Connolly got up off the bench, energised suddenly. "We're talking about an organiser, a co-ordinator, a super terrorist. He'd probably be a mujahedeen. An Afghan-Arab. Might have state support. Could be on the list you fellers keep. Perhaps a weapons specialist. Might even have experience on mobile launchers. Maybe even a pilot. Met the Russian deserter on the front back in the '80s, kept up correspondence the way they all do." Connolly checked himself, lighting up another cigarette, captive to the excitement of a new idea. "These perpetrators, the ones they chopped; you said they were Saudis." Jay hadn't but he concurred anyway. "Sunni or Shia?" Connolly continued.

Jay honestly didn't know. No names had been released as yet, only numbers. "Why would that make a difference?"

"'Cause I've got a theory." It was a prelude, Jay knew, the moment you signed on or took off. It was Connolly's personal test of loyalty. You either bought in right at the top or you were cast out forever as an unbeliever. Jay waited for the rest.

"You boys know about the Bank of Doha, right?" Connolly didn't wait for Jay's answer, plunging right on. "Regular World Bank of International Terrorism, was owned and operated by no less than the Government of Qatar. Osama bin Laden was using it to wash his funds through. Well, he's not the only one. A feller I know has been running Afghani drug money through it, setting up legit operations in Europe to buy parts and weapons for the Taliban."

Jay interrupted. "I don't get it. What's the connection?"

"This feller, he's Shia. Kind of unusual given the circumstances." The two men were silent, each waiting for the other, Connolly still reluctant to entirely forgive his former student, Jay wondering if there was more.

Jay spoke first. "Give me the name, Brian," he said quietly.

Connolly brought his face down to Jay's, his mouth close enough that Jay could smell the stale smell of cigarette. "Tell me, Jay. Do you really want to do something, I mean get in there and buck? Or are you just stringing me along? Uh?"

"Tell me what I've got to do and I'll do it."

"See, if you're just one of them, one of Lorenz's Robocops looking to bag another Mohammed then you can take the proverbial flyer. Once I let you in, you're in all the way. Understand? I've got good friends out there who wouldn't be too happy if you turned out to be something I said you weren't."

"I understand, Brian."

"Right then. This feller, his name's Bax, Khuda Bax. Problem is, that's about all I can tell you. The Bank of Doha hasn't returned my calls if you know what I mean. If you want to know more, you'll have to go see a friend of mine. He was in London last time I spoke with him. Not in the inner circle but a good man all the same. Got the Afghani connection down flat. Go to London and wait for his call. Can't call him; it's a visit, face-to-face. Then call me. That a problem?" Jay shook his head. Connolly straightened up. "And you won't go telling Mr. Bob Lorenz all this now, will you?" The question was accompanied by a wheezing laugh, Connolly enjoying his own small joke.

"No, Brian. I understand the rules."

"There you go, Jay." Connolly clapped a hand on Jay's shoulder. "We'll make a believer of you yet."

It was a small gesture but to Jay it was the last push that propelled him all the way over the safe perimeter of the world he knew into outer darkness.

CHAPTER 7

Paris

There is a stubbornness in certain plants, in certain species and types of human behaviour that overrides any resistance, any influence for change. Human need for intoxication is one such behaviour. No matter how many steps the subject takes or, at some future time, how many genes may be mutated, addictions will survive. Just so the poppy. In the stony fields of central Afghanistan, the red gash of poppies in bloom bleeds across the rocky surface. Subsistence farmers, their hands black with gum, their backs bent, move through the flowers lancing the poppy bulbs and squeezing the juice into collecting sacks. Other hands, more slender but just as nimble, the farmers' wives', sisters' and daughters', mould the sticky harvest into blocks, black bricks redolent with the scent of the earth's secret oils. It's an activity that has survived wars and droughts, survived even the methodical and tempting rewards of the United States drug eradication programs.

Follow the bricks from the shadow of the walls against which the women lean as they work, along the pot-holed roads to the village markets, on to Afghanistan's decayed cities. Under the watchful eyes of Taliban militia, the bricks are carried from cart to truck, US dollars passing from brown hand to brown hand at each exchange. It's an ancient, primitive economy. Along the way, edges of the dried bricks are broken off and crumbled into a chewable wad here, a crudely-made cigarette there, the consciousness of the smoker drifting upwards with the smoke for a few brief moments of forgetfulness.

The route the black cargo follows shifts with the tides of war and alliance but its direction never alters; westwards always westwards, into the setting sun towards the great cities of Europe and the cities of the Americas beyond. There, as if passing through some magic curtain, black becomes white, the opiates distilled down and purified into white powder that will be consumed in clubs and penthouses, men's rooms and street corners, wherever the user's need and the line of delivery intersect. The transformation requires the skill of a chemist and a crude but efficient laboratory. A slip of the hand or a miscalculation of ingredients can result in sudden and total immolation of plant, chemist and product. It's a delicate balance. But, like the addiction itself, the fruits of the labours of farmers, shippers, chemists and distributors are heady indeed.

The face reflected in the window of the elegant clothing store on the rue Faubourg Saint-Honoré considered all this, considered, too, the irony that the fervent Taliban, so eager to eradicate temptation amongst their own beleaguered population saw no contradiction in cultivating and exporting the forbidden crop. It was God's mystery, God's own handiwork, destroying the unbeliever with the fruit of God's own good earth.

Ibrahim turned away from the window and looked across the street at the row of cabs. As Ali Hussein he could easily take one. But as Ibrahim he had time. He would walk.

The police had pulled him over, of course: a single Arab male arriving from Ankara, how could they not. A woman had rifled his overnight case, picking through the few shirts, the light jacket, checked and re-checked his United Nations passport, asked to see how much money he was carrying, an address where he was staying. Reason for visit: Official. Turn on the computer. Was it his? A gift Ibrahim said. He turned it on. There was nothing much to see: a folder of official documents, the few applications.

The express bus from Charles de Gaulle Airport was half empty. Ibrahim sat alone at the back looking out at the rain-swept streets of the French capital, taking in the crush of traffic, the narrow buildings, the grey skies.

At the terminal on the Invalides, Ibrahim collected his case and walked across the Pont Alexandre III. He would be stopped again, he was sure, but he had nothing to hide, no reason to object.

His Adidas bag slung over his back, Ibrahim crossed the Place de la Concorde where a French king and his court had lost their heads, through the Palais Royale where Molière had induced other heads to roll, down the once-bloody rue St. Antoine and across the Place de la Bastille, empty of its fortress, and along the broad boulevards down which helmeted hussars had charged make-shift barricades one way and a conquering German army had marched the other.

None of this invisible history mattered to Ibrahim. He saw only the scornful look of an Algerian waiter setting out a café-au-lait and its appurtenances – the glass of water, the folded linen napkin, the heavy cutlery – at an outdoor table as he went by. He saw the elegantly-dressed woman on the Place de Vosges step sideways to leave as much room between him and her when they passed as she could without stepping into the street. It was not until he had walked over the crest of the Buttes Chaumont and down along the Canal de l'Ourcq and into the north-east quarter that Ibrahim began to see a resemblance between his own narrow face and the faces of others on the street. The blue dyes of tattoos on the women from North Africa, Egypt and Morocco, the ebony skin of the street sellers from central African states, and, at last, in a corner café at the intersection of rue 4e Settembre and the rue Jacquard, a face much like his own, the face of a true Arab.

Ibrahim read the café's name from across the street: Café Relais, rue Jacquard. He crossed the street and entered. A girl stood behind the tiny bar reading "al-Hayat". Otherwise the café was empty, the only sound the low, wailing chant from the juke box in one corner.

"Is Mr. Mohammed here?" Ibrahim asked.

The girl looked Ibrahim over once, folded her paper onto the counter and pushed through a bead curtain at the back of the small room. A moment later a small, plump man appeared in place of the girl.

"Mr. Mohammed?"

"Yes," the little man replied guardedly.

"I am Ali bin Fatta al Hussein and I have arrived."

The little man eyed the other man suspiciously for a moment then burst out laughing. "So you have, my friend, so you have."

A cautious display of identification followed, an exchange of names, then Mohammed led Ibrahim around the corner to an open entryway. As they climbed the winding stone stairs, the outer treads worn down by years of use,

Mohammed kept up a running commentary of unnecessary advice and warning.

"Always carry your papers. The 'flics' will stop you anywhere, anytime. If you have no papers, they will arrest you. Stay away from the department stores in the centre of the city. Even if you have money in your pocket, they will arrest you for shop-lifting before they will ask you what you are looking for. If you need to buy something, buy it here. Here you are among friends. If you need to phone, use the phone in the café or the public phone in the Post Office."

Ibrahim read the names on the doors they passed as he followed the puffing Mohammed up the stairs: El-Abrahim, Hussein, Mobarra, Khalid. Finally, at the highest landing, Mr. Mohammed stopped before a wooden door with no name.

"Here is the key," the little man said producing a large door key. "The tap and toilet are across the hall. If you need hot water, you must boil it. There are public baths on the rue Mansard but they are open only on Wednesdays and Saturdays. Good fortune, my friend."

Ibrahim watched Mohammed disappear down the narrow stairs then faced the unmarked door. Turning the key, he let himself into a small, low-ceilinged room. At its centre was a table with a single chair. A small gas-cooker was perched on a shelf by the window. Against the wall a mattress was spread out on the floor. Ibrahim set down his bag and looked around him. There were no pictures, no ornaments, only a bookcase. He perused the titles carefully, pulling a book from the middle shelf. He opened the book at the title page. In Arabic it read: "Clear Evidence of the Apostasy of the Saudi State" by

Abi al-Maqdisi. Sitting at the table Ibrahim began to read. He could do no more, only wait for the man Khuda Bax and for the rest to arrive. It was well. He had time.

CHAPTER 8

London

Jay stood on the shore, a girl next to him. They were both silent, looking out to sea, watching the sunset. The huge orange ball was melting, dripping fiery liquid onto the dark line of horizon. The ball erupted, blowing upwards and out-wards, pushing a wave of flame towards them. Jay snapped his head away from the blast, towards his companion. It was Dana. As he looked, she too evaporated in an explosion of orange flame, the dark ring of her mouth screaming silently. Instantly, Jay was awake.

It was night, the glow from the streetlights leaking through the small window and washing the room. The phone beside the bed was trilling.

"Yeah," he said.

"This Jay Peterson?"

"This is he."

"Short here. Our friend said you'd wanted to reach me. Gave me your number."

"Right," Jay said, suddenly awake. After his meeting with Connolly, he'd left word with Lorenz that he was taking him up on his offer of time off, then booked himself on the night flight to London out of Dulles. He'd found a small tourist hotel in Kensington, called Connolly, then settled in to wait.

"This a hotel?" the voice at the other end said.

"Yeah," Jay said

"Do me a favour then, will you Jay? Find a pay phone and call me back. Same number."

He swung off the bed and six minutes later was dialling Short's number from a phone booth, the second he had passed, three blocks from the hotel. It was raining heavily. Water dripped from his spectacles, blurring his vision. The back wall of the booth was plastered with card-size advertisements for prostitutes. "Shandi, 19. Real photo. Hotel visits. Games, toys." The strangeness of the invitations, the emptiness of the street added to the sensation that he was treading air.

"Short."

The voice gave him a rendezvous, a pub south of Dublin. Jay was to rent a car, find his own way down. "Nothing personal," Short assured him. Jay wasn't reassured. He considered calling Connolly then thought better of it. He looked out on the rain-swept street again then back at the leather-clad women on the phone booth's wall in front of him. He was wet, he was tired and he was alone. He'd moved from the centre to the edge, from the middle of some secure room to its outer perimeter. Now he felt himself passing through its walls.

The Brazen Head pub stood in the centre of Sandycove, a coastal town twenty minutes south of Dublin. Jay had found the pub the following afternoon by the noise, the action spilling out onto the street. He parked the rental car on the adjoining block and walked back.

"You'd better start with something serious to warm you

up," said Tim Short, Connolly's "name." The gnome-like man, a reporter on the Irish News, had suddenly appeared at Jay's side, his head craning up to Jay's.

"The young man is drinking with me, Danny. Be sure to make it a real drink. None of your little thimblefuls now," Short berated the bar-tender. He turned back to Jay. Where Brian Connolly was lanky and fair, Viking Irish, Short was dark and squat, "black" Irish, a true Celt. And he was angry. There was an edge to him, a hint of rage bubbling under the cheery exterior. "You're Brian's star pupil then," he started.

"Is that what he told you?"

"No, but I'll bet you are." Two glasses of Guinness appeared on the bar before them. Short slid one over.

"Have you known him long?" Jay asked not quite sure where he should begin.

"Oh, yes. Brian and me go all the way back. Remarkable mind. Can recite you the names of the Gypsy Kings, all eight of 'em. Knows how many books there are in the Long Room in Trinity College Library. Can quote, by heart mind, three different translations of the first fifty two lines of Homer's *Odyssey*; I've heard him do it. But, the poor bugger is still single. So, what's the good of that? Sláinte," Short toasted, hoisting his glass. He wiped his mouth, placing his Guinness on the bar before him. As he did, a man put his hand on Short's shoulder, directing a toothy smile at Jay. The man whispered something. Short said something back but the answer was drowned out by the roar of conversation all around them.

"Have you seen the tower yet, Jay?" Short asked, throwing some money onto the bar.

"The tower?"

"The Martello," Short offered cryptically as they headed

out of the pub. "Brian would slaughter me if you didn't see that." Outside, Short said: "We'll take your car. You can drop me back after."

They drove down wet streets, past Dunleary Harbour and the ferry terminal for England to a parking lot beneath a pepper-pot-shaped granite tower overlooking Dublin Bay. Jay pulled the car to a stop at the tower's base.

"This," Short said authoritatively, "is *the* Martello Tower where he stayed for six days as the guest of Oliver St. John Goagarty in September, 1904, and where, if you will pardon my national pride, the greatest work of modern fiction began."

"And *it* is?" Jay inquired meekly, confessing his ignorance.

"Why *Ulysses,* of course," Short said in mock indignation.

"Of course," Jay said. They sat for a moment watching the lights of a ferry heading across the Irish Sea towards them.

"Phil said you weren't alone."

"Your friend back there?" Jay queried; "the one at the bar?"

"Aren't you the sharp one," Short said, the mocking tone still present.

"Try to be."

"He said you had a tail – or a baby-sitter; one or the other." It was news to Jay but instead of making him feel secure, the knowledge or absence of it only unsettled him. He had seen no one, noticed nothing. "So;" Short continued, "now we've dispensed with the pleasantries, why don't you tell me which arm of the all-powerful, all-seeing, God-Almighty American government you work for. DEA, is it? Or the FBI?"

Warily at first, trying to dull some of Short's sharp edge, Jay explained why he was there, told him about Dana, said this was more of a personal mission. He dodged Short's question about profession saying only that he had worked investigations before which was how he knew Brian. Short smiled at that and Jay guessed Connolly had given Short the full résumé anyway and Short already knew.

"Brian said there was a drug connection you'd identified. Said he had an idea that one of the Middle East operators he had been tracking and you knew about, a guy named Khuda Bax, was laundering drug proceeds for the Taliban through the Islamic Bank of Doha and setting up European companies to wash the money and buy arms. He reckoned there might be a connection."

"That's Brian for you," Short said, ducking low so he could get a better look at the top of the Joyce landmark through the windshield. "Always got some new villain in his sights. Truth is, Jay, there are a lot of fish swimming out there. Big ones, little ones; predators and prey. Spotting them is one thing. Catching them; that's a different matter altogether." Short opened the car door and climbed out. A stiff breeze blew in the smell of the sea. Jay got out his side and walked round to the front where Short was standing. "Look," Short said, pointing upwards at a lumbering Aer Lingus on final approach to Dublin; "that'll be the Boston flight. Full of Micks come home to see their mams and drink a few jars. Innocent as lambs. Second biggest group of illegal workers in the Northeastern US, the Irish. Did you know that? God Bless America. Keeping the light of freedom burning. Small arms for the Rebels, cash for the Cause, heroin from Afghanistan to keep the lads in the States happy."

What Jay did not know was that Short took more than just a professional interest in the drug traffic that washed out of Asia through Ireland's ports and airports on its way to the US His own son, a medical student at Trinity College, had died of a heroin overdose from injecting a lethally potent strain that had hit the city's streets a few years earlier.

The wind whipped at their hair, the sea spray damping them. Jay looked at Short, waiting for more, then said: "Brian thought you could help me, give me a lead."

"And if I did, Mr. Jay Peterson," Short parried, "what would you do with it? Take it back to your precious FBI and add it to your other pile of toys?"

"Listen," Jay said, his tone matching Short's now; "my sister died out there in the Gulf. That may not count for much back here but where I'm from family is all we have. If you won't give me the name, I'll get it somewhere else."

Short laughed loudly, the wind whipping the noise away. "Oh, Jay. That's a good one." Short clapped Jay on the shoulder. "'Course I'll give you the name for God's sake. We're on the same side, more or less, aren't we? That crazy bugger in Georgetown has vouched for you. I was just having my little fun is all." Jay didn't see the joke. "So, here's the deal," Short went on lightly. "The big man? The shark? I can't tell you that. I'm getting close but I'm not there yet. I have got one name though. It's a chap who works for Khuda Bax; a banker, sort of. Oldham, Roger Oldham would you believe. Probably fudges his books, holds your man's company registers that kind of thing. Works out of London, Old Bond Street. Pretty fancy shop, too. He'd be the man to see. I've been trying myself but hacks like me don't quite heft the weight you pros do, if you know what I mean." Some of the edge was still there but Short was clearly won over. "Come on back to my place and I'll show you what I've put together so far. Not much. Some names, faces. If you've got the time, that is?"

"Sounds good to me," Jay said, relieved to find himself no longer alone.

They drove back through the same dark streets to the pub and Short's car. The crowd inside had thinned but the pub was still open for business.

"Just give me a second," Short said getting out. "I'm over there. You can follow me." Jay watched the little man jog across the street towards a battered Ford Prefect parked in the shadow of the pub's wall. Short opened the unlocked door and got in. For an instant, his face was lit by the overhead dome-light, his black hair gleaming. Jay watched Short reach the key down from the visor, push it into the ignition and turn.

Short's car erupted in a ball of fire. And everything seemed to slow down. Jay couldn't move, was mesmerised by the mass of flames ballooning towards him in the night. The shock wave reached him first, the safety glass in his own car shattering inwards, the vehicle's body rocking forward and back as the tyres exploded. His face was on the steering wheel, pressed hard into his cupped hands. Then came the huge sound of the explosion clattering in his ears. Through the death-like silence that followed, he heard a voice very close insisting: "Let's go. Now." He felt a hand bunch the collar of his jacket, wrench him sideways away from the burning wreck on the street and out into the cold air.

CHAPTER 9

Northern Ireland

In Tim Short's bestiary, his food-chain of swimmers in the sea of drugs and arms, Roger Oldham was a bottom-feeder. Oldham had become a familiar figure in the shallower waters of this sea: The casino in London's Harrington Gardens where the sons of Arab oil men dropped their fathers' profits on the green baize, the fashionable restaurants along the King's Road, the apartments in Mayfair whose leases the fathers had purchased and the permanent suites in the Ritz in Paris their fathers maintained. Oldham's Bentley, a lurid aquamarine Turbo R convertible, could be spotted outside any of these places late into the night and on into the early hours of the next morning. It was Roger Oldham's fate, however, to be drawn always to the dark abyss where the great predators stalk and the promise of boundless wealth summons the prey.

Roger Oldham's mind was on fate as he drove the Bentley, its top down, north from Dublin. Only fate, after all, could have thrown an old acquaintance as wealthy as Neil Greyson his way. Oldham had known Neil Greyson since their days in service in the British Army. They had shared the rigors of guerrilla warfare in the desert hills of Yemen but found little in common then or since. Greyson had always treated Oldham with an indifference bordering on contempt.

Oldham heard through the ever-shrinking grapevine of old soldiers who showed up year after year at the regimental reunions to trade stories and drink ever larger quantities of alcohol that Greyson had been spectacularly successful in the intervening years. Security in the Gulf it was rumoured. Those who knew told Oldham that security translated into arms-trading with various Gulf States, primarily Qatar and the United Arab Emirates.

It was a trick of fate, then, laced with sweet irony that Oldham should be on his way to collect money from Greyson a considerable amount of money, money that for a period at least would be Oldham's to hold. And right now, Oldham badly needed to hold onto something.

Oldham had never had a good head for business. He would be the first to acknowledge it. But he did know a good thing when he saw one. The property on London's Canary Wharf had certainly looked like a good thing. Arab money was flooding the London property market back then and the developer was anxious to strike a deal. The good thing had gone bad when the real-estate boom went bust and Oldham had been left holding the bag. Off-loading the properties at fire-sale prices had not satisfied his creditors and that had launched him on a brief but perilous career buying genuine and highly-priced prints and adding their creators' famous signatures to increase their value at auction. His activities had attracted the unwelcome attention of the Serious Fraud Office and brought him very close to the brink. Only the generosity of one of his "marks," an Arab called Khuda Bax, had rescued Oldham from a vicious mauling by creditors and authorities.

Khuda Bax was an arms-importer/exporter and contrac-tor, at least that was what Oldham had been led to believe.

Khuda Bax regularly exported huge amounts of cash from the US for various clients in the Gulf. Given the US's stringent banking laws requiring its institutions to report cash deposits in excess of $10,000, and its investment brokers and casinos to file Suspicious Activity Reports on the consistent use of money orders, wire transfers or third party deposits, Khuda Bax shifted the money through what he referred to as "alternative" channels. Like all highly-successful businessmen he needed a personal banker. Until recently, that banker had been the Islamic Bank of Doha.

Charges of embezzlement, of which Khuda Bax assured Oldham he was entirely innocent, had brought Qatar's Minister of Finance onto the Board of Directors. Right behind the Minister had come the Americans because Qatar was the site of the US's largest prepositioning supply base outside of US territory with 10,000 troops and 5,000 vehicles. Khuda Bax had not only been obliged to take his financial business elsewhere, he had also been cut out of the bidding on the $178 million contract the US had put up for upgrading the supply base. That left Bax with a problem that Roger Oldham could easily have lived with: an enormous and ongoing cashflow with nowhere to bank it. As fate would have it, Roger Oldham, scrambling through his Rolodex to find a saviour to bale him out of his latest financial crisis had turned up Khuda Bax. Khuda Bax had explained the job opening, Roger had applied, and so had embarked on yet another short-lived but spectacular career.

At fifty six Oldham was still an imposing figure. He could certainly have passed for a banker, an international man of business, and, if he had been careful, simply couriering the cash in the expensive leather pilots' briefcases he bought for the job to its various destinations, totalling the receipts, deducting out the expenses, billing his client a reasonable sum for his services, he in time might have matched substance to style. But it was not Roger Oldham's nature to live and die in the shallows. The darker waters beckoned. On one of his frequent flights from Boston to the warmer climate of the Caribbean, Oldham had come across advertisements in the airline's in-flight magazine promising instant wealth. Had it not been that the business being touted was the business he was actively engaged in at the moment, offshore banking, he might have ignored the promises. It was one of those moments. Oldham had seen another good thing and he knew it. He picked up the phone on the back of the seat in front of him, called for the literature, and within days Offshore Management was born.

It was an "a" to "b" sort of thing, occupied a minimum amount of time, and promised incalculable wealth even though technically the wealth belonged to someone else. He purchased corporate names from offshore registries, opened accounts in sovereign states happy for the cash and not too concerned about its source, had flown to the Cayman Isles, the Turks and Caicos, the Channel Islands, the Isle of Man, and even the Solomon Islands. He had hired a full-time corporate secretary and accountant, the chronically overworked Andrew Starling, and opened for business with one client, Khuda Bax bin Abdul Aziz.

The cash, some of it from the US, much of it from Europe, had been changed into money orders and wired as bank-to-bank transfers to Offshore's forty one banks world-wide, most no more than a numbered account in a foreign capital and individual articles of incorporation in Oldham's Bond Street safe. Deposits were characterised to those bank officers curious enough to ask as profits from Offshore's client's rapidly expanding agricultural businesses, notably the wonderful Camembert produced at farms in Normandy. Where possible the accounts were opened by mail using the signatures of Khuda Bax's many close relatives and several wives, Oldham maintaining power of attorney at Starling's insistence. That will allow Offshore, the emaciated young man had explained to Oldham one night over drinks at the pub they frequented, to keep the balance in each account as low as possible by shifting assets electronically. "Never more than $10,000 though," Starling said. "Because?" "Because anything more could trigger an investigation by an examiner. We call it 'smurfing'." "Do you, indeed?" Oldham had said, hoisting his tumbler of single-malt. Starling had also advised opening a second level of accounts using fictitious European names for the account holders to avoid the "political" flag raised by the distinctly Islamic sound of the names of Khuda Bax's relatives. "Then we can 'sanctify' the money by passing it through European front companies: you know, restaurants, real estate, things like that, and making legitimate investments in their names and/or purchases." Oldham, barely able to contain his excitement, became as familiar a figure in corporate brokerage houses in New York as he was in the restaurants along the King's Road.

Oldham never questioned the source of the cash. It was not his style. "That'd take the fun out of it," he had told an anxious Starling at another of their nightly sessions at the Turk's Head, drowning the young man's misgivings in a bottle of expensive champagne. "To Mr. Khuda Bax and all who sail in her," Oldham toasted. Had he known that the primary source of Khuda Bax's wealth now came from Afghani heroin, he might have expressed shock. But the profits made a very persuasive argument and he would have found a way eventually to accommodate the new information without putting too great a strain on his conscience.

The good thing had started to turn bad soon after, when the same Khuda Bax had introduced him to the tricky but immensely profitable oil futures market. Starling had figured out a complicated derivative based on future oil contracts that essentially bet against the price of oil rising in the short term. Basking in the warm glow of Khuda Bax's trust and profiting from his insider knowledge, the flood of cash, and the relatively stable situation in the Gulf, he had watched gleefully as Saudi Arabia sank deeper into debt and his own wealth at last began to swell. It was money for jam, a bet he couldn't lose. With Starling's expertise and reluctant connivance, he began shaving larger and larger sums off the accounts under his management. There were so many accounts and so much money that Khuda Bax had no idea how much money there really was much less where it was. Recycle the money, cream off the profit, put the money back – some of the money back. It was an ascending spiral that lifted Oldham skyward.

Then the unthinkable happened. The fucking Americans let one of their ships, the carrier Harry S. Truman, get into the sights of some trigger-happy mujahedeen with a rocket-launcher and the price of oil went through the roof.

Oldham's overextended margin positions were wiped out in one day, his hedges flattened the next. The first couple of days, he and Starling had been able to check their terrifying plunge by shuffling cash through Khuda Bax's nominee accounts. Then, everything that hadn't already happened seemed to happen at once. His brokers called his margins, the price per barrel hit another high as a hyper-inflated and understandably nervous market corrected, and some pint-sized Irish reporter showed up and started asking a raft of embarrassing questions. If the man found anything, and he probably would, Andrew Starling not being the staunchest of souls, the shit would really hit the fan: Inland Revenue, who knows what. Worst of all, just when he had finally found his pot of gold some bastard was about to pluck it out from under him. Desperate times called for desperate measures. The shallow waters Oldham had left so recently suddenly seemed a long way off and dark shapes had begun to circle.

So, on this spring morning that still promised so much Oldham headed into Northern Ireland on a desperate quest to find new money to plug the leaks. He swung the big Bentley through the narrow curves of the abandoned border-point between North and South at Newry, its barbed wire rusting and concrete blockhouse boarded up, and along the sea lough to Greyson's. It would indeed be an irony beyond ironies if it were Greyson's money, en route to Khuda Bax's accounts, that rescued Oldham's sagging fortunes. The only nagging question was how much, exactly, it was going to be.

Preparing himself for whatever fate was about to cast his way next, he pointed the Bentley up the long allée of copper beech that bordered the driveway of the majestic mansion, Ballynahinch House.

CHAPTER 10

Ballynahinch

The long driveway opened finally onto a wide gravel circle with a perfectly-cut ring of emerald grass at its centre. Away from the house, a wide lawn sloped down to the water's edge, the view giving onto distant hills shrouded in low cloud. Ballynahinch was classic Georgian: tall windows, slate roof, solid salt-stained walls fashioned out of the yellow sandstone of the hills against which it sheltered. Also part of the hereditary estate Oldham had no doubt. He pulled the Bentley to a halt on the far side of the circle only then realising that the driveway contained a number of cars of all kinds: a Rolls, a '60s-something Porsche, a battered Land Rover. True wealth Oldham knew, and he was an expert after all, never had to flaunt itself.

He stepped out of the car, pulling one of the empty leather pilot's cases out of the passenger side with him. There were two more in the trunk but better not show too eager, he thought to himself as he approached the house. The room to the right of the main door was clearly the dining-room. It was filled with guests. A drinks party by the look of it. Oldham entered the glassed-in porch that sheltered the double front doors, pulled once at the tarnished brass bell-pull and let himself in.

The stone-flagged hallway was itself big enough to accommodate a decent-sized reception. Portraits of Greyson ancestors eyed Oldham suspiciously from the walls. A huge canvas by the society painter Stubbs dominated the entrance from its pride of place over the staircase. The picture was so wide that the horse it commemorated tended by a top-hatted owner, a Greyson no doubt, seemed to have been elongated, giving it the appearance of a monstrous Dachshund. Point taken, Oldham thought. His attention was drawn from the portrait to a girl sitting on the stairs, her face partly hidden by the banisters. Very attractive, Oldham thought: late twenties, dark-haired, slim, short black skirt. The legs to wear it, too. A real beauty.

"Halloo there," he called invitingly.

The girl turned her face towards him, scrutinising him through the gap in the balustrades. She had been crying but her face, puffy as it was, had a luminous beauty. Mediterranean, Oldham thought. The girl looked at him for a second then away.

Oldham's confusion was covered by the appearance of an old man in a suit that might have been fashionable in the '40s. As the man came though the door from the dining room where the party was Oldham was hit by a wave of sound. The man closed the door carefully behind him and approached Oldham, a frail hand extended.

"I expect you're a friend of Neil's," he said.

It's a wake, Oldham thought suddenly noticing the black tie. "Yes, indeed," Oldham said. General Gordon Greyson, Oldham remembered, had been one of the most highly decorated members of Britain's Special Air Squadron before his retirement, a remarkable achievement in an élite company where indiscriminate bravery was the price of admission. The stooped figure before him turned, indicating the dining-room door.

"I'll let Neil know you're here, shall I?"

"Would you, please?"

"You all right up there, Lis my dear?" the old man asked, noticing the girl on the stairs.

"Yes, I'm fine, thanks." She flashed Oldham another cursory glance but said nothing more. The General shuffled back the way he had come releasing another roar of conversation from the dining-room as he entered. Moments later, Neil Greyson appeared. "Roger." Greyson made the name sound slightly ridiculous and his greeting meaningless.

"Hello, Neil. Look, I had no idea. I should have called ahead but our friend did say . . ." Oldham's voice trailed off. He cursed himself for apologising. It was a trick of Neil's to somehow always make you feel as if he were doing you an enormous favour by just letting you stand in front of him. Preoccupied, Oldham missed the momentary hesitation in Greyson's answer.

"It's fine. Really. Want a drink? Something to eat?"

"No thanks. Already ate on the way up." Oldham hadn't but again he found himself involuntarily playing courtier to Greyson's monarch. "I'm just here to . . ."

Greyson cut him off. "We can talk in here," he said, shepherding Oldham into the library on the opposite side of the hall. Neil Greyson at forty-nine was in his prime, a tall, squarely-built man with wide shoulders and farmer's hands. A badly-reset broken nose – boxing he'd once told Oldham – jutted like a granite promontory from the sloping plane of his forehead. Where Neil led, most men seemed instinctively to follow.

"I feel like a perfect fool asking, but . . ." Oldham said as Greyson closed the door behind them.

"An old friend of Dad's, a journalist. They served together in the war. The funeral was this morning. Dad insisted on having everyone over here afterwards. You know the way he is."

Oldham nodded, but quite honestly had no idea if it was the General's manner or not since the Greysons had pointedly avoided having anything to do with Roger Oldham from the moment his name had registered on their collective screens. Oldham's hand went to a jacket pocket and produced a pack of cigarettes.

"Someone I might know?"

"No," Greyson answered, his tone clearly stating both his opinion of the deceased and the press in general. "Some little prick at the Irish News – Tim Short."

It was Oldham's turn to register surprise. He had a hard time covering it. "Mind if I smoke?" He waved the pack toward his host.

"Go ahead," Greyson said.

Oldham put down the flight case and sat heavily into one of the armchairs that surrounded the large and ornate fireplace. He took a swift inventory of his surroundings: the inevitable scimitar on the wall, the photos on the piano, Neil and Gabrielle, his stunningly pretty Swedish wife, Neil in Arab head-dress standing on the hood of a jeep from their days in the desert. The usual stuff.

"How . . .when did it happen?" Oldham asked, his voice steady now.

"Three days ago, south of Dublin. A car bomb," Greyson said flatly as if he had already answered the same question too many times.

"Good God," Oldham said, taken off guard again.

Greyson sat himself on the window seat, the sea at his back, his face hard to read against the light. "Short was an investigative reporter. He claimed he had some inside story on the arms-for-drugs traffic between the Near East and the US Claimed Dublin was a way-station. Since, as you probably know, I have a considerable interest in security matters in the Gulf, he locked on to me as one of his prime suspects. Pretty pathetic really. Anyway, once he'd got onto that track, he started attracting the attention of the IRA The rest, as they say, is history."

Oldham leaned forward in his chair, lightly brushing a fleck of ash from the leg of his blue silk suit. "I can't believe it, Neil. These're things you only read about in the paper."

"Neil would rather you didn't even read about it in the papers. Isn't that right, Neil?" Oldham turned. It was the girl on the stairs standing now in the open doorway of the library.

"Roger," Neil said from his seat by the window. "This is Lis Charnay, a friend of ours, a friend of Tim Short's really." There was the slightest hint of ice in Greyson's voice. "Lis, this is Roger, a friend of mine from army days."

"Glad to meet you, Lis," Roger Oldham said, turning on the charm. Charnay ignored him pointedly.

"Neil thinks this is all an IRA plot, don't you Neil? Just the fucking Catholics taking a sideways poke at his dear old dad. Right, Neil? He'd rather the whole thing just fade away. Rather we'd all go away, leave him and his precious house, his beautiful estate in peace." Charnay placed heavy emphasis on the possessive. "I've been talking to your old man, Neil. Sweet guy. He told me that he's actually left this thing, this whole beautiful fucking two thousand-acre thing to all four of his children, you, your brother and sisters, Neil. Old Neil here believes in primogeniture," Lis went on, turning to Oldham. "Thinks it's all his. Right of the firstborn. Basically, Neil's a major arsehole but no one round here has the nerve to tell him that to his face."

"Lis just got back from the front in Afghanistan," Greyson explained coolly. "I'm afraid she has taken up the late Tim Short's cause. He was something of a father to her. She's taken this whole thing pretty much to heart."

Oldham realised the young woman was not only very upset, she was also more than a little drunk. She carried a full glass of the General's Bushmills in her hand. It shook slightly. "Well, don't let me spoil your fun. I'm sure you've got plenty of old war wounds to compare," Lis said tartly, gulping down some of the whiskey and heading back into the hall.

"American?" Oldham asked.

"Lebanese actually, though she's spent most of her life in the States. Works for some cable news channel."

"Beautiful girl," Roger Oldham commented, admiring Lis's slim form retreating.

Neil Greyson ignored Oldham's comment, instead cutting straight to the point. "I suppose you have the appropriate credentials to show me. Why don't you bring your bag there and follow me. And you'll need another." Greyson led the way through an arched doorway in the wall of bookshelves, Oldham following expectantly.

Lis Charnay entered the dining-room and threaded her way through the crowd of mourners to the sideboard. That morning they had all stood silent in their dark suits, their bowler hats, their uniforms, the mist drifting in from the sea. The night before, over their strangely festive dinner in this same dining-room, General Greyson had told her: "We're all up there. The first Greyson was buried in 1634. We buried my wife there, too. He'll be amongst friends." He was so sweet, trying so hard to make it all seem part of the measured pace of life in this house where Greysons had lived, at least on the site, for three hundred and fifty years. But the General's gentle recital of family history and the slight pressure of the pitifully thin hand on her arm as the six men had lowered Tim's coffin into the grave hadn't helped, had even made it worse in ways. Tim Short's body had been incinerated. The image it recalled was of the crisped body of the drug-dealer at the terrorist camp in Afghanistan. Her best friend had died in a senseless local border-war while she was off in left field chasing shadows, snagging the likely suspects for an image or two. Lis poured more whiskey from the crystal decanter, her hand shaking uncontrollably now.

"Are you all right?" a voice asked. It was a pleasant, shy voice with the faintest lilt of Irishness that delivered the "all right" as "awrite." A pale face with a shock of red hair came into focus. Lis stared at the young man but said nothing. "I'm sorry," he said, reddening. "I just wondered if you were okay."

"I'm not. Okay? None of us fucking are. Okay?" None of them would be ever again, she was sure. The horror had come home to roost for each one of them. Except, of course, for Neil. "I'm sorry," she said, sniffing hard. "Let me guess, you're one of Neil's army friends."

"Actually, no. I'm not – a friend, I mean." The blush rose on his neck and accentuated the colour of his hair and the paleness of his skin.

She had noticed him earlier, watching her intently as she moved through the room. "Not a friend and not in the military. You can't be on the General's staff because he doesn't have one and you're not one of Tim's friends because none of them wear Marks and Spencers suits."

The young man was, in fact, a Special Branch "watcher" who under normal circumstances would already be safe in his Metro and headed back to Dublin to type out his unnecessary and unread report: no incident, no strange faces. But General Greyson, veteran of plenty of seemingly pointless watches in his time, knew immediately who the young man was and, without undermining the boy's already shaky professional confidence in the least, had insisted in his easy manner that the "watcher" stop in for a drink before taking off. The young man was silent, dazzled by Lis's head-on assault.

"Okay. Let's just settle for a name. Red hair, Paisley tie: I'd say a Robert."

"It's Stephen, actually," the young man managed. "Stephen Thompson."

"Stephen," Lis repeated the name as if the young man who went by it had seduced her utterly. "And since I did so well with the name, and since you haven't talked to a single person in this room except for me, I'm going to guess you're a Greyson cousin."

"I'm afraid not," Thompson said, apologising again

He was so real, so much of the present, not of the past, as if he had risen fresh on some moon tide, washed ashore on a virgin beach, that Lis had an urge to let her grief for Tim, for the cause they pursued so relentlessly, and the rage she felt engulf him.

"Nothing to be afraid of," Lis replied encouragingly;

"who'd want to be related to this crew." Her right arm, the one holding the drink, encompassed the silent ancestors in their frames around the walls. As she gestured, her arm knocked against Thompson's shoulder and most of the liquid spilled onto his suit and shirt. "Oh shit. I'm sorry."

"Really, it's fine," the young man reassured her, trying to brush it off but making it worse.

Lis ignored his protest. "Let me take care of it." She grabbed Stephen Thompson's arm and dragged him through the crowd to the sink in the butler's pantry off the dining room. Wetting a dishcloth under the tap, she mopped first the suit then the shirt. The strangeness of the activity, the sudden quiet of the small room, closed-off from the din by the heavy swing-door, her own acute pain overcame Lis suddenly.

"I'm sorry. I'm just, I just can't . . ." Lis managed, both hands dropping onto the moist shirt, her voice beginning to break. Thompson, startled at his own audacity, wrapped his long arms around Lis's shoulders. She looked up into his puzzled face, not a hint of guile clouding it.

"Take me home," Lis whispered. "I have to go home."

As Neil Greyson walked Oldham out of the study and across the stone-floor to the front door, Oldham now weighted down with two gleaming black-leather flight bags but still the consummate salesman, laid an elegant green and gold business card printed on vellum on the circular mahogany table. "Just in case, old boy. You never know what next." Greyson nodded. "Give my regards to your father, won't you. I don't want to disturb him," Oldham said easily, shaking Greyson's hand.

Greyson opened the door just in time for the two men to see a rather battered Metro making its way down the tree-lined driveway. Oldham was quick to notice that the passenger was Tim Short's blunt-spoken friend, Lis Charnay. Pity, he thought; I'd have liked to have got to know her better.

"So long, old boy," Oldham said, trying to make light of his disappointment. Unable to contain himself at the sight of the treasure-trove in Greyson's ample safe, Oldham had momentarily crossed the line and asked Greyson if he'd mind adding something to the pile in the bags for Oldham personally. "Just a temporary fix to carry me over. Took a bit of a beating on the markets. I'd get it back you, of course." Greyson hadn't seemed put out, had just been very direct, blunt even. No funds were available. Too bad. As Oldham walked back to the Bentley, Greyson picked up the phone on the hall table and punched in a Dublin number. Offshore Management, Ltd. he read off Oldham's card; Roger Oldham, President. Funny what the tide could wash in, he thought.

CHAPTER 11

London

The tide was coming in for Roger Oldham faster than he knew. While he was engaged in his desperate efforts to plug the leaks with fresh infusions of cash, the heart of his operation, his office in London, was under attack.

The windows in the Bond Street office off Piccadilly were uncurtained. The tenants on the street, renowned for the high-priced art displayed in its galleries and equally high rents, had everything to gain from being seen. The man inside the second-floor office at number 32 had everything to hide and was doing his best to avoid discovery. Crouched in one corner of the room, his back to the window, he tried vainly to mask what his hands were so busy at.

In keeping with current tradecraft all the office lights were on. This suggestion had met with a snort of disbelief from Max Skinner, the retired pro now practising his craft again. Skinner had been breaking safes legally and illegally since he finished his National Service in 1953. The idea of opening a "piece" as he called the safes he worked on in broad daylight or the next best thing was ludicrous. The two men who had approached him had been adamant. They had even supplied the overalls Skinner now wore. City Cleaning Corp. emblazoned his back in swirling red letters and the side of the panel van parked on the street. The cart containing cleaning materials in the outer office completed the subterfuge. Skinner sat back momentarily on his rump. He checked his watch, allowed himself a glance at the window. "If the law is watching, at least they're getting a good view. Bloody Do-It-Yourself time on the TV!" He scratched the side of his head, dislodging the ear-piece that attached to a wireless pack on his belt. Irritably, he pulled the device away from his ear and stuffed it in his top pocket before picking up the flexible probe from the tool box at his side and kneeling before the safe again.

The two men who had visited him in his Ladbroke Grove flat had been more than generous, agreeing to all his suggestions. He had spent the next day shopping, the most expensive item being the flexible endoscope he now used to probe the safe's interior. "Same thing your doctor sticks up your old back passage, innit. All fish and chips these days," he had rambled on then stopped to explain. "All computers and circuit boards." The two of them didn't seem too quick, though. Didn't get it. As for these gadgets, there was no knocking them. "You can look right in and count off the numbers pretty much." Skinner made a final adjustment to the mini-terminal at his side then carefully entered the eleven-digit sequence on the keypad on the safe's surface panel. The safe's locking mechanism whirred softly for a moment, a dot of green light shone on the panel. Bingo.

Directly across the street in an office much like the one Max Skinner now busily plundered for his employers, though by contrast completely dark, two men standing well back watched the man work.

"Does he always do this?"

"What?"

"Talk to himself?"

The other man smiled. "Every time."

The safe-cracker checked his rubber gloves once more then pushed the "Open" button on the soft-key pad. The heavy door of the safe swung steadily open. "What a beauty," Skinner said to himself. "Chubb SuperTech. State-of-the-bleedin'-art. Bloke must be rolling in it."

He picked up a Polaroid camera from his tool box, checked the flash was taped over, and snapped the safe's interior twice. Setting the prints aside to develop, he began removing the items one by one. Envelopes, a couple of videos, porn most likely, always is, a pile of computer disks, cash, wads of cash but leave it alone, always leave the cash, a packet of what looked like stock certificates or bonds – "Bearer bonds," Skinner said flipping through them – and, of course, the 'black book.' "They always choose black, don't they." He opened a portable easel with a gooseneck quartz-iodine light at each top corner, clipped the book open at the first page then switched on the two lights. He checked his watch. One fifteen. Snap the book, use the fancy copier in the front room for the papers, copy the disks onto the laptop and over to the Jaz drive. "Done by four thirty, home by six. Nice work if you can get it." He began to whistle softly through closed teeth as he worked the digital camera with its self-focusing close-up lens.

"How much longer?" Jay Peterson whispered to his companion. His eyes were beginning to ache. He shifted the horn-rims onto his forehead to rub them, carefully avoiding the scars on his face.

"An hour, maybe more. He should be done by five anyway." Jay had spent close to three days with the man standing next to him but had learned little more about him than his name. "Sam Clemens," he'd offered as he leaned over Jay's bed in the Dublin Hospital where they had taken him after Clemens had pulled him from the car. Jay's eyes, the only part of his wounded face he could move without causing agonising pain had asked the obvious question. "Yeah. Like Twain. It's a long story." Jay hadn't asked again.

Jay didn't know how long he'd lain on the gurney while the young Indian doctor had extracted fragments of the windshield from his face and neck. "It is a good thing," the liquid voice had said, "that you were wearing your glasses." Jay tried not to imagine the alternative.

Later, while the doctor picked at Jay's hands with the shining forceps, the man named Clemens made his own meticulous examination of Jay's recent past. How long had he known Short? Had he seen anyone else that night? Anyone in the pub or the street? At first, Jay assumed Clemens was official, but when a Special Branch officer had joined them and asked Jay the routine questions, Clemens had identified himself only as a friend. After the man had left, Jay had mumbled a comment that had brought Clemens' ear intimately close to Jay's mouth. Moving his lips at all required an effort of will: the combination of Novocain that paralysed his face and the pain caused by the slightest movement of his features limited communication to the barest necessity. "Have we met?" Jay mumbled again.

Clemens' usually emotionless face was lit for a moment by a warm grin but he made no comment until the doctor had left to answer a phone call. "Bob Lorenz called me. Asked me if I'd keep an eye on you. Hope you don't mind." Jay could hardly object since Clemens had probably saved his life, certainly had saved his eyesight. In spite of the debt, Jay had been hesitant about telling Clemens much about Short. He told him that Short was a journalist specialising in arms- and drug-traffic, a contact given him by a friend in Washington. Short, in turn, had passed Jay Oldham's name suggesting he take a closer look. It came as a surprise then, a shock even, when 24-hours later, Jay and his newly-attached "watcher" boarded a plane for London and wound up across the street from Roger Oldham's office engaged in what could only be characterised as an illegal entry.

During their long night's watch Jay had succeeded in squeezing out of Clemens that he had qualified as a para-rescue jumper, making it through a hellish eighteen months of survival training, high altitude parachute jumping and freefalling onto glaciers only to be permanently retired after a near-fatal car crash on graduation night in which the driver, a fellow student, had died. But his questions about the connection with Lorenz, whether Bob had condoned the night's work, if Clemens was with the DEA or the FBI were all rebuffed with the same quiet smile and an elusive "not really" or "maybe."

By four fifteen Max Skinner had finished work on the black book and had begun transferring the information from the three and a half inch disks stored in the safe, methodically removing one from the stack, slipping it into the floppy port of his laptop, dragging its contents to the laptop's hard-drive and waiting for them to copy over. He was two-thirds down the pile when Sam Clemens' cell phone trilled. He flipped it open.

"Yup?" He snapped it shut again. "Company."

The street had been quiet all night. A garbage truck had worked its way noisily up the street at around one. At two a private security car had cruised by, a flashlight from inside playing on the street doors it passed. Otherwise, only an occasional black London cab had broken the monotony of their watch. Now, a white panel van turned into the street.

"Their second pass in five minutes," Clemens said. "Better hurry him up." He turned up the gain on the two-way radio and pressed the transmit button. "Cleaner to Craftsman, Cleaner to Craftsman." Peterson and Clemens waited for Skinner to react but the old man across the street carried on with his routine, inserting a disk, copying the contents over, ejecting the disk, placing it on a second stack.

"Cleaner to Craftsman, Cleaner to Craftsman," Clemens repeated, his tone more insistent. "Shit!"

The brake lights glowed on the panel van as it pulled to a stop four doors up. The van reversed suddenly, its gears whining as the driver accelerated backwards. Peterson and Clemens watched the van stop in front of Offshore's building, saw its lights go off. Then, nothing. In the lighted window, two floors above the street, Skinner worked on. After a minute, the back doors of the van swung open and two men got out. A heavy-set man in warm-ups and running shoes looked up at Offshore's windows while the other glanced up and down the street. They walked over to the door. The big man pulled a slip of paper from his pocket and holding it out before him to catch the light used a podgy finger to punch in a code on the keypad on the door-frame. Taking one last look behind them, the two men entered.

Max Skinner had always done things his own way. As a

young man, his mulishness had landed him in permanent trouble; now it saved his life. Peterson and Clemens had insisted on openness. If there was an interruption, Max was to use his cover as the cleaning service. Skinner, however, had filed his own insurance by dragging the office copier across the glass front-door. Watching the hands on the tiny clock on the computer's desktop tick away the seconds before the contents of the disk inside were copied over, Skinner caught a brief flash of reflected light on the screen. He didn't miss a beat. He pocketed the disk he was holding, leaned across the desk, his backside rising off the seat simultaneously, and began tidying up the scattered items before him, whistling loudly all the time. An elbow deftly closed the lid of the laptop and the vacuum cleaner hose and nozzle appeared in his hand as if by magic. Pushing the cleaner out in front of him, the appliance's body trailing behind, he moved into the outer office in time to see the larger of the two men putting his shoulder to the door and shoving.

"Just a tick," Max called; "I'm coming."

The big man on the other side of the door watched in disbelief, undecided, but his companion had already voted, taking off down the stairs two at a time.

"Sorry," the big man mumbled, "wrong place." The accent was thick Irish.

Across the street, Peterson and Clemens watched in amazement as the two intruders stumbled out of the street door and scrambled back into the van while their own "intruder," unruffled, watched their progress from above. Coolly placing the vacuum cleaner hose back against the table edge where it had been leaning, Max Skinner returned to his seat to finish the night's work.

Above the squeal of van's tyres as it took off up the street, Clemens heard the old man humming now over the wireless speakers transmitting from the window mikes Skinner had placed.

"It wasn't even on," Clemens said.

"What?"

"The vacuum cleaner. It wasn't even on."

CHAPTER 12

Portree, Northern Ireland

The young man lay outstretched on the bed, his arms spread slightly and turned upwards to show the long lines of the arteries, blue against the pale skin. A sparse cluster of curly red hair surrounded each nipple, a darker and fuller thicket covered his crotch. His breath was even, shallow, his lips fractionally turned up at the corners. He slept like a baby, defenceless, guiltless. The woman beside him lay on her back, too, but had pulled the sheet to her neck, her eyes wide and staring straight up. She too barely breathed but her broken face was streaked with tears, the sheet beneath her chin soaked.

Lis Charnay and Stephen Thompson lay side by side on the double-bed of Lis's hotel room at the Fraser Arms in Portree, five miles down the road from Ballynahinch House, the young man spent, Lis still awake in the first light of dawn. Images piled one on top of another. Again and again she saw Short's car erupting silently in a balloon of red fire with Tim's screaming mouth at its centre. Lis's whole body shook as she sobbed, her grief for Tim, for herself and the many lonely nights she had spent in strange, empty rooms like this one, for the cumulation of a thousand images of violent death, pain and suffering, all at once crashing over her like wave, rolling her up and hurling her down, gasping for air.

Sitting abruptly upright, the sheet dropping from her body, she turned over the top of the young man at her side, grabbing his head by its curly red hair with her right hand, her left arching over his shoulder to prop up her body, pounding the head up and back on the pillow beneath it.

"Why didn't you fuckers do something? Why didn't you?" she yelled in the startled man's face, his blue eyes staring wide, trying to focus on the face above as his own rose and fell against the pillow. Lis straddled Thompson, sitting on his stomach, pushing down on his chest with her arms so that the young man could hardly breathe.

"Why?" Lis's last question, howled into Stephen's face, dissolved into uncontrollable sobs as her arms collapsed and her body fell onto his.

Thompson lay on his back with Lis's lithe body now hunched like some strange animal on his chest. He didn't move, barely breathed. Lis's cropped black hair, redolent with the smell of some flower, tickled his nose, the warmth of her breasts pressed into his chest making him suddenly aware of the icy cold of his exposed toes. Lis hoisted herself off Thompson's chest.

"You're a fucking policeman. Why didn't you save him? You know who did it. Why don't you go and arrest the bastard and blow him up? Blow him fucking up!" Lis stared wildly into Thompson's callow face, the startled blue eyes, the faint shadow of red beard on the chin. "You don't know, do you?"

Thompson managed a faint reply: "No."

"No, you don't know," she repeated, still staring directly into his face but less wild now, beginning to think, beginning to realise what she had hold of, this young, infatuated Special Branch policeman who would likely never get over this wildest night of his life. "But you could find out." Thompson, still paralysed with amazement, lay thunderstruck.

"What exactly do you do?" Lis began.

"What do I do?" Thompson repeated stupidly.

"Yes, Stephen, you. What exactly do you do?" She was her wiliest now, her sexiest, reassuring, cajoling, stroking his hair the way an attentive mother might soothe a sick child while the luckless Stephen Thompson exposed all the small secrets of his profession that he was ever to know.

There had been an investigation, yes, but he hadn't been part of it. Well, yes, it was his office that was leading it and, yes, of course, he did hear things from time to time. What sort of things? Well, it had been a bomb. A bomb? Yes. Mr. Manktilow, his boss, had him working overtime on the database the night of the bombing. What database? There are these databases we can cross-reference that will match past incidents with locations, dates and types of explosive and triggering mechanisms and so on.

"And what kind of device was this, Stephen?" Lis coaxed, still stroking Stephen's hair. It was the young man's turn now for remorse. Gently sniffing, he betrayed the closely-guarded details of his office's investigation to this exquisite temptress. "A UCBT."

"A UCBT?" she prompted.

"An Under Car Booby Trap," he whispered.

"And which car was this UCBT placed under?" Lis continued.

"Under his car, under your friend's, Mr. Short's"

"It was the IRA, wasn't it?" Lis said. Thompson hesitated. "Wasn't it, Stephen?"

"Mr. Manktilow doesn't think so."

Lis's long fingers stopped in mid course, gripping the boy's hair again. Thompson's body tensed, preparing for another onslaught. Instead, Lis resumed her stroking, asking gently how he knew. The boy's eyes were fixed in hers as if reading his text there. The device was too sophisticated for the IRA It didn't match their signature. And the material used, non-detectable Semtex suggested the bomb had originated overseas. Non-detectable? It gave off no detectable odour. That particular type of Semtex was no longer produced. The Czech manufacturer now added a trace scent so that dogs could detect it. Remaining supplies had been hoarded by the Libyans, over one thousand tonnes, though isolated caches were believed to exist in France, the Middle East and Afghanistan. The utterance of the last name stopped the steady flow of questions for a moment; then the drum-beat began again.

"And how would somebody trigger this UCBT?" Lis continued. Suddenly, Thompson's frame was wracked with a sob, a hiccup of air. Lis pulled his body up to hers, bringing his face in towards her chest.

"I shouldn't be telling you all this. You shouldn't be asking me," Stephen managed to choke out.

"Shh," Lis soothed. "What sort of trigger?"

"A remote."

Lis Charnay covered the young man's body with her own, her mouth covering his, her hands pouring over him like a warm, soft river that stilled his conscience and aroused him to one final crescendo.

CHAPTER 13

London

Roger Oldham's life was laid out on the narrow bed in Jay's hotel room, a mosaic of receipts from expensive restaurants, airline charges, hotel bills, scrambled notations of amounts subtracted from individual accounts or amounts owed them, Jay wasn't sure which. The names on the accounts ranged from the ludicrous to the exotic, John Smith to Ali Hussein. The totals were more serious, never less than six figures. If there was a pattern it was going to take a forensic accountant to find it. Connolly and Short's "name", Khuda Bax, was nowhere visible, not even in the pages of the black book where names, phone numbers, women, men, dates, appointments were entered in no apparent order. The document Jay had hoped for, the master ledger with a summary of all accounts that might tie Khuda Bax to some recognisable entity either didn't exist or was missing. It looked like Brian's theory was just that. He turned to the official report Clemens had added to the stack.

The two men had driven Skinner home just after six then on to the US Embassy in Grosvenor Square and into its subterranean garage. "Best if you stay down here," Clemens had said and gone upstairs, presumably to transmit the product of their night's work to Washington. Clemens hadn't said and Jay knew him well enough by now not to ask. Jay had slept fitfully in the front of the cleaning van until just before ten when Clemens climbed back into the driver's seat. The other man had handed him copies of the material, the pages and pages of print-outs and the rest without a word, then driven Jay back to his hotel, the grubby little place in Kensington with Albanian help and airless box-like rooms.

There were three pages to the official report on Bax, a summary in the impersonal style Jay knew well. Under the heading Khuda Bax Abdul Aziz, the report began with a quote from an unidentified informer:. "He speaks Urdu, English, French, and Arabic, three with an accent, one without. Not to be trusted in any."

Jay scanned the document. Khuda Bax it seemed was a relative-by-marriage of King Fahd of Saudi's clan and something of an embarrassment to his in-laws. Among his better advertised exploits was his purchase of potentially valuable property overlooking the Holy Kaaba in Mecca. He had taken over the deeds then forced the occupants out without payment. There had been bouts of drunkenness and lewdness, reports of wild nights abroad and ill-considered associations at home. Overall, these excesses must have been slight or Khuda Bax's eligibility wildly overrated. His father-in-law, Prince Hashem bin Nayef al Safar, the King's nephew, dished out $2 million for the wedding to his daughter Liala. Khuda Bax had duly entered the protective but watchful inner circle of the royal family, swelling its charmed membership by one.

In the mid '90s Khuda Bax had been cut into some of the smaller so-called "security" deals by his father-in-law, a

Defence Ministry insider, but had never really tapped into the big time. He'd been shut out of the $3.2 billion allegedly kicked back by Lockheed to phantom Saudi companies for the sale of $30 billion-worth of F-16s that Saudi pilots would never be allowed to fly armed. Fahd's close family was supposedly so paranoid they had ringed their palaces with Stinger missiles. No, Khuda Bax was not one of the chosen few. Instead, he had been kept busy in the less glamorous liquidation of a bankrupt Russia's armoury, buying the arms with US dollars, everything from tanks to the ubiquitous AK-47, and brokering them to second-tier markets: Somalia, Congo, Nigeria. Competition was fierce, cheaper versions of the AK-47 coming out of China and Egypt undercutting his market, bigger fish swimming in smaller ponds. Khuda Bax had taken a heavy loss in Bosnia where the "the world's peacemaker," the US, wiped out his margins when they landed a boatload of $100 million-worth of M-60 tanks, a squadron of UH-1 helicopters and 45,000 M-16 rifles, the first of an ongoing re-armament. So much for peace.

Khuda Bax had turned elsewhere for his profits then and found a riskier and homelier dancing-partner: Afghanistan. The newly ascendant Taliban were desperate for weapons and desperate for cash, an insoluble equation that Khuda Bax had solved. He proposed, and by various accounts had succeeded in convincing the intransigent Taliban to trade arms for heroin. Clemens had attached a note to the document in his own hand-writing that read: Afghanistan 2nd largest opium producer in the world. 80% to Europe balance to US. DEA still trying to ID Khuda Bax's distributors.

Drug trafficking in Saudi was punishable by death, Jay knew; in Taliban-controlled Afghanistan, too. Khuda Bax was not only alive but apparently kicking in both countries according to the report. The US State Department showed a twenty five percent jump in opium production in 1998. Khuda Bax? And if so, so what? Jay wondered. Khuda Bax's Afghan connection certainly placed him in the most lawless region in the world and close to some of best-stocked pools of terrorists outside of Iran: the Hindu Kush, Baluchistan, the Khyber Pass, Peshawar, Darunta. But with no hard evidence, no point of contact, Jay was no nearer finding a connection than before.

Three thousand miles to the east, an unscheduled non-commercial flight had cleared Iraqi airspace en route to Paris after a tortuous detour to avoid the no-fly zones. There were only two passengers. One, a squat, frog-like figure in a cheap suit was asleep, his head slumped forward on his chest. Across from him sat Khuda Bax humming tunelessly, his thin voice rising and falling in a soft chant, his gaze resting nervously on the figure opposite for a moment and then just as quickly flicking away. A white-coated steward, recognising his employer's anxious mood, placed a large, ice-filled glass on Khuda Bax's arm-rest without comment, then padded softly back down the aisle to the galley.

Fate was nobody's mistress, thought Khuda Bax; she could not be wooed. One moment she was soft in your arms, the next a screaming fury at your ear. He peered through the porthole at the desert of white clouds below. He enjoyed these long flights in the Challenger as a rule. He could relax, could do as he pleased, dividing his time between uninterrupted contemplation of his multiple businesses and an occasional dalliance with one of the entourage of boys who usually accompanied him. Now, nothing could console him, not the boys nor the guilty glass of forbidden alcohol at his side.

The meeting had been arranged by phone. The Taliban commander with whom Khuda Bax only spoke when he absolutely had to for the sake of commerce had introduced a Mr. Ibrahim and then put him on. Mr. Ibrahim had appeared courteous at first, complimenting him on his astute handling of the Taliban's traffic in opium. He had risen to the bait in spite of himself and luxuriated in the praise. Then the trap had snapped. Mr. Ibrahim had need of Mr. Bax's service, his "pipeline." Would Mr. Bax object? How could he? Mr. Ibrahim, it seemed, had a particularly close relationship with the Taliban. Mr. Ibrahim did not want Mr. Bax's enterprise to suffer, it went without saying, nor would he ever want the Taliban's success to be put in jeopardy.

Khuda Bax was left in no doubt as to the consequences should he refuse. The creature sitting opposite him now had been offered by the ever-thoughtful Mr. Ibrahim as "protection" though it was clear whose interests the thug was protecting. There were plenty of other urgent reasons to persuade Bax to comply. He would lose the lucrative trade with the Taliban, he was sure. But, worse, his traffic in forbidden drugs would be revealed to his in-laws. That, he knew, would bring a sudden end to his comfortable life within the protective walls of King Fahd's guardianship. God knows what evil creatures lurked without or what harm they would visit on Khuda Bax should he be cast out.

Having no choice, Khuda Bax asked meekly what small service he might willingly render Mr. Ibrahim. Mr. Bax, Mr. Ibrahim knew, had ways of transporting items across international borders without interference from curious officials. Was that so? Khuda Bax could hardly deny it. Details were elaborated, a calendar set.

And that was that. And now, here he was en route to Paris with this vileness before him. The flight into Baghdad International had been uneventful though interesting. They had been "visited" several times by American and British fighters, sleek shapes that darted into Khuda Bax's vision like giant fish, close enough so that he could see a bulbous head turn his way from the cockpit of the other aircraft. Then, just as suddenly, the fighter had winged down and disappeared from view. Even the arrival had been free of anxiety. Mr. Ibrahim had instructed him that his duty was simply to have the plane land in Baghdad. Various cargo would be loaded into the hold and he could then continue on his way to Paris. No cause for concern. The cargo was under United Nations seal and was anyway humanitarian in nature. Khuda Bax was willing enough to accept the explanation. Then, just before departure, he had been joined by his passenger.

Without invitation Nasir Abu Massoud had occupied the seat opposite. When Khuda Bax had got up to go to the bathroom, Nasir had risen soundlessly and accompanied him, a pace behind. Khuda Bax had tried to close the door but the man had blocked it with his foot and he had been obliged to relieve himself in full view of Nasir and a steward who was passing. So it had gone for the remainder of the flight. There was never any physical violence, just the threat, always the threat. Nasir was a coiled spring that might snap open at any moment.

Slumped now in the wide armchair on board his Challenger, a blandly pornographic film playing unwatched on the overhead monitor, the usually unflappable Khuda Bax hummed tunelessly on. The drug traffic he wanted. Smuggling the raw opium across the Afghan border into Turkey at Sadaruk and by truck across Europe had been a hugely profitable business in spite of the overheads. Not least of these were the new and increasingly punitive duties levied by the local Mafia in the Republics who oversaw the safe transit of Khuda Bax's precious cargo through their territories. The opium business was certainly an easier monopoly to protect than arms. The margins were better and the drug was making a comeback. It was in high demand. Drug traders were anyway better payers than governments.

The phone in Khuda Bax's armrest warbled. He picked it up, casting a nervous glance at the sleeping Nasir first. A hiss of static gave way to a faint voice.

"Khuda Bax?"

"Yes?" he said in accented English. A moment's pause gave him the time to recognise the caller.

"I'm afraid we have a small problem our end." The caller's emphasis landed heavily on the "we." Khuda Bax was silent, hoping the caller would elaborate. Instead, the voice at the other end simply said: "Call me when you can. You understand?"

"Yes, I'll call," Khuda Bax said. "Yes, of course."

The connection went dead and he replaced the receiver in its cradle. As he did, he was aware of Nasir's gaze on him, a wide grin stretching the frog-like face.

CHAPTER 14

London

Ripples on the water's surface foreshortened the submerged body beneath. The body was naked, the greenness of the water adding an eerie luminescence to its flesh. One leg rose slowly then dextrously turned off the tap on the miniature heater above. Lis Charnay's face emerged at the other end of the narrow bath, her cropped hair slicked back, the water running down her neck and collecting in the hollow above her breasts.

The bath was almost cold but she wasn't ready to get out. The water soothed her, helped her think. She sank again, hearing the faint rush of early morning traffic, then what sounded like the crackle of a motorbike exhaust on the Embankment through the thin wall of water.

The houseboat in Chelsea Harbour off Cheyne Walk was Lis's base of operations when she wasn't on assignment. She couldn't really call it home. The houseboat, an old de-masted sloop, was more of a box on water than a boat and had never once moved from its mooring between the Johnsons' boat against the quay and Arthur Sullivan's boat between it and the Thames.

She let her body rock with the light swell of the river, thinking of Tim Short. They had met at the network's Paris offices five years before and had quickly discovered an affinity. They were fired by the same spark. There was a fearlessness, a need to know that urged them both on whatever the odds, a fire that forged a deep and enduring alliance. Where Lis was impetuous, however, Tim was staunchly conservative and he finally returned to print journalism. The network's approach was too superficial, he lectured Lis, too casual. Real investigative journalism required a patience and dedication that TV news didn't have time for. In spite of the professional breach, they had developed a deep trust, continuing to share information and work each other's stories, most recently on the traffic in Afghani opium and arms.

Lis's body settled, the memory of the adventures she had shared with Tim overcoming her pang of loss. Then, a tap of wood on wood brought her sharply back to the present. She opened her eyes underwater, staring up at the ceiling. The tap was followed by a squeak on the deck above. Her neighbour, Arthur, always called before he even set foot on the boat. He was so sweet. He'd been here for years, dabbing away at unsaleable paintings of watery sunsets. The decking creaked again.

The boat's main cabin and sleeping quarters were covered by a raised hatchway with narrow storm ports running front to back. It was still dark out but light spilled in through the ports from streetlights along the Embankment. Lis pulled herself upright, water dripping off her shoulders onto the floor. She turned her head to the strip of window above her. Silhouetted against the light was a man's shoe. It disappeared instantly and was followed by another creak.

There had been a prowler once. The young man, it turned out, had intended to relieve himself over the edge of Arthur's boat but hadn't made it further than Lis's. He had spent the rest of the night curled up on the hatch cover where he had fallen, wrapped in one of her blankets.

Lis pulled herself out of the bath, reaching for a towel and wrapping it tightly round her. If this was another drunk, she wasn't going to give him any more pleasure than he'd already had that night. There was a heavy thump overhead as if someone had dropped a weight. She waited for a second, barely breathing, then crossed the cabin to the cockpit door at the stern. As she reached for the handle, her face now level with the window in the top of the outer door, she froze. Squashed flat against the glass was the bloodstained face of Stephen Thompson.

Lis stifled a scream then pushed hard on the door. It wouldn't budge. Thompson's inert body was blocking it. "Stephen, you've got to get up," she called through the glass, trying again to dislodge him. Thomspon didn't stir. She stepped back down into the cabin and ran forward to the sleeping quarters, a narrow bunk on one side, the bath on the other. Overhead was a long disused skylight which she now heaved up and open. A clatter of breaking flower pots followed. Clutching her towel tightly with one hand, she pushed herself off the bunk and into the early morning air.

A thin fog hung over the water obscuring the lights on the far bank. No lights showed in the other boats yet, no one was visible on the Embankment. She climbed onto the deck and ran the few steps back to the cockpit. Sprawled drunkenly against the door, just as she had seen him, was Stephen Thompson, his legs hooked over the coving around the edge of the well, the rest of his body crumpled tight in the bottom.

"Oh, my God," she said aloud as she saw the wide stain

of blood across Thomspon's back. Stepping down into the cockpit, she gently pulled the boy's body back, opening the door at the same time with her free hand. Thompson groaned slightly as she hoisted him up but his eyes stayed closed. A smear of blood stained the pale face, its bright crimson clashing violently with the crop of red hair above it. She grabbed Stephen under the arms and unceremoniously pulled him down into the cabin, his heels rapping against the stairs then lowered his head to the floor, smoothing the hair away from his brow the way she had not three days before in the hotel in Portree.

"Stephen, what happened?" She looked at his face and the front of his jacket, then down to the lake of blood welling in the pit of his stomach. "Oh, Jesus." She stripped the towel from around her and crumpled it into a ball. He was clutching something against his body, a manila envelope soaked now in his own blood. She pulled it from his hand and pressed the towel gently against the boy's middle. He groaned again, his eyes flicking open.

She whispered to him, her voice soothing. "Stephen. Sweet boy, what happened?" The young man's mouth opened slackly, the breath so slight she thought at first he had died. A sound came from low in his throat. "What?" Lis said, her ear to his mouth. The boy exhaled again, this time arching his neck slightly against her hand. Blood bubbled from the wound in his stomach, Lis's bunched white towel now a shocking crimson. "Olam," the boy uttered, the effort racking his whole body. Lis felt it shudder under her hand, then go limp. "Stephen? Stephen?"

There was no reply. The boy was dead, the blood from his wound pooling on the floor of the cabin. Lis gazed unbelievingly into the young face, her nude body shaking from the cold or the shock or both.

"He's dead."

The suddenness of the man's voice shocked her upright, her breath drawing in with a strangled shriek. The man stood on the lower step of the hatch stairs watching her, his wide eyes behind round horn-rimmed glasses unable to resist the attraction of her nakedness.

"I don't fucking believe this. I just don't fucking believe it," Lis said, drawing heavily on the cigarette the man had found for her. They were sitting in the rear of a black Ford just up the Embankment from the gangway that led down to the boats. Thirty minutes had passed, no more, from the time Stephen Thompson had slumped against her door and this stranger had waited for her to dress then led her up to the car.

The sky over the river was beginning to pale, softening the glare of the streetlights above them. She watched two men in grey overalls carrying Stephen Thompson's body, unrecognisable now in the plastic body bag, and lifting it into the back of the van ahead of them. One of the men walked round to the driver's side of the cab while the other closed and secured the rear doors. Lis read the cursive letters: City Cleaning Corp. The truck pulled away leaving Lis and the two men alone.

"Okay, Sam," the man beside her said; "let's go." The car pulled off the sidewalk and started in the direction of Westminster.

"Who the fuck are you guys anyway? Cops?"

"Jay Peterson," the man beside her answered. His voice

was soft, almost apologetic. "This is Samuel Clemens," Jay said, indicating the driver.

Lis took another heavy drag on her cigarette and exhaled the smoke into the front of the compartment. The man beside her turned his head almost imperceptibly. "So?" Neither man replied, the silence filled by the swish of tyres on the wet street.

"He was shot," Jay Peterson said.

Lis managed a laugh. "Well, that clears that up. You're right. He was, wasn't he."

Jay ignored the rebuke. "A block from where you live." It was Lis's turn to consider, wondering why she hadn't heard the shot, then realising she had.

"What the fuck is this?" she erupted. "CIA?" A little sheepishly, as if he weren't used to the action, Jay drew out his wallet and showed Lis the badge inside. "FBI?" Lis was curious in spite of herself. "What're you doing here? What're you even doing in England?"

"We, I came to see you." Jay looked to Clemens for help but the driver wasn't offering any. "Have you any idea why he, why the young man was on his way to see you?" he asked tentatively, almost shyly, as if it was really none of his business.

Lis ignored him, realising now that Thompson hadn't just shown up in the hope of extending the great adventure he had begun in Portree. He had brought her something. "We have to go back." Clemens gave Jay a quick look in the rear-view mirror then back at the road.

"We can't," Jay said. She began wrestling with the door lock. Jay's hand reached across and took her by the wrist, the grip surprisingly strong. "I guess I'd better explain," he said.

Ten minutes later, they sat facing each other over a narrow table in an all night café in Pimlico favoured by cab drivers. Jay began telling her about the night Short was killed, how he, Jay, had been there, seen it happen, and how Clemens had provided the link to her. Lis made out the silhouette of Clemens waiting patiently in the car, occasionally looking in their direction.

"So you know who did it?"

Jay followed Lis's gaze. "Sam is something of an expert in these things. He says it was some kind of booby-trap. Officially, they've placed responsibility with the IRA" Jay stopped. He was getting ahead of himself, giving up information before he had obtained any.

"But it wasn't, was it" Lis shot back. She noticed the scars on his face for the first time, the wounds showing like tiny white birds on the dark skin. "I know, as you probably do too by now," Lis went on, "that Tim was killed by a remote UCBT. That's not IRA signature. They don't go in for high-tec."

"Who told you this?" Jay's question was so unassuming that Lis found herself telling him. She looked into the brown eyes. The horn-rims made them seem larger, giving Jay a slightly startled look as if he didn't quite believe what he was hearing. Perhaps that was what persuaded her.

"Stephen, Stephen Thompson. He worked for the police. Special Branch. Tim and I were working on a story on the Afghani drug trade. It was his project but I helped out where I could. He had a special interest. His son died of an overdose. Did you know that?" Jay didn't. Lis went on. "He said he was close to naming an Irish connection, the main man. And he didn't make claims like that lightly. He was old school, straight down the line." Lis paused, remembering Tim's lectures, his fierce anger. "And I was there, in Afghanistan, in the camps. I saw them do that, blow up a car with a remote." Jay didn't react. "Don't you get it? That's where the weapon came from, from the Taliban. They have non-detectable Semtex. Tim had already confirmed that. It's hard to come by. Either they did it, one of their operatives, or they passed the weapon on to whoever their contact, their delivery point in Ireland, is. Tim was too close so they killed him. Just like they killed Stephen."

Lis looked across the table at Jay, the dark eyes now filled with sympathy. There was nothing hidden there, a gentleness perhaps but no guile. His long fingers were wrapped around the cup of un-drunk coffee in front of him. His eyes followed hers again. "It's not much good, is it?" she smiled.

"Certainly isn't," he grinned back, pushing the cup away, one slender finger inadvertently touching the back of her hand. "Did he say anything to you . . .?" He hesitated.

"Lis, please. Everyone calls me Lis."

"Lis. Did he say anything?"

She watched Peterson's face. "He said 'Olam.' Just that. Then he died." There was a catch in her voice. A man across from them looked up for a moment then went back to his paper.

"I'm sorry," Jay said, his hand covering hers now. "I know how it feels." It was his turn now. He told about the Truman, about Dana and his trip to Ireland. It was unofficial, he explained; a personal thing. Then he talked about Short and what he had told him. That brought him to Khuda Bax. He stopped. "Look, I know this is going to sound strange." Lis waited for Jay to get out the rest. "But I don't think it's safe right now. For you to go back there, back to your boat. Maybe I could offer you my room. It's not much but you'd be okay there until we can, you know, square things away."

"You don't waste much time, do you," Lis said wryly.

Jay looked a little hurt. "What?"

In the car Sam Clemens took another look at the two figures inside the café then huddled further down in the front seat of the Ford. It had been another long night. It looked like it was going to be a long day.

CHAPTER 15

A city

Saeed bin Sayyaf held the future in his hand. The boy who had stood shivering from the cold or from fear or perhaps both on the Doha Road was a man now. And the man, Saeed, had been called to duty. After the roar of the rockets in the cement plant and the sudden almost simultaneous arrival of the Qatari police, Saeed had been quickly separated from the rest of the group and taken to a private house in the residential quarter. The fear he had felt at the separation from his comrades, the men who had accepted him into their company as one of their own, respecting him for his rudimentary knowledge of computers, respecting him for his dedication to their cause, was nothing to the fear he felt then, sitting alone in an upstairs room awaiting his fate. And that fear could not equal his surprise when two men entered the room, grabbed him roughly, then pushed him into a waiting car below and hours later pushed him out again onto the street in front of his home. Fate had a hand, he knew, but it was the hand of his brother who protected him always. Of that he was sure. As sure as he was of what the future held now.

The airline ticket had been delivered five days earlier along with a passport, a credit card, clothes and a suitcase, the driver of the pickup handing the items over without comment. His little sister had asked to hold the passport, had laughed at Saeed's serious face on the inside cover. His mother had only looked, said nothing, then turned her face away. When the cab to the airport pulled away from their shabby little house in a cloud of dust no one had waved. This city, the dark glass-fronted skyscrapers climbing endlessly to the sky, the wide boulevards flanked by palm trees, the big American cars, would not notice his going either.

Saeed rarely came downtown, his family never did. His lowly job at the chemical plant outside the city didn't call for visits to luxurious corporate offices or lunches at expensive restaurants. No one in his family shopped at the big stores: Armani, Yves Saint-Laurent, Versace. Downtown was a place of myth, a foreign country no less alien than the city inscribed on his ticket. He pulled it from the inside pocket of his leather jacket once more.

There was a time when Saeed could never have worn a jacket like this. It spoke of Hollywood, of luxury. Growing up, after he came of age, he had worn the traditional thobe, the white robe all Saudi men wore. He and his friends had been inspired then. They had joined the al-Tabligh, proselytising from door-to-door, encouraging whoever they met to observe the precepts of the good book, to follow the path of the Prophet. It was blasphemy to think it but secretly Saeed was following the path of his brother. It was a confession he had made to no one. He worshipped his brother.

The day had come when his friend, Musa Aziz, had been arrested for distributing anti-government leaflets. There was nothing in the pamphlet that in the least warranted what happened to Musa next, nothing you could not read any day in al-Hayat. The Saudi secret police had taken Musa to the

Ministry of the Interior. There his sandals had been ripped from his feet and, while two men held him, a third beat the soles of Musa's feet with a rod. Fallaqa, they called it. Their employers, the King and his thousands of relatives, treated their camels with more respect. Musa had been unable to walk for three weeks and never straight since.

Saeed's sister was the next victim. She had been spotted by the matawwa, the religious police, picking up a piece of paper in the shopping mall. The man who seized her insisted it had been dropped by a boy and had the boy's phone number written on it. For this infraction, his sister was given forty lashes on her bare back. No one in Saeed's family had dared protest, not Saeed, nor his sister.

Saeed and his friends had been good Saudis once, dutiful sons, loyal subjects. But, as the Imam said, you can beat a camel once too many times. The first of them, Musa, had left for the training camps in Pakistan in 1987. It had been a challenge to the rest of them to follow. Ahmed had been seventeen when he left in the winter of 1988. Saeed, just twelve and the youngest of their group, had remained at home.

Two years later and many years older, Ahmed had returned to find his friends and his home much changed. Nothing, of course, was really different. The royal family still pressed its combined will on the people of Saudi Arabia, demanded strict obedience to its rule and the laws of Sharia while its own members demeaned the honour of the Prophet, the women sporting make-up and Western clothes, its men squandering the nation's wealth on vast armouries of weapons that served only to support the economies of the foreign governments that manufactured them. They had invested in all manner of Western decadence from Euro

Disney to Michael Jackson. All that was the same, it was Ahmed's eyes that were different. For the first time he could see.

When the rulers had invited the Americans inside their borders, the government-owned newspaper al-Riyadh had pronounced sententiously that it was a temporary measure only to protect the kingdom from the foreign aggressor, Iraq. But Ahmed had not been fooled. The Ruler and his clan needed the Americans to prop up their own faltering hold on his kingdom. And it was Islam itself that was desecrated. Infidels trod the ground on which the Prophet himself had walked. A thousand holy Imams had gone to jail for daring to protest. What would be next? Infidels permitted within the walls of Makkah itself? Musa had died in the snowy foothills of the Hindu Kush and Ahmed had taken his place as the older brother of their little group, had heard the call and led them forth.

Saeed had come to know the route to the Yemeni border very well. Long, hot hours in the dust-choked cab of a Toyota pickup on desert roads, and a heart-thumping run across the border at night. More hours then, haggling in the arms market, paying too much for aged Kalashnikovs that no one, Ahmed said with authority, would have deigned to pick off the ground in Afghanistan. In abandoned rooms they had cobbled together their bombs and timers in the fashion they had been taught and the explosions that they and others like them had detonated had been heard all the way to Washington. Their number had been cut down, the head of Muslih Ali al-Shamrani rolling ignominiously on the square at the feet of the infidel journalists, Riyad al-Hajiri, Ayid al-Riyadh, and all the others, following him to blessed eternity.

Only Saeed was left now of the original group. Now, he was alone again.

The cab turned into the airport and pulled to a halt. Foot-high letters proclaimed the airport's name: King Khalid International Airport, Riyadh. Saeed bin Sayyaf was leaving his home without regret. He knew he could never return, never see his family or friends again, safe in the company of the holy ones. Yet, deep down in the secret place to which each of us goes when the storm is at its height, he was frightened beyond words.

CHAPTER 16

London

"Is this it?" Lis asked, surveying the miniature hotel room.

"All the taxpayer could afford," Jay wisecracked lamely. Lis squeezed her way into the narrow space between the bed and wall, Jay following. They looked at each other, her face in shadow, Jay's accented by the wan light from the small window behind Lis's head. His dark skin was almost blue in the daylight, the brown eyes now invisible behind the glasses. There was a strangeness to their intimacy, one they were both aware of, a sense that in some other time or place the urgency they both felt would have propelled them together. Now, they were separated by events. It was as if the bodies of Tim Short, of Dana and now Stephen Thompson were crammed in there with them.

"We're wasting time here," Lis said, breaking the moment. "I have to go back to the boat. Find what Stephen was carrying." She was interrupted by Clemens calling on the house phone from downstairs. "Jay. They're beeping you."

"What will you do with Stephen?" Lis asked. They would dispose of him, she thought, the words coming uninvited. Jay caught the change in her tone.

"I'm not sure." he said. "I'd better go. You'll stay here?"

"Sure I will, Jay," she answered. "And I won't leave the

room or let any strangers in or answer the phone." Jay grinned. "That's the first time you've smiled," she said, her voice almost a whisper. "Since this morning, I mean." They stood for a moment more, then Jay left.

"Where to?" Clemens asked as Jay climbed into the Ford that he had parked down the street from the hotel.

"Where's the van?"

"Hyde Park. Underground parking lot off Park Lane."

Twenty minutes later, the Ford nosed down the ramp of the US Embassy's underground garage on Grosvenor Square, the van in convoy behind it.

"I'll be a while," Jay said as Clemens pulled the car to a halt.

"Give my regards to Bob."

Jay wasn't looking forward to the call to Lorenz. The last time they had spoken, Lorenz had warned him off in no uncertain terms. Since then, he'd been witness to two murders and one grand larceny, the product of which Lorenz must have already seen.

"You did what?" Lorenz's voice erupted down the line.

"We picked it up."

"You picked it up? You should have left it there, you fucking idiot. The British still have a police force, don't they? It's not your problem."

The lobby of the Dorchester Hotel, a few blocks down Park Lane from the Embassy was empty but Jay took the precaution of closing the door of the elegant booth with his foot anyway. He let Lorenz's rage boil for a moment then let him have the second barrel. "I've got his," he hesitated for an instant, "his girlfriend in a safe-house."

This time Lorenz connected with his apoplectic self and fired off a string of expletives that crackled in the receiver. Jay held it away from his ear. "Wait a second, wait a fucking second. You've got a dead man in the garage and she's where?"

"In my hotel. She's a target, Bob. There's no question that whoever shot Thompson, the boyfriend, will be out to get her, too."

There was a pause at the other end of the line, the receiver filled with the hiss of static. Then, Lorenz was back, his tone suddenly deliberate. "Use her," he said.

"What?"

"Use her. Bait the trap."

Jay was about to protest but the line was already dead. He put the receiver back and wedged his way out of the booth.

In the cab, Jay considered Lorenz's instructions then thought of Lis. In the few hours he had known her, the balance of his life had shifted irrevocably. He had walked through a wall into a room where all the people who had once been strangers, the love-sick, all the victims he knew but had never recognised, suddenly had names and faces. The cab cut across Kensington High Street and into South Kensington. He would go with her, of course, back to the boat. He'd go wherever she led. Her cause was now the same as his. The cab pulled up at the hotel.

He took in the few details of the room's interior in a second: the side table, the bed, the small window. The bed. Empty. Then the note on the bedside table. "Gone back to the boat. L."

*

Lis stood at the top of the embrasure that opened onto the Chelsea Harbour gangway. She had sat in the back of Jay's car in almost exactly the same spot just this morning. She looked up and down the sidewalk for a telltale stain, for yellow police ribbons, a crowd of curious spectators. There were none. Everything seemed the same and yet everything had changed. She felt exposed, as if the familiar landmarks around her each hid some imminent danger.

"G'day," a familiar voice broke in. Arthur Sullivan's head stuck out of the cockpit of his boat.

"Hey, Arthur." The man had a streak of paint on his brow, a garish pink. "Anyone come by this morning?"

"Didn't see anyone."

Arthur's head disappeared and Lis made her way down the gangway, across the stern of the Johnsons' boat to her own. She stopped at the cockpit. It had been scrubbed clean. It was as if Stephen's body had never lain there. Lis took one last cautious look up at the Embankment and, ducking her head under the hatch, climbed down into the main cabin.

"Hello, Lis," a voice said from the narrow corridor leading to the forepeak. "The door was open so I let myself in." Neil Greyson emerged from the shadow, filling the cramped cabin.

"Bloody hell, Neil," Lis said, drawing in a deep breath; "you scared the shit out of me. How long have you been here?"

"Not long," Greyson replied.

"Oh," was all Lis could manage. Then, to cover her confusion: "Well, sit down. I'll make some coffee or something." She busied herself with water and coffee-maker then looked over at Greyson sitting now on the companionway. The close-

120

set eyes were studying the photographs he held in his big hands.

"Where did you find those?" she asked as casually as she could.

"Under the steps here. You know either of them?"

He held up the black-and-white 8-by-10s. There were three photographs, the top one smeared with a crimson stain, though the faces of the two men were still quite legible. The photographs had most likely been taken by a long lens. The background was barely distinguishable. It might have been an airport or an outdoor café. Lis didn't know the younger man. He was dark-haired, Arabic. His face was soft and bore the marks of late nights and repeated indulgence. The older of the two was European. Lis recognised him immediately. It was Neil's army friend, Roger. She looked at Neil again, the anger settling her.

"Roger," she said simply.

"Roger," Neil repeated. "Roger Oldham." Greyson let the photographs and the envelope that had contained them drop to the floor.

The shock of recognition paralysed her. At the wake for Tim, Neil had introduced Oldham by his first name only. She had never bothered to ask his last name. It didn't seem important then. Now, the intelligence was beyond value.

"No milk, right?" she said, her voice tight but firm.

"Right."

Greyson's big hand wrapped around the mug of coffee setting it on the step beside him. They sat in silence for a minute, neither touching the coffee Lis had poured. She stared at the spot at Greyson's feet where Thompson had lain then back up at Greyson.

"I hear you're still working your own investigation on Tim Short's death," he said at last.

"Where did you hear that?" Lis fired back, wondering which of Neil's "fraternity," the old-boy network of serving and retired intelligence officers, had informed him.

"Special Branch. They wanted to know if I knew where you were. They seemed quite interested. Apparently, they're after Roger, too. I thought you might want to get there before them." Neil reached into his jacket pocket, the sudden movement startling Lis. It was irrational, she knew, but all at once it seemed no coincidence that Greyson had sat on the companionway leading to the deck, his bulk blocking her exit. "He gave me this." He passed her the elaborate business card Oldham had left on the hall table at Ballynahinch. "You should go see him. He lives just up the street"

Lis took the card, then said: "You remember that boy?"

"Which boy, Lis?" Greyson asked. There was heavy irony in his voice.

"The one at the funeral, Stephen Thompson."

"What about him?"

"He's dead."

Greyson's face, shadowed by the closed hatch above his head, was impossible to read. "I'm sorry to hear that." Greyson's narrow eyes fixed on Lis. Lis held his gaze.

"He was shot," she said. "In the street. He died here." Her eyes lowered to the spot at Greyson's feet again. He looked too, his foot shifting the photos to one side, then up at her.

"That might be a problem, Lis; a big problem." He got up off the stairs, his body seeming to fill the small room now. "Thanks for the coffee, Lis. See you." Greyson turned and climbed the few steps to the deck. Lis heard him stepping onto the Johnsons' boat, the clank of his shoes on the gang-plank. She crossed the cabin and picked up the blood-stained envelope from the floor, cradling it gently.

CHAPTER 17

London

The first working phone Lis found after leaving the boat was in a coffee shop on the King's Road. The place was noisy but the crowd felt comforting. She dialled the number Jay had given her.

It rang once more then a recording picked up. A polite American voice chimed: "For Consular inquiries, press one. For passport applications, press two. For the Public Information Office, press three. All other inquiries please stay on the line. An operator will be with you shortly." The woman's voice was replaced by an orchestra playing the title theme from Beauty and The Beast. Welcome to Disneyland Lis thought.

It hadn't occurred to her until Greyson had shown up on the boat that they had all been looking in the wrong direction. She'd known there was a connection missing, some link that needed to be made. Thompson, Short, Greyson, Jay had all pointed to one man, the man in Stephen's photograph: Roger Oldham. The equation was so simple she wondered why she hadn't figured it out before. Greyson with his long-standing ties to the Gulf, the intelligence background, the old-army connection, the arms, the Semtex – the drugs. It had all suddenly coalesced into the kind of knot she was good at unravelling and explaining on camera. After Greyson left, Arthur had appeared. She gave him instructions in case Jay showed up, scrawled Oldham's address on the envelope for him.

She waited now for the US Embassy's phone system to connect her. The drone of music was interrupted by a live voice. "Embassy. How can I direct your call?"

"Yeah, hi. I'm trying to reach one of your people, one of your officers. Jay Peterson. He's part of the FBI's operation here."

"I'm sorry, ma'am; this is the United States Embassy. We don't handle FBI matters."

"Who does, then?" Lis said doing her best to remain civil.

"You'd have to call the agency in the United States for that information, ma'am."

Lis called the hotel, waited. A sweet-voiced Italian receptionist, the girl who'd welcomed her and Jay with a grin when they had walked in told her that he had left the hotel.

Fifteen minutes later, Lis Charnay stood at the corner of Cornwall Crescent and Gloucester Road, the address on Oldham's card. In her time as an investigative reporter Lis had participated in her own stake-outs in hotel lobbies or the reception halls of ministries or government agencies; but never on the street and never like this. It wasn't her style, watching from the shadows, waiting for the suspect to make a move.

Lis tried to "read" the street, watching for the tell-tale signs. There were none. She headed briskly down the sidewalk towards the middle of the block. As she neared number fourteen the large blue front door swung open and Roger Oldham appeared. He was obviously in a hurry. He turned to double-lock the door behind him, an overnight case and bulging briefcase clasped in his free hand.

"Roger," Lis called. Oldham looked up, startled. "Roger," she called again. Oldham had come down the front steps of the house and turned down the sidewalk to face her. "It's Lis Charnay. We met at Tim Short's wake in Ireland."

"Oh, yes," Oldham suddenly remembered. "Look. I'm in a bit of a rush right now, I'm afraid. Got someone waiting in the car. There's a fire in the engine room if you know what I mean."

"I need to talk to you," she said, grabbing onto his arm. "Now. It can't wait."

"Right. I see." Oldham continued looked anxiously up and down the street. Whatever it was that was pursuing him was invisible to ordinary eyes. There was no one in the crescent, no traffic save for a cab at the far end, its engine running, passenger door open, the driver waiting for the passenger in the back to find change. "Why don't we do this somewhere else. I'm headed out of town. We can talk on the way to the station." He began to guide her towards the aquamarine Bentley parked on the opposite side of the crescent. It glowed like some exotic plant among the duller shades of the cars parked either side. Its single passenger, Andrew Starling, Oldham's accountant, sat nervously in the front.

They skirted the gardens, the older man escorting the young woman. They might have been a father and daughter, an uncle and his niece. At the top end of the crescent Oldham stopped, putting down his cases for a moment and patting his coat pockets for his keys. Lis could now see past the Bentley all the way down the street. The cab was still there, the rear door open.

"Got 'em," Oldham said and Lis suddenly understood.

Intelligence is of value only as long as it is current. Once it can no longer be acted upon it is history. The intelligence that Lis had gathered in the last minute, the position of the cab, Oldham's hurried exit, the passenger in the Bentley, was still current. She acted on it without thinking. She pulled Oldham off the sidewalk, dragged him towards the narrow mews to their right, and shoved him through the opening.

"What . . .?" Oldham protested, staggering under the force.

"Go," she yelled pushing him on, "go!"

The two of them were under the arch leading into the mews, the end of the street still just visible. The cab was there, Lis could see, its rear door closing, the vehicle beginning to reverse backwards out of the crescent. An arm was visible, pointing in their direction. In the second before they ducked behind the shelter of the mews wall Lis thought it was aiming a gun.

The buildings either side of the cobbled mews they were running down rose two stories only, apartments above what had once been carriage houses or stables now living rooms and kitchens. For a second it seemed as if the whole short street was bathed in the afterglow of the setting sun, a warm orange reflected back off the windows. Then, too suddenly to determine the lapse of time between one event and the next, the glass in the windows erupted outwards, the flowers in the window boxes were flattened, a front door crashing inwards under the force of some invisible hand. Chips of glass rained on them as they ran on, the shock of the blast behind propelling them forwards. And then, finally, came the sound of the explosion, a howling roar that cracked against the walls, erupting in their ears.

They had made the train with just sixty seconds to spare thanks to the deft manoeuvring of their cab driver and the £20 notes pulled magically from Oldham's pocket.

"Ridiculous" Roger Oldham said; "Neil wouldn't hurt a fly." He didn't sound convinced. Lis and he were sitting across from each other in the first-class compartment of the Paris-bound Eurostar.

He had been too shaken at Victoria to put up any opposition to her accompanying him to Paris. While she detailed her suspicions of Neil Greyson's implication in the death of her friend and Thompson, daring Oldham to disprove it, the Kent countryside sped past the window in a blur of darkening green fields and cone-capped oast-houses.

"I'm really at a loss here. I realise this whole thing has been a bit of a shock but, believe me, you've completely lost me."

Lis levelled her face with his. "I don't know what kind of shit you're in, Roger. But if it has something to do with Tim's death and the death of an innocent young man and I find you're holding out on me, I'll blow the whistle on you so fucking loud that whoever's after you would have to be on another planet not to hear it."

Oldham recoiled. A man sitting two rows down slapped the page of the pink financial paper he was reading as he folded it down. Lis went on. "What were you doing at Neil's place anyway?"

"Visiting."

"Why?"

Oldham sighed. His impulse to accommodate this young woman had turned into a heavy weight that now anchored him before her. "I was there to pick up funds. Some cash, mostly bearer-bonds actually. Know what they are?" he asked, his voice resigned.

"Come on, Roger," Lis snapped. "You don't have to be coy. Who were you bagman for? I know it's not your money."

Oldham looked hurt, as if the revelation were news to him. He sighed again. "Lis, I'm just the banker. I collect the money and I deposit it for clients at their instruction."

"Which clients?"

Oldham balked "Let's have a drink, shall we?. I think we both deserve one."

"Which clients, Roger?" Lis demanded fiercely, her hand diving on Oldham's wrist, clamping on to it.

Some wall in Oldham's compartmentalised life tumbled at that moment, knocked down by the fearsome proximity of death in the quiet London crescent. His desire for honest tenderness and his terrible hunger for wealth, always separate before, business and pleasure, suddenly crashed together like opposing tides. The show was over and the magician was finally pulling off the loaded jacket with its secret caches of coins, silk flowers, and cards.

"Look, Lis. I've had a long run but I think my time may be up. You don't know this, I expect. Maybe you do." Oldham paused. "My offices were broken into, ransacked. Now, this, this explosion. I'd love to help you. God knows, if I was ten years younger I'd do more than that. But I've run out of road, you see. Run out of road." He repeated the phrase to himself, looking through her.

"Tell me, Roger," Lis pushed. "Tell me."

"Let me have that drink?"

So, for the price of a large scotch and soda, Oldham exposed the deep secrets of his ambition. Lis learned how he laundered and banked money for several clients, principal among them the man who had summoned him to Paris, Khuda Bax. He related how his gamble on oil futures had taken a disastrous turn leaving a longer and longer string of nominee accounts bankrupt. "If the calls had paid off," he said; "my God, that would be a different story. Tonight's my last chance, you see. If Khuda Bax will cut me some slack, I can plug the leaks."

The train was under the Channel now, the rounded sides of the tunnel flashing by the windows as the express descended to the lowest point of its trajectory. "Khuda Bax, the man you're going to see; what does he sell through Neil? Arms? Drugs?"

Oldham took a gulp of whiskey, draining off his glass. "I suppose there's no harm in owning up to it," he said. "Arms. Neil and I both used to dabble a bit in the old days. Just light stuff, you understand. Never drugs though. Wouldn't go near them. Khuda Bax neither. He's a bit of a player but not one of those, not slime." He nodded to the bartender who began setting up another drink. "Bit of an embarrassment really. He's asked to see the books. Caught with my pants down, you might say. Someone rifled my safe five days, no six days ago. Couldn't call the boys in blue. Sensitive business, you see. They showed up anyway. Someone must have tipped them a wink. Andrew had the back-ups with him in the car, the codes and accounts. The poor little sod. Not a bad chap really. Just, you know, a bean-counter. Bit of an embarrassment as I say."

"You'll take me along, won't you?"

"To see Bax?" Oldham shook his head then realised her company might actually be to his benefit. Some of his former panache returned. "Of course, dear girl. You can be my niece and I'll be your wicked old uncle."

Imperceptibly, the Eurostar began its ascent towards the French coast.

CHAPTER 18

Chelsea

The Earls Court Road was a parking lot. Cars, double-decker buses and delivery trucks crawled past the betting shops, the pubs, the travel-agents, filling their doorways and lobbies with exhaust. Only the couriers, gunning their BMWs and Hondas up onto the sidewalks, cutting back in perilously close to the sides of the stalled vehicles, made any headway. Jay Peterson sat in the back of a cab, his body pitched forward to urge the traffic onwards.

"How much further?"

"A mile maybe. Won't free up till we cross the Fulham Road though," the cab driver offered from the front. Some incident to the south of them had diverted traffic to the west and east, he said, forcing them out along Kensington High Street. "Nuvver of those bombs I should expect. You'd think the Irish would learn to give it a rest."

"I'll get out here," Jay said

He paid off the cab and started to run. He had phoned a message into Clemens' pager right after his call to Lorenz wishing now he'd talked to Sam in person. He stayed on the sidewalk for the first few strides, then, as he stretched out, switched to the street. He crossed the Fulham Road, dodging a fire-engine heading east, checking his pace momentarily, then picked up again. Six minutes later, he was standing at the head of the gangway to Lis's boat.

He hesitated for a second then walked slowly down the catwalk. The hatch doors were locked, the shutters drawn across the glass, no sound from below. He dropped full length to the deck to peer through the storm ports into the cabin. It was empty. Edging forwards, he checked out the bedroom. Empty, too. Lis had either come and gone or was still on her way.

"See anything you like?" a voice above him said.

Jay rolled over. A balding man in tight swimming trunks, his belly bulging under a paint-flecked T-shirt stood over him, a rusty boat hook pointed at Jay's throat. "Don't tell me you're from the City Council."

"I'm looking for Lis Charnay," Jay said.

"People usually knock first round here, look afterwards."

"I'm sorry. I just . . .Look," Jay reached into his back pocket and pulled out his wallet, flipping open the badge. The action was becoming a regular habit.

Sullivan read the inscription gravely: "Jay Peterson, Federal Bureau of Investigation," then gave Jay a knowing smile. "Bugger me. The Seventh Cavalry. Why didn't you say so?" Sullivan was already back in his boat. He emerged seconds later with the manila envelope and Oldham's card. "She told me to give you this if you showed up. Said she's gone to Oldham's house. Said to meet her there."

Jay slid the photographs from the envelope. He recognised Khuda Bax immediately but not his companion, knowing all the same that he was looking at Roger Oldham. Jay had a terrifying flash of precognition. He remembered Stephen Thompson's last word to Lis spoken here on this boat:

Oldham. He wheeled, vaulting the gunwale of the inside boat and ran for the gangway.

"Don't you want to know how to get there?" Sullivan called after him. Jay was already gone.

"Sorry, sir. You can't go in there."

A stocky policeman in white shirt and flat, chequered cap, an automatic machine-pistol in his hands, blocked Jay's entrance to the crescent. He could see a scramble of emergency vehicles beyond, lights still turning, heard the crunch of boots on the shards of broken glass. At the epicentre, Jay knew, would be Oldham's car. A neatly dressed grey-haired man appeared at the policeman's shoulder. "Mr. Peterson?" the plain-clothes man asked.

"Yes."

"Would you like to come through?" He motioned to the yellow tape barring Jay's way. "Thank you, Constable." The man put a boot on the strip of ribbon stretched across the road and Jay stepped over. The air was thick with the choking stench of burning plastic, a wash of charred debris still floating down like black snow. Ambulances were parked off to one side, back doors flung wide, empty. Fire trucks formed a solid wall of red paint and brass connectors. Beyond the barrier of emergency vehicles stood two others daubed an anonymous grey-green. Along their armoured side-panels Jay read: Metropolitan Police, Bomb Disposal Division.

The blackened ruin of the car was set off by the glaring white of the foam residue that still clung to it. Three men in heavily-padded protective suits picked carefully through the debris, removing minute pieces of material with foot-long

tongs and placing them in plastic evidence bags. In the passenger seat of the vehicle, tilted comically, was a scorched pillar, Starling's corpse still exuding a faint vapour.

"Car bomb?" Jay asked, suddenly seeing Tim Short again,
seeing the debris hurtling towards him out of the fireball.

"Yes," the other man said. "Careful where you put your
feet."

He led the way up a flight of stone steps to a blue front-
door, the house number displayed in brass figures below an
elaborate knocker styled in the fashion of a Saracen castle.
Inside the house, plain-clothes and uniformed officers were
picking through book cases, letter files, desk drawers. A
woman operated a communications station on the drawing-
room coffee table, an ornately-carved door of a mosque
mounted horizontally on a brass stand.

"In here," Jay's guide indicated. It was the dining-room of
Oldham's house, perfectly appointed in silver ornaments, fox-
heads, pheasants, and several ancient-looking oil paintings of
ships at sea. From its window Jay looked out over the chaos in
the street, his eyes drawn to the skeleton of the car and its
silent occupant. The man closed the door behind them. "I'm
George Manktilow," he said. He motioned Jay to a high-
backed dining-room chair, its back to the window, seating
himself at another. "You came here looking for someone."

Jay turned away as if he might find her there among the
wealth of oils and precious metal then asked: "Was that her?"

"In the car?" Manktilow said, looking beyond Jay. "No.
That was Andrew Starling, Roger Oldham's accountant."

Jay twisted in his chair to survey the wreckage in the
street again, then back. "It was a remote, wasn't it."

"Mr. Peterson," Manktilow said; "I appreciate that you

have a job to do over here but since I've been good enough to let you go this far, I think you might return the courtesy."

"What do you mean?"

"Let's start with Stephen Thompson. Your embassy delivered his dead body early this afternoon. He'd been shot. Savagely. I have every reason to believe he died at the home of an associate of yours, Elise Charnay. And I expect you could tell me more than I already know about how his body got from her house-boat to your embassy." Jay made no reply. "Miss Charnay is an accessory to the murder of Stephen Thompson, a very serious charge in this country, no doubt in yours, too. If you know of her whereabouts, I could arrest you here and now for obstruction of justice. And even if you don't know where she is, which I suspect right now you don't, I'd have no trouble booking you for grand larceny."

Jay couldn't let the new charge go without a challenge. "On what pretext?"

"For the disk or disks you didn't return to Mr. Oldham's office safe the night you or someone in your employ opened it. I get the impression from your superiors at the embassy that they wouldn't put up any resistance to your arrest."

Jay suddenly felt cold, a stranger in a strange land. He had launched his own investigation and whatever product he had accrued had been appropriated by someone else for their own ends. He recognised that his own quest now was simply to find Lis, to shield her from whatever avalanche he had set in motion. He was saved for the moment by a knock at the door.

"Come."

A plain-clothes officer appeared in the half-open door. "American gentleman to see Mr. Peterson, sir."

"Let him in," Manktilow said. The officer stood aside to

let Sam Clemens into the room. He nodded to Manktilow then to Jay.

Sam had been there at all the right moments, always a step ahead. Now he was here again. There were connections that Sam had made or knew about that he had chosen or been told not to pass on. Jay didn't know whether to feel betrayed or just plain stupid.

"Mr. Peterson," Manktilow said. "I think it's time you started co-operating. If I cared to, I could have you and Mr. Clemens on the first flight back to Washington at the very least. We seem to be pursuing the same quarry and you seem to have made a little more progress than we have, albeit in some unconventional ways." Manktilow's gaze turned to the street.

"Was he on your command?" Jay asked sensing the note of despair in Manktilow's voice.

"Thompson? Yes. You could put it like that. He was just a young lad, really. Hadn't been with us a more than a year."

"I'm sorry." Jay said. "When I find her, I'll tell you. Will you return the favour?"

Manktilow managed a thin smile. "If you like."

"And you may want these back." Jay handed over the bloodied envelope with the photographs inside. It was an exchange of prisoners of sorts.

Outside the elegant room, a score of policemen and women moved slowly over the street and the fenced garden it encircled, picking over the splinters of glass, the shreds of metal and rubber. Somewhere in the carpet of debris that had dropped so recently from the sky, one of them would eventually find a piece of moulded plastic, burned black and shattered but still just identifiable as part of the dummy exhaust manifold that had contained the explosive Semtex.

CHAPTER 19

Paris

The breast was firm and conical, its shape and texture reminding Lis of a dessert, a sherbet topped by a cherry. The nipple, pink with rouge, was pierced through at midpoint by a small silver circlet. A few tiny curls of hair sprouted from the areola. As the girl leaned back from the table where they sat, the other breast came into view completing the symmetry. Her name she had told them when she first appeared at their table was Aube. She had said it in English too, pronouncing it "Don." Aube set down another bottle of champagne and walked away carrying the drinks-tray at shoulder level. She wore a red Moroccan leather bodice laced at the back that pushed her small breasts up and out, her buttocks down.

"To Dawn and whoever is lucky enough to see her come up each morning," Roger Oldham toasted.

Aube's appearance had not been the guests' first surprise that evening. It was clear to Lis, when she and Oldham entered the club, that the men seated around the table were not expecting to see him that night. But the surprise had passed quickly, covered by loud greetings and back-slappings. Oldham had taken a seat to Lis's left. Beyond him sat Pierre Cabannes, a dark-skinned Armenian. To her right was Cabannes' companion, Jean-Baptiste de Jonge. Lovers or co-conspirators, it was hard to tell. "Arms dealers," Oldham whispered.

To de Jonge's right was a young man, probably Pakistani, no more than twenty, pretty and shy, saying nothing and not introduced. And directly across from Lis was Khuda Bax. He was taller than he seemed in the photos, leaner. His thinning hair was combed straight back from his brow giving his face a polished appearance. His eyes were deep-set, topped by darkly expressive eyebrows over a hook-like nose. His most remarkable feature was his smile. It was a beacon, flashing both a greeting and, like a lighthouse on some rocky point, a warning.

They had arrived at the exclusive supper club, the Club Zizi just off the Champs Elysées, a little after nine. It was now past eleven. Their dinner had been cleared by Aube but Oldham and the two Armenians continued to drink champagne steadily. The young Pakistani had eaten nothing and had contributed nothing to the lively round of conversation during the meal. Fifteen minutes ago, after a whispered conference with Khuda Bax, the young man had left without a word. Khuda Bax grinned widely to the rest of the company explaining the boy was tired. "Today's young people don't have the staying power of us old war-horses, isn't that so, Roger?" Oldham agreed, lifting his flute of champagne in a toast to maturity. Lis's own glass shone a mysterious blue as she raised it.

The source of the luminescent colouring was a huge cylindrical fish tank that dominated the club. A girl, entirely naked, appeared through the opening in the ceiling and swam to the bottom of the tank with two or three powerful strokes. She was joined almost immediately by another girl, also naked. The women embraced, their sleek bodies inter-twining, sliding over and around each other.

"Zey are vairy beeg feesh," Cabannes commented glee-fully in heavily accented English. Every vestige of hair had been shaved from the women's bodies and a silvery paint applied overall giving them a sleek and fishlike appearance.

The first girl propelled herself towards the surface, disappearing through the opening above. She was replaced by a small grey-tipped shark that circled the perimeter of the glass. The second girl ignored it, instead draping herself with a small Pacific octopus that seemed oblivious to her and what she did. Eventually, she too kicked for the surface leaving the octopus to drift down to the bottom of the tank.

"Come," Cabannes ordered. "We muss feed zees feesh." He pulled Oldham from his seat and accompanied by de Jonge climbed the spiral stair to the floor above.

"You must go, Miss Charnay," Khuda Bax said from across the table. "You will find it most entertaining."

"No, thank you," she replied.

"Another drink, perhaps."

She covered her glass. "Roger didn't tell me what it was you did, Mr. Bax. Something fascinating I imagine."

"Please, let us be friends. You must call me Khuda Bax and I will call you Elise. May I?" His large hand extended to cover hers. She resisted the temptation to pull it away.

"Roger said you do business in Afghanistan."

Khuda Bax's smile broadened. "You must not believe everything he tells you."

"So you don't do business in Afghanistan?"

"I do, yes. On occasion. And elsewhere, of course." Khuda

Bax was on the defensive for a moment, perhaps not ready for Lis's direct questions. When Aube appeared at his shoulder to replenish the champagne, he waved her away without ceremony.

"Are you the kind of trader, Mr. Khuda Bax, Khuda, who could get anything anyone wanted? Say I wanted to buy weapons. Would you trade me some of those?"

"Why would a beautiful young woman like you want weapons?"

"To protect me from dangerous criminals."

"The police will do that, my dear."

"They couldn't protect Roger."

Khuda Bax's manner changed, his beaming smile replaced by a mask that hid all expression. "Roger is a very dangerous man, Elise, a dangerous man to be with. I don't know what it is that brings you and him together but take my advice, stay away from him." He rose from the table, his face still a blank. "Au revoir, Mademoiselle Charnay. It has been a pleasure. Perhaps we will have the opportunity again some time." Without waiting for a reply, Khuda Bax turned and headed for the club's cloakroom.

Lis went looking for Oldham.

"Fucking bastards," Oldham stammered as he and Lis walked together from the club. "Fucking, fucking bastards." A motorised street-cleaner whirred past them throwing a spray of water at their feet and scrubbing the gutter with its circular brush.

"You have to understand, Lis," Oldham started in, a little unsteadily, "these guys, Cabannes, de Jonge are just spectators. They're not players, just spectators. They know nothing about what's really going on."

Charnay and Oldham turned into a side street, walking now in the roadway. Oldham needed the room, bumping into Lis then righting himself once too often. "God, I'm tired," he sighed. Ahead, the narrow alley was empty save for a few of the plastic trashcans that dot Paris's byways. A shrill squeal sounded from the far end of the alley. A car's headlights caught the two of them in its yellow beams.

"It never stops," Oldham continued, stumbling slightly, unaware of the approaching car. "You get one lot sorted out and another lot come out of nowhere."

The car, straightening, picked up speed and headed right at them.

"Better get out of the way, Roger," Lis said, eyes on the car, her hand pulling at Oldham's coat sleeve and guiding him onto the narrow sidewalk.

"Never stops," Oldham continued, looking up and seeing the headlights for the first time. The car, now fifty feet from them and accelerating, had two wheels mounted on the sidewalk, its offside doors inches from the wall. "Jesus!" Oldham's voice was barely audible over the car's revving engine. Lis clung to Oldham's arm, seemingly transfixed by the headlights of the oncoming car.

"Jump!" She propelled Oldham and herself sideways feeling the rush of air, the whack of metal plate on her thigh and shoulder as she and Oldham rolled off the car's hood, aware for a second of a dark face before she and Oldham plunged into the roadway. Lis staggered up, pulling Oldham with her.

"Get up, Roger. Get the hell up."

She hauled him up, Oldham pushing with his right arm.

For a moment they were two comics in some drunken routine. Lis heard the double concussion of the speeding car as it careered off first one wall of the alley and then the other, finally coming to a halt with a squeal of tyres. The sound brought Oldham to his feet. The car was stopped, its brake lights burning red, its engine revving. The driver's face in deep shadow turned to observe them. Lis looked round the other way, the way they had been heading. No chance. They couldn't outrun it. The car's white rear lights came on.

As the car accelerated again, reversing towards them, Lis felt herself lifted by the front of her blouse and planted against the wall, the bulk of Oldham pressed against her, suffocating her. The car screamed by them again, gaining speed, swerving back the way it had come out of the alley. As it turned backwards into the boulevard Roger Oldham's free hand came up, Lis saw the silver body of an automatic levelled at the retreating vehicle. The gun kicked once, twice as Oldham fired off two shots, the first whining off the back of the car, the second whacking into an overturned trash can. The car's tyres squealed again, the vehicle out of their vision now executing a 180-degree turn on the boulevard, the sound of its roaring engine diminishing. A dog barked in the growing silence.

"I don't believe this," Lis said finally.

Behind the wheel of the battered Peugeot, Elhassan Mohammed jerked the gear stick down hard and accelerated across the red light two blocks along the boulevard.

CHAPTER 20

Paris

Three cars had crossed the Place Vendôme in the last twenty minutes, the most recent a police car responding to a report of gunshots in the rue des Saints. Oldham and Lis had drawn back into the shadows, their faces lit only by the spinning blue roof-light.

A light drizzle had begun to fall and in spite of the arch above them their hair and the shoulders of their coats were already damp. Neither paid any notice, their attention instead fixed on the well-lit entrance to the Ritz Hotel on the western side of the square.

"I certainly have to thank you for an exciting evening," Lis said wryly; "a real gentleman would escort a lady to the door."

"I'm the target, Lis," Oldham protested. "You'll be quite safe, believe me." Oldham, quite sober now, had come up with a new stratagem. He'd been trying to convince her since they had left the rue des Saints.

"Why should I believe you, Roger. You haven't told me a word of truth since we met this afternoon."

"I've told you what I know."

"Bullshit," she retorted.

His plan was simple. Khuda Bax's father-in-law, Prince

Hashem, maintained a suite at the hotel. Since the Prince was rarely in residence, Khuda Bax had extended an open invitation to his banker to make use of the rooms when he was in Paris. Oldham hadn't hesitated, finding as many reasons to be in the French capital as he could. It had taken the near miss in the alley to remind him that the suite's safe contained a large sum of cash belonging, of course, to his client, a couple of passports issued by grateful governments, host to his numerous accounts, and records of recent transactions he was trying now to convince Lis would allow her to skewer Khuda Bax.

"This is ridiculous" Lis said. "Let's just walk across the street into the hotel and carry on this discussion like a couple of grown-ups in the comfort of his suite or in the lobby, if it'll make you feel safer."

"You know I can't do that, Lis."

"Then tell me who's out to get you, Roger. Why not start with that?"

"You might show a little sympathy you know. I may have landed myself in this mess but you don't have to be such a bitch."

"And you don't have to be such a bad liar." Oldham began to protest but Lis stopped him. "Don't, Roger, not with me. I know you didn't have anything to do with Tim's death, not directly anyway. And if you've been picking Khuda Bax's pockets more fool him. But don't try it with me, okay? I know and you know that if you did get the cash you'd be gone, right?"

It was Oldham's turn to study her. Lis Charnay had hardened. What Oldham considered a lack of sympathy was rather a determination that extended beyond her quest to identify Tim's killer, a desire for revenge for its own sake. Oldham looked away, unable to meet her gaze.

A cab pulled up at the hotel's main entrance. A couple got out, the man slamming the rear door hard. The pair walked a little unsteadily into the hotel.

"So how do I get into this room and how do I open the safe?" Lis said. Oldham fished a card from his wallet and passed it to Lis together with the safe key. "Give me twenty minutes. If I'm not out then, I'll need some way to reach you," she said.

"Here,." He wrote a number on a card from his wallet. "This is a pager number. Leave your number and I'll call you back wherever you are. I think you'd better take this, too." Oldham slipped the gun from his pocket and handed it to Lis.

"You need it more than I do, Roger."

"Take it," he said. "It's loaded. All you do to fire is slide the safety catch forward like this, see. To clear the chamber just push this button, take off the magazine and pull back on the barrel like this. Got it?" She nodded, setting the safety catch on again.

"Now," Oldham said leading her back the way they had come, "if you go up to the right there, follow the building to the corner, turn left, you'll come to the back of the hotel to the service entrance. There's a door there they leave open all night. It's actually the cooking school."

She nodded, sliding the heavy gun into her coat pocket. "Will you be all right?" she asked.

"Of course. I've been in worse fixes than this, dear girl."

Lis took a deep breath and walked fast up the narrow street, the great wall of the Palais de Justice looming beside her, expecting at any second to hear the smack of a shot, feel its

blow on her back. She turned the corner. The back door of the
hotel was clearly visible, a glass canopy projecting out over
the sidewalk. The street was empty.

The back door led through a dark corridor into a brightly-
lit service area. She turned left and started up a flight of stairs
she guessed would lead to the lobby. Two men sat at the night
desk, another stood by the front door looking out across the
square. She crossed the lobby, the movement catching the eye
of the man at the door. He turned and gave her a look that
was part curiosity, part disdain. She nodded back, ready to
run, then saw her reflection in the mirror opposite. She
looked a mess, a wide scuff mark on her skirt, another on her
jacket, her black hair plastered to her forehead. A bath would
be nice, a long sleep would be better. She leaned her back
against the tapestried wall while she waited for the elevator.

The sixth floor hallway was empty and Lis' shoes made
no sound on the thick carpet as she turned left towards
Oldham's borrowed suite. There were two doors. The first,
602, was the primary entrance, which Oldham had explained
led into a lobby and the living room. Beyond were a kitchen
on one side and a small hallway on the other that in turn gave
onto the bedroom and bath. Down from the main door was
another unmarked door leading directly to the bedroom. It
was this that he had instructed her to use. If anyone was waiting for her they would expect her to enter by the main suite
rather than the bedroom, at least that was his theory.

She slipped the plastic card into the slot on the handle,
watched the green light flashing as the lock whirred back,
and, turning the handle, slipped quickly into the darkened
room. She stood listening. A street-sweeper, maybe the same,
passed on the street below, the flash of its orange warning

light playing across the ceiling for an instant. She waited. No sound came from the other rooms. She squeezed out of her shoes and crossed to the hallway without turning on the lights. The pistol was in her hand now, her other hand stretched before her protectively. She began to relax, breathing more easily as she tiptoed across the hallway to the main living area. She stood for a moment, lowering the gun to her side as she surveyed the empty room then walked slowly through the archway.

The arm came up and round in one motion, pushing her chin back and up, choking her breath. A hand snapped to her wrist, its thumb and fingers tightening like an iron cuff and pulling her arm down.

"Drop it now," a voice barked at her ear. "Now!" it repeated.

The gun fell with a dull thump to the floor beside her, the hand at her wrist twisting her arm up behind her, forcing her down to the floor. A light came on.

"What've we got?" a voice over her said.

The hand at her neck pulled her collar back roughly bringing her face up into the light.

"Oh, fuck," a second voice said.

Three men were in the room. Lis didn't recognise the first man; late fifties, American by the look of him. The others she knew instantly.

"Lis, we had no idea." Jay said from across the room. "Let her go, Sam."

Sam Clemens helped Lis to her feet. She was too stunned to speak for a moment but the shock passed almost instantly. "What the hell are you all doing here? You could have fucking killed me!" The side of her neck felt as if it had been hit by a baseball bat.

"Sorry, Miss Charnay," Clemens apologised quietly.

"You could have just asked, for Christ's sake. I might be armed but I'm not dangerous."

"We didn't know that," the third man said gruffly.

Lis moved to the long sofa by the window and eased herself into it. "So, Jay. Are you just going to stand there or are you going to introduce me to your friend. I assume he is a friend?"

"Yes, of course. Bob, this is Elise Charnay. Lis, Bob Lorenz."

CHAPTER 21

Paris

"You can't get croissants like this in the States. Why is that?" Lorenz asked.

"The water," Lis said.

It was five-thirty in the morning. The three of them sat around the room, Jay off to one side of Lis and looking miserable. Clemens haunted the lobby.

"So, let me get this straight," Lorenz started in again.

"I already gave you the whole story," Jay interjected.

"I know, I know," Lorenz said. "I just want the story from Lis herself. All right if I call you that?"

"Go ahead," Lis said.

"Okay, Lis. Here's what I got. Your boyfriend, Tim Short . . ."

"He wasn't my boyfriend."

"Whatever. Tim Short is killed in a car-bomb explosion. That's a pretty unusual event for someone working the crime beat."

"Not anymore."

Lorenz pushed himself out of the sofa. "Okay. So he treads on someone's toes, we don't know whose, and he or they blow him up."

"Look," Lis interrupted, her voice shrill. "I just came up

here to get something for Roger Oldham, okay. It's not my room, nor yours. Just let me get it and get the fuck out of here."

Lorenz waited for her to finish, then continued unfazed. "And your contact, Stephen – what?"

"Thompson."

"Then this guy Thompson expires on your front doorstep. Now, why do you think that might happen?"

"I've already told you. He came to give me some photographs. He gave me the photographs of Khuda Bax."

"Lis made the connection, Bob. She's the one who tied them all together," Jay said. Lorenz gave the younger man a look that told him to stay well clear.

"So Mr. Peterson here does you a great service, disposes of Mr. Thompson's remains at our government's expense, offers you shelter in his hotel room and what do you do? You take off."

"I went back to get the photographs."

"Next thing we know, you and this guy Oldham are almost blown sky high by another fancy bomb planted in his car – in the centre of London this time – which you just happen to notice before it goes off though you can't describe the trigger-man. What do you do then? You make a run for it on the train with our friend Oldham. Pretty weird." Lorenz stopped himself in midstream, something new occurring to him. "How did Bozo get his gun by security? I thought they had gates?"

"We were late. They let us in through the exit on the platform level. Maybe he knows the conductor. I don't know."

Lorenz filed the thought away and continued. "You jump on the train with this character and you and he and a bunch of oddballs finish up at some fish club where you have dinner with a man who is widely known to be a drug dealer. You and Oldham then take a little walk back to his hotel or his boss's and, bingo! Out of the blue comes some unmarked car . . ."

"I didn't say it was unmarked. I said it was a Peugeot without plates."

"Some unmarked car that tries to run you down. Whereupon Mr. Oldham, obviously unused to the way people drive in Paris, looses off a couple of rounds at the driver and gives you the gun. Being the gentleman he obviously is, he sends you up to this room which, in fact, isn't his, isn't even his boss's to get this." Lorenz scooped up a pile from the mantelpiece and flung it down theatrically on the dining table next to Lis, scattering passports, neat packets of one hundred U.S. dollar bills and three fat manila envelopes. "Francs," Lorenz said, "and Saudi riyals plus your friend's highly questionable accounts or some of them. Conspiracy theories, Lis? Been there, done that. Your buddy's a thief, a scam artist. Nice guy. Carrying an unlicensed weapon may not be such a big deal in gay Paree, even shooting up passing traffic, but breaking and entering, especially in this hotel, is going to get the *flics* real upset when they find out. You want to call them? Go right ahead. Phone's on the table. Jay, can I talk to you in the other room?"

The two men disappeared into the hallway leaving Lis alone. Maybe Lorenz was right, she thought. Maybe Roger was just a desperate, sad old man no wiser than she was. After all this, the blood, the shooting, she still had nothing that would explain why Tim had died. Not even a reliable witness. She felt depressed and very tired.

Jay was suddenly at her shoulder, gently holding her, his

voice in her ear: "It's okay, Lis, it's okay. It's just his way. It's what he does, the way he works." She was standing up, her arms pressed to his chest, his arms enfolding her, the quiet reassuring voice continuing: "It's okay, okay."

She had been asleep, having nightmares but now she was awake, a bright wedge of light piercing the curtains where they didn't quite close at the top.

"Feeling better?" a voice asked from a dark corner of the bedroom. Jay.

"A bit," she said, sitting up in the bed, pulling the sheet up to her neck. She was wearing only her bra and panties, "How did I get into bed?"

"It wasn't Lorenz," Jay said quietly.

"If it was, he'll wish he'd taken the gun away."

"He did."

Lis slumped back again on the pillow, the bruise on the side of her neck throbbing, the pain around her wrists registering, her hip hurting. "How did you find this place? I mean, how did you know where to come?"

"Bob Lorenz had Oldham's phone bills. A whole bunch were billed to this suite but Oldham had billed them back to Khuda Bax. Then Bob discovered who was leasing the suite. Khuda Bax's father-in-law is in the Saudi Ministry of Defence. Next thing I know he's over here. Sam told me right after I missed you in London." Jay stopped. "I'm sorry, Lis. About all of this. Once he's on a roll, he's like a bull. There's no stopping him."

"That's okay," she said, "that's okay . . ." slipping off again.

She dreamt Lorenz was driving her in the Bentley, its interior somehow filled with blue-green water. She was in the back, the water chilling her naked body, Lorenz's eyes leering at her in the rear-view mirror. There was someone beside her, another passenger but she couldn't turn her head to see. All she could do was look down at the floor. It began to shift, transforming itself into a face, Neil's face, the great T of his flattened nose and brow staring back at her.

Lis jerked awake again, her mind racing, her eyes wide open. The room was dark. This time no wedge of light sliced in from the curtains.

"Miss Charnay?" It was Sam's voice from a corner of the room.

Lis sat up, clutching the sheet around her. "Where's Jay?"

"He and Mr. Lorenz went out. Would you like something?"

"What happened to my clothes?"

"Mr. Peterson sent them to the laundry, ma'am."

"Good for him." Without pausing, Lis threw back the covers and strode across the room to the window. She yanked back the curtains, her slim body silhouetted against the pale afternoon light.

"I'm going to take a shower."

"Yes, ma'am."

Twenty minutes later, her hair washed and wrapped in a towel, one of the hotel's monogrammed robes tight around her, Lis came back into the bedroom. It was empty. Her own freshly laundered clothes were laid out on the bed. Beside them lay a cream-coloured Chanel suit and a blouse. On the floor, a pair of Celine shoes. Her own clothes, clean as they'd ever be, seemed as worn out as she was. She set the elegant clothes aside, putting on her own short-cut skirt and loose jacket. Sitting on the bed, she pulled on her black ankle boots.

Lorenz and Jay were at the dining table working through the pile of spreadsheets that spilled out of Lorenz's briefcase. Clemens was gone again.

"Hey. You look terrific," Lorenz greeted her cheerfully. Lis ignored him, instead speaking directly to Jay.

"I've been thinking while I've been in the shower and I've decided that I'd be better off taking Neil's advice." Lorenz looked to Jay for help.

"Neil Greyson, a family friend." Lorenz nodded.

Lis went on. "Neil said I should just let the police take care of it and I've decided he's right. I don't know what you're all messed up in, Jay, you, Roger, Khuda Bax. Whatever it is, I'm getting out of it before anyone else gets killed. I just wanted to find out who killed Tim Short and I probably never will. If you do, let me know, okay? If you're ever in London, drop by. Alone! And, by the way, whoever bought the suit, thanks but no thanks. Right size, wrong colour. Cream was yesterday."

Lorenz looked at Jay again then at Lis. "We change the colour, you give us another shot?" Lis didn't answer. Lorenz got up from the table and came round to face her. "Wait a second. You're not going to quit because of me, are you? I'm not in charge here; they just let me out on Tuesdays. He's the one with the brains, Mr. Personality over there. Our problem, his problem is that he can't get in to see Mr. Bax but he thinks you can. Better still, the reason Mr. Bax was so anxious to see Mr. Oldham again was so he could get all his precious files back." Lorenz nodded to the heap on the table. "We've just been keeping these ones safe for him. Copies, I'll grant you, but good enough. So. You could do everyone a favour. Square Bozo's account with his boss, make Mr. Bax happy, make Jay here happy and make me happy by settling this thing once and for all and getting him off my back."

Lis looked at Jay. His face was impassive making no appeal. He had already taken sides, had picked his target. It almost didn't matter to her anymore: Lorenz, Roger. They were all the same. She looked back at Lorenz. "It should be black. And two pairs of shoes, not one."

Lorenz winced. "You're a hard woman, Lis Charnay. The taxpayers'll never forgive me."

"They'll learn," Lis said.

CHAPTER 22

Paris

"If you want to get out, get out now."

Bob Lorenz's blunt warning echoed in Lis Charnay's head as she stood before the metal door at the back of the courtyard reading the brass plate over the intercom: Sulaiman Properties. It was now or never. She had telephoned last night from the hotel as instructed by Lorenz. A man speaking heavily accented French asked her what business she had with his employer. She had a packet that Mr. Oldham was supposed to deliver to Monsieur Bax but she would deliver it in his place. Certain documents. There was a pause then, improbably, she was asked if she could come round at 12 o'clock for lunch. Mr Khuda Bax would like to see her. She had turned to Lorenz and Peterson who were listening in on the other telephone. A brief nod from Lorenz and she had accepted.

"I'll be up front with you," Lorenz had said. "It's a long shot. You're pretty much going to have to play it by ear."

Late into the night and again this morning Jay and Lorenz had prepared her for the meeting, showing her where dates of deposit suggested payments that might have been made in exchange for services rendered at around the time of the attack on the Truman, large round figures, wire transfers to a bank in Peshawar. They gave her markers, specific references to certain accounts and certain transactions. Try not to make them accusations, Lorenz said. Make it sound as if you've looked at and understood the financials. Watch for his reaction. You'll know if you've hit a nerve.

"There are always other ways," Jay said. "Like Bob says, there's no guarantee this'll pay off."

"There are always other options," Lorenz agreed.

"Thanks," Lis said. "I'm flattered."

Sam Clemens had carefully taped the wire to her half-naked body, clipping the tiny microphone into the front of her brassiere and leading the thin wire round her back, taping as he went, to the miniature battery pack at the base of her spine. The other two men had sat on the bed, watching.

"I hope you're having fun," Lis said. Jay had looked at his feet but Lorenz's stare had been brazen, admiring Lis's slender shoulders, her half-exposed breasts.

She stood now, the sacrificial lamb, brushing a speck of lint from the skirt of the black Chanel suit. Now or never. She pressed the intercom button under the brass plaque. The metal door in front of her slid open revealing a wood-panelled elevator. There was a single gold button inside. She pressed it.

As she came out of the elevator Khuda Bax was standing halfway down the stairs. "Welcome to my humble abode, Miss Elise." Lis surveyed the wide hallway, its walls covered with what looked like originals by various European masters.

"Hardly humble, Khuda, but thank you," she said.

Khuda Bax led the way up the sweeping staircase to a gallery on the second floor then ushered her through double doors into the mansion's principal reception room. It was what every house should have, a well-known architect stated, a "Jesus" room. When you entered it, your only response could be: "Jesus." From the high domed ceiling, an impressive array of barely clothed gods and goddesses smiled down. Along the walls ran glass-fronted cabinets containing what Lis's host described as "little things I have picked up on my travels." Lis saw Russian icons, ancient Egyptian figurines, museum pieces every one. Then she saw the window. It ran from the floor to the ceiling through two floors perhaps twenty feet high and filled the whole northern and part of the western wall. Lis could see the Pont du Carousel across the Seine at her feet, the top of the Palais d'Elysée to the left, directly up ahead the glaring white dome of the Sacre Coeur on top of Montmartre. She could even see the Place Vendôme and suspected that from the upper gallery she might even be able to see the Ritz.

"Jesus," Lis said under her breath.

They were five at lunch on the upper gallery. Khuda Bax sat at the head of an oval mahogany table, Lis to his right. Across from her was a young Arab man introduced to her as Saeed bin Sayyaf.

"Saeed is from Riyadh and is very angry," Khuda Bax said introducing him. There was an edge to Khuda Bax she hadn't noticed at their first meeting, an uncertainty. The beaming smile was more in evidence than ever. "This is Mohammed Rafi," indicating a much younger boy to Saeed's left. Next to Lis sat the same Pakistani youth she had seen at the Club Zizi. As before he was not introduced and, as before, sat silently. While Khuda Bax gave instructions to a white jacketed manservant Lis smiled hesitantly at her companions aware that anything she said would be overheard by Lorenz and the others.

"Are you a student in Paris, Saeed?" she asked the young man across from her. Saeed eyed her carefully.

"I am a student of the truth," he replied cryptically in broken French effectively stifling further conversation.

Khuda Bax came to the rescue. "Saeed is a veritable wonder with computers. He has been introducing us to many delights." Lis wasn't sure whether Khuda Bax meant computer games or other distractions. "This is what you teach students at your universities, Miss Charnay?"

"You went to school in the US?" Lis asked Saeed in English.

Saeed blushed. "The University of Michigan," Khuda Bax provided with a hiss. "See how beneficent is our Ruler. And Saeed chooses to return his generous gift by abandoning his studies after just six months." Lis guessed it wasn't what Lorenz was looking for but there was definitely some very bad feeling between Saeed and Khuda Bax. Khuda Bax's expression lightened. "Now we eat."

There was no small talk. At this rate, Lis thought, I might as well disconnect the wire. The silence was broken by high-pitched screaming from an adjoining room. The waiter appeared and gave Khuda Bax a whispered message. Lis caught the words "enfants." Khuda Bax shoved back his chair and angrily left the room.

Lis turned to Saeed. "A student of the truth?" she said.

Saeed glared at her. "The truth is in the eye of the

beholder says the wise man. Mr. Khuda Bax says you are an American," he said spitting out the adjective as if it had a bad taste.

"Mr. Khuda Bax doesn't know everything then, does he?"

The young Saudi stared at Lis, his eyes unabashedly taking in the slim form, the black hair, the dark eyes. Lis touched the edge of her jacket instinctively as if to cover herself and the treacherous witness she carried beneath her clothes.

"You are French then?" Saeed said.

"Lebanese," Lis said repeating an old refrain. "Born in Sidon, school in Switzerland, college in the States. Now you know more than Mr. Khuda Bax, don't you."

"Mr. Khuda Bax says you are a colleague of Mr. Oldham," Saeed said, giving his "Oldham" about as much quarter as he had given "American."

"Like I said, Mr. Khuda Bax doesn't know everything. I'm a journalist, a reporter, though it's none of Mr. Khuda Bax's business."

"What is the truth that you seek?"

Lis stifled a laugh. Saeed's question was so earnest, so innocent. Not truth, she told Saeed, a killer. She was looking for the killer of her friend, Tim Short, also a reporter. He had been murdered in a car-bomb explosion.

The explanation had a sobering effect on Saeed. He sat back in his chair, pondering a question. Before he could ask it, the door opened and Khuda Bax entered the room.

"I am sorry," he said expansively. "A little domestic dispute. My sons." He shrugged as if that explained everything.

The meal concluded in a dribble of conversation. Saeed remained at the table briefly then left. Lis did her best to probe Khuda Bax further but he was too troubled by whatever indiscretion had taken place behind the closed doors and didn't seem interested in the records Lis had brought with her.

Finally, she excused herself. "Well, this has been really different. Thank you for your hospitality."

"My pleasure," Khuda Bax said dryly, leaving her at the top of the stairs to find her own way. As she was waiting for the elevator, Saeed appeared in the hall, his manner furtive.

"We will meet again," he said his voice almost a whisper.

"We will?" she said.

He thrust a flyer into her hand. It announced a meeting for that night at a church hall in the north of the city. The speaker was Rashid bin Khalifa al Said, a well-known London-based Saudi dissident who was much in favour of driving the Americans out of Arabia, preferably by force.

"You want me come to this?" Saeed didn't answer, fixing her again with his brown eyes. "Thanks anyway," Lis said, giving him her hand. She might have given him a dead bird for the look of amazement on his face but he shook it. "For nothing," she said to herself. She clutched Oldham's precious packet of codes and accounts numbers to her chest and, crossing the stone-flagged yard, let herself out at the street door.

CHAPTER 23

Paris

The rue des Saints Pères is one of those particularly Parisian streets on the left bank of the Seine that promises nothing yet delivers magnificently. The massive bulk of Paris' Ecole des Beaux Arts keeps it in shadow much of the day but its northern end at the Quai Voltaire opens onto a panoramic view of the Louvre and the river. Lis turned up it now, her back to the river and the light. Ahead, a Chevy Suburban dwarfing the smaller Citroëns and Renaults either side of it, was crammed against the wall, two wheels on the roadway, two on the sidewalk. Lis had to step into the street to get around it.

"You okay?" Sam Clemens asked as she climbed in.

"Fine," Lis replied. A man she didn't know was sitting in the back of the van taking off his headphones. "Did you get anything?"

"Loud and clear," Clemens said. "See you back at the hotel?"

Lis nodded.

Lis let herself in through the bedroom door of the suite at the Ritz. It felt like coming home somehow, even after the trauma of Clemens' ambush and Lorenz's interrogation. The bedroom was empty but she heard Lorenz's voice from the main room. He was ripping into Jay. She dropped the packet of bank records on the bed and crossed to the adjoining door.

"This is not up for discussion. This is a matter of national security and out of your hands." Jay began to answer but Lorenz cut in again. "Son, I've been there, done this. These groups come together then fade away." Lorenz's voice rose and fell as he paced the room. Lis heard him moving objects around restlessly as he talked, shifting the phone, moving a coffee cup. "You heard the wire. Khuda Bax is too busy fucking his little boys to care. The accounts don't mean a thing." Lorenz's tirade was interrupted by a knock at the main door and Clemens' arrival. "Did you bring her back?" Lorenz snapped.

"He did thanks," Lis said appearing from the adjoining hallway. "The suite has two doors, remember?"

Lorenz barely acknowledged her presence, turning back to Clemens. "We're out of here, Sam. I want this place clean inside the hour. Any bills direct to me. This is off the Embassy's screen. Understand? Get Frank up here and strip out all your little bugs – all of them."

"What about me? Don't I get a vote of thanks or something?" Lis asked.

"Thanks, Lis. You did just great," Jay said. "Bob's under a bit of pressure here and we're working some things out."

"Jay," Lorenz interrupted; "you and me will meet back at the Embassy at three. We're gone tonight. Miss Charnay, nice to meet you. Sam will take care of your expenses." Lorenz stalked from the room leaving the others to pick up the pieces.

"What's up with him?"

"Like I said," Jay said, "he's under a lot of pressure. Developments in the US" Jay's grin couldn't hide his embarrassment. Lorenz had earlier recounted in painful detail how far out on a limb he'd gone to defend Jay's extra-mural activity. The hounds on the Hill, cheered on by Enrico, were just getting wind of this latest initiative. "I guess he's terrified someone's going to find out he's been shacking up at the Ritz for the last two days."

They stood in the middle of the big room under the chandelier suddenly at a loss. "So is this 'Good-bye?' You going back to the States and me sorting out my 'personal problems?'"

"I don't know. I haven't really thought it through. I mean . . ." Jay wanted to say more but Frank, Clemens' technician, stepped between them, rolling back the carpet to remove one of the tiny microphones placed around the room. "Look, Lis. I don't want this to end right here." He handed a business card to her awkwardly. It had several numbers in the States printed on it, his name and address.

She took it. "Maybe next time I'm in the States. We can have a meal or something."

"No. I mean, this looks like my last day here. For now anyway. Can we meet?"

Lis considered for a moment. "I can't. I'm sorry, Jay. I already have a . . ." She hesitated. "A date. But I guess you and Bob already know that, right?" Jay said nothing. Lis moved closer to him. She held his lapel gently in her hand and kissed his cheek. "'Bye, Jay. Another time, another place perhaps. You're a sweet man but you've got terrible taste in your friends. I guess I can't handle both at the same time." She kissed him again, picked her things off the bed and left.

It was seven thirty the same night and a hundred or more people were crammed together under the police floodlights outside the Eglise St. Denis in the northern quarter of Paris. Counting the CRS in riot gear, the TF1 and network news teams and the plainclothes DGSA agents recording the events with their own camcorders, the total was probably closer to one hundred and fifty. The doors to the church ahead opened suddenly and the crush of people began to shuffle forward.

"Take your fucking hands off me," Lis yelled in French, one arm shielding her face as she fell back into the press of people. The expressionless CRS corporal just shoved her again, pushing the end of his night-stick into her chest. Charles de Gaulle who had founded the special police force and used them to bust the 1968 student riots in Paris had insisted the rank and file be recruited from outside the city to ensure loyalty. The thug assaulting her had to be from Outer Mongolia.

"Miss Charnay," a voice from in front called.

Saeed bin Sayyaf was standing by the door, hanging on to the hinge to prevent himself being swept along with the rest of the crowd. He led the way into the lobby then up winding stairs to the gallery. A young man about the same age was keeping two empty seats at the front of the balcony against lengthening odds.

"Here," Saeed announced triumphantly sitting next to Lis. "The man who is speaking, Rashid Khalifa, is a very important man," he went on excitedly, his voice raised against the wash of conversation around them.

The hall below them filled quickly, every chair taken, men sitting in the recessed windows along the side aisles.

Most were in their thirties or forties, a few older men and younger boys were evident here and there. Some of the older men wore traditional dress, a Berber in robes and burnoose prominent in the front row. Otherwise the uniform of choice was white shirt, slacks and leather jacket. Lis glanced at Saeed. He wore a leather jacket too. The boy next to him, the one who had saved the seat, wore a sweatshirt. Its front read: Hard Rock Café, Beirut. The universal dress code made the cluster of men in suits stand out even more. They were lined up in twos and threes against the wall under the windows, some wearing sunglasses.

"They are Saudi police," Saeed told her. Others had obviously identified the intruders too. Hissing filled the disused church. One of the men took the hint and left the room, the others brazened it out.

"Brothers, Brothers," an amplified voice rose above the hubbub, first in accented French, then Arabic. Lis suddenly realised she was the only woman present.

"That is Mr. Rashid," Saeed said and Lis heard the name whispered through the audience. Rashid Khalifa was a focal point of Saudi dissidence abroad. Three years ago he had launched a long-distance war against the Fahd regime by fax and e-mail from his base in London, citing royal indiscretions, unwanted foreign intervention and government sacrilege. Now he was calling for open revolt. It was a fiery performance, received with rapt attention by the audience during its delivery and wild cheering on its conclusion. Rashid, his face glowing with sweat, stood down from the pulpit. An organiser thanked him, embracing the little man warmly, then announced the next speaker, an Algerian. Lis noticed the Saudi plainclothes men had been joined by the

DGSA agents from outside, guessing the next topic might be closer to home.

Suddenly, she saw one of the men turn to look directly at her. The stare was unabashed, the man removing his dark glasses to get a better look. There was no hostility, no curiosity, the small eyes merely recording her face. The man replaced his sunglasses.

"Saeed? Who is that man?"

"Which man?" Saeed asked. Lis looked again for the squat figure by the wall but he'd vanished. "Come," Saeed tugged at her sleeve.

They pushed their way up the short flight of stairs to the back of the gallery then down to the lobby. Outside the CRS lounged against their armoured buses and riot vehicles ignoring the small group of Parisians who were adding their voice to the wave of protest. Several carried crudely written signs urging "Dirty Arabs go home NOW."

"Rashid Khalifa is a very important man," Saeed said again as he and Lis edged their way through the cordon of police and onlookers and into the empty boulevard beyond. "But he is wind only. He says but he does not do."

Lis stopped walking and put a hand on the young man's leather-clad arm missing what he was saying. "At Khuda Bax's house this afternoon, when I told you about my friend's death; you already knew about it, didn't you?" Lis said.

"I don't know what you are talking about."

Lis pulled him to a halt. "You've heard the name before. Where?" Saeed seemed ready to resist but Lis held both of his arms now. Further along the sidewalk on their side of the boulevard a group of Arab boys was approaching. Saeed glanced nervously in their direction then back at Lis.

"It is not your business," he said; "not your business. Now, let me go." Saeed shook himself free. The group of boys passed, looking at Saeed and Lis, laughing. Saeed walked off leaving Lis standing, her own image suddenly visible in a store window, her face a blank mask.

CHAPTER 24

Paris

A man lay curled in the shape of a question mark, the body hooked, the legs bent. Two figures stood over him, one beating him with a club the other kicking his back. Lis had picked so many similar clips from so many stacks of video-tape that she wouldn't have been able to identify the location if she hadn't seen it herself.

It was eleven o'clock in the evening and the demonstration at the church was running third in the news behind a depressing set of jobless figures and a boiling ministerial scandal. Lis watched the scene from the bed in the room of her new hotel, the less-than-luxurious Hotel Américain. Feast or famine, she thought. At least there was a shower.

Lis got up and switched off the set. She was tired, tired of all this, tired of men like Lorenz and his bullying. She began to unpack, hanging the suit she'd extorted from Lorenz behind the door, setting out her few cosmetics on the sink. It was an old habit learned from long days on the road, flying out overnight to wherever the story was breaking, arriving at the hotel sleepless, the producer already on the phone wanting to know when to expect the tape, where the uplink was. She stacked the wad of account records and codes on the television and thought, suddenly, of Alain, the network's legendary archivist in the Paris bureau. These people had histories, public lives. Wealth attracted attention. She looked at the digital clock by the bed: eleven thirty. Too late to call him now but not too late to call Roger's number. She pulled her jacket from the closet.

The café at the corner of the rue Plantain was still open. A young couple in the window held hands and stared into each other's eyes. She thought of Jay. The boy let go of his girlfriend long enough to walk over to the juke-box. He slipped a coin in and the undulating wail of a popular Moroccan group filled the room, the music from the speakers competing with the sound from the television now playing a rerun of the earlier news.

The *patron* gave her a token for the phone and pointed to the booth at the back. She wedged her way in. Pulling Oldham's contact number from her pocket, she dialled. There was a tone, then a voice in English. "Welcome to WorldPage." She keyed in Oldham's voice-mail number and waited. Roger's own voice came on, urging the caller to leave a message and a number. She gave the number of the phone she was calling from.

"I'm expecting a call."

"Oui, Mademoiselle. Vous voulez quelque chose à boire?"

She ordered a café allongée and sat down to wait. Eleven fifty. She'd give it another ten minutes then call one more time. As if on cue, the phone at the back of the café rang. The *patron* looked in her direction for a moment then back to his sports page. She walked past the lovers and picked up the receiver.

"Hello?" There was a sound of laboured breathing at the other end, no voice. "Uncle? Is that you? Say something."

"Lis?" His voice sounded far away and Lis realised he might not even be in the country anymore.

"Can we meet?" Another long pause.

"There's not much point, my dear. In fact, there are a couple of very good reasons why we shouldn't."

"For old times sake?"

Another pause, even longer this time. Lis could hear the music distinctly now. A chansonneuse, French, plaintive. He was still here then, in Paris or in France anyway.

"The Musée d'Orsay? Know it?"

"Yes."

"One? One thirty? Tomorrow?"

"Yes. Where? Upstairs? In front? Roger?"

The line was dead.

Lis put down the receiver and slid out of the booth. The jukebox had stopped, the couple gone. She paid for her coffee, waiting by the counter for the change. She never thought she would need company so badly. Any familiar face would do, any voice. The television was playing an old Clint Eastwood movie as she left the café. The face of the lean actor, eyes shaded by the brim of a stained cowboy hat, filled the screen. "Je m'appelle Josie Wales," the dubbed French voice said, the clipped syllables not quite matching the actor's barely moving lips, the tone too bright. No man's land.

"Lis! Mais c'est toi?"

Alain Barais, the video archivist at the network's Paris office, was known throughout the organisation. His passion was his job and his job was cataloguing the hours of raw footage shot by reporters in the field. He lived with his mother, at least eighty, though Alain claimed he'd forgotten, in a house just outside the city. Lis had been one of the chosen few invited home and had raised the old woman's hopes that Alain might yet bring home a bride but Alain had spent the evening showing Lis his collection of books and gadgets. He was a geek.

Barais' knowledge of current events was as encyclopaedic as his reported collection. He could place a name, story or date without hesitation, but Alain's knowledge was not to be bought. One wrong word could leave a producer scrolling through endless feeds from the network's outstations in search of the right sequence or quote. If Alain didn't like you, there was no appeal.

"Alain!" Lis returned Alain's embrace. "It's been a long time."

"My God," he said stepping back. "Look at you." Lis was wearing the black Chanel suit. "Did you marry an American?" He wrapped his arms around her again, his mouth close to her ear. "I heard about Tim short, chérie. They should roast the pig who did that. He was a true friend. These shits here," Barais said, hiding his emotion with a toss of his head at the network's logo, "didn't even give him a ten-second tribute."

"They forget us all when we're gone," Lis said, the depression of last night lingering.

Barais shrugged. "What are you doing in Paris, chérie? I thought you were in the Middle East."

"I was but they let me out. I'm, well I'm sort of on a leave of absence."

"You are working on something?"

Lis charted the course of her investigation for Barais. He listened attentively, his enthusiasm picking up with each new twist. She skirted around Stephen Thompson's death and her own close-encounter in London but filled in enough of the detail on Oldham and Khuda Bax to give Alain a start. When she was done, he sat down at his computer, his fingers clattering over the keyboard. An index of names appeared, he clicked on one. A window with archive references appeared on the screen. He scrolled down the abbreviated list and noted an index number. "This is your man here, Khuda Bax. There's a CBS feed we never used and this profile done by TF1 that we excerpted for the International Conference on Drug Enforcement. It was held here last year."

"Why did Khuda Bax figure in that?"

"You'll see. He's supposed to be a big wheel in opium imports from Afghanistan. So the American DEA. says. That's probably history now. The Taliban clamped down in Afghanistan and the French connection was busted last year. Most of the heroin that gets into the US comes from Colombia via the Caribbean these days anyway. You want to see the footage?"

"Sure."

Lis waited at one of the monitor booths while Barais ordered up the tapes. She looked at her watch. Ten thirty. She had two and a half hours before her meeting with Roger. Time enough. The CBS report was gathered for a *60 Minutes* segment on Islamic politics in the US and its airing had caused a furore in the States. The raw footage included coverage of political gatherings in the US that presented Muslims as a potential source of danger within the country as well as without. Then suddenly and for no more than five or six seconds there was Khuda Bax.

The footage had to be several years old but the smile was

unmistakable. He was getting out of a car, a Mercedes, and shaking hands with an official delegation of some sort. The brief appearance came just before a breathless report by a man standing in front of a hotel in Peshawar, the Pearl Continental. Khuda Bax, the reporter announced, was responsible for hundreds of thousands of dollars in contributions to Islamic groups in the US, the proceeds of his activities in Afghanistan, the reporter conjectured. What these activities were was quickly established by file footage shot before the Taliban take-over of subsistence farmers in the Hindu Kush collecting liquid opium from poppies planted among the wheat and corn on the hillsides. The camera zoomed in on the bulb of a poppy flower as the farmer made a vertical cut to let the latex drain out.

She ejected the cassette from the player and pushed in the second of Barais' offerings. This was a French report, more raw footage, with still images only, of Khuda Bax and several other alleged kingpins. The report confirmed beyond doubt that Khuda Bax was a key-player in the drug trade whatever Roger might say to the contrary. A graphic flashed up on the screen and she paused the tape, the freeze-frame flickering on the screen. It was a flow chart of sorts, arrows interspersed with poppy flowers charting the route taken by the opium exported from Afghanistan through Turkey and into Europe. A large white question mark hung over France and another over Ireland, a broader arrow pointing in the direction of the US.

"Interesting, non?" Barais said.

"Why is there a question mark in the graphic in the last tape?" Lis asked rewinding the tape and pausing it over the map.

"The old network was taken apart but this is a new route apparently. They are supposed to be introducing a pure strain into the market, very powerful, very lethal. They haven't seen stuff this good since the sixties. It's so pure the kids are snorting it and smoking it and dying, of course," Barais concluded with a shrug.

"Who did the French coverage? It's quite good."

"A lot of it's file," Barais said, sitting himself on the desk in Lis's booth, "but the core of it, the stuff on your friend Khuda Bax and the new route was done by Didier Falon, the lead reporter."

"He's at Antenne Deux, no?" Lis asked.

"Was. He was found dead three months ago in the Canal St. Martin. Suicide, apparently. Death by drowning."

CHAPTER 25

Paris

The Lautrec canvas hung in the upper gallery of the Musée d'Orsay, the blues and greens of the interior depicted in it capturing some of the tints from the arched skylight of the former railway station. The woman at the centre of the picture gazed back at Lis, her look stale with fatigue or resignation, she wasn't sure which.

It was one fifty and Lis had briefly abandoned her post at the entrance, looking again for Roger inside the gallery. Tourists in twos and threes drifted in and out of the side galleries, a flashbulb popping once and a uniformed guard appearing from nowhere to chastise the offender. Roger wasn't coming she suddenly realised. The museum was too exposed or he was too scared. Maybe he was already floating face down in the Seine, the silver hair twisting in the current, the body beginning to bloat. She walked back to the stairs, her eyes still fixed below, steadying herself for a moment with one hand on the metal banister. Her hand slid off the railing absent-mindedly as she walked the few paces to the last flight and reached out for the next. It never completed its journey.

The man dragged her sideways through a service door marked "Employees Only/Do Not Enter." In the three beats it took them to enter the adjoining service corridor she realised it was Roger. "Jesus, Roger. Take it easy."

"I'm sorry," Oldham said, his voice hoarse.

She could see him head on now. He hadn't shaved, white stubble covered his chin and cheeks and wisps of hair had begun to sprout over his collar. His shirt was wrinkled, his tie awry. He looked like he had slept in his clothes.

"You look terrible. Where did you spend the night?"

Oldham didn't answer, just kept going. "I'm up against it, Lis. I used the cell phone, see. Didn't think. They have scanners. Could have picked me up."

"Slow down, Roger. Who? Who's got scanners? Bax?" Oldham tugged her again, drawing them out of the passage and into one of the storage rooms. Its interior was crammed with slim cases stacked on edge. The afternoon sun shone dimly through a dirt-streaked skylight washing the colour out of Oldham's face, tinting the hand raised for silence to a faint blue. He listened intently. A door down the hall opened then closed again. He swayed slightly where he stood then suddenly slid to the floor, his back against the wall, his head slumped forward on his knees. Lis thought he might have passed out. "Roger?"

"God, it's good to sit down." he said. "Just to sit for a minute." She crouched down next to him, sliding her arm round his shoulder extending what little comfort she could. His hand reached up to hers. "Just like this." They sat in silence for a minute, the elegant young woman in her tailored suit, the dishevelled man beside her, forming their own odd picture.

"What happened?"

Oldham didn't answer right away as if he needed to rerun

the events to be sure they had really happened. "I reckoned I'd be better off on a train," he began. "Not the night before, last night. There's an overnight to Nice. Friend of mine gave me the idea once. If you need to disappear for twenty four hours, take one train down another right back. Thought I was safe, cops everywhere. The train was just leaving when this brute came out of nowhere."

"Who?"

"A big black guy. He tried to kick down the compartment door. My God," Oldham said his hand shaking.

"And?"

"I managed to wedge the door, got out the window onto the track, got away. I'm not even sure how, really. If I had some real money I might still make it but now . . ." Oldham let the thought go.

Lis realised she had little chance of pulling him back but knew she had to try. Very slowly, as if she were telling a story to a child, Lis started telling Oldham everything she knew, hoping that even now he might deliver some piece she had overlooked. She wasn't even sure he was listening. It didn't matter. "After I called you last night I went walking. I started over from the very beginning and suddenly saw what Tim had been looking at all along: Neil Greyson. Neil was declared *persona non grata* in the Gulf two years ago. Did you know that? A rumour got started he couldn't shake. That he was involved in drug trafficking. Seems his righteous clients couldn't handle that." Something got through to Oldham at last. He said nothing but she knew she had his attention, knew he was listening now.

"So Short started digging," Oldham whispered to himself.

"I guess it all led to you," she said; "Khuda Bax."

A flash of the old Roger Oldham shone through. "I swear, Lis. How could I possibly have known? I only handled Khuda Bax's accounts and a couple of his arms-buyers' in the third world. I swear."

Lis cut in. "This wasn't arms, Roger. This was drugs. Opium. Heroin."

The idea stilled Oldham's ripple of protest. "My God, Lis; you can't be serious. Neil's, Neil's . . ."

"Neil's what?"

"We served in the Army together."

Lis thought about the funeral, the big house in Ireland, the estate, thought about the sham of it all. And then she thought about the man sitting next to her and the paintings around them, worth thousands, hundreds of thousands of dollars for all she knew. She thought about Saeed and his anger. None of them belonged anymore. There were no tribes, no borders anywhere. "Tim made the connection: from Khuda Bax to you, to Neil and back to Khuda Bax. Maybe it was a chance meeting, a phone call to the house. Something or someone tipped him off.

"I have to take off, Lis my dear."

"Wait Roger," she said, standing up. Oldham shook his head and, using both hands, pushed himself off the floor to his feet. "Roger!"

"Lis," he said. "You know I can't help. My chances are slim as it is. I'm sorry." He started to open the door, more relaxed than when he had entered, resigned perhaps to the fate that awaited him outside.

"No one counts, do they? Everyone betrays everyone else. There are no rules, no loyalties," Lis countered.

Oldham led the way down the back stairs to the service

entrance on the rue de Lille. The guard at the desk didn't even look up as they passed through the lobby and onto the street. Oldham pulled his coat closer around him and began to walk quickly.

"You just needed someone to run your errands for you, didn't you; someone to take the bullet," Lis said, keeping up with Oldham. "You, Greyson, Bax, Lorenz, you're all the same. Different skins but the same snakes." Lis's voice rang out along the street ahead of them.

"That's not true, Lis. I didn't have to come back," Oldham said without slowing his pace, a hint of self-pity in his voice.

"So why did you? You came back for these, right?" she said pulling the bundle of accounts from her pocket. "You know what? I actually don't give a flying fuck whether you get blown to pieces or not."

Lis's outburst had carried them behind the Ecole des Beaux Arts and round the back of the Institut Francais onto the Left Bank by the old Mint. Oldham stopped under the statue of the Marquis de Condorcet, author of the Theory of Probability. The Marquis was handed over to his friend, Robespierre's Revolutionary Tribunal by his lover, Madame Vernet. Oldham was apparently no more conscious of how exposed he was now to the probable dangers than Condorcet had been of his own.

"That's not it, Lis," he said. His red-rimmed eyes were welling with tears. It might have been from the wind off the river or something else. Lis couldn't tell. "I came for you. No one's ever been there for me, dear girl, ever. I came for you, don't you see, for no one else."

She looked into the tired face, wisps of silver hair blowing across the eyes. He was like a little boy just wanting to be believed. She slipped her arm through his, pressing the sheaf of bank records into his free hand and guiding him through the traffic to the far sidewalk. "We need to get you a cab," she said trying to spot one in the traffic.

Oldham lingered in front of one of the bookstalls that cling to the wall of the embankment. He picked up a tinted engraving from the counter, studying the face in the frame for a moment. "'When good Americans die they go to Paris.' Incredible wit, wasn't he. He died here, you know," Oldham said and then, almost to himself: "Good for him." He dropped the engraving back onto the stall, flashed a smile at the stall-holder and moved away leaving Lis looking at the picture of Oscar Wilde. As she turned to catch up, she heard a roar from behind, a motor revving, and a scream, then another. The bookseller grabbed her, pulling her back against the stall as a motorbike accelerated towards them along the sidewalk from the direction she and Oldham had just come.

There were two men, the man on the back barely visible behind the driver. Then he leaned out from behind the driver at an angle. Lis thought he was going to grab her but then suddenly she knew what was happening. It was as if she had seen it all before.

"Roger," she screamed, "Roger."

Oldham no more than eight or nine paces further up the sidewalk stood with one foot on the bottom step of the entrance to the Pont des Arts, the narrow, pedestrians-only bridge spanning the Seine and leading to the Louvre on the far bank. He half turned, whether at the sound of her voice or the bike's engine she couldn't know. The bike was abreast of her now and for a flash she saw both the driver and the passenger in profile, their attention fixed on Oldham. As the bike roared past, a staccato rattle cracked in her ears.

"Roger," she screamed again.

Oldham's body jerked up and sideways as the burst from the gunman's machine pistol stitched a line diagonally across his back from his hip to his shoulder, the bike and its riders already past Oldham before his lifeless body crashed forward to the sidewalk, the papers in his hand scattering. The rider pulled the bike to the right, the two men leaning into the turn, the engine revving to a scream, then gunned it up the steps onto the bridge, smoke jetting from the tyres. The gunman looked back at the body, his face obscured by his helmet. Lis didn't have to see the face to recognise Oldham's killer. It was the man she had seen at the rally, the same squat body.

The bike rose into the air for a moment then crashed to the deck of the bridge, scattering a few startled pedestrians. The gunman's head came up, looked her way then, his arm swinging back for leverage, he flung the gun upwards. It arced out over the side of the bridge and plunged down to the river.

Lis ran the few steps to Oldham's body, knowing he was already dead but picking up his shoulder, rolling him onto his back. Oldham's face was slack, the lower lip pushed upwards in a curious contortion, eyes staring upwards, empty, already dark. The noise around her began to register, a squeal of tyres, voices yelling. She saw the legs of people collecting around her, the shoes, a little dog staring at the body inquisitively, then, looking up, she saw the gendarmes running down the road towards her.

"Got to go now, Lis," a voice at her ear said firmly. "Now."

A hand helped her up, guiding her to the open door of a vehicle, lifting her up almost bodily into the interior, the man's body pressing in behind her, pulling the door closed. The engine revved and the vehicle pulled away fast. She said nothing, staring back through the tinted glass at the remains of Roger Oldham's hopes, the bank records she had handed to him, lifting in the breeze and beginning to blow out over the river.

"Where to?" the driver asked.

"Don't care, Sam" Jay Peterson said. "Just get the fuck out of here."

CHAPTER 26

Paris

They sat silently, Sam Clemens at the wheel, Jay and Lis on the back seat. A passer-by able to see through the tinted glass might have said they were on a date that had turned out badly, the driver looking doggedly ahead, the couple not speaking.

The section of the Bois de Boulogne where Clemens had parked was habitually patrolled by prostitutes, male and female. One approached them now, tapping on the windshield. Clemens got out, taking up station on the passenger side to ward off any other intruders.

Lis broke the silence. Not looking at Jay, she said: "You could have saved him."

"Not possible."

"You could have intervened." Her face was empty of expression.

Jay reached a hand out then said quietly: "It was a matter of time. Even if we had got to you earlier, someone was going to get him eventually. You know that. The Bentley, the hit-and-run. They were desperate to see him dead." There was good reason now to believe that Thompson, Oldham, Starling and Short had all been killed by the same hand or under the same direction. The problem, as always, was how to substantiate their theory and explain its purpose. Jay was no nearer finding the organiser of the attack on the Truman and no nearer to Khuda Bax. As it was, he and Clemens had barely been keeping up. When he hadn't met Lorenz at the airport, he knew he had blown his last chance. There wouldn't be another reprieve. It would only be a matter of time before Sam was pulled off the case. Without back-up it was a wonder they had even been able to keep up with Oldham and to pick up Lis.

"I've only seen two people die," Lis said; "I mean, before all this. There was a woman in Texas. They put her to death with an injection. And my father. They did the same thing. Isn't that strange? He was dying of cancer and they gave him morphine. The doctor never said: We could just give him a little bit more. He just said: We just want to be sure there's no discomfort, no pain. That's what it's all about, isn't it; no pain."

Gently, Jay returned to Oldham's killer. "It's possible the man who killed Oldham killed Stephen Thompson, too. We'll know when they find the shells." Or someone will, he thought, realising he was outside the circle. He owed Manktilow a call.

Lis's tone didn't change, the same level voice as if she were far away from what she was seeing in her mind's eye, far from Jay. "He was at the rally, in the hall. He looked right at me."

"You saw his face?"

Lis didn't answer. Instead, she said: "Roger said good Americans come to Paris to die. That was the last thing he said."

"The rest of us die in America," Jay said.

Lis looked at him for the first time since Oldham's killing.

"*A Woman of No Importance.* My professor was, is Irish. He said *all* Irish go to America period. Wilde went too." Lis looked away. Jay tried again. "Last night wasn't the first time you saw him?"

Lis ignored the question. "He killed Tim."

At first Jay thought she was making it up. "How can you be sure?"

"Greyson and Khuda Bax are in the same business. Khuda Bax, Greyson, Roger – all one big happy family." A cold smile crossed her face.

Jay tried to keep up: "Neil Greyson? What connection does he have to Khuda Bax?" Lis said nothing. Jay took her hand, held it tenderly as if it might break. "Lis. Listen to me very carefully." She looked at him again, still far away. He went on. "Whoever killed Tim, whoever killed Roger . . . You're a target now, too. We have to get you out of here fast!" She stared at him, through him. There was a tap at the window. Jay looked up, expecting to see another painted face leering at them through the windshield. It was Clemens. Jay lowered the window.

"We're attracting a little heat. Nothing special, just the boys in blue. Thought you should know."

Jay saw the patrol car reversing down the avenue, it's passenger turned back towards them. "Let's get out of here. Lis, we're going to take you to a safe place until we can sort all this out with the proper authorities. Understand?"

"I need to pick up my things."

"What things?

"At the hotel."

"Sam can get them later."

"I need to pick up my things!" There was an edge to Lis's voice that warned Jay off.

"Okay, it's okay. We'll swing by the hotel, get your stuff and then go to a safe house. All right?" Lis didn't respond. "Where were you staying?" Jay asked her.

"It's on the rue Plantain," Clemens said. "Hotel Américain."

They drove by the entrance slowly, Clemens and Jay registering the unoccupied cars parked in the streets, the empty lobby. Clemens turned the Suburban at the end of the block and circled back.

"Park it here," Jay said. "I'll go up with Lis."

"No!" she said, her voice rising over the rumble of the engine.

"Why not? It's just in case."

"No!" she said again, her voice shrill.

Jay looked to Clemens for help but the driver just shrugged slightly. "Okay. Sam and I'll wait down here. But if you're more than five minutes we'll come looking for you. Okay?" Again Lis made no response, instead opening the rear door and getting out. Jay watched her crossing the street oblivious to the traffic. "Stay here, Sam," Jay said; "I'll follow her up." He got out of the car and followed Lis across the street, pausing until she was inside the hotel. In the lobby the reception window was open. A woman sat at a desk.

"Bonjour, monsieur," she said as Jay entered.

"Bonjour," he mumbled not stopping.

"Monsieur," the woman called; "je peux vous aider?"

Jay ignored the question and started up the stairs. They

were narrow and steep and Jay took them two at a time so as not to lose her. On the second floor he stopped, listening for Lis's footsteps, not wanting to overrun her. He could hear her on the next flight and he turned the corner quickly, his foot already on the first step. A man was coming down, almost on him two steps above. The last thing he registered was the man's build, compact, round. On the outer edge of his vision, he saw something coming down hard and straight. He turned, one arm beginning to lift to deflect it but it was going too fast. It hit him high on the shoulder near his neck. The pain never even registered.

Sam had the radio scanner on listening to the chatter, mostly in French, some police. The crackle of static fading in and out was suddenly overridden by a very clear signal from somewhere close by, the nasal French replaced by something guttural and fast. Turkish? Israeli? Clemens turned off the engine so he could hear better. The signal came in bursts, two voices, brief, staccato, like a message or instructions. The voices died and were replaced by the background chatter.

He reached to turn on the engine but stopped as he saw a Mercedes pull up on the other side of the boulevard and the driver open the trunk from inside the car. Sam could see the man was dark-skinned. Tall. He didn't get out, just stayed inside with the engine running. Sam looked across at the hotel lobby again and then at the service entrance, a barred metal gate leading to a narrow alley that ran down one side of the building. The other driver was watching it too. Two figures appeared at the gate carrying a bundle, the one in front pulling the gate open with his free hand. The two men shuffled round to the back of the Mercedes swinging their package up and into the trunk. It looked like a carpet at first then Sam saw it was a blanket wrapped round with silver duct tape. It sagged in the middle as the men tossed it into the back of the car.

Clemens reacted instinctively. He pushed the door open with his foot, one hand reaching under his jacket to the back of his belt where the Browning was holstered. One of the men on the other side of the street looked up. He was squat, pear-shaped almost. The man's arm lifted, the gun in his hand flashing. The windshield shattered, glass chips spraying over Sam as he threw himself flat on the bench seat. He heard a car door slam, a squeal of tyres. He sat up fast, throwing the Suburban into a U-turn across the boulevard, its front wheels screaming in protest, the front door swinging shut again. The right fender bounced against a parked Deux Chevaux. Clemens slammed the vehicle into reverse, tearing loose from the car in front and hearing the blast of a horn and the crash of glass as the car behind barrelled into the back of him. The force propelled the big wagon forwards as he accelerated and launched it down the boulevard in pursuit of the Mercedes.

Ahead of him the saloon turned hard right, a small cloud of smoke streaming from the nearside tyres as the driver threw the car into the turn and the rubber burned for a second on the cobbles. Clemens was a hundred yards behind them, no more. He pushed his foot all the way down, the V6 engine on the Suburban revving and the 4-wheel drive thrusting the vehicle forward. Cold air buffeted him through the shattered window, dirt and dust blowing into his face. Ahead, the Mercedes, now less than seventy five yards in front, accelerated through a stop light, its progress marked by a fanfare of angry horns. Clemens pulled the Suburban around a dawdling Renault and straight for the intersection, his hand on the horn blowing a continuous warning.

He saw the police van a clear two seconds before he reacted. It had entered the intersection and hesitated fractionally as if the driver was deciding whether the Mercedes was worthy game or not. If it had kept going or if the driver had made the turn, Sam might have been alright. But for that one instant he wasn't sure which way the police van was going. He had no choice. He threw the wheel over, the Suburban doing its best to obey the instruction but beginning to slide already, its whole body sweeping sideways like a great steel wave straight at the side of the police van. The Suburban smashed into the van's side with a spectacular thump, glass shattering, the metal sides of both vehicles crumpling, the rear doors of the van springing open. The impact thrust the other vehicle across the intersection and into the market street beyond, the police van falling on its side onto a produce stall, splashing vegetables and fruit onto the sidewalk before coming to rest against a café window, an amazed customer staring through the glass at the flashing blue light inches from his face. The man posed for a second, his coffee cup raised as if in a toast before the Suburban, still moving irresistibly sideways, caught up with the van and drove both vehicles through the plate-glass window with the crack of a gunshot.

In the stillness that followed Sam could hear the patter of falling glass like rain on fall leaves. Then his world went black.

CHAPTER 27

Paris

The Préfécture of Police on the Ile de la Cité in Paris faces the grim towers of the Palais de Justice and the Conciergerie. From the third floor offices of the chief of the Rapid Response Team a visitor can look down on the elegant Cour du Mai and beyond to the steps on which les tricoteuses, the knitters of France's revolutionary terror, counted off the kingdom's aristocratic heads as they were guillotined.

Sam Clemens looked away from the window and assessed his own damage. The pain in his ribs and down his left side had turned out to be only heavy bruising. The wounds to his face and hands were pretty much superficial. The rest of the damage went deeper. He had made a mistake. He knew it as soon as he had swung the truck round in pursuit of the Mercedes. He should have stuck with his charge, with Jay. Those were his instructions. He had chosen wrong. Now he was paying.

By the time the police doctor had picked out the glass from his face, stitched the gash on his cheek and cleaned off the blood, the Paris police attending the scene of the accident had identified Clemens and notified the US Embassy. Inquiries by the Embassy had revealed Clemens' presence in the French capital to be unauthorised and he had been brought to the Préfécture. There, a US consular official, Bernard Schulz, no rank given, had advised him to remain silent. That was fine by Sam. He had managed to take some liquid through a straw at the medical centre but opening his mouth now the Percaset had worn off was like washing his face in fire. The door behind him opened. It was Schulz again.

"How are you doing, Sam?"

Clemens managed a muffled "okay" in response.

"Good," the consul's man beamed. Schulz was all papers and procedure, a typical consular type. He swung his briefcase onto the empty desk between them and snapped the catches. "They still won't let you go just yet I'm afraid Sam, but we're working on it. In the meantime it would help your cause a lot if you could just tell me again what you are doing in Paris anyway. I realise it's painful for you to talk so you may just want to write it down." Schulz pulled a yellow legal pad from the briefcase and offered it to Sam with a pen. Sam took them and wrote "shopping" before handing the pad back to Schulz.

"Very funny, Sam," Schulz said stiffly. "Look, I'm doing my best to clear up this mess. So let's not be childish, okay? You and Mr. Peterson have some explaining to do. Shall we?" Schulz gathered up his case again and gestured to Clemens to lead the way out of the office.

"Hi, Sam," Jay said. "You look worse than I feel." Clemens tried to grin but the searing pain stopped him. Jay turned to the smartly dressed young man seated under the portrait of the President. "Josh Redman, this is Sam Clemens; Sam, this is Josh Redman, US trade representative."

Clemens heard the warning immediately. The chances were more than good that the only trade Redman represented was foreign intelligence for the CIA.

"Sit down, Mr. Clemens," Redman said pointing to the couch where Jay was sitting. "You might as well know, since I've already told Mr. Peterson the same thing, that part of our arrangement with the French is that you'll both be returning to the States at the first opportunity. There's a Continental flight leaving Charles de Gaulle in three hours. You'll both be on it."

Sam looked at Jay and then away. He knew how desperate Jay had to be. He had watched the two of them, Lis and Jay, collide, watched Jay throw over everything to stay by her. Jay wouldn't go quietly.

"I don't intend to have you make statements here at this time. You will be fully de-briefed on your return to the States."

"Understood, sir," Jay said. Jay's willingness to comply struck a false note but Clemens was the only one to hear it. "Just for the record though, you should know that Agent Clemens was acting entirely on my instructions."

Redman ignored Jay, getting up and going over to the desk. "I need you to sign this." He pulled a typed sheet off a pile of papers and handed it to Jay.

"I can't sign this, Redman; not without representation. You know that," Jay snapped. Redman took the document back and offered it to Clemens. "Don't touch it, Sam. Not without a lawyer present." Redman made no comment, simply replacing the document on the pile and making a note on the pad in front of him.

"Who put you up to this, Redman? Enrico? Or did you just feel like practising the writer's craft? Redman's little fiction here," Jay said turning to Clemens and indicating the document on Redman's desk, "has it that we deliberately obstructed justice and knowingly aided and abetted a terrorist. They want us to agree that Miss Charnay plotted Oldham's death. Take a look for yourself." He reached over and slid the document off the pile before Redman could intercept him. "While we're waiting," Jay went on, "I'm going to need a secure phone so I can call my boss."

Redman shook his head. "Sorry, Mr. Peterson. That will have to wait until you're back in the States. I've been given specific instructions that you're to talk with no one till you get back. It's part of the deal."

Clemens sensed Jay winding up for a big hit then just as quickly backing off. Instead, Jay stretched out, settling deeper into the couch and massaging his neck carefully. "So, Redman. What's the news from home? Have we won the war yet?"

The Continental Airlines flight to Newark, New Jersey with onward connection to Reagan-National in Washington D.C. was scheduled to depart at one forty. By one o'clock, Sam and Jay with their "keepers," Redman and Schulz, were assembled in the VIP lounge at Charles de Gaulle Airport. Apart from the meeting earlier in Redman's office, Jay and Sam had been kept apart, not strictly under arrest but left in no doubt by the presence of the US Marine in each room that they weren't free to leave either. Now they sat across from each other with Redman and Schulz beside them. Schulz was working on some papers in his briefcase, Redman next to Jay was watching the news on CNN.

"The search for the organizers continues in the recent attack on the US carrier Harry S. Truman in the Gulf with bipartisan pressure mounting on the White House for a change in leadership of the investigation. Meanwhile, the FBI continues to insist it is making progress. From Washington, our foreign affairs correspondent Alex Martin." The scene switched to a reporter standing across the street from the FBI. building. He noted the Bureau's absence of results and the increasing pressure on the agency to stand aside. Bob Lorenz's scowling face flashed momentarily on the screen.

"Maybe we should let you lot take a crack at it," Jay said to Redman. "What do you think, Sam? Think they'd get any closer?" Clemens said nothing.

The rest of the report was drowned out by warning chimes from the roof speakers followed by an announcement in English: "Continental Airlines is pleased to announce the departure of Continental Airlines Flight 57 for New York's Newark Airport. This flight is now ready for boarding through Gate 14."

Sam pushed himself up. "I need to pee," he said.

"Go ahead," Schulz said not looking up from his papers.

Sam hobbled across the lounge to the bathrooms, a single door accessing both men's and women's.

Redman watched him. "If you have to go, you'd better go now," he said to Jay. Jay shook his head.

A couple of minutes passed. A second announcement was made for their New York flight. Redman began to jiggle his leg. "Think we should check on him?" he asked. Schulz looked up. "Clemens. He's been gone three minutes at least."

"If you want," Schulz said.

Redman got up and crossed the lounge, pushing the bathroom door open a little too violently, banging it against the wall. He disappeared inside. Schulz put down his papers, interested at last, watching the door. Redman reappeared in the doorway, waving Schulz over.

"What's up?" he said, his tone that of the senior man taking charge.

"He's not here," Redman said.

The two men entered the men's side. The room was empty.

"He's got to be here," Schulz said looking at the ceiling helplessly, at the tiny window high in the wall. "Have you checked the women's?"

The men pushed out of the men's bathroom and into the women's. A woman was standing at the sink, her startled face visible to them in the mirror.

"Mais, qu'est-ce que vous faîtes ici?" she said.

Redman froze in the doorway but Schulz plunged in pushing open one door then the second. There was no sign of Sam. Schulz backed away, apologising in rapidly deteriorating French. At the door into the lounge Redman blocked his view. Schulz gave him a shove to one side then realised what had brought Redman to a full stop. Across the room, Sam was sitting in the same seat Jay had occupied before, innocently watching them watching him. The expression on his face inquired if anything was wrong. Schulz saw immediately what it was. Jay Peterson was gone.

CHAPTER 28

Paris

Jay's exit from the Continental VIP lounge had been quick and easy. He had expected some kind of police blockade but there had been nothing. Maybe Redman was too embarrassed to admit losing his charge. In the cab on the way back into the city he thought about Sam, feeling he'd betrayed a friend. In the ten days they had spent together, he and Sam had developed a subtle bond. Jay was the novice, Sam the expert, Jay's baby-sitter, his guiding hand. He had staked out the rally with Jay, followed Lis back to the hotel. Jay had been embarrassed. He felt he was intruding, violating her privacy. They had covered her visit to the café, picked up the call to Oldham on the scanner, noted the rendezvous. They had followed her to the network's offices on the Champs Elysées, watching her back all the way. It had been an educated guess that had put them at Lis's side when Oldham was gunned down, no more; a lucky break. Jay had had a good teacher, one of the best, but far too little time to learn. Now he was on his own and running.

The wide boulevard in front of the Gare du Nord, where Jay had told the taxi to stop was busy with traffic, a line of taxis blocking the curb, a bus double-parked beyond them. Jay threaded his way through to the far sidewalk, turning left.

He passed a café, the Brasserie Anglaise, then a news-stand. The morning edition of FranceSoir carried a photograph under its banner, a grey heap almost indistinguishable from the background of the sidewalk, its bulk outlined by a darker pool. It was the body of Roger Oldham. He walked up the block to a phone.

"Yes," a voice answered, muffled, not fully awake.

"Brian?"

"This is he. And who the hell are you to be calling me at this godforsaken hour?"

"It's me, Brian. Jay. I need you to call me on a secure phone in thirty minutes." Connolly said nothing for a moment as if weighing Jay's situation or maybe just lighting up his first cigarette of the day. "You still there?"

"Yes," Connolly said finally. "What's the number?"

Thirty minutes later Jay was on the same café phone in the rue Plantain that Lis had used two nights before. The phone was ringing as he entered the café, Connolly on the other end. Jay gave it as briefly as he could. Connolly swore softly then fired off a round of questions finding the financials more intriguing than the individuals, probing Jay for missing pieces.

"She went through the wall, Brian. Don't you see it? There was a heroin pipeline, Khuda Bax at one end, some kind of Irish Mafia at the other. But that was shut down. They had no reason to abduct her, no reason to pull her unless she'd broken through."

Connolly laughed, the laugh turning to a cough: "You're starting to sound more like me every minute. You've got names, right? Give me some names."

"Saeed bin Sayyaf. Saudi. Twenty-two, twenty-three possibly. Lis met him at Khuda Bax's. They went to a rally together. The guy who killed Oldham. Smallish, five foot seven, compact, used an MAC II or something like it, very professional, back of the bike. Threw the gun over the bridge on his way out. Could have been the same one who hit me. My partner thinks he was in the car that took Lis."

"Busy little bugger."

"Please, Brian."

"Okay, okay. Where am I going to reach you, supposing these freaks don't reach you first?" Brian sounded like a worried parent.

"I'll call you."

The concierge at the Hotel Américain recognised Jay the moment he walked in. He knew his cause was hopeless as soon as she picked up the phone.

"Non, Madame. Je vous en prie."

His plea went unheeded and the woman behind the counter kept dialing, her heavy-lidded eyes daring him to come any closer. He could make a break for the room but didn't rate his chances.

The Quai Voltaire extends east west along the Seine's Left Bank from the Quai Conti where Oldham had been gunned down. Tourists strolled the sidewalk pausing to pick over the cheap magazines and trashy books, ignoring the most famous of the sites the street offered, the house where Voltaire had been born and died eighty four years later. The sage would have appreciated the irony. Just short of it, Jay came to Khuda Bax's house. He crossed the street to get a view of the pent-house, its huge two-story picture window catching the afternoon sun, an ugly satellite dish marring the roofline. Khuda Bax had certainly got the best house on the block.

Jay checked the street in both directions. If the house was being watched it was unlikely he was going to spot the watchers. He gave it an extra five minutes anyway before crossing the boulevard and going into the courtyard. Across from him was a metal door covered by a video camera. Sulaiman Properties. The place was a fortress. Jay pressed the intercom.

"Oui?" The voice was metallic, distorted by static.

"Mr. Khuda Bax?"

"Il n'est pas là. C'est de la part de qui?"

"I'm a friend of a friend. Jay Peterson. You may remember Miss Charnay? She was here to lunch two days ago."

The intercom went dead but Jay knew he was still being watched on the video monitor. Taped too probably.

It was after five now, over twenty-four hours since they had taken her. At the FBI's academy in Quantico the trainers had told them that most people being interrogated cracked on the first day. The thought only increased his sense of despair.

The lobby of the offices on the Champs Elysées was hung with oversize headshots of the network's US anchors, their perfect teeth and carefully piled hair giving them freakish aspect. The decor was New York corporate rather than French, an English-language newscast playing on the monitor in the upper corner of the room. The receptionist asked for his name, asked him who he wanted to see. He told her he was here to pick up something for Elise Charnay, something she left when she was here yesterday to see Monsieur Barais. The woman gave him a look but lifted the phone and dialled anyway. Jay waited.

"Jay Peterson?" The man was dressed in jeans, sneakers and an improbable FBI sweatshirt. He gave Jay a careful inspection. The look on Barais' face told Jay he'd failed the first test.

"I came about Lis."

"Lis?" Barais said.

"You know she's missing?" Jay tried.

Barais stared at him. "Maybe. Why should you care?" Barais read the answer from Jay's expression. "Do you want to come on back?" he said holding the lobby door for Jay. He led the way past a line of cell-like editing booths to a cramped office at the back. It reminded Jay of Connolly's office in Georgetown.

"Are you a friend?" Barais asked, pointing Jay to the only chair.

"Yes. A good friend."

"And you're looking for her?" Barais asked.

"Yes."

"You're not the only one."

On cue the view on one of the monitors above Barais' desk cut to the scene of Oldham's death the day before, the spot Jay had just passed. The voice-over chronicled the events then said police were looking for a young woman believed to be a prime witness.

"They won't find her," Jay said turning back to Barais. "Look, we don't have time to fence. I'll be straight with you. Lis is out there alone. There's a slight chance that she's still alive and there's an even slimmer chance I can get to her before they kill her. I'm her only hope right now. I need your help."

Barais regarded Jay quizzically, a small smile collecting at the corners of his mouth. "Monsieur Peterson. You haven't told me everything."

"I haven't had a chance," Jay said.

"No, you misunderstand. You didn't tell me you're, how do you say enflammé – nuts about her."

CHAPTER 29

Paris

"Vous êtes marié vous?" The old woman sat erect in the bed, her head towards the television, white hair piled like spun sugar, newspapers and magazines scattered over the bed-spread. The question fired point-blank at Jay stopped him dead.

"Maman!" Barais shot back. "Don't worry about her," he told Jay. "She has only one thing on her mind ever. C'est un copain, Maman. C'est tout. Up here." Jay bobbed his head to Barais' mother by way of greeting then followed Barais upstairs. The house in Billancourt where Barais and his mother lived was a small, flint-sided construction of the type the French call a *pavillon* right across the River Seine from the Renault car factory. Pictures of Barais' parents dressed the walls of the narrow staircase.

"This is Papa," Barais said pointing to a photograph of a young man dressed in civilian clothes standing on top of a burned out German tank. "He was in the same Resistance cell as François Mitterand. He always said there was only one side to be on – our side."

The trip from the centre of Paris on Barais' Kawasaki had taken a little less than fifteen minutes, Barais weaving expertly through the evening traffic along the river front. The tapes Lis had looked at before going to meet Oldham were at his house, Barais said. He hadn't told Jay about his mother.

"He must have been quite a man," Jay said, stopping to look at the picture for a moment. At the top of the stairs, Barais unlocked one of the bedroom doors. "This," he announced with a flourish, "is my rec room." Barais' English was good, much better than Jay's French. His "rec" room as he called it looked a lot like his office with a few exceptions: four TV monitors not three, an expensive-looking computer with two monitors and minitower hooked up to two VTRs, even more videocassettes, DVDs and CD-ROMs, stacks of American catalogues and a wall full of books on the Gulf and Arabian Peninsula, their politics and peoples. The world of what Connolly called "terror groupies," those outside the professional circle who tracked trends and shifting alliances, techniques and targets, was a small one but mightily equipped.

"This is an on-line digital editing system," Barais said, proudly displaying the monitor and its attachments, "and this is my hobby." He indicated the books and catalogues. Jay's spirits sagged. Quark International Ltd., he saw, offered a digital voice masker on its cover, a low-profile beacon transmitter and a tie-clip camera on "special." Jay wondered if he had made a terrible mistake.

"Do you know Brian Connolly?" Jay asked, wondering if Barais was one of the "contacts."

"The author of *Blood and Oil*? Sure. I've got his book right here. I've never met him but we talk a lot on the e-mail. You?"

"He was my college professor."

The images flicked across the computer monitor in miniature, Barais occasionally freezing a frame at Jay's request. He had digitised the footage on the hard-drive when he'd seen the first report of Oldham's assassination to make it easier to manipulate. "Those jerks don't even know what they have," he said dismissively.

"Did she say anything about what she saw? Did you talk at all?"

"A little," Barais said. "She said Tim Short had identified an Irishman, Neil Greyson. He was the one who killed him, she said."

"Because?"

"The drugs, of course. Greyson was next in the trail, non? Afghanistan, Bax, Greyson, the States. Elementary. It's always drugs or guns and usually it's drugs. Is that who's got Lis, then, this Irish man?"

"No," Jay said, more unsure than ever. "No. It's a cell, Saudis maybe." Jay looked at his watch. "I need to call Brian Connolly. Could I use your phone?"

"Why didn't you say?" Barais scolded. "We could have been talking all the time." Barais switched to his e-mail and posted a message to Connolly. Within minutes, Connolly was at the other end of the connection, feeding the information and images he had amassed at Jay's request to Barais' terminal. No rest for the wicked or for the wired, Jay thought. "See?" Barais said triumphantly.

First, Connolly communicated, there was no trace of Saeed bin Sayyaf on the FBI's "Afghan" list, the database supplied by the Saudis to the Bureau of activists who had served on the Russian front. He wasn't on the US immigration service's "watch" list either. Connolly had come up with an academic record, a social security number and driver's license. A Saeed Sayyaf, no "bin," had dropped out of the University of Michigan last year after an incomplete year in biochemistry.

He had listed Riyadh, Saudi Arabia as his home address. No family connection with Khuda Bax, no known attachment to dissident groups. Clean kid. Older brother killed in Afghanistan, Connolly noted.

"That fits Lis's description," Jay said. "Has to be the same guy."

Connolly's transmission continued, the text interspersed with several images of active "assassins," each compressed image accompanied by a caption. "The usual suspects," Connolly had footnoted the files explaining they had been screened by favoured method of execution, country of origin, group association and current whereabouts. Barais downloaded the individual files busily pulling them into the video sequence he was building and printing out the text. He was clearly getting a big kick out of this. Connolly ended with a cryptic "Keep the faith" directed to Jay. The transmission was unsigned.

Barais clicked on a button on the screen and the sequence he had pieced together began to play. He hadn't included all the footage but had cut in parts of the TF1 and CBS profiles. Barais had kept the sequence just as Lis would have seen it: the shot of Khuda Bax, the journalist's field report from Peshawar.

"Stop there," Jay said. "He's in Paris, isn't he?"

"Who?"

"Khuda Bax. Isn't that Paris?" Barais re-ran the few seconds of footage of Khuda Bax getting out of a Mercedes, freezing on a wide angle of the car and its exiting passenger and the building in the background. The architecture wasn't immediately recognisable but the face of the man welcoming Khuda Bax was. "My God," Jay said.

"What?"

"Roger Oldham," he said, answering Barais' look. "How about the car's plate?"

Barais executed the same manoeuvre, this time selecting the back of the Mercedes. The license number was distinct enough to read, the last two digits, 50, now clearly visible. "Interesting," Barais said. "The car's registered in St. Lô in Normandy."

"How can you tell?"

"Each department has its own identification. Paris is 75, the suburbs 93. 50 is St. Lô. It's where Maman is from."

The "live" sequence ended and the monitor was filled with the headshots Connolly had modemed minutes before. There were four in all. Two of them were identified as Iranian or as working for Iran. One had been charged in the assassination of a Turkish diplomat in Paris but was believed dead. The other was serving a life sentence in Germany on a similar conviction in Berlin. The third consisted of a blurred picture and physical description. Under characteristics the file listed "Race" as "Negroid," "Height" as "6'3."

The fourth was their man. Various aliases were listed but Connolly had highlighted Nasir Abu Massoud. Nasir claimed Syria as country of origin and small arms as a speciality. A brief biography noted time spent in the Imam Ali terrorist training camp in Tehran, height as "5'6", build squat and powerful. Above the caption was a face, the same that Lis had probably seen in the church that night in the north of Paris, the man on the back of the bike. It was quite round, the head shaven, the eyes hidden behind heavy lids. Current whereabouts unknown.

"That's the man. That's who we're looking for."

"So," Barais said. "Why don't we start?"

"Where?"

"Easy. We look for the owner of the Mercedes."

CHAPTER 30

Quettebec, Northwest France

There is a state between sleeping and waking when a sleeper can will herself back to sleep, refusing consciousness. Lis Charnay stood now at this threshold. Her eyes were closed, her slim body coiled into the shape of a shell. Had there been an observer, he could not have helped seeing the child in her. She looked younger than her twenty-six years, her skin pale, her black hair unbrushed, spiked with dirt. One hand was at her mouth as if to prevent her from saying something she didn't want overheard. She still wore the elegant black suit, crumpled now, stained. Only the blanket underneath her, protecting her from the bare earth of the cellar, suggested she had chosen to lie there or had been set down there.

The room was completely silent and pitch dark. When Lis did open her eyes, finally accepting reality whatever the price, she was unsure if her eyes were indeed open or if they were still shut. She closed and re-opened them carefully, taking stock. She put out a hand, feeling the blanket beneath her, picking at the tape that had secured her in its roll. She lifted a corner, the adhesive separating from the wool with a tear and a dull flash of fluorescence. She brought the hand back to her mouth, her mind beginning to focus.

She felt hungover, drowsy. The images were still running

as if she were seeing them projected on a screen, the motion slowing and speeding up indiscriminately, the only sound the shallow breathing through her mouth. Dry. It was very dry. She needed water, something to drink.

She saw the door, her door at the hotel, her hand on the latch, pushing the handle down, saw the door swinging open and the light from the window shining at her like a flashlight and the shape of the man's head, the silhouette coming towards her, filling her vision, the taste of his hand on her mouth like oil or gasoline but the hand dry, blocking her nose. Then the panic rising, her eyes wide, the sting, a needle, a blow in her back like a fist or an elbow and the long fall into the deep, the light fading as if she were sinking, her breath roaring in her ears, and faintly, so faintly, a voice from far away speaking. French. "Attrappez-la," it said; "catch her."

Safe. She was safe here. The voice wanted to help her, to catch her before she fell. And she was not cold. She was thirsty. A small chamber in her brain, a tiny shred of will urged her to work on that. That was real, the thirst. And the pain. A bruise where the elbow or the fist had hit and some other pain, a tiny point of white light in the back of her upper thigh just below the buttock. The needle.

Gradually, she pulled herself away from the safe place the drug had created, pushing her hand into her back to locate the bruise, circling the needle mark with a finger. She forced herself upright, leaning on one arm. Her body felt loose as if the bones had melted under the flesh, as if it would dissolve if she tried to get up. She was sitting up, her eyes unblinking, staring straight out into the darkness, desperate for the slightest spark of light. She pulled at the tape again, the tiny flash reassuring her.

She was kneeling now, her body swaying slightly. She knew she wouldn't be able to stand. She was too feeble. But she could crawl.

The darkness all around was impenetrable. She wished she smoked, wished she had a lighter or matches but there was nothing, just her clothes and the blanket beneath her. She began to move then stopped immediately. A furious discussion broke out in her head. What if she couldn't get back? Since she didn't know where she was, it didn't matter. The argument resolved itself. She dragged the blanket with her: like a baby, she thought.

The ground beneath her was flattened earth, cool to the touch but hard, hard on her knees and bare hands. She slid one hand out along the ground, testing the area in front of her, bringing a knee up to the hand, creeping forward. The darkness seemed to fill her senses, to weigh in on her. She had no sense of progress. Hand out, knee up, one. Two. Three. How far? Three feet, four? Her left hand went out, the fingertips suddenly connecting with something, recoiling as if they had touched a bare wire. She almost lost her balance. The sensation was wrong, the signal her hand sent telling her that it hadn't touched the ground, had touched something that gave, something soft like flesh. Charnay took a deep breath and willed herself to extend her hand again, edging it forward over the floor until it came into contact with the obstruction. This time she kept her hand where it was. She was touching another human.

"Hello?" she said, her voice tiny and hoarse, reaching her hand an inch further, feeling bare skin. She pulled the hand away, listening, waiting for an answer, for the sound of breathing. "Hello," she said more firmly this time, pushing with her hand, feeling the flesh give way, the body shifting slightly. And suddenly the weight of an arm fell on her hand, shocking her backwards, her scream tearing up the darkness, screaming until she had to draw breath then screaming again. A blinding white light scorched her eyes, spilling onto the dirt floor in front of her and the shape she had been exploring. She saw the figure in perspective, horribly foreshortened, the feet closest to her, the bare belly and hairless chest, the rolls of the neck and the face, saw it as if it were a flash photograph. And, abruptly, darkness again. A sack went over her head, blocking out all the light, stifling her. Hands reached under her, hoisting her to her feet, the image of the naked man lying dead in front of her burned into her retina. The naked man, face, chest, arms spattered with his own blood and excrement, the hooked nose squashed sickeningly flat, the soles of the feet pointed towards her, purple from beating. It was a man she knew. It was Khuda Bax.

She was standing, the hood over her head. There was a faint haze of light, a relief from the blackness of her cell. Her arms were held above her, the muscles aching, her hands throbbing. The first time she had tried to lower them someone had hit the back of her legs with a stick, something thin and whip-like that had smacked as it had come in contact with the skin. She had spun around to face her attacker, stooping off balance. Hands had caught her, pushed her upright, forced her hands above her head again. She shifted the angle of her head, trying to find a chink in the cloth. A hand jerked it back into place.

"When did you first meet Roger Oldham?" The voice,

always the same. Not unpleasant, accented. When did you meet Oldham? How long have you known Jay Peterson? Where are the files you gave Khuda Bax? The man always asked her the same questions, over and over. He wasn't interested in her, in her life, only in what she knew. At first she had resisted, perversely refusing to speak. No one had threatened her, there had been no subtle cross-examination, no prompting, just the shaking. Hands had grabbed her arms, pressing them to her sides and began pushing and pulling her, her head snapping back and forth like a rag doll's, her teeth biting down on her tongue. Just as suddenly, the shaking stopped and again the same questions. At last she had begun to respond, telling the truth. She had nothing to lose. Roger was dead, Jay would take care of himself. That was when the realisation had come that she was alone. No one was looking for her, no one riding to her rescue. She was alone.

She had met Roger in London, she said, had come to Paris with him. Why? Because she thought Roger could help her. How? To find Tim Short's killer. Who is Tim Short? And on, and on. When the man had finished with one sequence of questions, he began again from the beginning. Why did you come to Paris? Why did you go to Khuda Bax's apartment? Sometimes his voice was near, coming from behind her; sometimes it was far away. And then she was being dragged backwards, her heels banging down the stairs, upright again and waiting for the moment when a shove in the back would send her sprawling face forward onto the dirt floor, the hood yanked off at the same time, back into that place with the thing her only company. She was terrified they would throw her onto Khuda Bax's body, that she would fall sprawling over the decaying carcass, the putrefying naked skin, the flattened nose. She had not tried to explore again, remaining in the spot where they threw her down until they came again. How long? She didn't know. Hours? She didn't know.

She sat sometimes, sometimes knelt. Her head sagged with exhaustion, not sure if she were sleeping or awake. She dared not lie down again, obsessed now with the idea that the body of Khuda Bax would come crawling towards her, would smother her. She spent hours peering around her, her neck aching with the effort. She became convinced she could see the corpse glowing, luminescent with a wan light. Then, suddenly, the door opened again and in that instant before the hood was pulled over her eyes she saw the wall in front of her, the heavy dark grey stones of the building's foundation. The body was gone.

There was no food, no water, no one else spoke to her, only the man with the hoarse voice. After a day or a week for all she knew she managed to count the steps, managed to concentrate long enough to remember. Ten steps along a corridor, twelve stairs, her bruised feet counting the twelve edges as they pulled her up, ten more steps to the door of the room of pain. The door opening, falling forwards, pulled upright, the door closing behind her. Then they changed the routine.

She counted ten steps from her cell then her body was twisted by the unseen hands, spun like corkscrew. The paces continued, Lis stumbling between the bodies on each side of her as they pulled her forwards. She was panicking, terrified now that some new danger waited her, some unimagined pain that she had no way of predicting. She whimpered uncontrollably, uttering little yelps of anguish, unable to think, unable to balance or co-ordinate her movements, a trickle of urine running down the inside of her leg. The forward motion halted, hands shoved her into a room and the same interrogator started his repertoire of questions all over again, forcing her this time to stand on one leg, some unseen hand whipping her again with the stick if she staggered. How long had she worked for the FBI? Who was her superior? She told him anything now, two years, ten years, fifteen. Her superior was Jay. Her superior was Lorenz. She worked for Neil Greyson, for Oldham, for Khuda Bax, for Thompson. She babbled incoherently, unaware of the beatings to the back of her bruised and bloody legs, her leg screaming, her arms above her head throbbing, collapsing, being dragged up again.

And then, suddenly, nothing. No voice, no sounds, no feeling. Death is soft, she said, as she fell for the last time, not knowing if the sound were locked in her mind or if she were screaming it out loud. Death is soft.

CHAPTER 31

St. Lô

The journey to Caen took just over an hour and a half. Why Caen? Barais had ignored Jay's question and continued loading the bike. Jay had no idea a motorbike could bear so much gear but Barais kept bringing it out, strapping down the packages he carried from the house with fierce efficiency. Jay saw knives, a crowbar, a high-intensity spotlight each being found a place in the mountain of equipment. He was reminded of a knight riding out to battle.

"I don't know what it is you're planning exactly, Alain, but shouldn't we cover the dealerships here in Paris, wait till they open? At least take a look around Khuda Bax's property, the parking lots, side streets; see if the car is still there."

Barais finished pulling on his leathers, dramatising his own sense of purpose with vigorous tugs on the zippers. "Fine by me, Jay. You do your thing, my friend. Okay? I'm out of here." Barais swung his leg over the bike's saddle and kicked it into life, running the big engine up with a roar. No wonder his mother was deaf, Jay thought.

By four thirty that morning they had driven round Khuda Bax's neighbourhood twice, had made a pass along the garage parking lots on the Left Bank and even gone through the Ritz garage under the Place Vendôme. There were plenty of

Mercedes, none with plates from the Manche, the Department in which Khuda Bax's car was registered. Then, like a rocket shooting out of earth's orbit at its far off destination, the Kawasaki accelerated north around Paris' Peripherique and headed west. Jay had quickly found that mounting and riding the bike had as much to do with balance as muscle. At first he had gripped Barais tight around the waist. The Frenchman had curtly suggested that Jay might be better off holding onto the seatback behind him. Jay thought about Sam Clemens, wondering where he was, which reviewing committee had him trapped in front of its desk. Mostly he thought about Lis. He leaned forward, sculpting his body round Barais' back, willing the bike forward.

They stopped in the main square in Caen off the Boulevard des Alliés, Barais unzipping his leathers and taking off his helmet before taking his place at the counter of the Café de Ville. The route had some ancient significance for Barais and the ritual would not be denied. Jay, chilled to the bone in his suit, skipped the croissants and coffee to fax an update to Lorenz. He found a machine at the bank of public phones off the square. Barais was already suited up and waiting when he got back.

"When they run the plates they usually do it through the central registry in Paris," he said. "Each Department in France issues its own vehicle permits though, collects its own road taxes. So, instead of going through the main computer, which we can't do, we go to local records for the Department in St. Lô."

"Couldn't you just phone?"

"Jay, it's six thirty. No one is at their desk until nine, maybe nine thirty."

Up on the bike, the sun at their backs now, Jay thought about Lis again, tried not to think about her. He tried to focus instead on Nasir. He was a real person with a real history, a professional with a paymaster. Someone would be funding him. Khuda Bax? It was a start, a point of entry. Jay took assurance in the thought of Connolly hacking his way now through every electronic wall in pursuit of his quarry, the smoke choking the air in his basement office.

The rush hour jammed the narrow streets of St. Lô, filling its central square to capacity. Barais guided the Kawasaki through the buses and Renaults and into the courtyard of the Préfécture. The two men climbed off the bike, Jay stretching, Barais already heading up the steps.

"I thought no one got to their desks till nine," he shouted after him. Barais kept going, Jay behind him now.

"Bonjour, Cécile."

"Alain! Tu vas, chéri?" The blond woman behind the first floor reception desk reached over to embrace Barais, clearly pleased and a little surprised to see him.

"My cousin," Barais said introducing Cécile to Jay.

"Et ta maman? Ca va?" she said.

"Ah, mais oui," Barais said. "Comme toujours, merci. Comme toujours."

Then he explained what he was after and the woman led them up two flights and through a glass-fronted door labelled *Véhicules*.

"We have no year, but I'd guess seven or eight years old," Barais said. "Let's begin with his last name."

They hunted through the Bs for Bax then the Ks. They even tried the Os for Oldham. "Does it have to be registered in person?" Jay asked.

"What do you mean?"

"What if it's a corporate registration, a business?"

They tried Oldham's company then the holding company that owned Khuda Bax's apartment in Paris and nominee accounts in Oldham's web of offshore deposits: Sulaiman. And there it was. A 1993 Mercedes registered to Sulaiman Produce, Inc. with a business address in the Channel Islands and the local address, as required by law, in Carenton. Three other vehicles were also listed, a Renault van and two trucks. A fleet.

"Where's Carenton?"

"Fifteen minutes," Barais said already on the move.

"Any relatives?" Jay asked half kidding.

"Sure. My sister-in-law. She works at the real estate office."

Barais's sister-in-law, Monique, an attractive woman in her thirties, had her own office in the real estate company's townhouse in the centre of town. There was another round of polite introductions, Barais embroidering the notion that Jay was a rich American expatriate looking for a country property. Then Barais steered the conversation round to the address on the Mercedes registration, 23 rue Vassy, Carenton. That could be interesting, he said. Monique didn't bother to ask why and went across the hall to see if it was listed.

She came back two minutes later with a file folder and three listings which she set down in front of Jay. "Just in case, you see?" One was a modern construction at Lessay with a view of the English Channel or La Manche depending on which side you were on, one a ruin outside Carenton, the third a massive turreted mansion dressed with local flint. It was a farmhouse of sorts though the listing described the building grandly as a château. You couldn't actually see the Channel from the property but you could if you climbed the hill behind, Monique assured Jay. Plenty of land too.

"Rue Vassy is a rental," Monique went on. "I expect it could be purchased if your friend is interested." She gave Jay a coquettish tilt of the head and a little wink. Barais pressed her for rental history. Monique found a date that corresponded to the registration of the Mercedes, a six-month rental by Sulaiman Properties. Monique hadn't been at the office then. She thought the broker who had made the arrangements had moved to Paris, she couldn't be sure. No forwarding addresses for the renters. "Would any of these other properties be of interest?" Monique asked, getting back to Jay.

"No," Barais answered. "Thanks anyway, chérie. Regards to that jerk my brother." He exchanged rapid kisses with his sister-in-law while Jay looked over the two property listings, his panic surging again. He had screwed up badly. Screwed up with Lorenz, screwed up on his own. He'd better face the fact, now or later, that Lis Charnay was already dead and he, Jay Peterson, pretty close to it professionally.

"You coming, Jay?" Alain said.

Jay flipped the first two listings over and took a closer look at the third, the flint-covered farmhouse in Quettebec. He looked at the price distractedly, trying to figure the exchange rate, his mind holding onto anything to prevent it spinning off into space. He worked the numbers, the taxes, the square footage. Then he spotted the name under "Seller." There is a God, Jay Peterson knew, and he had just heard him speak the seller's name: Mrs. Gabrielle Greyson.

CHAPTER 32

Quettebec

The village of Quettebec, or what there was of it, was centred on a dilapidated concrete memorial to France's dead and flanked by a café and a row of three houses on one side, open fields with scatterings of dirty black and white cows on the other. "Welcome to Quettebec," Barais said racking the bike up on its stand and leading the way into the darkened café. Jay took a seat while Barais negotiated with the owner.

"There isn't even a restaurant. We have to go to Cherbourg. But monsieur here," Barais indicated the *patron*, "has agreed to rent us his room. You don't mind sharing a bed." Jay looked the owner over carefully. "If you're worried about word of us getting around, my friend," Barais said with a smirk, "don't. Normans can't even say good morning till they've had a shot of Calvados. The locals are noted in France for their natural hostility." The *patron* set Jay's coffee down in front of him without a word and disappeared into the back. "Point taken," Jay said.

The room above the café was cramped but would serve their purpose. A double bed took up most of the space in the room, a bureau under a faded picture of Mont St. Michel occupying the rest. Jay put his carrier bag on the bureau. They had stopped in St. Lô on the way and Jay had bought clothes:

jeans, sweatshirt and some cheap sneakers. Barais threw one of his cases onto the bed.

"Voilà," he said snapping open the top. The foam lined interior was crammed with gadgets. Barais began removing them, identifying each as he set it down. "Nightscopes, miniaturised digital video camera, alarm detector, electronic eavesdropper, transmitter, and this little sweetheart," he said lovingly removing parts of a long-barrelled gun from the centre of the case.

"What the hell is that?" Jay asked in wonder.

"Dart gun."

"Where did you get all this?" Jay asked then remembered the catalogues. Every piece was unused, a few still in their original wrapping.

"Not bad, huh?" Barais inquired. "Lis used to send me the catalogues from the States. See?" He offered Jay the video camera. The unit was the size of a cigarette pack and, Barais assured him, could download QuickTime images directly onto the laptop fitted snugly into the top of Barais' second case.

"Why do you have all this?" Jay asked.

"My hobby," the Frenchman said. "Everyone should have a hobby, right?"

A visit to the Mairie behind the café gave them the only background they were going to get. A previous owner had set up a processing centre for Camembert cheese at the château. Architectural drawings had been duly filed with the mayor's office and the renovations completed. Discreet questioning by Barais confirmed the building had just come onto the market, the female clerk venturing that she thought it was empty but could locate the real estate agent if they were interested. Barais said that really wouldn't be necessary but if there was a floor plan available they might just run out and take a look. An outline was retrieved from the Mairie's archive and handed over with a shy smile.

"Time to go looking," Barais said.

The road from the village split a couple of kilometres out, one road descending into the valley, the other following the ridge. "Take the small road on the left," Jay said reading from the instructions the clerk had given them. The road narrowed, high stone walls blocking their view on either side. "There it is." They drove slowly past a track on their right, the farmhouse appearing briefly below them through a gap in the wall. Barais continued up the road pulling onto a dirt track half a mile further on.

"Now what?" Barais asked.

"Now I go and take a look." Jay said. He took only the floor-plan they had acquired at the Mairie and Barais' binoculars. "I'll be a while," he said. "If someone comes by look busy. Fix the motor or something."

As Jay crested the rise, the farmhouse came into view half a mile below. A number of outbuildings surrounded it, a few derelict greenhouses, wrecks of farm machinery, drums of chemicals or fertiliser and a pile of old tyres with some kind of sludge pit beyond. There was no sign of activity, no movement around the house and, importantly, no Mercedes.

It was a relief in some ways. A crazy notion had come to him on the way out that he would see Lis's body down there, splayed out in the courtyard. He had wanted to make the discovery alone. He walked along the ridge for another hundred yards and came to a stone foundation, its roof long gone but parts of its wall still standing. He had a clear view of the sur-rounding countryside from its vantage point. He could pick up anyone approaching a ways off. He settled in to wait.

It was late afternoon and the day was beginning to cool, the heat haze lifting off the opposite ridge, the horizon widening. Jay traced the valley road to the intersection they had passed through, locating the next village between Quettebec and the sea and further off Cherbourg and the Channel. If this was a waypoint on Khuda Bax's heroin trail, the site indicated by the bold question mark on the video Lis had viewed, someone had chosen well. The château could be accessed from three different directions. A level field to one side of the main building would make a handy landing strip. Cherbourg's cross-channel ferries to England and the Channel Islands and its small airport were just twenty minutes away. Almost the last thing Lis had said, her last words to him, were Khuda Bax and Neil Greyson are one big happy family. She had told Barais that Greyson was the Irish connection, had had Tim Short killed. Jay had put off calling Manktilow. He wouldn't put it off any longer.

A movement in the still landscape caught his eye. A figure was crossing the courtyard from one of the outbuildings towards the main house. Jay levelled the binoculars, keeping his head low to the wall. The man was dressed in farmer's cov-eralls, legs tucked into green rubber boots. He wore rubber gloves and was carrying some kind of headgear, a mask. The man climbed the steps to the door of the main building and disappeared inside. Jay checked his watch, then focused the binoculars on the windows of the house.

"You recognise him?" Barais had moved up beside him so quietly that Jay didn't know he was there till he spoke. "Can't be making cheese," Barais went on, taking the binoculars from Jay and surveying the surrounding area.

"What makes you say that?"

"You need milk to make cheese. Cows make milk. I don't see any." Barais was right. The countryside was bare of livestock for a mile or more. "And if the château is empty, what's he doing there?"

"One of the local farmers making a little extra money off someone else?" Jay ventured taking the binoculars back.

"So who's paying the electric bill?" Barais asked. As if on cue a light went on inside the house. Even at this distance Jay was able to see the man inside quite clearly. He was standing in what was probably the kitchen looking in their direction, a cell phone pressed to his ear.

"Farmers round here use cell phones?" Jay queried.

"Sure. Maybe," Barais said hedging his bet.

The man turned off the phone and threw it onto a couch, talking with someone else in the room, someone Jay couldn't see. "Two of them," Jay said handing the binoculars off to Barais. The night had set in now, the air beginning to chill. Venus rose on the horizon. A reddish glow to the north blossomed over Cherbourg.

"We know the other one," Barais said quietly. Jay waited while Barais studied the second figure silhouetted now in the château's lighted window, taking the binoculars back quickly when they were offered. Barais was right. They did know one of them. Connolly had got them a likeness. It was Elhassan Mohammed.

CHAPTER 33

Quettebec

Jay's feet were on the pillow, his head at the bottom of the bed. He was staring at the picture on the wall. The *patron's* mother and father? Not a good sight to wake up to.

"Jay?" It was Alain. "Are you awake?"

"What time is it?"

"One."

Jay swung his legs over the edge of the bed and stood up. They had watched until ten, waiting for an arrival, an event. Barais had dubbed the first man they had spotted, the man in coveralls, "Hot Dog" for his cheap zipper boots and fake Western shirt. A *voyou*, Barais said, a local punk. Hot Dog had stayed inside watching TV. The other man, Elhassan, had come outside around nine, smoked a cigarette at the top of the château's steps then gone back inside. The light in the kitchen had gone out immediately, the TV half an hour after.

"I've got Connolly," Barais said excitedly.

"What?"

"See," Barais turned the screen of his laptop towards Jay, showing him the active connection with Connolly in the U.S. "Wireless modem. It's patched into my box at home and the channel's network. Cool, *non*?"

Jay thought of Madame Barais sitting in her bed downstairs in Billancourt, her hair piled on her head, eyes fixed on the silent TV, while overhead millions upon millions of electrons careered outwards from Barais' digital deflectors like demonic fireflies.

Jay read through Connolly's transmission while Barais busied himself with the nightscopes. "No gadgets, okay Alain?" Jay said. "Please. Take the gun if you know how to shoot it but just the gun." Barais shrugged. Jay went back to the laptop.

On the screen was the biography of the third profiled "active assassin" who Connolly now confirmed as Elhassan Mohammed. "A bit of a bullshit artist," Connolly had footnoted the file. He had been or still was employed as a trainer at one of the newly opened camps in the Hindu Kush. No known distinguishing features, age 53, heavy build, dark colouring. Speciality: Remotely triggered explosives. So now they knew. Jay hit the close button on the computer, shut the lid and got off the bed. "Alain! What the fuck are you doing?"

Barais had put on sixty pounds in the few minutes Jay had spent on the computer. He wore a black jacket with loops and pockets, a pair of what looked like black painter's pants, a black baseball cap reversed on his head and combat boots. The night goggles, the nightscopes he had shown Jay, were shoved up on his forehead. The crowbar was strapped to his leg, a knife stuck in a shoulder holster, another in his belt. He carried a flashlight in one hand, the gun in the other.

"You can't do this," Jay yelled. "This isn't funny." It was obvious Barais thought it was deadly serious, too.

The moon came up at two. They had taken the thin blankets off the bed at the café and wrapped themselves against the

damp night air. Jay, facing the farm, saw it first. The huge silver orb pushed its way up over the horizon, its naked glory
shrouded temporarily by scant wedges of cloud. As it lifted
into the sky, its brilliance was caught by the thin strip of road
leading from the north. In the stream of silver Jay made out
the white stars of headlights coming in their direction.

"Alain." Barais stirred, his equipment clicking against the
stone. Barais adjusted his goggles and followed the direction
of Jay's arm. There was a long pause. The moon rose further,
its great sphere shrinking and brightening, Jay tracking the
approaching car with the binoculars. "The Mercedes," was all
he said.

The car pulled into the château's courtyard two minutes
later. Floodlights went on, throwing the outer buildings into
deep shadow and washing out the moon. The driver got out
first. "Hot Dog Two," Barais said. The man was almost a twin
of the first. He wore the same cheap clothes, the same zip-
pered ankle boots. Then the passenger door opened. Jay could
hear Barais' shallow breathing suddenly loud in his ear.
Elhassan appeared on the château's steps. He flicked a half-
smoked cigarette into the darkness. A cap of black hair
appeared over the car's roof, a slender neck, slim shoulders.

"Pakistani," Barais said. "Or Indian." He flipped the goggles onto his forehead and slumped down against the wall. It
might be Khuda Bax's silent partner. It was not her.

Elhassan and the new arrival chatted for a few minutes on
the château's steps then Elhassan went down and backed the
Mercedes into an open shed at the side of the house. The
other man, the Pakistani, walked over to what Barais was now
calling the Cheese House with its bright new extractor fans in
the roof and tall aluminium chimneys, the building they had

seen Hot Dog One come out of earlier that afternoon. The man gave the building a cursory inspection then, quite unexpectedly, unzipped his fly and relieved himself against one of the open yellow drums that stood against the wall of the outbuilding.

"What's he doing?" Barais asked. Jay passed him the binoculars.

By four the sky had clouded over. A cold mist covered the valley floor. Barais snored quietly. Jay took one more look at the scattering of buildings below. They'd start with Barais' Cheese House then move on to the château.

"Here's what we do," Jay said after he'd shaken Barais awake. "We go down the left of the hedge there in front of us. We'll be in deep shadow and out of sight of the house most of the way. That'll get us to the Cheese House. Once we get there, I'm going in alone. You keep your eye on the house. Okay?" Barais nodded uncapping a small flask he'd taken from his breast pocket. He offered it to Jay. "What is it?"

"Calvados." Jay shook his head.

Jay led the way down the slope, Barais' crowbar in one hand, the knife in his pocket. A bird started in the field, its cry ripping the silence. The two men paused for a moment then stepped softly onwards through the damp grass, finally reaching the Cheese House. Jay pointed to the corner of the building indicating where Barais should take his position. Barais edged forward, Jay waiting until he was in place then turning right along the back wall of the building.

They had seen the padlock on the rear door from their vantage point. The lock was new and heavy. Whoever had installed it had done a good job. The door's hinges however had been ignored. The wood of the door-post looked soft. Jay fitted the crowbar under the top one, testing it. It gave slightly. He covered the hinge with his free hand and yanked down hard. The screech of the screws pulling out of the rotten frame sounded much too loud. Jay waited. Barais' anxious face appeared round the corner of the building. Jay yanked again. This time the three screws holding the hinge gave without protest, the top of the door flapping open.

His way was blocked by a double layer of heavy-duty plastic fixed tightly over the wall. If the rest of the building was insulated in the same fashion, he was going to have to work his way around to the front, come in the other way. He looked at his watch. Nearly four fifteen. No time for that. He pulled the door to one side then took Barais' knife from his pocket and cut a tear from above his head to waist level. The plastic hissed as he cut through first one layer, then a second. Closing the knife, he peered into the long room. The air smelled overpoweringly of ether or some solvent. One thing was for sure. Whatever they were making in here wasn't Camembert.

Jay pulled out Barais' Maxilight and, adjusting the beam to its narrowest, inserted it through the hole he had cut in the plastic. The whole interior was sealed off in a double-layered plastic envelope, floor, ceiling, all four walls. The hiss he had heard had been escaping air. So how did Hot Dog get in and out? To one side of the envelope, the side of the building where Barais was stationed, there was a crude airlock consisting of heavier sheets of plastic and airtight seals. Jay looked at its plastic roof. It looked as though high-pressure power-washers were rigged in the ceiling of the compartment, hoses connected to a generator outside the envelope. The narrow beam of light flashed on a stainless steel housing. Jay recognised the international diver's symbol, the purple flag with a white diagonal line through it. An air compressor. He looked around the room, picking out more of the yellow drums. Then he saw the suits on the outside wall beyond the airlock. They were NBC full-body suits, the nuclear bacteriological/ chemical gear that had entered the popular imagination with the germ scares of the early '90s. He suddenly felt very cold and very vulnerable. He was standing unprotected next to what could only be a high infection area. As if to confirm his fears, an alarm went off.

He went back to the door and stared into the darkness. The alarm seemed closer now, its insistent beeping louder. Barais' face appeared suddenly around the corner of the cheese house, eyes wide. "The fucking thing went off just like that," he whispered. Jay looked at the small device Barais was holding up, its red light still blinking dully. A motion detector. "Sorry," he mouthed.

Jay dragged a finger across his throat and flicked a thumb towards their shelter up the hill. At the same moment the floodlights went on in the courtyard. Jay drew back into the deep shadow along the wall as Elhassan came slowly down the front steps of the main house into the courtyard. He was carrying a pump-action Winchester shotgun, a flashlight taped to its barrel. He stood with one foot in the yard, one foot on the last step, listening.

"Qui est là?" Elhassan called out. The question was answered by a scuffle of steps. Jay knew Alain was making a break for it. The shotgun boomed, stray pellets splintering the glass of the front window and smacking into the wooden wall behind his shoulder. Elhassan began to move, raising the shotgun and racking up another cartridge as he ran. Alain wouldn't stand a chance once the man got round the side of the building. Jay reached down and picked up the nearest heavy object, a fire extinguisher, then broke cover. Elhassan came charging across the courtyard, whipping the Winchester round in Jay's direction and loosing off another shot. The roar was deafening, the muzzle of the gun no more than ten feet from Jay's head. Jay felt the swarm of lead whistling over him as he pitched forward, heard the clatter of exploding glass behind him and the racking of another cartridge as he finally found his balance. Diving forwards he swung the extinguisher's tank in a low arc, connecting with the man's legs at knee height. Elhassan toppled sideways, the gun clattering to the hard ground.

Jay grabbed the gun, rising to his feet. A movement off to his right brought the gun's barrel up and around. Hot Dog One and Two were stumbling down the steps across the yard, one man barefoot, shirtless, the other wearing no trousers. Jay lifted the stock to his shoulder, aiming high, and pulled. The two men took off at a run. Jay pumped the gun again, the spent shell tinkling on the stones. Where was Barais? He searched the dark wedges of shadow beyond the oasis of brilliant light in the courtyard.

"Arrêtez!" a high-pitched voice behind him yelled. Jay began to move, trying to turn at the same time. "Arrêtez!" the voice yelled again, sharper this time. Just a few feet more and he'd be round the corner of the building. He located the voice at the same instant, saw the raised pistol pointed at him. It was the Pakistani, standing in front of the shed where Elhassan had garaged the Mercedes. Jay knew in that instant that he could never beat the bullet. He heard a sharp pop, once, twice and, miraculously, the Pakistani folded at the waist and fell. Seconds passed. Then Barais' voice: "Jay?" The long-barrelled dart gun was in his hand. The Pakistani was crumpled on the bonnet of the Mercedes, two of Barais darts sticking from his face like bees, one on the lower lip, the other in his cheek. "Sleeping," Barais said.

Jay turned and ran up the steps into the château. He made a quick search of the ground floor rooms and then, his panic rising, went up to the bedrooms. There was no sign of Lis, no trace. There was one place left.

The door to the cellar gave off the back of the kitchen. Jay turned the flashlight on the shotgun back on before easing open the door. It gave way with a squeal. Jay was hit by a wave of rank air, the sweet sour smell of decay. He knew then that he had reached the end of his journey. He took the stairs one at a time, the scent of death rising to meet him. At the bottom step, he worked the flashlight's beam over the dirt floor.

The flashlight's beam cut across the darkness, Jay knowing it would reach her eventually, would catch the pale skin, shine on the black hair, the eyes. There was a dark pool in one corner as if groundwater had welled up through the earth. Jay swung the flashlight's beam into the other corner and felt rather than saw the shape as the light caught it. It was a blanket, just a blanket.

He knelt to touch it. And something in the wall caught his eye. A scrap of pale silk was stuffed into a crack in the big river stones the house rested on. He reached over to prise it out. It was a label bearing a maker's name. Chanel.

"Where is she?" Elhassan screamed as the butt of the shotgun cracked against his knee. "Tell me where she is."

When Jay had come out of the château, he had found Barais by the Mercedes, his face ashen. The Pakistani was taken care of, Barais signed to Jay, patting the trunk of the car. He gestured over his shoulder to a second group of buildings beyond the garage. On the open side of this second yard was a foul-smelling lime pit the size of a small wading pool. In the wan light of the coming dawn Jay saw what Barais had found minutes before. Face up, belly pregnant with decay was the body of Khuda Bax.

"Where the fuck is she?" Elhassan screamed again as the gun's butt smashed into his shattered knee.

"They took her with them. Saeed and the other guy."

"Where?" Jay raised the butt again.

"I don't know, man. Please. I don't."

The butt crashed down on Elhassan's groin expelling the answer from the man's bloody mouth.

"The airport."

By five thirty he and Barais were back in Quettebec and by six in Cherbourg. "No way we will get passenger lists or flight plans right now, Jay. There are only two people in traffic control and one's asleep. The other one isn't too happy, no one in the charter offices," Barais reported.

They stood by the bike, he and Barais watching the sun rising over the Channel behind Cherbourg Airport. Barais was looking at his hands, wondering at the fruit of their night's work.

"You'll go back to Paris. You don't have to say anything,

do anything. I'll call our people in Paris and Washington. They'll confirm whatever you tell the police when they get to you. Just tell them the truth. It'll be fine."

Barais looked up. "You?"

Jay said nothing. He was smoothing out the scrap of material he'd found, stroking it flat.

"What is it?" Barais asked. Jay placed it carefully in the other man's palm. "It was hers. Lis's. We bought her the suit."

Barais nodded, handing the material back. "We were good though, no?" he said patting the cases strapped to the bike.

"Yeah, Alain. You were very good. Thanks."

As the turbo-prop swung out over the Channel and onto its heading for Paris, Jay imagined the tiny figure of Alain Barais crouched over the Kawasaki below. He wondered what Barais would tell his mother.

CHAPTER 34

Dublin

Phoenix Park in Dublin is home to one of the world's oldest zoos and, less conspicuously, the headquarters of Ireland's Special Branch. Jay had made the call to George Manktilow from Paris and the older man had graciously sent a car to the airport to collect him.

"I was instructed to give you this fax," Manktilow said. "It's from Mr. Lorenz." Jay took the envelope. "I thought you might need a little peace and quiet. I cleared some space on my desk. Bit of a mess otherwise, I'm afraid," Manktilow said, ushering Jay into an elegant office with a view of the US Ambassador's residence. He made no comment on Jay's appearance, said only: "I'll have someone bring you coffee if you'd like. It's quite good, really."

"Sure," Jay said. He'd had six hours sleep in the last forty-eight. Even coffee seemed undrinkable. But, it was a peace offering of sorts and Jay accepted it.

Lorenz had been efficient and swift. Heads would have rolled, Jay was sure, cages rattled. It had been a bare seven hours since Jay had sent his report from Barais' computer at Cherbourg. It would have arrived at the Director's home after midnight. Jay guessed no one on Lorenz's watch including his own unit would have had much sleep.

There were four pages, each carrying Lorenz's signature, each bearing the warning: Top Secret. Lorenz acknowledged Jay's transmission and attached the report the French authorities had relayed through the US Embassy in Paris, adding his own comments in the margin. Jay allowed himself a moment's pleasure at the thought of Redman's discomfort when he had been told to pass the document on to Washington.

The report began with a brief recreation of the events that had likely preceded the scene that confronted local police on their arrival at the château. It was predictably sketchy but, under the circumstances, surprisingly accurate.

Between them, the FBI and the DGSA, the Direction Générale Surveillance Extérieure, had identified all suspects except one. Elhassan Mohammed, aka Washington Harvey, headed the list. He was believed to have been the driver of the Mercedes that Clemens had pursued in Paris and that was found at the farm. He was under guard in Cherbourg's Hospital of Pity. The man in the Mercedes' trunk, the Pakistani, had yet to be identified. The body recovered from the lime pit was indeed that of Khuda Bax. Death had been tentatively set at the previous Thursday, three days prior to discovery. The subject died from a 9mm bullet fired "execution style" from a Spanish Gammalondo automatic bearing the unidentified Pakistani's prints and removed from him by an American agent present at the scene, name withheld pending authorisation.

Jay recognised Lorenz's thoroughness. He was a master at getting everyone looking in the same direction when it came time. The subject, Khuda Bax, was revealed to have received multiple abrasions and severe bruising over much of his body prior to death. Concentrated traces of blood matching the deceased's type found in the château's cellar suggested that death occurred there but blood on a blanket in an adjacent area did not match. Analysis of clothing fragments and hair pointed to a second victim or captive.

Why would they kill her? Jay thought, searching the rolling lawns outside Manktilow's window for the answer. Why would they keep her alive? A seagull dived into view, hovered for a second then dropped out of sight.

Two other suspects who had turned themselves in earlier that morning were already known to local authorities. Local Mafia, Lorenz had scrawled in the margin. Jay flipped to page three, headed: "Physical Evidence." A detailed inventory of the château's contents followed. The Mercedes he knew about. Title to the property was registered in the name of Mrs. Gabrielle Greyson. Cases of pre-printed labels and round cheese boxes had been found in Utility Building B. The list of items removed from the Cheese House, or Utility Building A as the French report had designated it, was chilling.

The "hot" room created by the plastic sheeting Jay had cut through had been analysed for an initial batch of trace elements as had the compressors and other equipment removed by the hazardous materials team specifically requested by Washington D.C. Jay's skin crawled as he read over the list. Chlorine in solution was present in quantity. That would be for the scrubber. Traces of ammonium and sodium carbonate and an abandoned production line gave strong indication that the premises had been or were intended for the production of heroin. Confirmation subject to ongoing investigation.

So? Jay questioned silently as he turned to the next page.

Initial analysis of a so-called transfer station at the site indicated trace elements of a nerve agent, possibly VX or Sarin, type to be confirmed, also present in various drums outside the site, identified variously as being of Iraqi and Russian origin by their markings. Jay set the report down on Manktilow's desk. The Bureau had been very busy in recent months upgrading response capability to domestic terrorist attack by bio-chemical/biological weapons. The effort had included an ongoing program to educate officers likely to encounter such threats. Jay had tried hard to focus on the memos relating to the effects of various agents that had been added to the never shrinking mountain of unread material in his "to read" pile. Were symptoms detectable within hours or days? He couldn't remember. There were too many agents, too many variables.

Sarin. That was what the Aum Shinrikyo had used in the Tokyo subways. Experts had testified that if the group had spent even a few more days purifying the gas, the victim count would have gone into the thousands. And VX? Jay couldn't remember its properties, only that the US no longer manufactured it. That was what was in the drums? Elhassan was a "shooter," Nasir, if he had indeed been there, was an assassin. But Saeed was a biochemist. Saeed bin Sayyaf, Khuda Bax's lunch guest, Lis's protégé. Nice little Saeed brewing up Sarin in a farmhouse in France and shipping it. Where? There was one more connection in Khuda Bax's heroin pipeline to be made. He dropped the report on Manktilow's desk and made a run for the door, almost bumping into a young man in shirtsleeves carrying a coffee tray.

"Sorry, sir," the young man apologised. "Shall I come back?"

Jay didn't bother to answer. He and Mr. Manktilow had a pressing engagement.

CHAPTER 35

Ballynahinch

So this was it, this was what all the fuss was about. Jay had wondered sometimes, leafing through magazines and seeing the fictional life the clothing manufacturers created for their models, the old world aristocracy, the entitlement. Wearing the designer's $600 sports coat wouldn't win you entry into these exclusive ranks; it might let you live the fantasy.

The tyres of Manktilow's black Rover crunched on the gravel circle in front of Ballynahinch House. Jay, sitting next to him in the back seat, took in the wide lawn sloping to the water and the distant hills. The view seemed to belong to the owner of the house, too. Jay got out, a manila folder in his hand, joining Manktilow at the glassed-in porch of the house.

Neil Greyson was taller than Jay had expected, broader in the shoulder, heavier. Like his father who had first greeted them, the younger Greyson was as gracious as all of his class, fluent in the light compliment, the lazy gesture that put a guest at ease.

Manktilow and the General, old comrades in arms, had headed for what Jay supposed was the dining room. General Greyson insisted the Special Branch officer try a glass of the extra "fino" an importer friend of his had brought in from

Jerez. Courteous to the bone. That had left Jay and Greyson standing awkwardly in the hall.

"It's rather a fine Stubbs, isn't it," Greyson commented, seeing Jay's attention drawn to the huge canvas above the stairs.

"I wouldn't know," Jay said.

"Let's get on with this, shall we? I'm dining with friends tonight. Sorry to rush you."

Jay followed Greyson into a room that was obviously the library. The view Jay had admired from the driveway was perfectly framed in the high windows, the late afternoon sun flashing a brilliant gold on the grey waters.

"Sit down, please. Mind if I smoke?" Jay did but said, "Go ahead."

"George, Mr. Manktilow said you had made some progress in the investigation into Mr Short's death. I must admit I had pretty much given up hope that it was ever going to lead anywhere."

Jay said nothing, let the silence hang. Then he flipped open the folder in front of him and slid out the head shot of Khuda Bax that Washington had modemed. "When did you last see this man?"

Greyson craned his neck round to see the photo then looked back at Jay. "I didn't. Never seen him to be honest."

"How about this one?" Jay slid out a photo of Elhassan Mohamed.

"Can't help, sorry."

"I don't have time to screw around, Mr. Greyson. There are other lives at stake besides yours," Jay said, pulling a grainy police photograph wired to Manktilow's office late that morning. It showed Khuda Bax's battered naked body half-submerged in the lime pit at the château. Jay laid it carefully on the coffee table between them. Greyson studied the picture, his face giving nothing away. "Are you threatening me?" Greyson said.

"No," Jay said then changed his mind: "Yes."

"I don't know which particular government agency you hail from Mr. Peterson," Greyson said giving Jay's stained jacket and dirt-streaked jeans meticulous study, "but in this country there are certain laws we abide by, certain rules . . ."

"There are no fucking rules, Greyson."

Greyson stood, working up to some big finish but Jay never gave him the chance, pulling documents from his folder and slapping them one on top of the other like winning cards. "These are the financial records of Sulaiman Properties procured for me by Mr. Manktilow's officers showing you to be a direct beneficiary of the proceeds of smuggling heroin into and out of Ireland and into the US over an extended period. Title to a property used in the processing of narcotics. Depositions of witnesses apprehended at the same property this morning. A transcript of an intercepted phone-call. Voice prints match your voice and Khuda Bax's. Transcripts of other numerous calls to the man you claim not to know." Jay paused. "There's more but I know you're pressed for time."

Greyson didn't move, the cigarette in his fingers burning down unnoticed.

"What do you want?" he asked finally.

"I want a name and I want the truth. I don't have time to come back here and ask you again."

Greyson's gaze was focused on the file of evidence as if he could will it to disappear. "Short wasn't supposed to die. They were just supposed to scare him off, give him a fright. Khuda

Bax said he knew someone, someone who was good at that sort of thing, a professional. They weren't meant to kill him."

"Elhassan Mohammed, Nasir Abu Massoud. Those names register?" Greyson. "And Oldham?"

"I had nothing to do with that, I swear." Greyson was pleading now. "Roger showed up out of the blue. He got himself into a squeeze. But I didn't do anything to him, I swear to God. He was a . . ." Greyson's voice grew quiet. "He was in my regiment."

Jay kept on. "Who cleared the goods this end?" Greyson looked at Jay stupidly as if he were speaking in another language. "Who was your insider in Dublin? The shipper."

"I can't tell you that. They'd kill me."

Jay stood up, moving in very close. "As far as I'm concerned, Mr. Greyson, you're already fucking dead. Who was the shipper?"

"Sean Ferguson at the overseas freight desk," Greyson said, sitting down hard. "And Katie Conway, his assistant. They cleared everything through the Port of Dublin. Look," Greyson went on, brightening a little, his hand on the pile of evidence; "we can fix this, can't we? I mean, there's a way to do this without bringing the family into it, isn't there? They were the reason I got involved in the first place. With Khuda Bax. No one else was doing a damn thing to save this place. My brother and sisters just sat around on their hands whining. It would have been sold up if I hadn't done something. You see that, don't you? It's been in the family for generations. Greysons have been here since the 1600s."

"You'd better ask Mr. Manktilow that, Mr. Greyson. I really don't give a shit," Jay said as he nodded towards the

Special Branch officer standing now in the open doorway of the library.

Sean Ferguson's office in the customs building at Dublin airport was decorated with helpful advice to travellers. Above the man's head was a warning in bold black letters on a yellow background: DANGEROUS ARTICLES NOT PERMITTED IN BAGGAGE: COMPRESSED GASES (DEEPLY REFRIGERATED, FLAMMABLE, NON-FLAMMABLE, AND POISONOUS) SUCH AS BUTANE, OXYGEN, PROPANE AND AQUALUNG CYLINDERS. It struck Jay as more than appropriate.

The interview conducted by Manktilow with a senior customs officer present and Jay sitting at the back of the room was brief but thorough. Katie Conway had revealed her small role immediately and pointed the finger at her superior. Ferguson quickly realised he had no room left to manoeuvre and more to gain by co-operating. A double entry had been kept, the shipments consigned to a Boston agent acting for Greyson's transport company, Northern Freight. All Ferguson did was route the shipments through special handling. Refrigerated, see? They had to believe him. He had no idea what was in the containers beyond what was marked in the manifest: French cheeses. Pre-cleared this end for Department of Agriculture in Boston. How did they pass through customs in the US? He didn't know. When was the last shipment? Ferguson hunted through the records on his computer, going out of his way to be as co-operative as he could, guiding them through the intricacies of his double entry system. There, he said, four days ago. The only one this month, he noted helpfully. He pointed to the single entry on the spreadsheet on his screen. Special handling. Twelve cartons refrigerated under seal for forward shipment. Inspecting officer: S. Ferguson. Consignee's name. Weight. Provenance: Port of Cherbourg. Inspector's name. Charge to: Address, Name. Greyson's name, an address in Dublin, a standing order account with an off-shore address. Pretty blatant, Jay thought; don't even bother to bill me, just charge the account. They had been doing it so long they had become careless.

There it was. Twelve cartons. And all they had was one name: the handling agent in Boston. Jay knew before he even picked up the phone to call Lorenz while one of Manktilow's runners went to book his flight to Boston that whoever the consignee in Massachusetts was, the chances of his being alive were zero. No better than Lis's. He picked up the phone and dialled the thirteen digits anyway, his hand steady, his heart ice cold.

CHAPTER 36

Boston

She was a diver rising towards the light. She could see the surface approaching, the pressure lightening on her ears. She wanted to stay down here, didn't want the glare in her eyes, the voice. Stay down.

Fragments of the journey her body had undergone followed Lis Charnay to the surface like air bubbles. She was in a chair, a wheelchair; it had been a wheelchair. And the voices, like the rustle of papers, a strange, rapid mixture of soft and harsh. Arabic, they were speaking in Arabic and overhead, a face smiling. Irish, jolly. Welcome. Good, she felt good, deep down. Was she smiling? She hoped so. She felt so good. And the car, her head on a shoulder, warm voices, no anger in them, and the crawling in her arm, always the same arm, the flood of cool fire through her body and sinking. Good, it was good. She sank, her body dropping soundlessly into the dark water.

All that was so long ago, so many days. And now her body was rising, the light brilliant in her eyes, the voice whining from somewhere else, pleading. A high, anxious voice grating on her ears. Her eyes opened. A white tiled ceiling and the buzz of neon lights. She was in a room, an empty room like an office. She turned her head to the right, saw a door closing, someone leaving her. She tried to call out, wanted to say: Wait, I'm awake now but the words wouldn't come. She opened her mouth, exploring her lips with her tongue. They were dry and chapped, her mouth and throat sore. She felt sick. Her stomach was tight, screwed up in a ball. She raised an arm to shield the light from her eyes. It was too bright, too insistent. And she saw her arm, bare, unexpected as if it belonged to someone else. She touched her face, her throat, reached over and felt her other arm. Her skin was hot, sticky to the touch. Her ring was gone, her watch, too. No socks on, but jeans and a shirt. Not hers but clean. And below her the same voice pleading.

"You will not suffer now."

Another voice was by her ear. At first she thought it might be her own but it was rougher, a man's voice. She turned her head slowly. She could move nothing fast. He was sitting by her head, just behind her so she couldn't quite see him. She turned some more. Had she seen him before? It was the man she had seen at Darunta. "You?" she said, trying to puzzle it out, her neck stretching to get a better view of his face. It was the man she had met at Darunta. Was that it? No answer. Her body began to shudder, her hands shaking uncontrollably. Where was she? Panic came diving at her, gripped her. Someone was screaming, crying. Why was she in hospital? Where? Where had she been? Who had she been with? And then the doors began to open in her mind as if the wind were sweeping through the house, bursting them open. The cellar. The beating, her body screaming at them to stop. The body. That was what she had seen the last time. When the door had opened and the light had shone into the dark room, the room she thought stretched to eternity she saw suddenly was just a cramped cellar, the underside of the wooden floor above, with the nails sticking down towards her and the man's body that been her constant companion.

A hand, a strong hand took her arm, held it. "Okay, Missy." The prick of the needle, oh yes, the pressure of the liquid forcing its way in like a snake, yes, and then the glow spreading, her body sinking back, letting go. Her breathing slowed, her eyes opening again. The ceiling, a man's face swimming over hers. She recognised this man. She was sure.

"Saeed? It's you, isn't it." It was Saeed. His face came into focus above her, looking down, the soft brown eyes half-closed, a slight frown creasing his brow. She moved her arms slowly, very slowly and pushed. His hand was behind her back, helping her, and she was sitting. She looked at her arm again. The inside was stippled with small blue bruises. She pushed one in, watching the skin go white, watched the blood flow back in when she released the pressure.

"What are these?"

"Marks," he said. And then the voice that had woken her, the voice from below screamed, stopped, screamed again, high like a bird. She lifted her head to find the voice, trying to shake the voice out of her ears. And she saw him in the doorway. It was the man who had killed Roger, the man at the rally. He grinned at her, his hand lifting and shaking something at her, teasing her. The needle.

"Why?" she said.

"We need to go down," the man said, his voice a low growl, the Arabic harsh. Lis understood "Go down" only, watching him at the door, watching the needle, unable to look at his eyes. Saeed walked across the room and out into the corridor without looking back at her. The other man closed the door behind them leaving her.

She rocked her body, sitting on the bed, backwards, forwards, the motion finally bringing her to her feet. She crossed the room, reached out for the handle. She turned it slowly, opened it. The noise was loud again now, the voice downstairs whimpering. A corridor, stairs down to the left, another room, a door closed across from her. It wasn't a hospital. It was someone's house. The carpet was gold, the walls panelled. She smelled mildew.

She crept down the stairs, the room opening below her, a table, three men round it. Saeed, the man from Darunta and another man she hadn't seen before. They were watching television. That was the voice, that was what she had heard. There was a picture of a man, a dark naked man, his hands raised above his head. The room he was in was very familiar. She knew the room. She knew him, knew the man. Khuda Bax. The voice didn't seem to be coming from him. His body was twisting, writhing. He looked like he was scratching his back against the wall, like a bear. And whimpering. Then Lis saw his hands were tied together. He was hanging, twisting.

She looked away, looked at the window, her attention drawn by the lights in the dark of the night. She could see traffic, cars, pick-ups, a truck. The headlights swept across the ceiling, lighting up the room in flashes as they whipped by not fifty feet away. An overpass, the great metalled arc of it glowing orange in the street lights. The side panel of a tractor trailer suddenly filled the window frame blocking out all the cars. Boston Seafood, it said. She was in the US She was in Boston.

"Sit down, Miss Charnay," the man from Darunta said pointing to the chair beside her. "Join us."

CHAPTER 37

Boston

"It's good to see you, Jay," Clemens said shaking Jay's hand, keeping his professional distance. Jay said nothing, wrapping his comrade in a two-arm embrace and holding on hard. Jay had been first off the plane at Logan, following the flight attendant down the service stairs of the jetway onto the apron and finding Clemens standing by his vehicle, its motor running. It was another Suburban.

"Hope you take better care of this one," Jay said. Sam grinned, shifting into drive and heading across the concrete at speed, the removable red light on top of the SUV flashing. "Where are we headed?" Jay asked.

"Boston office," Sam said. "Lorenz's got the place wired. They don't know what he's like when he gets fired up like this." They drove on for a minute saying nothing, stopping briefly at the security booth then pulling onto the public road and the Sumner Tunnel that led downtown.

"How did you make out finally?" Jay broke the silence.

"It was okay," Sam said, "once they'd got over the bill. It certainly helped when Lorenz got your call. Anyway, I gave you most of the blame."

"Thanks."

"No problem," Sam said, grinning again; then: "Did you find her?"

"I found this," Jay said, taking the dress label from his jacket. Clemens glanced down but said nothing. "It was stuck in the wall. She was there."

"They're still running European entries back from Sunday midnight."

"What about flights from Cherbourg. Did they cover those?"

"Scheduled flights. You'll have to ask the boss about charters. Nothing yet."

The FBI field-office in Boston unlike its monumental and highly visible Washington counterpart is in an anonymous glass building on Centre Plaza in downtown Boston, a suite of rooms on the sixth floor. Lorenz had hit it like a tornado. The usually unoccupied conference area had been turned into a temporary command centre. City and suburban maps covered the walls, three specialists flown in from Washington manned phones at the crowded conference table. Lorenz hovered round the hive of activity like an angry bee.

Jay crossed the lobby and stood in the doorway of the conference room, listening to the electronic frenzy, the phones, the computers, thinking of Alain and his gadgets then of Khuda Bax's body, trying to connect the two, the virtual and the real. "Jay," Lorenz said, putting the phone down with a bang. "Get in here." That was all the greeting he would get for now, Jay realised. He stepped into the room.

"Frank, this is Jay Peterson, the young man who got us into this mess. Jay this is Frank Morrelli, SAC in Boston. And this is Professor Smith. Felicia's a biological-weapons analyst at MIT. A specialist in nerve gases. Right, Felicia?"

Smith nodded politely, shaking Jay's hand. "Pleased to meet you," she said. "Mr. Lorenz has been telling us all about you." Jay could only imagine what she might have heard.

"Barbara," Lorenz said to his assistant, "we're going into Frank's office. No calls except from the chief. He gets through, no one else." Lorenz led the way to the corner office. When they were all seated Lorenz closed the door and started right in from where he stood. "You can bring us up to speed in a second, Jay. I want you to hear what Felicia has already given us on the French findings and the stuff you sent. You'll just have to listen to this again, Frank. You may learn something new. Felicia?"

Morrelli was obviously not used to Lorenz's full-throttle style. He seemed put out. His office had been commandeered, his routine upset. Smith was unfazed. She might have been trading gardening tips the way she now described the lethally dangerous weapons that were her chosen area of specialisation.

"We're assuming," Smith began, directing her comments to Jay, "that the provenance of the chemicals discovered at the farm in France was Iraq, possibly Russia. We have the codes on the drums which we assume to be original."

"You've established the agent then?" Jay said.

"There are two possibilities. VX or Sarin. Both share some of the compounds detected at the farm. Phosphorous, isopropanol, methanol. Only VX requires ethanol." Jay remembered the biting odour in the Cheese House. "It's quite obvious the inert VX was being pressurised and transferred to individual containers. Mr. Lorenz tells me you're still attempting to identify what these receptacles might be."

"Twelve of them. Refrigerated," Lorenz confirmed. "That was what was on the way-bill. Felicia thinks they might have used scuba-tanks, the kind they use for mixed-gas diving. Pony-tanks you called them. Right?" Felicia Smith nodded again. "Tell him the effects, Felicia, what contact can do."

Lorenz was in his element, at the centre of the drama. Jay had seen him turn a roomful of reasonable men and women, any one of them capable of out-thinking Lorenz under normal circumstances, struck dumb by his punch-and-duck style.

"VX gas or Soman as it's sometimes called has an unusual property. When it was developed by the British at the Ministry of Defence's chemical weapons laboratory at Porton Down in the '50s . . ."

Lorenz interrupted again. "Just the facts, Felicia; not the history."

"Mr. Lorenz, you'll have to restrain yourself. I cannot give Mr. Peterson the necessary information if you keep interrupting." Lorenz was silent but unchastened. "The British scientists at Porton Down saw right away that it was a very potent weapon. When manufactured to maximum potency, twenty pounds of VX in the water supply could destroy the population of a medium-sized town. The British passed the process plans on to the United States. We built a plant at Newport, Indiana, run by the Pentagon."

"Was it ever used?" Jay asked.

"Oh, yes," Smith replied evenly. "We had manufactured at least four to five thousand tons by 1967 and loaded it into land mines, artillery shells, aircraft spray tanks, missile warheads."

"If the French supply, the stuff at the château came from Iraq, how did they get the formula?" Jay said.

"We're talking over thirty years on, Mr. Peterson. Its structure was published in 1972. No one can keep a weapon that potent secret for that long. Russia acquired and disseminated it to others. Iraq, as we all know, acquired the ingredients to manufacture tons of high-grade VX before the Gulf War."

"More lethal than Sarin?"

"Absolutely." Smith surveyed the three men. "It's more stable, at least ten times more potent and – this is the most disturbing feature of this substance, gentlemen – it's soluble in cold water." Jay didn't get it immediately, asking why that was significant. "Other G agents like Sarin, Mr. Peterson, evaporate. VX in its pure state is heavy and viscous and has a much lower volatility. It could lie in puddles and remain active for weeks. It could be introduced into the water system or carried airborne as a vapour. A TNT detonation, the most effective form of delivery, could release it into the atmosphere. It's a very versatile agent."

The men were silent, trying to grasp the enormity of what Smith was saying. Then Lorenz prompted soberly: "Tell Jay how this agent affects humans, Felicia."

"All G agents interfere with vital enzymes. VX is no exception. Unlike Sarin, however, VX can penetrate the skin and can be inhaled in vapour form. The subject, the victim that is, only needs contact with the agent in solution. A low dose, a very low dose, would produce tiredness, slurred speech, hallucinations and nausea. In higher concentrations, the symptoms are very unpleasant: vomiting, involuntary discharge of urine or defecation, broncho-constriction. Then, of course, the subject exposed to VX in sufficient concentration would experience paralysis and consequently suffocation."

"How long could this take?" Jay asked.

"It depends. Each of us is more or less susceptible. For the most sensitive individuals, the lethal dose of Sarin, for instance, is 100 milligrams per cubic meter per minute. That's fatal density in about one minute. Ten or twelve lungfuls."

"And VX?"

"Oh, almost immediate even in small doses. Deterioration and death would be almost instantaneous."

"Say, worst case, the drums that were found in France contained VX in pure form or maximum concentration. And say that their contents were introduced into a city water supply. What would be the effect?" Jay asked.

"Deadly, Mr. Peterson. There was enough there to destroy the populations of Los Angeles and New York together."

"And the antidote? Is there one?"

"Yes and no. These nerve agents have an extremely rapid effect. If medical treatment were to serve any purpose, the oximes that would be used to treat victims would have to be introduced immediately. The Swedes developed a very clever little gadget, an auto-injector that someone could use always assuming the antidotes were available at the time of contamination." Smith waited attentively for the next question but none came. Lorenz broke the silence.

"Right. Thanks, Felicia. Stick around. We're going to need you. Jay? Frank?" Lorenz was already out the door, Barbara at his side immediately.

"I've got the University of Maryland on hold and the other bio-weapons analyst called back. Said she'd try you later. She faxed the list of known manufacturers to the Washington office."

"Nothing more from France?"

"Uh-uh."

"Tell Maryland I'll call back. Frank? You hold the fort here, okay? Reinforcements are on their way. We're going to have to cover every rental, every self-storage, anywhere they could store these things assuming they're all still in one consignment. And keep the pressure on at Logan. They're not there now, so they were picked up or shipped on somewhere else. And I don't give a fuck who's on strike, whose feast-day it is. We need that address." Morrelli grunted assent and took off back to the conference room. "Barbara, have them forward the calls to the plane. No point in sticking round here. Meet us downstairs. Jay, you and I are going to Washington."

On the way downstairs Jay wondered how long it would take Felicia Smith to realise Lorenz had abandoned her.

CHAPTER 38

Washington D.C.

From the air, Cape Cod looks like a muscular arm flexed at its eastern elbow, Chatham. Jay looked down from the window of the jet at the long feathered wake of a ferry heading out from Hyannis on the south shore of the Cape to one of the islands, Nantucket or Martha's Vineyard. Barbara, Lorenz's assistant, Sam Clemens and Ken Masami, one of the team leaders on the Bureau's new biological-threat module, were asleep in the rear of the plane. Lorenz was on the airphone. Jay tried to focus on the capsule report Professor Smith had given them.

The characteristics of the agent shipped along Khuda Bax's heroin route could give them some indications as to intended targets: cold water, extreme potency, longevity. They could mean nothing. Maybe the agent was the only one obtainable. Maybe the group, Saeed's cell, whatever they were, had access to a whole range of agents and would pick selectively according to their goal. How long had they been stockpiling? What else had been shipped in? Jay's attention drifted back to the window, his thoughts on Lis.

"Yes, absolutely correct. I'll do that. Yes, sir." Lorenz hung up the airphone, his face set in thought. There was only one man who could command that degree of civility from Lorenz:

the Chief Executive. The news of a potential home-grown terrorist strike leaked to the media last week had turned out to
be a damp squib, ill-researched and then badly reported. Now
it looked like they had hold of the real thing. Jay knew the
President would cut loose any political liability before it had
a chance to singe him. It was the nature of the beast. Lorenz
would be the first to go, his Director next.

"Bob," Jay started in.

"Don't even, Jay. Not now." Lorenz was surprisingly subdued, his voice low. He crossed the aisle and slumped into the
seat next to Jay. "What you did was incredible, son," Lorenz
said, his big hand gripping Jay's knee. "In Dublin, in London,
back there in France. Incredible. I mean it. Just don't expect
any medals. You're lucky you're not in jail." Lorenz paused,
breathing in deeply. Jay had never seen him like this, realised
he really didn't know him that well. Just knew the raging bull.
"I know," Lorenz said, "believe me. I know what you're going
through. You can't explain Dana's loss, can't forgive yourself.
You feel guilty that you're alive. You meet a girl and then she
goes missing. But we have to go on. I know it sounds corny.
So, it's corny. It's our job. Okay?"

Jay nodded his head slowly. It was the pep rally, the call
to arms, and it was Lorenz's job to deliver it. Jay knew that.
That didn't make what Lorenz said any less true. "So?" Jay
said.

"Jesus Christ, Jay." Lorenz laughed out loud, finding some
of his usual fire. "You are one tough nut. You know that? My
mother was easier to please than you are. While you were out
there shooting up the town, they were crucifying me back
here. Enrico's still after my hide for what you did. One day
son, you'll be sitting where I'm sitting. No, it's a fact. And

you'll know then." Lorenz twisted in his seat, looking back down the aisle, checking the others, then began again quietly. "There have been a few developments in the last twenty-four hours. First off, Nasir Abu Massoud, our killer."

"One of them," Jay interjected. "For what it's worth, Elhassan triggered the bomb that killed Tim Short and set up the bomb that killed Oldham's accountant. His 'wiring.' George Manktilow is sending you the details."

Lorenz nodded. "So the other one, Mr. Nasir Abu Massoud. Turns out he makes his living cleaning houses."

"What do you mean?"

"He was on the CIA's payroll, not directly of course, but he got paid just the same. Remember the botched hit on Saddam Hussein our sisters in Langley dreamed up? When was it? '96? Managed to expose most of the domestic resistance but failed to reach the target. Saddam is alive and well, the rest are history. Another thing John Enrico doesn't like to talk about. None of our side got hurt of course. He'll tell you about that all right. So, there were some loose ends needed to be tied up. Abu Massoud was the man."

"The same guy?"

"The same guy," Lorenz said.

Lorenz leaned his head back, breathed out hard, his hands moving over his chest, his face, his belly as if he were wiping something off. The action was ritualistic, some kind of stress relief Lorenz had been prescribed.

"Another thing. The Frogs transmitted records of Cherbourg traffic. Private jet. A Challenger. Filed a flight plan like good boys. Cherbourg departure time, outbound heading, destination."

"Whose plane?"

"Khuda Bax's. At least the one he was using. It belongs to his father-in-law. They picked up the registration when they finally got around to running the personal property Khuda Bax had registered in France. Nifty list. The big house on the river, another in Cannes – he liked to produce movies apparently, the dirty kind – a yacht. Two up on the flight deck, four in the passenger compartment. No cargo."

"Four?"

"Right, four."

"They flew into Boston?"

"They flew into Boston." Lorenz lifted his arm looking at his watch. "About sixty-some hours ago."

"Wait," Jay said. "Go back."

"She could have come in too, Jay, I guess. It's not on the cards, you know that. But she could have. The old patient on a gurney trick? The passenger taken ill in flight, a wheelchair called to the ramp? Christ, these days they're crapping on the food carts. Who'd notice a pregnant woman or an invalid?"

The Gulfstream dipped suddenly then levelled into its glide path. "Twenty minutes out, ladies and gentlemen," the captain announced. "Beginning our descent."

"What about INS? What's on their entries? She was a citizen, remember."

"We're running them," Lorenz said patiently. "We're looking for the names we have. And the names we don't." Lorenz glared at Jay. "There was somebody else involved, one over the six the Saudis executed."

"Connolly's seventh samurai?" Jay was caught off guard. The two men were separated in his mind. "He told you?" Lorenz nodded.

Jay took a moment then said: "They executed six because

they needed to show us a head count. But someone got shown the back door, the organiser, the co-ordinator. It was someone bright, someone with a technical background. It had to be Saeed," Jay said remembering the starkly lit courtyard, the stainless-steel cylinders, Khuda Bax's comment on Lis's wire about how clever Saaed was with computers.

"Like I said," Lorenz assured him, "we're running the entries." The plane stooped again, waking the others. "Just you and me in on this, Jay. Okay?" Lorenz said quietly, his hand gripping Jay's knee again. "Just you and me."

It was like being back in school. Jay might have been away for months. He had been away for two weeks. Ragged applause pattered round the clustered booths as he came in. Jeff Cohen was there, Judy Barron, the others, standing. Jay waved a hand, sports-star-style, acknowledging the greetings, embarrassed for them, embarrassed himself.

"Way to go, Jay," Cohen said.

"Right," Jay said shutting the door of his office and taking a deep breath. He sat at his desk and started to go through the pile of faxes, memos, envelopes. Requests for contributions, Princeton Alumni, stuff, a brown envelope with British stamps, clumsy hand-written address, another bunch of kids in London wanting something for their school project most likely, more stuff.

"Jay?" Barbara was at the door leaning against the frame, smiling. She always seemed so elegant, so collected, even under pressure. He looked down at the cheap blue-jeans he had bought in France, the mud-stained sneakers, knew she was probably wondering about his suit jacket.

"Guess I should regroup," he said.

"Don't bother. Bob needs you," was all she said.

CHAPTER 39

Washington D.C.

"Stirred or shaken, Mr. Bond?" Connolly asked.

"In the can is fine," Jay answered.

Connolly threw him a beer from the cooler at his feet. They were in the back yard of Connolly's town house, a room-size patch of yellowing grass with a patio of concrete flagstones at its centre and a palisade of tottering wooden fencing round its edge. Connolly was standing by the outdoor grill in shorts and Hawaiian shirt poking at three charred hamburgers. He squinted against the smoke. Jay and Connolly's current love-interest, a political science major from Denver called Cindy, sat in beach chairs around the TV Connolly had carried out from the study. They were watching a round-table discussion on Muslims in America. Jay was wearing a clean pair of jeans and there was no sign of the jacket. Cindy, wearing only a structurally-challenged string bikini, was making the most of the afternoon sun.

"There's a moment in the evolution of an immigrant community, of the immigrants themselves, when they have to cross over," a spokesman for the American Muslim Alliance, Fariq Barak, was saying. "People come here and think they're only going to be here six or seven years, get an education, make some money and go back. Even when they get citizenship they're still here but not here. Then, when their kids start going to school, start making friends and getting entrenched, they have to ask themselves – am I a migrant worker or an American?"

"And this applies to the Muslim community, you think?"

"I know. There is no group in the US so strong and yet completely locked out of the electoral process. Americans need a Muslim viewpoint in politics."

"They're planning to run two hundred or more candidates in the state and national races," Connolly commented, prodding the hamburgers viciously as if they might stand up and protest. "More power to them I say," he added sticking a paper plate of blackened meat into Jay's hand. Jay politely offered it to Cindy beside him but she declined. "I'm a vegan," she said, her perfect white teeth crunching into a carrot stick from the bowl in front of her for emphasis. Connolly pulled a chair alongside Cindy, holding his cold beer can against her thigh.

"Ow!"

"You're not eating either?" Jay said.

"Wouldn't touch it," Connolly said. "This is the only food that nourishes." He held up the can of Fosters Lager. "Cindy's reforming me. Aren't you my love?" He patted the girl's bare thigh with his greasy hand. She protested again, wiping off the residue with a napkin.

"This is not about religion. What we're talking about here," another panellist interjected, "is about race. Why is it that every time there is a bomb-scare the FBI comes directly to our doors. The first suspect they held in the Oklahoma bombing was an Egyptian just because he looked like me and was flying home to Cairo, because he had an accent. My God.

We all have accents. The FBI, the media, they all think Islam and fundamentalist are one and the same word. It isn't about religion. It's about race."

Connolly walked over to the television and switched it off. "Go tell that to the judge, Jay," he said. Cindy looked at Jay curiously. "Jay's a fed, my love, a federal agent. Doesn't look like one but who does anymore."

"I'm an analyst," Jay corrected; "a specialist, that's all."

Cindy didn't seem to mind either way, pushing herself up from the chair. "I'm going to take a shower."

"You do that. Mr. Peterson and I will continue to address the problems of the world while you anoint your lovely body with the oils of the orient. If we discover any answers in the meantime, we'll come up and tell you." Cindy ignored him pointedly.

"Lovely girl," Connolly said watching Cindy retreat towards the house. "Sharp as a pin. A geek. Says she's only interested in my mind. Ah, the sweet joy of youth." Connolly drained the last of his beer, crushed the can and threw it back into the cooler. "So did Lorenz fire your ass this morning or just send you back to school?"

"I didn't come here for the food, Brian."

They decamped to Connolly's study, a cramped room at the front of the house.

"You've run the list again?" Connolly asked. The list was the FBI's database of active and inactive terrorists and groups. It was co-ordinated, or was supposed to be, with similar data-bases at the CIA and State Department.

"Yes, against every fact sheet we can including Mossad's active list."

"Nothing on the ground?" Connolly asked, expecting the answer.

"Not according to the Saudi Interior Ministry. They'd like us to believe they have no active terrorists."

"Going back now. Just for me. How do you know this is Saudi based and not Iraqi or Libyan, if you don't mind my asking? I mean you've got this guy Saeed. There's Khuda Bax, or there was. There's Elhassan and the other feller, Bax's boyfriend. And Nasir Abu Massoud. Except for Khuda Bax, Saeed's the only one with a Saudi connection. Any record?"

"Nothing. The French did get him coming into Paris on his own passport."

"Ticket?"

"Purchased on Khuda Bax's American Express card."

"Point taken. So," Connolly said blowing smoke at the window. "Motive? Contacts? College friends?"

"Nothing yet. What's got everyone cranked up is that Saeed's just a kid. He had a brother, Ibrahim, but he went to Afghanistan when Saeed was eight or nine. The brother was killed. Saeed's too inexperienced is the word, too new. But there's no one else. We've accounted for just about every known active and any group with access to or knowledge of this kind of weapon. We can cross-reference just so much. If they're not even on the grid, we'll never get them."

Connolly and Jay had done this before, sitting in Connolly's front room or his office at the university, sometimes in Jay's apartment on Capitol Hill. There was a known universe of active and inactive terrorists, dissidents, activists, foreign and domestic and there were various matrixes the list could be plotted against: historical, behavioural, social, procedural. Some groups operated only in certain areas, others stuck to practices they knew well: car bombings, letter-bombings. There weren't many multifunctional groups or individuals. Ramze Yousef, the World Trade Centre bomber, was something of a rock star, a super-terrorist.

"Let me get this straight," Connolly said stubbing out his cigarette. "You know you have an active group, you know how they're armed more or less. You just don't know who they are or what they plan to hit and when. Right?" Jay nodded. "And Bob Lorenz's got every Mohammed on every block in Anytown, USA walking the plank to tell him?"

"Pretty much."

"You know the group is in the US."

"They've got four passengers entering Boston on a private flight: Saeed, Nasir maybe." Jay said. "The other two? I know it doesn't make any sense, the risk of bringing her in. Why would they? But she's still alive. I know it's crazy but there's something about this, something about her. I guess I'm the only one left who thinks so."

"You think so?" Connolly asked. "Not anymore." He walked to one of the three monitors along the back wall of the room, keying in an Internet address and waiting for the site to appear.

"It's one of the top ten, did you know that? More hits than any other." The FBI logo unfurled on the screen and Connolly clicked on one of the selections offered, bringing up the Most Wanted list. He clicked again and there was Lis Charnay's face, the photo from her press pass that Lorenz had taken off her at the Ritz with a chronology and biography added. "Fifteen minutes of fame," said Connolly. "And twenty five years to life on the inside." Jay's face was expressionless. "He didn't tell you, did he?" Connolly deduced.

CHAPTER 40

Nashua, New Hampshire

The kitchen was more for show than cooking. New copper pots hung from a rack above the island, dried herbs adorned the window. An oak table stood in the middle of the room, six chairs round it. The man from Darunta sat at one of them. She paused in the doorway, uncertain whether to go in or not.

"Coffee is on the counter, cups above. Milk and sugar are in the refrigerator," he said not looking up from his laptop. "There is bread." His voice was soft, the accent barely detectable. Lis hesitated a moment more then crossed to the counter, poured a cup of coffee and, after considering, sat opposite him. He went on working, occasionally pecking at a sequence of keys with two fingers. "Did you sleep well?" the man from Darunta asked looking up from the keyboard.

Lis nodded. The ride from Boston in the van had been long and uncomfortable. They had got badly lost and a fierce argument had broken out between Saeed and the fourth man, the bearded man from Boston. His name, Lis had learned, was Mahmoud. When they reached the house in the early hours of the morning, while the others were unloading the van, Saeed had led her to a room upstairs and helped her onto the bed. She was barely conscious. Daylight had woken her half an hour ago.

"What time is it?" she managed at last, her voice small and dry.

"Eleven thirty. You slept for a long time."

The sound of a truck outside drew her attention. She could see its familiar brown paintwork and the golden logo. She recognised Saeed's voice outside, the voice of the UPS driver, a shuffling of feet on the driveway, the sound of the engine revving and the truck pulling off, a scent of diesel floating through the open window.

"Who are you?" she asked.

"My name is Ali," the man said slowly; "Ali Fatta Hussein."

Lis studied Ali's face, the widely separated eyes, the slightly flattened nose. His right eye drooped a little, a prominent scar running across his brow close to his eye, evidence of an earlier accident. It was the face of an academic or an accountant, someone who lived by his mind not his hands.

"Why am I here?"

"Because you wish to be here, Miss Charnay; because you are curious to know answers to certain questions you have been asking."

"What questions?" she asked, genuinely unsure of what questions she might have asked, when she would have asked them.

"How you got here, what business we are engaged in, who we are, such questions as those." Ali's manner was composed, his voice quite polite. He seemed to know her very well, knew what she was thinking.

"Am I a hostage?"

"How can that be?" he asked. "You are not being kept against your will."

"So why am I here?" This time she yelled the question, her restraint caving in under the weight of her frustration. A face appeared for a moment in the doorway behind Ali. Lis recognised it immediately. "That man killed a friend of mine," she said.

"That is possible but quite unlikely," Ali said turning. "Nasir is a devout man. Perhaps you made a mistake, perhaps your friend did not die." Ali waved him away then closed the lid of his computer as if to protect its contents.

They walked then, away from the road across the fields behind the house, she and Ali side by side, Nasir several steps behind. The warmth of the sun restored her strength a little though she stumbled often, Ali once catching her by the elbow to steady her. She asked Ali if she was his only victim. He told her she was not a victim, commiserating with her when she recalled the beating she had been given, talking to her the way a friend would if she had fallen and grazed her knee badly. Her anger surged, rolling in like an ocean swell then subsiding. They returned to the house, Nasir always a pace or two behind. There was no sign of the packages delivered that morning, no sign of the van in which they had driven from Boston.

"Where is Saeed?" she asked. In answer to her question a door at the far end of the hall closed. Lis was just in time to see the young man's back and in the room beyond a computer monitor and hard drive. They went into the kitchen and sat down round the table. Nasir made tea. As the afternoon light drained from the sky the realisation came to Lis that one of these men, Ali or Nasir, or Mahmoud, the bearded one, would eventually kill her. Not Saeed. He was her hope for a future beyond this place. No, not Saeed.

Later, upstairs, she woke to the sound of voices. She recognised Saeed's voice and Mahmoud's. The effect of the last dose of morphine was beginning to wear off. The dizziness was coming back, the cramp in her stomach. She was beginning to learn, to predict its cycles. She sniffed hard, wiping her hands on the blanket. They were clammy with sweat. She pulled herself upright and crossed to the door. They kept her shoes downstairs, a curious precaution or some cultural prohibition, she couldn't be sure which. The window in her room had been nailed shut but she could see it was fully dark. She tried the light switch. There was a soft click but no light. The voices downstairs continued.

She opened the door, moved quietly across the landing and down the stairs. The kitchen door was ajar slightly, just enough for the raised voices to drift out into the hall, clear enough now for her to make out the words.

"It is not good for the woman to be here. It is not right." It was Mahmoud, his voice a staccato growl. Lis could recognise key words, enough to decipher his rapid Arabic.

"It is not your business." Saeed's voice, higher, insistent. "It is Ali's business." Confirmation which she didn't require that Ali was the leader of this odd foursome. The bickering continued. Nasir and Ali remained silent. A smell of cooked vegetables permeated the house. Lis looked at the front door then back down the corridor to Saeed's computer room. The door was closed. She hesitated then walked purposefully towards it.

The room was dark except for the glow of the screensaver with the letters "W O W" rotating on the monitor of Saeed's computer. A printer stood off to one side and Ali's laptop, cabled into the back, sat precariously on top of the monitor.

She touched the trackball and the screen came alight. Several different windows were opened, one of them displaying what looked like an outline diagram of a connector or nozzle with an assembly sequence, another displaying written instructions. Only part of the Arabic text was visible under the borders of the top window but she caught the English words "canister" and "separator valve", tying the text to the diagram. Her finger rolled the ball to the left. At the same instant a hand clamped onto her wrist, wrenching her arm up behind her back and bringing the owner's face next to her ear.

"Won't you come eat with us, Missie?" It was Nasir, his breath sour with garlic. He turned her round towards the door and shoved her hard into the corridor.

Nasir served them, carrying the pre-packaged meals of couscous and vegetables from the microwave and placing one before each of them. Glasses of water were set out and a loaf of bread passed from hand to hand, each man tearing off a chunk.

"It is very good bread," Saeed told her, "but Nasir's cooking is not top quality." Only Mahmoud laughed.

There was no reprimand given for her intrusion into Saeed's room. Instead, a passionate debate continued over faltering religious observance and economic despair in Saudi Arabia. Saeed and Mahmoud were still the only contributors.

"The Saudi people are stupid like American people are," Mahmoud said.

"They are not stupid," Saeed countered; "they are sufferers but they are not stupid. Each of us is a sufferer. What am

I? I am a biochemist. What do I do? I work in a warehouse with Pakistani pigs for scraps of bread."

"You are not a biochemist," Mahmoud retorted. "Prince Walid gives money to young boys like you to study in America so you will be corrupted like him with your computers, your Internet and your pornography."

"He is demented. Ali, tell him. I am Saudi, Mahmoud, like you. The computer lets us talk without the Ruler hearing or seeing. We can be modern. That does not make us western. The Holy Book does not tell us we cannot use a modem."

"The computer tells you to lust after women, to read apostasy."

"Mahmoud, you are possessed. Because I eat chicken at Kentucky Fried Chicken does not make me American. It is cheap food, like dirt, but it is food. Being in this American house does not make you American or me American, seeing by this American light does not make you an infidel."

Ali Hussein watched Lis from down the table as the two men argued back and forth, watched her brow furrow as she tried to follow the flow of words. She noticed him and looked down at her food.

"And the Americans who work for the government?" Mahmoud queried. "Mr. James Baker and all his economists who work in the Saudi Finance Ministry, the King's American business advisers. They tell Fahd, he tells you to buy American cigarettes and American cars and American computers. It is Saudis like you, Saeed, who buy these things. The computer you use, the food you and your family eat, the Macdonald's. Isn't our food good enough that you have to eat Americans' food?"

"It is just food, Mahmoud. Like this food," Saeed said.

"And they are just films, and just warplanes, and just atheist soldiers. They are the apostate," Mahmoud spat out, banging a fist on the table. A look from Ali quietened him and brought the two-sided debate to a close. Nasir collected the empty packets, throwing them into a grocery bag and sweeping the bread crumbs off the table onto the floor. Saeed left the room, going down the hall to the room at the back, while Mahmoud went outside. Lis heard the van pull up outside the door.

"We will be leaving shortly," Ali said to her.

"Where are we going?" She said expecting her fate to be read out to her now.

"You will discover," he said.

"I need fresh clothes. Or need to wash these. I need a shower."

"You will have them. Now you must join Mahmoud in the van."

Nasir came to her side. Just having him near was enough to persuade her forwards. Was this it? Was this the moment? A torrent of inconsequential thoughts flooded her mind. Her last meal had been dried vegetables out of a packet. Her assassin had cooked the meal. She should have participated in the discussion, said something at least by which they would remember her. Would they drive her somewhere in the night now, throw her body out onto the road with the flattened racoons and possums? She began to shiver.

"Come on, Missie," Nasir said.

CHAPTER 41

Washington D.C.

Lorenz had called the briefing for seven. He was late. There were thirty or so people in the bullpen, the largest available open space to offer at least a semblance of closed-door security. The elements of the "Truman" task force had grouped themselves loosely by function and activity. The interagency emergency support team co-ordinators stood round the water fountain, the response module leaders by the coffee stand. Lorenz's foot soldiers, the "brick" agents, stood in twos and threes round the edges of the room. Jay raised a hand in salute to Sam Clemens standing on his own by the door. Jay's own unit stood round Jeff Cohen's booth. Conversation was minimal and came to an abrupt halt when Lorenz, his deputy and aides, his "immediate family" as Connolly had once characterised them, entered the room. Lorenz launched directly into his address.

"You all know part of what this is about. Some of you I've talked to directly, some of you have heard about it in the corridors. I'm going to meet with team leaders again when we're through here to co-ordinate tasking. They'll meet with each of you and your teams after that. But I want all of us to understand right now that this is the real thing. A minimum of four persons, the mother cell, entered US territory within the last four or five days; Friday most likely. They have access to unknown quantities of a lethally dangerous nerve agent, VX. That's why we're going to full alert just for those of you here who wonder why you're not at home watching the game."

Lorenz had his audience right where he wanted them. They were his team. For the next two days, two weeks, two months, however long it would take, he would lead them into the charge. Relationships would collapse, life outside the office cease to exist.

"And that's not half of it. These people don't even have to move. All they have to do is let it be known what they are capable of and they'll have every right-thinking citizen in this sacred nation of ours scared witless. And that's all they want. They don't want hostages. They don't want to read a manifesto on primetime. They don't even want their name in the paper. They just want to bring the whole fucking intricate well-oiled machine we call daily life to a grinding halt and they're going to do it if even a hint of what we've got here finds its way into the press. We'll be working with more agencies on this than you've even heard of: the Federal Emergency Management Agency, the Office of Emergency Preparedness, and twenty odd others. It's your job, you people here, to ensure the rest of them understand exactly what we're up against. You hear someone with loose lips, smack 'em. Send me the bill. Give their lawyer my home number. Understood?"

Lorenz notched his delivery down a peg, moved in towards them. "We've had some false starts," he said sharing the embarrassment, taking his part in the blame. "We all know what they are and we all know how we can correct them. The Bureau has spent millions of dollars and thousands of hours setting up our interagency teams. I hope to Christ we don't have to deploy them. 'Cause if we do, we're looking at more fatalities than this nation has seen on its own soil since the Civil War. And you can bet your sweet ass every detail, every kid's bloated corpse will be all over the evening news. We can't afford to let these fuckers get even close to that point. Not within a million miles. You read me?"

No one spoke. Lorenz knew he had done what he had to do: put the fear of God into them. It wasn't what the management manuals recommended but it worked for Lorenz. "Right. Get something to eat if you need to. Make your excuses at home if you have one. We're in here for the duration."

The meeting broke up, Lorenz heading for the door, Jay at his heels. He caught up with him in his office, the door wide open. Jay didn't knock. Lorenz was already back on the phone.

"Tell them I don't give a fuck how much it costs, Frank, or who's feelings get hurt. We don't have the manpower." Lorenz was standing at his desk, holding a print-out of the digital match-up of Mahmoud bin Mubarrak's prints lifted from the row house in Boston's North End and the prints he had given the INS for his Green Card. A copy of Mahmoud's Massachusetts driver's license and a blurred headshot were attached. "I want every beat cop in Boston on this. Every car rental, every truck rental. And whatever you do, Frank, keep the papers out of this. No press, no comment." Lorenz slammed the phone down. It rang immediately. "Where's Barbara? Where the fuck is Barbara?"

"She's at the dentist's. It was an emergency," Jay said.

"What're you doing here, Jay?"

"You knew Lis had come in all along. You gave me some bullshit about how they could have smuggled her in and you knew all along."

Lorenz glared at Jay, one hand on the ringing phone. He looked as if he might throw the instrument at Jay then relented. "Okay, okay. The INS came through with three positives. Saeed bin Sayyaf, Nasir Abu Massoud, our assassin, and Elise Charnay. Fourth passenger a United Nations passport. They're not permitted to screen or record those documents apparently. Why not? I don't know. Most of them have got to be spies. I would have got round to telling you eventually but you may have noticed we are in the middle of a fucking national emergency. You are not my first priority right now, Jay. We don't have stars in this division. We are a team. Frank Morrelli may be a dick-head but he's our dick-head. Since we left him he's identified their safe-house or whatever in Boston. Nice little row house in the North End. Mahmoud's. Rent was paid by a Saudi charity he thinks, but doesn't know which one. I swear, these guys are unbelievable. They enter the country on their own passports, they leave fingerprints all over the sink."

"Hers?"

"We don't have anything to match them with yet but, yes, there was a fourth set unaccounted for."

"And the containers? Gas tanks?"

Lorenz sighed, knowing he'd have to go through this anyway and might as well get it over with now. The phone stopped ringing at last. "Fire extinguishers. That's what the manifest listed. They got it screwed up, had it filed under the shipper's name or some bullshit. Couldn't find it."

"Fire extinguishers?"

"Fire extinguishers. The Frogs are already crawling all over the map trying to find out where they bought them."

"So why did you put her picture on the web site, Bob? It's a death warrant. You know that. If they don't kill her, the first dumb cop with an itchy finger is going to blow her away as soon as they spot her."

"It's none of your business, son, that's why," Lorenz yelled. An aide paused in the doorway of Lorenz's office a pink phone message in her hand then faded away. "I've been doing this job for thirty seven years one way or another and I'm doing it the only way I know. I've got every cop from Boston to Bar Harbor asking anyone with a tan where they hid the body. Right now what I don't need is some infatuated kid who can't keep his mind off his dick telling me how to do my job. You've done plenty already. And I'm grateful. Truly grateful. Now it's time you did your job. You're an analyst; analyse. Tell me if I'm dealing with the Islamic Movement for Change or the Islamic Fucking Front for Free Food Stamps before the shit really hits the fan." The aide was back, standing silently inside the door now waiting for the right moment to interrupt her boss. "What?" Lorenz fired off at the girl.

"Mr. Rosen called from National Security. They want to move the meeting up to eight. And Karen Goldberg's on line two. She says it's urgent." Goldberg was Lorenz's co-ordinator for the interagency support teams that were right now being deployed to meet the coming emergency. She was a petite matronly woman in her fifties and Lorenz's equal in every way. Barbara had once told Jay that Karen had out-cursed the Director two for one on their very first bout. Lorenz picked up the receiver and punched in the line button.

"Karen?"

"Hey, Bob."

"What's up?"

"We've hit a snag on the antidote injectors. The original target quantity was twenty thousand per region, eighty thousand in all. The stockpile was being held in Virginia but was shipped to the Gulf three months ago when Saddam started waving his sword. It'll take at least two weeks to get them back here or to brew up a new batch of antidote and we don't know how long till we get the auto-injectors from Sweden."

"Find an alternative."

"There isn't one, Bob."

"Find one." Lorenz dropped the phone in the cradle, picked up the stack of faxes that had accumulated on the desk in the minutes he had been away, cursing his assistant's absence once more, and headed for the FBI command centre. His exit was blocked by Jay. "Let it go, Jay. There's a war on. I have a division to run here. You've got a job to do. We'll figure out who owes what when they bring the bill." Lorenz's momentum propelled them towards the elevators, Jay still at his boss's shoulder.

"If you'd stopped long enough to listen," Jay said his voice hard, the anger controlled, "they would never have got this far. You weren't prepared to listen when we were in Paris and we're paying for it now."

"Don't give me that shit, Jay. I saved your ass in Paris. Went to the wall for you and haven't stopped paying for it since." Their altercation had attracted the interest of others on the floor. Conversations had stopped, a head appeared round the corner of an office door to see who Lorenz was chewing out this time and as quickly withdrew. "You're a hell of a guy, Jay; you've got balls of brass. But this is a whole different game. These guys are criminals, crazies, and whatever it is they're cooking up it's our job, yours and mine, to get to them before they have a chance to make their play. If that means your girlfriend goes down in the ship with them, then I'm sorry. Those're the rules of war."

They were at the elevators now and the bronze doors slid back to reveal Barbara, Lorenz's assistant, one side of her face slightly swollen. "Don't even ask," she lisped.

Lorenz stepped into the elevator. "Stay where you are. We're headed for the command centre then the White House. Keep me posted, Jay." The doors began to close on Lorenz and his assistant. Barbara gave Jay a little wave of her hand, part greeting, part encouragement.

"Mr. Lorenz, sir?" The aide who had interrupted Lorenz earlier appeared round the corner.

"Don't tell me Rosen has changed his mind again," Lorenz said.

"No, sir. It's Morrelli. He said to tell you they've found the rental in South Boston. Quincy, he said. It's a U-Haul. Positive ID on Mahmoud's headshot."

"Fantastic," Lorenz beamed. "Tell Morrelli I'll call him right back." Lorenz looked at Jay as the elevator doors began to close again. "What did I tell you, Jay? Teamwork."

The doors slid together with a sigh.

CHAPTER 42

New Jersey

She twisted the strip of red rubber on itself and pulled it tight with her teeth. The vein rose like a long blue highway from the crook of her elbow to her wrist, the purple needle marks standing out. She jetted a tiny quantity of the precious liquid into the air then laid the tip of the wet needle against her skin. It felt cold. She jabbed it inwards the way Nasir had shown her, not too hard, not too deep. She gasped more from surprise than pain then worked the plunger out slowly, watching fascinated as her purple blood flowed up into the syringe. She was in the drug, it was in her. She pressed the plunger down feeling the pressure building in the vein. A second, two. Then the rush of warmth, the wave engulfing her, her right hand dropping into her lap, the needle hanging from her arm.

It was late night on the New Jersey Turnpike just beyond New York City. They were driving south past Elizabeth and Carteret, the pungent gases from the oil processing plants along the roadside filtering into the van's cab, the lights from the docks lighting up the faces of driver and passengers. Ali Hussein was at the wheel of the white U-Haul, Lis by his side. Nasir, Mahmoud and Saeed were asleep on the bench seats behind. She would survive another night, she realised. She had known as soon as they had pulled out of the driveway, watching Saeed loading his hardware into the van's caged cargo area and Ali Hussein locking the front door of the house, carefully hiding the key. Saaed had driven first, then, just before New York, had switched with Ali. It had been Ali who suggested she ride in front with him.

The drug washed over her, melting her body, but let her mind rise halfway to the surface again. "Am I the message you are sending, Ali? Am I the lesson you are teaching Americans?" She looked down at her arm, finally releasing the rubber tourniquet and slipping out the needle.

"Americans do not need lessons, Miss Charnay. They know everything, always."

Lis leaned her head on the window, her eyes on the galaxy of lights outside. "So you are teaching Saudis a lesson then?"

"That is possible, yes."

"What is this lesson you are teaching them, Ali Hussein?" she said drowsily. Something in her tone caught Ali's attention. He turned towards her, momentarily taking his eyes off the turnpike ahead, studied her face for a second in the yellow light of the overhead lamps, then turned back to the road.

They watched the lights ahead for a while, wrapped together in the safety of the night. Then he said: "There was a place once, a village. That place had a name and the people in it knew each other, knew their families, their children."

"What was the name of this place?"

"It has no name now."

"And the people, the families?"

"They are gone elsewhere." As they continued south, the names of the New Jersey towns spelled out on the green highway signs flicking past, Ali described the Shiite village which she guessed had been his, one of many in the eastern provinces of Saudi Arabia, he said, that had been razed to accommodate the oil drillers, the cracking plants, the pipelines.

"Was it your home?" she asked.

"I have no home, Miss Charnay. This is my home." He patted the seat between them. "This is my family," he continued, indicating the sleeping men in the back.

Ali told her about the Saudi poor, the "invisible" who lived in shacks on the fringes of Riyadh but were not supposed to exist, who could not be filmed or photographed, eking out an existence in the shadow of billions of dollars of unused American armaments. He talked about the enclaves of the Saudi rich, how they bought time-shares in Disney's gated community in Orlando, about the images of wealth and luxury beamed in on satellite TV from all over the globe spreading the corruption, composting the soil for the video-game parlours, the karaoke bars, the disintegration.

Lis caught herself looking at Ali in a new light, not as a tormentor but as someone's child, as some mother's son. What they were doing, driving down the New Jersey Turnpike, was such an American thing, something every American who drove had done or most likely would do at some time in their lives.

The lights of the petroleum processors receded, the green mile markers slipped by, a service station was announced. Ali said: "This country, the USA, trained us to make missiles. The CIA trained us to make bombs out of household detergents in Afghanistan, trained us to load and shoot grenade-launchers against the Russians. We shot, we killed. We died for you there, but we died for our cause. We didn't know, no one knew the enemy was all around us, was behind us, beside us. We were the warm bodies. That was what your Congress called the mujahedeen, me, my brothers."

Ali paused for a second only then repeated: "The warm bodies. Those men in suits with their comfortable homes, their rootless children, their stocks and shares in Lockheed and Raytheon. They say they know, say they understand but still they drive the same big cars, write the same big cheques, send the same soldiers and sailors and airmen to guard the oil. They do not consider the people of that country, their families, their lives. We must be left to our own destiny. The US used us in Afghanistan to fight their war with the Russians, thought little of us as we died. But what they did do was to turn my brothers and me into a fighting force. One of your senators called us blowback. We may not have the planes, the missiles but we have the patience and the will. We are a small army, Miss Charnay," Ali said indicating the four of them, "a very small army but at our backs are many more 'warm bodies,' thousands and thousands. And we have a path now, a road to follow. And we will keep coming, keep fighting till there is not one of us left standing."

This is the time, Lis thought, and this is the place. This is how it happens, when you throw yourself into the curve, when you dive head first off the building. The worst has happened and the worst is yet to come, here in this place. "On the New Jersey Turnpike."

"The Turnpike?" Ali queried.

"Just thinking out loud," she said, then: "And you're going to die for all that. Because you are going to die, Ali; you and Saeed and Mahmoud and that pig in the back seat, Nasir, sleeping so peacefully. He will be the one to kill me, won't he? You know that already. You, Ali, will tell him to do that, right? Little nod of the head? Well, I'll go down fighting, Mr. Ali Hussein, Ali Fatta Hussein. Okay? I'll fight every inch of the way. I'm a survivor, a fucking survivor."

Ali turned towards her again. "You will not die, Miss Charnay. Remember, you are my messenger."

"So if I'm the messenger, what's the message?" she fired back.

He felt inside his jacket and brought out a videocassette. "This. You will take it to CNN and NBC. They will believe you. They will know what to do with it."

She stretched her arm out to take the tape, her hand trembling slightly from the shock or from the drug singing in her blood, she wasn't sure. It was her reprieve, her ticket to life beyond, but Ali withdrew it, put it back in his pocket before she could grab it, both hands gripping the wheel now, eyes lifting to the rear-view mirror and what he saw there.

CHAPTER 43

New Jersey

The whirling red light behind them brought an instinctive rush of fear to Lis before she realised the light was her salvation. Ali slowed the cargo van and pulled over onto the shoulder, the van slightly angled against the guard rail. The deceleration woke the others. Nasir turned to watch the approach of the police car. The full beams of the cruiser's flashing headlights lit up his round face like a full moon.

The door locks snapped down and at the same moment a hand from the rear seat settled on her shoulder, the faint pressure of a thin blade, a knife, pushing against the side of her neck. "No talking, Missie. Okay?" Nasir snarled at her. Ali reached across her to the glove compartment in front of her. "No speaking. You understand? It's just a routine thing. No problems."

Ali pulled out the rental agreement Mahmoud had signed in Quincy then extracted his own driver's license from his wallet. The siren died, the spinning light filling the van's interior with a blood red glow. They sat silently the five of them, waiting, the six lanes of traffic washing by north and south, the van rocking slightly as a truck went by. The trooper stayed in his car checking their number plate. There was a movement from the back seat of the van as one of the men shifted behind Lis. "Wait," Ali said, his tone commanding.

The trooper was getting out of the car now, putting the pioneer's hat on his shaved head, his right hand moving to the holster at his belt, his free hand picking up a flashlight from the passenger seat. Lis, the pressure of the blade still there, shifted her eyes to watch his approach in Ali's wing mirror. The man was in his early twenties, lean and eager. An ex-Marine maybe, a veteran of the Gulf War perhaps. There was a slight strut in his gait as he moved along the side of the van, working the flashlight over the passengers in the rear then stationing himself just behind Ali's elbow at the open driver's side window.

"Good evening, officer," Ali said easily. "There is a problem?" The flashlight blazed on Ali's face then dwelt for a moment on Lis, the blade at her neck hidden in deep shadow, someone's breath loud in her ear.

"Driver's license and registration," the trooper said without answering. Ali handed over the rental registration and his license. The trooper inspected the license. "You Mr. Ali Hussein, sir?" the trooper asked.

"Yes, officer," Ali replied.

"Where did you rent this van, Mr. Hussein?"

"In Boston," Ali replied.

Lis kept her head forward, her eyes straining down to the trooper's hand at the window trying to see Ali's driver's license and the name on the pink rental slip.

"Any of you in here a Mahmoud Mubarrak?" the trooper asked sounding out the name with difficulty. The flashlight beam picked out the faces in the back. No one spoke. The beam crossed Lis's face again. "You all right, ma'am?" the trooper asked. Lis nodded slightly. "You wait here," he said turning and walking back to the patrol car. Lis felt the blade's edge release, scratch her neck then switch to the left side and press suddenly hard into her skin. She stretched away from it involuntarily. There was a click from the seat behind her and a sudden wash of warm air from her side of the van.

They sat waiting for a movement from the car behind, Lis watching in the rear-view mirror above her. The trooper got out again, repeating his routine, his hand this time unsnapping the leather holster guard. Another small sound from the rear of the van turned Lis's head instinctively to the right but the blade switched sides again forcing her to stop and a hand squeezed so hard against the nape of her neck that it choked her. She strained to check the rear-view mirror. Nasir was no longer in his place by the door.

The trooper was back at Ali's door, his automatic out of its holster and held straight down by his right leg. "Get out of the van, sir," he said, "hands where I can see them. Rest of you hands on the roof, now." Lis's view of the rear of the van was blocked by the trooper's body so she never saw Nasir slip round the back of the truck, never saw his arm raised, never even heard the soft pop of the Beretta over the roar of a passing tractor-trailer. All she saw was the trooper's body collapse and Nasir's framed suddenly in the high intensity beams of the cruiser's lights. Someone must see, someone had to see.

Ali slid out of the driver's seat. Lis heard the left rear door slide open, a grunt of effort from the two men and the door slide closed again. The right passenger door shut softly then Ali's door closed too. He revved the van and swung hard into the nearside lane, the sudden manoeuvre provoking a chorus of angry horns and a flashing of headlights. He ignored them, accelerating as he went. The violent movement of the truck jarred Mahmoud's hand. The razor-edge cut into Lis's neck. She screamed, her hands moving to the sides of the seat to steady herself. The blade was retracted but Mahmoud kept her head jammed into the head-rest of the passenger seat. She felt blood trickling down her neck.

"Sit on your hands," Mahmoud's voice growled at her ear. "Sit on them."

"Why did you do that?" It was Saeed, his voice shrill. "You should not have done that."

They were silent, Ali intent on the road ahead and the traffic behind. Just when she thought her neck might snap from the pressure, the van slowed and the glow of the orange lights of a service area lit the interior. Ali navigated slowly through the parked cars and trucks, finally pulling alongside an empty camper with Virginia plates at the rear of the parking lot. He backed the U-Haul in beside it and cut the engine, leaving the headlights on. The rear door on Nasir's side opened then closed again. Then the door on Saeed's side opened and closed. Mahmoud remained in place, his hand still anchoring Lis's head to the seat.

They waited there for five minutes, Mahmoud behind, Ali and Lis in the front. The rear doors of the cargo area were opened and Lis guessed that whatever had been loaded into the van at the beginning of their trip was being taken out. The van's horn sounded suddenly, a short, sharp warning. Mahmoud released his grip letting her see the plaza, the rows of cars, the improbably cosy lights of the restaurant and an overweight man in flip-flops, a tray of food in one hand, keys in the other, shambling towards them, the weight of his body rolling slightly from one side to another in time to his shuffling step. When he was near enough to see her, Lis made her best effort to warn him, rolling her eyes to the right, mouthing a silent "No." He didn't even look her way.

The man balanced the tray of food and drink precariously on the roof of his vehicle's cab and slid a key into the door-lock. "No," Lis yelled, the sound of her voice loud enough through the glass to pull the man's head around. He stared at her open mouth, saw Mahmoud's hand clamp over it, watched her head pulled back against the seat, not connect-ing what was happening with the danger behind him.

The bullet entered the rear of his head where the scant ring of thinning hair gave way to bare scalp. His body col-lapsed like a punctured balloon against the side of his camper, dislodging the tray of food he had so carefully carried from the restaurant. The hamburger, French fries and a black shower of cola and ice rained down on the red pulp of the man's face, the eyes staring sightlessly at the downpour. Nasir stepped round the fallen man, pulled a wallet from his back pocket, then dragged the body by its legs around the back of the U-Haul and stuffed it unceremoniously underneath the chassis, kicking an errant foot, still exposed to the night, back under the truck.

Ali and Saeed finished the transfer of their gear to the back of the camper, slammed the door hard, then Ali climbed in behind the camper's wheel. Mahmoud yanked Lis from her seat in the U-Haul and round the front of the vehicle to the off side of the camper. The rear door opened from the inside, Saeed holding it open. Mahmoud pushed her roughly from behind, following her in, ramming her flat on the camper's floor.

"Leave her," she heard Mahmoud say to Saeed. Saeed

protested then dutifully took his place on the camper's bench seat. The front passenger door banged shut, the tyres squealed briefly and the vehicle pulled across the plaza and out onto the highway. Beneath the abandoned U-Haul cargo van the bloodied shirt of the camper's owner, pressed tight against the hot exhaust, began to singe, a faint scent of seared flesh mingling with the smell of scorched fabric. On the floor of the passenger compartment directly overhead, the body of the young trooper lay wedged between the seats, a metallic voice calling uselessly to him from the receiver clipped to his lapel.

CHAPTER 44

Washington D.C.

Dawn broke over the Potomac River. The first rowing shell was already out on the water tracing a wedge of golden arrow-heads across the surface, the four young scullers pulling steadily. Traffic was filling the city's bridges. Another Washington day had begun, a day that would not be like others.

Jay had been woken at five with the breaking news and reached the Counterterrorism's bull pen just after five thirty. He wasn't the first there. A couple of people looked up when he came in, the ceiling lights washing all the colour from their faces, ageing them. Jeff Cohen emerged from the maze of booths and handed Jay the AP wire then followed him to the conference area. The other members of their group, Ted Frankel and Hamad Amor, a Palestinian-American recruited under the Bureau's ongoing minority-hiring program, were already sitting at the table. Judy Barron was perched on the credenza. Jay read the wire reporter's account of the double murder while the others waited in silence.

"It'll make things easier," Judy Barron broke in. Her eyes were wide with disbelief, her face showing she couldn't relate the two deaths to the work she did every day. They were ana-lysts, the five of them. They compiled data, launched theories, shot them down. They tracked groups, watched movements evolve, picked over speeches for significant nuggets. "If they've broken cover," Judy continued, "they'll be easier to pick up. I mean it's not really our problem, is it? Jesus, I don't mean that, but you know what I mean." The others knew exactly.

"Has anyone out there," Jay nodded towards the Division's other offices, "updated us since last night?"

Frankel pulled a sheet of paper from his folder. "They gave us the identity of the guy who rented the U-Haul: Mahmoud Mubarrak, the same as the police report. Used his own name, can you believe. I ran his profile from the database for you." Frankel passed the sheet over. "The cell's leader has been confirmed as Saeed bin Sayyaf. Only other member to date, Elise Charnay." Frankel suddenly made the connection and looked up, embarrassed.

"Anyone else?"

"The police driver reported the driver's name, before he was shot – Ali Fatta Hussein," Frankel said.

Jay hesitated for a moment then launched in. "What the Director hasn't officially told us though I'm sure he'll get to it eventually," he said, "is that the route these guys used was established some time ago. There's a possibility the organisation has been stockpiling VX or other agents for weeks, even months. We have to assume that that tells us something about the group's targets. VX is most potent in its liquid form. Transferring it and pressurising it has to be extremely dangerous. They could have flown it in in the original drums. They didn't. Basically, we have a choice. We can either sit around waiting for the Director or one of his aides to pass on what the "bricks" turn up or we can do our own research."

The others leaned forwards in anticipation, Judy Barron leaving her place on the credenza and sitting at the table. "We have a when. That has to be very soon. They haven't been shy about leaving a trail up to now and they must know their time is running out. If they had a timetable, they'll have just collapsed it. The how is half answered: VX. There's no point in wasting time on the provenance of the agent. By the time anyone traces that it could be all over. Figuring out how they plan to deliver it, and where, brings us back to the question: Who?"

"And why?" Barron chipped in, her spirits lifted slightly now they were back on theoretical ground.

"They're Saudi, at least we know Saeed and Mahmoud are. So, it's not a military target. Why bother to make the trip to the US when you've got 20,000 US personnel right there in the Gulf?"

Anyway, they've already done that, Jay said to himself. He and his group could run Mahmoud down, figure out his association, his movements. He would prove to be a foot-soldier, most likely. Nasir Abu Massoud was a paid assassin along for the ride. Saeed? Not leadership material Jay had decided. Ali Fatta Hussein had to be their man. Had to be Brian's "seventh samurai" or at least Saeed's protector. Jay gave his group the edited version. "I want you to run anything you can find on Ali Fatta Hussein. Driver's license, social security, tax records, United Nations affiliation if you can find it. Assume he's Saudi for starters."

"Won't they be running that already?" Cohen asked meaning the agents on the case.

"Sure. So, we'll do it too. See who gets there first. We find out who he is, where he's come from and we'll find out what he's planning on hitting."

"He's the cell's head?" It was Amor's question.

"Let's assume so. Start with graduates of Afghani and Iranian camps. Iran stockpiles the stuff so they should know how to use it. The Iraqis are known manufacturers. Maybe someone purchased it for them. See if you can find a cross-reference to any of the names we have. Jeff, you and Hamad focus on Ali Hussein. This stuff is as dangerous to the user as the victim. The University of Michigan may be a great school but I don't think they taught Saeed how to set up a safe transfer station for VX. We're looking for a background. Someone out there knows what he's doing."

The sound of a ringing phone cut across the low buzz of the BBC World Service and Arab radio broadcasts. "Ready or not, here they come," Cohen said looking at his watch.

"It's for you, Jay," one of the other analysts in the bull pen called out. "I'll send it over."

The phone in the conference area rang, the others heading back to their desks.

"Jay Peterson."

"Jay, don't you ever sleep?" It was Connolly.

"More than you by the sound of it. When did you get up?"

"Didn't," Connolly said. "I'm still in bed. Say hello to Jay, my love." There was a grunt at the other end.

"Look, Brian. It's not the best time. Maybe we could meet later."

"I don't think so," Connolly said. "I heard the news on the radio. Not good. I think it's time we had a real chat."

"I thought we already had."

"That was just a warm-up. This time it's the God's honest. Can't do it on the phone."

"Your place?"

"Well I'm sure as shit not coming down to that place without a gas mask."

Cindy was nowhere to be seen when Connolly led the way into the narrow kitchen at the back of his Georgetown house. The radio was on, so were two TVs, one tuned to CNN, the other to C-SPAN.

"Sentimental reasons," commented Connolly. "The TV's for entertainment you understand. Coffee?"

Jay shook his head. "Where's the fire, Brian?"

"In me head, Jay, in me head and in me loins." He caught Jay's glance at the ceiling. "Sent her packing. Screamed like a vixen but that's life in today's army." Connolly poured coffee into his mug, ladling in three spoons of sugar. "I've got something to show you." Connolly's computer was humming, the screen lit. He swept a newspaper off the chair in front of it and sat. "Hate these fucking things," he said pecking at the keys. "Work of the devil." Jay waited impatiently, watching Connolly's search-engine slip through the walls of information. A home page built itself on the screen.

"See that?"

"University of Michigan."

"And who do we know at the University of Michigan?" Connolly asked, his voice alight with glee. Jay said nothing. "Now. Here's the trick," said Connolly. He hacked at the keyboard, countering the requests for access codes with a barrage of keystrokes. A directory of addresses appeared. He scrolled through the As and Bs to the Ws.

"Is this a game, Brian?" Jay asked wearily.

"Sort of. I had a little chat with the lovely Cindy last night. I told you she was a geek. Well, guess what? Seems every student knows this. Couple of old farts we are. Go to school these days and you get an e-mail account. Right? Go through the college's server. Then you move on. But wait! You've got used to having that little convenience. The college has suspended your service but, and here's the craft, you sneak back in, set up your own mail box or more than one and bill it to someone else's account. Now anyone can drop you a line when they want and you can chat with anyone you like for free."

"Cindy's doing this at the University?"

"She and every other grad she knows. Now, say you need a mail-box, a dead-letter box perhaps, and you don't want anyone seeing you delivering or picking up your mail because you come from a country where every phone is tapped. You can drop in, pick up the mail or send a note to anyone on the planet via the college. Better still, if you're particularly paranoid, you can suggest your correspondents go to one of the public libraries that still has e-mail enabled. Not easy to find anymore since most of the old dears shut theirs off when the patrons started stuffing them with junk. You can tap into the system from there. Keep moving around. That way, no one will ever find you."

Connolly had scrolled through the Ws and stopped at the initials WOW.

"History question. Who was the prophet's grandson?"

"Oh come on, Brian," Jay protested.

"Seriously."

Peterson thought for a moment. "Hussein, Hussein bin Ali."

"And he died?"

"Died in 680, no 681 leading a charge against the Caliph Yazid at Karbala."

"Very good. 10 Muharram. Holiest date in the Shiite calendar. Bet you don't know the name of the general's horse."

"Jesus, Brian. It's six a.m. Don't screw around, for Christ's sake!"

"*Ruh al Zal*. A white charger. So, big deal. Your library's keyboard has Arabic characters? Mine sure doesn't. Closest English translation I know is Wind of Wrath. It's his e-mail address."

Jay stared at the initials on the screen under the highlighted bar: WOW. "You're kidding me."

"You should be so lucky. Go ahead. Click on it."

Jay double-clicked on the entry and the file opened. It was a directory arranged alphabetically by location, each town followed by the name of the library, its street and e-mail address. "I don't believe this," Jay said.

"Our friend Saeed has been mailing his buddies at their nearest transmission sites. See. We even have his return address on this last one: Nashua, New Hampshire. I'll bet that's where they hung out before they headed south. Know what else?" Jay shook his head knowing Connolly had saved the best for last. "Next address between Cherry Hill, New Jersey where they had their little gunfight and here? Bethesda, Maryland, home of Lockheed Marietta, the biggest arms manufacturer in the US and principal supplier to the Kingdom of Saudi Arabia. I rest my case." Jay stared at the screen still unable to believe what he was seeing. "By the way," Connolly added as an afterthought. "10 Muharram this year falls on May 4, ten days from now."

CHAPTER 45

Bethesda, Maryland

The day that had begun with a promise of cool air and clear skies had deteriorated by noon into sultry overcast and climbing temperatures. Early lunch-takers in the business district of Washington's northern suburb were sitting out under the cherry blossoms. Drivers had car windows rolled up against the humidity, air-conditioners on.

Exhaustion and heat had taken their toll on Jay Peterson, too. He had ducked out of the proceedings across the street ten minutes before and was stretched out now on the front seat of Karen Goldberg's Chrysler, the air-conditioning blasting. He shielded his eyes from the sunglare off the glass-fronted high-rise opposite with the statistical report handed out by Lockheed's press officer. He felt only a little guilty. Karen, the FBI's chemical hazard co-ordinator, and her assistant were a match for Lockheed Marietta's management. Karen had pretty much ignored the press officer and within the next ten minutes had climbed rapidly up the corporate ladder, pulling in first the director of human resources then senior management. She never actually admitted that their building might have been targeted but she'd shaken them up enough to get their attention. Right now they were scouring the list of recently hired employees, looking for potential flags in the background checks Lockheed routinely ran on anyone new.

The group had been given a "cyber" tour of the building on an office computer showing access points to the water systems and sprinkler systems. Jay preferred the real thing and had left Karen and the others for a tour of the basement. He and the building's engineer spent half an hour figuring how an auxiliary container could in some way be attached to the sprinkler system inside or outside the building and its contents released at the same time the sprinklers were activated. It would call for precise co-ordination. It was too complicated, too hard to execute. The engineer rejoined the group upstairs. Jay went to get a file from Karen's car. He was still there, enjoying the rush of cool air and sorting out the chatter in his mind.

He had handed on Connolly's discovery to Lorenz who had been cautiously enthusiastic. He would get CITAC, the FBI's Computer Investigation and Infrastructure Threat Assessment Centre onto the case right away, Lorenz said. Jay was sanguine, his own enthusiasm dampened now. At best he figured they might get a directory or transmission log. Worst case they were going to pull in another army of Arab speakers emailing Saeed's address. Another dust storm, another diversion. Lorenz had grudgingly agreed to Jay's accompanying Karen and her team on its mission to Lockheed. Another reward, Jay supposed.

He lay back in the passenger seat, trying to answer an obvious but seemingly impenetrable question. Say you wanted to carry out a real attack on a building like this one across the street. You could copycat the World Trade Centre group or Timothy McVeigh and manufacture a truck bomb.

Not in the profile. The weapon of choice was chemical for whatever reason. The provenance? Russia? Iraq? Did that tell them something about the group's intention? Why VX under pressure? It was much more effective in water. A drop even in suspension on a subject's skin, Felicia Smith had said, could suffocate a victim almost instantaneously, too rapidly for any chance of intervention. The sprinkler system was already ruled out, the plumbing required making it too cumbersome. Water coolers? Fresh or grey water systems? Jay tried to see it from the terrorists' viewpoint, factor out what was not even realistic, concentrate on what was actually practical.

His attention drifted to the traffic. It was a token of just how little his father had left him. He had an early memory of the two of them by the road, Jay's arm stretched upwards to the big hand enveloping his, his father calling out the makes of the cars that went by. Jay found himself doing it now, thinking how most people knew the names of more cars than they did of trees or birds. A red BMW, tinted windows closed, went by too fast for the time of day and number of people about, a bass rhythm thumping from its interior. A couple of outsize sports utility vehicles with women drivers perched high on the driver's seat. Then a camper, a Winnebago, coming by more slowly, almost too slowly. The driver's window was down, the man's arm hanging casually over the door, the other hand relaxed on top of the wheel. The man kept switching his attention from the road to the parking lot. As the camper came along the line to Karen's car its driver caught sight of Jay. Their eyes met for a moment, the face of the driver registering a flash of recognition, the almond shape of the man's face contracting slightly in concentration, a livid scar by his eye showing against the darker skin. Arab, thought

Jay instinctively, the crop of unruly black hair, the dark shadow of a beard. The driver scrutinised Jay for a second more, the eyes steady, the face calm. There was no malice there, only deep curiosity, an almost animal intensity. Then the camper accelerated, taking the corner in a tight turn. Just before the vehicle disappeared around the blind side of the building Jay caught sight of a bearded, dark-browed man riding shotgun. He held a camcorder to one eye, the lens pointed upwards to record the upper floors of the Lockheed building. Then Jay caught sight of the license plate. The rear of the camper was at too sharp an angle to see the letters and numbers but there was no mistaking the state identification, Virginia.

Jay pulled himself into the driver's seat, cursing as he fumbled the ignition key into the steering column, trying to unlock it, taking it out again, reinserting it. He shifted into drive and was about to accelerate when the yellow side of a school bus filled the windshield. He leaned on the horn but the bus had come to a full stop at the light. He looked in the rear-view mirror. A car blocked his exit. He cut the engine, pushed the door open and took off down the street at a run. By the time he reached the intersection, the light had changed and the camper was gone. He stood for another moment, suddenly aware of the oppressive noon heat and the close air after the cool of the car's interior, seeing again the man's face through the open window. And it suddenly fell into place.

Karen's group had expanded to six when Jay burst into the tenth floor conference room. "Karen, I need to see you. And you, sir," he indicated the building's engineer.

Karen didn't miss a beat. "Would you excuse me a moment, folks. Seems we have a crisis." There was a murmur from the group but no move to follow the three of them from the room.

"Where's the air-conditioning plant?" Jay queried the engineer.

"Second floor," the man replied.

In the elevator Karen commented dryly: "Word is that you have an impulsive nature Jay Peterson. Seems the word was wrong. I would say tumultuous, catastrophic, explosive maybe. What's it this time?"

"Better if we wait till we're there," Jay said.

In the second floor utility room, the air-conditioning generator for the building took up most of the space, ducts leading from its top upwards and sideways like branches from a tree. For all its size, the generator ran surprisingly quietly.

"Can you override the building's climate from here? Any floor?" Jay asked.

"Sure," the engineer said the confusion obvious in his face.

"Can you lock it once you set it?"

"I guess," the man said. "Why would you want to do that?"

"Karen, can I talk to you for a moment?" Jay asked. They moved away from the man, Jay leading. "We're looking at a potential nerve agent attack," he began needlessly. "I've been sitting in your car trying to figure why they would choose an agent known for its peculiar property of being soluble in water. VX is not volatile and not easy to vaporise. So why go to the trouble? Say you did vaporise it, stored it in small gas cylinders, something very sturdy but portable, something quite ordinary like a tyre re-inflator or a fire extinguisher. How do you disperse the contents without becoming a victim?" Karen didn't answer. Jay demonstrated. "You puncture one of these ducts, the central one for preference, insert your nozzle or tube, seal the joint and release the gas. You leave it running while you lock down the air-conditioner to the lowest temperature. Result? The cooler air carrying the vaporised particles of the gas will condense once it hits the warmer air of the rooms its cooling, the agent air reconstituting as liquid and killing on contact. In the three or four minutes it will take the vapour to travel to its destination, you make your exit by the emergency stairs."

Karen Goldberg's face was ashen. The morning had been spent in academic discussion, outlining necessary precautions, trying to co-ordinate adequate responses, allotting space for decontamination units. The theoretical had suddenly become real, ugly and mechanical.

"Sir?" Jay said to the engineer standing by the open door of the utility room. The man turned. "Who maintains this equipment? Is a permanent staff assigned?"

The engineer shook his head. "We got a real good deal from an outside contractor. Made good sense. They guaranteed parts and labour. Haven't had any trouble so far this season."

"Who's the contractor?"

"Patuxent Industries, place the other side of the river. I've got the paperwork upstairs."

Karen pulled out her phone and began dialling.

CHAPTER 46

Washington D.C.

The parking lot looked smaller on the screen. The camera had shown it from ground level, from overhead, from in amongst the thicket of cars, trucks and uniforms. Last night the dark expanse of blacktop seemed to extend to infinity.

Saeed and Lis Charnay had watched the CNN report of the double killing three times on the portable television Saeed had brought from New Hampshire. Nothing she saw corresponded to the horror of the events she had lived.

Nasir had pulled the hood over her head as soon as the exchange to the camper had been completed and she had dutifully lain on the floor as instructed. There, she had initiated her own small rebellion. When Nasir, pulling off the hood, proffered the charged needle and the tourniquet she nodded acknowledgement then surreptitiously discharged most of the contents on the floor beside her, out of the man's sight. She had tied her arm as before, pumping up the vein then inserted the needle, drawing out the blood and pushing what little was left of the morphine into her. She would pay for her resistance she knew, but the killing had hardened her, burned off whatever sympathy she might have felt for her companions, whatever she had left for herself. She lay for three hours, four, the time didn't matter, the drone of the transmission at her ear. She tried to fix her attention on the sound, tried to ignore the writhing in her gut, the trembling in her hands, sucking on the inside of the hood, biting down on her finger to stop herself crying out. At last she slept, woke again as the camper slowed. The heavy rush of traffic that had swept them along the turnpike had diminished. They were still moving but slowly and intermittently. Her mouth was dry, her body drenched in sweat. She felt empty, light-headed. The air in the van was hot. She slipped the hem of the hood up over her mouth trying to free her breathing, not daring to raise herself. The van rolled to a stop. Doors opened. Warm air flooded the compartment. A hand pulled her upright, straightening the hood, guided her up stairs, brought her to this room. Saeed had taken off the hood then fetched her water. She had drunk it quickly then retched it up again. Nasir had come with his medicine kit, prepared the dose, then let her inject herself in the adjoining bathroom. He hadn't even bothered to stay and watch. She had shot the contents into the sink.

She sat on the battered couch now, Saeed beside her. She clutched a pillow to her to control the trembling, chewing on its corner the way she had on the hood. They watched the news for the fourth time. At least she knew what day it was, what time it was, that the clockwork of the world was running on. If Saeed would change to a local station she would even know where she was.

The latest CNN live report revisited last night's scene, a wide-angle view of the restaurant area in the morning light. The sequence cut to Bob Lorenz, his bulk suddenly filling the screen. He seemed to be reaching out to every viewer beyond the lens, trying to reassure them that he was personally in control, that the "scum" who had perpetrated this outrage were in his sights. Lis found herself leaning forward, willing Lorenz to see her. Saeed sat at the other end of the sofa toying with the cell phone. It was their sole means of communication with the outside world at present, Saeed's computer still packed up and waiting on the loading dock below. The remote lay between them.

Saeed was transfixed. Lis couldn't tell if he was fascinated or horrified, whether the images on the screen were real to him or some fiction that hadn't yet touched him. The report cut away from Lorenz and back to a pretty blond girl. She reported four people were wanted for questioning in connection with the killings. The anchor's face was superseded by a succession of four grainy headshots: Mahmoud's, Saeed's, Nasir's then Lis's. Saeed turned to Lis with a shy grin, a hint of embarrassment, a shadow of fear present.

"They'll get us sooner or later. You know that, Saeed, don't you. And that'll be the end. For all of us. For you, for me. You killed one of theirs, see. They won't spare any of us."

By slow degrees she extracted some history from him, learning about his younger sisters, his mother back home in Riyadh. She directed him away from the easy recitation of dogma where he was safe to the more unsettling areas of future plans, what his mother would think of him if he went back. He became angry, saying it didn't matter. She knew she had hit a nerve, continued to work at it, to pick away, to pressure him, switching from English into her faltering Arabic then back into English.

"They'll abandon you," she told him. "I've seen it happen." She hadn't. "It's classic. The young man with the future is the first to be sacrificed, the first to be jettisoned when

310

things start to go wrong. Things are going wrong; you know that, don't you. Ali's plans are really out of control."

Her comment produced a flash of defensive anger from Saeed. "You don't know," he snapped. "You have no idea what Ali Hussein has done. He is a genius."

"Tell me Saeed," she prompted. "I'm sure you're right. What has he done? He seems very capable, smart like you."

Saeed watched her carefully, knowing she was trying to trap him but at the same time anxious to share his admiration for Ali. "Ali Hussein will not desert me. He is a true brother. You cannot know, you could never know."

"Because, what? Because I'm a woman?" Lis said.

Saeed said nothing, looking at her much the way he had looked at her the first time they had met at Khuda Bax's, a mixture of longing and bravado. Now there was that hint of doubt in his face, a suspicion of fear. "Because you do not know this man."

"I'd like to," she said. "I find him very interesting. We got talking before everything went wrong last night. He told me a lot." Saeed kept watching her, distrustful as much of himself as of her, fingering the phone then putting it down next to the remote as if it might give him away. "Is he from Riyadh, too?" she asked, trying to make the question as innocent as possible.

But Saeed ignored her, turning back to the television and a commercial for weekend specials at a hotel chain. She fell silent too, her attention shifting from the television to the cell phone then back to the screen again.

There was noise of an arrival downstairs followed by a rapid outburst in Arabic. Ali was back and giving rapid instructions to Nasir. Lis tried to keep up but got only a little of what was being said. They were going to have to move. Things had changed. Ali asked where Saeed was and Saeed sprang up from the couch without being called.

She heard Nasir say: "What about her?" Ali Hussein didn't answer, began giving instructions to Saeed, a list of names, Arabic names, then suddenly in the clear as if spoken by someone else a single English word, "Atlanta." Whatever had happened during Ali Hussein's absence had triggered a new course of action. They seemed to have taken the events of last night in their stride, shrugged them off. This was something else, something or someone Ali Hussein had come across while he had been absent. It was time for them to act.

Lis looked down again at the cell phone knowing that even if she could turn it on without them hearing, she might never have time to say enough before Nasir, it would be him, appeared in the doorway. She had no choice. Her hand reached down, picking up the remote instead, changing from CNN to the music channel, VHF, her finger pumping up the volume, just enough she hoped to cover the sound of the phone being switched on, not enough to raise suspicion. She couldn't wait to find out, turning the phone on, the beep sounding painfully loud as the service activated. She paused a second only, listening to the voices downstairs, changed channels again, this time to "Baywatch," a favourite in Iran she had read, and punched in a number as rapidly as she could, the number he had given her in Paris praying now it was the right one, praying he wouldn't be home to answer.

Her hand was shaking again, the palm clammy with sweat, the withdrawal beginning to take over. The phone rang three times. And then, faintly under her hand, she heard Jay's voice, matter-of-fact, to the point, and the voices below growing louder as their owners climbed the stairs. "Leave a message I'll get back to you" then the beep sounding like a siren to Lis. She put down the phone, still on, still connected to Jay's answerphone. The voices were outside the door. The light on the phone. The red light was lit. She pushed the phone behind the cushions, pulling her hand out again just as Nasir came in, Ali Hussein behind him.

"I was watching the news," she said. Her voice sounded shrill. "I don't think they know where we are."

Ali Hussein looked at the television trying to reconcile the scantily dressed figures on the screen with what Lis was telling him then said in English: "Turn it off. We are leaving."

"Where are we going?" she asked, her tone still unnaturally bright, not obeying his order right away. "No point in asking, I guess, since I don't really know where we are. Baltimore maybe?" She tried being cute but her fear undercut her and the question came out sounding apologetic. Ali Hussein made no reply. "Do you know, Nasir?" she questioned. She knew she was overdoing it now, could hear the rising hysteria in her voice but she couldn't stop. "Did Ali tell you? Or does he keep secrets from you too?" she babbled. "I don't think Hussein's even his real name, do you? I've been thinking about that. I've had lots of time to think, you see, and Ali Hussein is like John Doe. It could be anyone . . ."

Nasir's hand swung hard across her cheek, the ring on his finger cutting her lip as it connected with her mouth. She gasped, recoiling against the side of the couch. Nasir said nothing, looking to Ali Hussein for instructions.

"She cannot stay here," he said. "Get her ready." Nasir grunted leaving the room. He was going for the needle.

"Please don't," she pleaded. "Please. I don't even mind

the hood anymore, Ali. Not the needle, not again." Nasir was back in the doorway, moving towards her, the syringe held erect in his right hand. "Please," she screamed. "Please, no." And then the room went black.

CHAPTER 47

Washington D.C.

There were four people ahead of Mahmoud in the line at the Delta check-in. An elderly woman at the front was battling with the clerk over a ticket issued for tomorrow's flight. She wanted the reservation changed to tonight. Directly in front of him, a mother and her two young boys were fussing over which toys would be kept out, which toys packed. Mahmoud was a patient man. He could wait.

They had abandoned the camper at the Montrose Metro, he and Ali coolly walking away from the vehicle as if it had been their own, locking the doors, throwing the keys in the trash. On the train heading into the centre of Washington D.C., Ali had passed him a quantity of money that Mahmoud had taken, placing it in his pocket without looking. He had accepted the small Adidas sports bag too and set it at his feet. Then Ali had explained his assignment, his voice low, the guttural Arabic purring in Mahmoud's ear. He was to go to National Airport, buy a round-trip ticket to Atlanta. Be sure it is round-trip, Ali insisted. Round-trip, Mahmoud repeated dutifully. Ali Hussein paused several times in his recitation, taking the time to observe other passengers then returned to his briefing. Mahmoud should use the new driver's license that Saeed had manufactured for him. If anyone should ask him he was to say he was an office equipment sales consultant visiting Islamic Centres in Atlanta and its suburbs. Stay at the Ramada Hotel, Ali said. I will make the reservation. Mahmoud nodded his big head again. He felt sure of himself, at peace. Saeed was a clever man with his computers and modems. Mahmoud turned the shiny, laminated Massachusetts license over in his hands, read his new name, Mansoor bin Musalim, traced the outline of his altered face in the photograph. Mahmoud had reluctantly trimmed his beard to correspond to the digitally altered face on the driver's license. He could not bring himself to shave it entirely.

He had parted from Ali at Metro Center, Ali going on to the Navy Yard stop, Mahmoud changing onto the Yellow line to National Airport. Before they separated Ali explained the safety device on the flower-decked aerosol can marked "Air Freshener/Désodoriseur" that Mahmoud carried in his bag along with the small extinguisher bearing the yellow "Demonstration Only/Inert" sticker Saeed had printed. Pull the plastic cap off the aerosol and depress the button on top. He should do this only in an emergency. It was quite safe otherwise. His contact in Atlanta would explain the rest. Mahmoud must buy a suitcase, Ali said. It didn't have to be large. He could buy it at the airport. Buy some sweatshirts, some books. Give the bag weight. Men travelling alone without bags are suspect. Do not be nervous, Ali said finally. Allah in his grace protects all his children.

Mahmoud looked down at his new case now, a black Samsonite. It was really quite handsome. Around him were other signs of wealthy extravagance, signs Mahmoud by now knew well. Stores, expensive clothes. The women he was still unused to and his eyes followed the bared legs and exposed cleavages of two young women as they passed. His look held a mixture of longing and disgust, regret and reproach. They ignored his stare and hurried on towards the small crowd gathering at the other end of the concourse.

The political animal is by nature and instinct a performance artist. The powerful Senator Aaron Starks, chairman of the Senate Intelligence Sub-Committee convened to investigate the attack three weeks before on the Truman, was not short of an audience now. The cameras and "sun" lights of three different networks surrounded him, reporters asking for clarification on a rumour probably put out by his office earlier that had called for the suspension of Assistant Director Robert Lorenz.

"Director Lorenz says he has a firm lead on the New Jersey perpetrators' whereabouts. Do you have any comment, Senator?"

"Bob Lorenz is a good cop," Starks drawled making the compliment sound like an insult. "If he can't bring them in, we have to call in someone who can."

"Any substance, sir, to the allegation that this group is the same that attacked the Truman."

Starks bristled. "I should remind you that my committee prosecuted a complete investigation of that outrage. Our findings were conclusive. The men responsible were apprehended and taken care of by our good friends the Saudis. End of story. Now gentlemen, I have a plane to catch."

"Senator, Senator . . ." Starks made a move towards his gate trailing press and staff in his wake but then stopped, unable to resist one more question, one more look in the public mirror. The question was lost in the confusion.

*

The old woman at the front of Delta's line had been assuaged, her money taken and a place secured for her on the 8:25 flight to Atlanta. Now the young mother and her restless boys were at the desk, the clerk checking the three bags, assigning seats. Mahmoud looked round him again, spotting the Emergency Services police for the first time, noting their body armour and riot helmets. The men carried automatic weapons at the ready. One of them returned his stare then looked away. Mahmoud felt a small worm of fear that he had not felt before, a tweak of apprehension. He fixed his eyes on the back of the woman in front of him. Ali had said there was no need to be nervous. He would not be nervous.

The woman gathered her tickets from the counter, grabbed the hand of a child in each of hers and headed towards the Atlanta gate. The Senator's ad hoc press conference was still in progress. It was eight fifteen, ten minutes till the flight.

"Next?"

Mahmoud pushed the suitcase towards the desk with his foot, the sports bag held gingerly under his arm. "I do not have a ticket," he explained in precise but accented English. "I wish to purchase a round-trip ticket to Atlanta."

"I'm sorry, sir. You'll have to go to Customer Services to purchase a ticket; this is for ticketed passengers only."

"A ticket," he insisted. "I wish to purchase a ticket."

"I understand, sir. If you'd just step over to your right one of my colleagues will take care of you." The clerk motioned to a desk three positions down.

"Next!"

"Wait," Mahmoud said shouldering the man behind him

back. "I wish to purchase a ticket for Atlanta. Tonight. I must fly tonight."

The worm of fear had grown in Mahmoud's stomach, the thought beginning to grow in him that he might miss the flight, might miss the appointment Ali had arranged, might disappoint Ali Hussein.

"Ben?" The woman called for assistance. A tall black man joined the clerk behind the desk. "This gentleman wants to buy a ticket. I've tried to explain he needs to go to Customer Service. I don't seem to be getting through."

Ben took quick stock of the situation and Mahmoud's mood. "Where are you flying to, sir?"

"Atlanta please."

"One way?"

"Round-trip, round-trip," Mahmoud insisted.

"When would this be for, sir?"

"For eight twenty five" Mahmoud said desperately, his eyes on the clock above the desk. "Very soon."

"Would this be Economy or Club, sir."

"Club is good," Mahmoud said.

Ben to his professional credit made no effort to dampen the blow when he announced the price. "That's going to be eight hundred fifty five dollars, sir. How will you be paying?"

Mahmoud drew the bills from his pocket and began to count carefully, the action forcing him to place the sports bag between his feet. The two clerks exchanged a glance then Ben said: "Do you have some form of ID, sir? A driver's license? We're going to need that for security." Mahmoud was still counting and preferred to ignore the question for the moment. "Sir?" Ben repeated.

The scene had begun to attract mild interest from customers on either side of Mahmoud. Mahmoud finished counting the fifty-dollar bills onto the counter top, replacing the roll in the jacket of his slightly outsize brown suit.

"The ID, sir?" Ben asked again.

"I will give it," Mahmoud said his usual careful manner suddenly abrupt. "It is always hurry with you people, hurry, hurry." He extracted the newly minted card from his jacket pocket and laid it on the counter along with the cash.

"Go ahead, Mary Ellen," Ben said. "Sorry to keep you waiting, folks. I can help someone over here." He went back to his position, picking up the phone on the desk as he waited for the first of Mary Ellen's customers to follow him over.

Mahmoud watched the man talk briefly into the receiver. The worm growing bigger now, flopping backwards and forwards. He had no way of stilling it, no way of quieting his fear. All around him were foreigners. They spoke a language he only half understood. There was a vocabulary of hidden exchanges, of secret looks and whispered hints that set him apart. Most of all he feared he would fail in his duty. Death he did not fear. Death was a welcome reunion. Failure was a permanent separation, an eternal exile.

"There you are, sir," the clerk said skipping the usual security interrogation and handing Mahmoud his ticket, boarding pass and luggage check attached. "Your bag's checked through to Atlanta. Boarding now through security to Gate Fourteen."

Mahmoud said nothing, taking the ticket and stooping to recover his overnight bag with its deadly contents. He started towards the security gate, aware of the two policemen again and, beyond, Senator Starks' entourage. Mahmoud shuffled past the police, placing his bag carefully on the security scanner's conveyor as requested but passing too quickly through the gate. The alarm sounded.

"Go through again please," the Indian security guard said.

Mahmoud was slow to react, understanding her meaning but preoccupied with the commotion in his gut, his energies and attention divided. He stepped back, bumping into one of the policemen behind. The man raised a protective arm to prevent him falling. Mahmoud half-turned, then stepped forward, steadying himself on the security gate. The alarm sounded again.

His sports bag had passed through the scanner now and another of the guards had collected it from the end of the belt, setting it apart on a carpeted table-top, one hand on the clasp to open it. Mahmoud reacted without hesitation. He continued through the gate, the female guard protesting, holding up a hand to prevent him. The cops behind Mahmoud shifted their weapons, their attention now full on him. In the domed concourse beyond, the Senator's party was moving again, the mother and her two children emerging from the gift shop and headed for the gate. Mahmoud reached for his bag.

"I have to look inside, sir," the man said resisting Mahmoud.

The animal inside Mahmoud bit down. He yanked the bag from the guard's grasp clutching it to his chest and headed down the concourse, at first striding out then, when the shouting began behind him, breaking into a shuffling run, seeing in his mind some place ahead where he could begin again, set everything straight.

A uniformed figure separated from the crowd further

down the concourse, then another. A woman screamed, a man behind a coffee stand ducked, people were scattering anywhere. Others watched open-mouthed. He was almost at the boarding area for Gate Fourteen, parallel with Senator Starks. The news crews turned, the lights on their cameras blinding him momentarily, throwing a monstrous shadow of his running body against the wall behind. Then came the first shot, a crack of gunfire from behind, then a second. The first round whined past his ear, the sounds coming together. A huge panel of glass twenty yards ahead of him exploded in a cascade of shimmering light. The second shot ripped through his chest, twisting him round and pitching him forwards. The spinning bullet continued through Mahmoud's body, through the thin fabric of the Adidas bag just missing the containers inside, out through Mahmoud's hand clamped to the bag, finally smacking into a neat display of best-sellers on the cart outside the concourse's bookstore, the round lodging in the bull's-eye under the book's title: *Carrier Attack*.

Mahmoud was falling, hearing Ali's instructions clearly now. His confidence rallied, the beast was back in its cage. He fumbled in the bag at his chest, breaking the plastic protector on the aerosol as Ali Hussein had instructed, pressing down hard and never hearing the crack of the detonator in the can and the subsequent explosion as his lifeless body hit the grey carpet and his contented soul rose lightly to a martyr's heaven.

CHAPTER 48

Washington D.C.

Jay opened the door to his apartment, kicking the junk mail away from the threshold. The place smelled damp, stale. He threw off his jacket, thought about running, thought twice, then pulled the last beer from the icebox. He sank onto the couch, screwing the top off the beer and taking a first mouthful. At least it was cold. He stared across the room at the poster of Jeddah, the Red Sea resort where he and Dana had spent a weekend at the government's expense. The white of the buildings in the picture was stained yellow and red by the streetlights outside and the slow winking light from his answering machine by the door. Lis would love Jeddah. He took another chug of beer.

It had taken Karen Goldberg and Jay forty minutes to get back to Washington. They might have crossed the emergency units heading out towards Lockheed but they didn't see any on the way in. At the office it only took them a minute to realise something more than a national alert was in progress. Marvin Frost, Lorenz's deputy, met them at the elevator. He ignored Jay, fixing his attention on Karen. Lorenz had stepped down temporarily, executive order, he said grimly. Frost was taking over for the interim. Nothing had changed. Same order of the day. Karen Goldberg followed Frost into his office leaving Jay to head back to the bull pen.

"Did you hear?" Cohen asked.

"What's going on?"

"Change of command. Someone's been swinging a bat in the Oval Office. Bob got hit."

"Why?"

"No one knows. Frost just gave us a business as usual and told us to go on doing whatever we were doing."

"Where's Bob?"

"Home, I guess."

Cohen brought him up to date on what he, Barron, Frankel and Amor had put together in the course of the morning. Ali Fatta Hussein could be any one of thirty or forty different hits they had made in their cross-referencing. There had been several Afghan-Arabs, all of them dead, a couple of local dissidents in Saudi Arabia's Shiite provinces, some politically active Arabs in the US.

"What about the UN?"

"Nothing so far. It's going to take a while. Probably a forged passport. Same with the driver's license. We did get something on the Nashua location before Frost pretty much cut us off."

"What?"

"They ran down the house. Fancy place west of town. Belongs to an economics professor at the University of New Hampshire. House is empty. He's on sabbatical in the Middle East. A Saudi no less. They're going over it right now for prints and stuff. No one there." Cohen's eyes said 'no bodies.'

"Jay?" It was one of Lorenz's aides. At least they hadn't cleaned out Bob's staff too.

"Yeah?"

"Marvin wants one of you, an Arab speaker, to make the run to Patuxent Industries. In case they need a translator." Usually, when one of the analysts was sent, they did no more than stand at the back while the agent in charge grilled the subjects through local interpreters, a friend or relative. This time Jay didn't mind going at all.

"I'll be right there," he said.

There were three of them in the car: Jay, the driver and the investigator, a man called Berk, a transfer from the Atlanta office. They made the trip out to Patuxent Industries, out beyond what was now the US-Air sports stadium, in heavy traffic. It wasn't till they got to the company's address on an industrial estate just outside the Beltway that they found out they could have covered the interview by phone. There had been two new employees, the service manager confirmed; two months ago and five months ago. One was on a job in Virginia, wasn't expected back tonight, the other had been fired a month ago. Home addresses and phone numbers were taken, cards exchanged and the team returned to Washington, back through the same heavy traffic now going the other way.

At the office he called Bob's home, got an answerphone, called Barbara, got another machine. He put his head round a couple of doors but got nothing back. Lorenz's demise was sudden and mysterious. No one who knew wanted to tell, no one else wanted to know. By five thirty he was ready to quit. Then Sam Clemens had called.

"You hear about Bob?" Jay asked.

"Yup," Clemens replied noncommittally. "We've got

some business down in the south-east and I wondered if you wanted to come along for the ride. I won't be driving if it makes any difference."

Half an hour later he and Clemens were sitting in the rear seat of another Chevy Suburban, part of a mini-convoy led by an unmarked Bureau car. The middle vehicle carried the hazardous materials specialists, the HazMat team, one of Karen Goldberg's modules. Their own truck brought up the rear. It was an armoury on wheels. A rack of seven M-16s, three MP-5 submachine guns, a 12-gauge shotgun, two M-79 grenade launchers, tear-gas equipment, ammunition, bullet-proof vests, helmets and shields with the agency insignia were stowed in the cargo hold, a wire-mesh grille separating it from the passenger area.

"I thought you said we were just going to talk to this guy," Jay said as they climbed in over the tough looking agent in the back.

"That's right. It's just he may not want to talk to us."

"The Patuxent guy from Virginia?"

"Yup."

No more had been said as they drove the short distance from the FBI garages to the industrial area on the Anacostia River not far from Jay's townhouse apartment. The silence was broken only by the occasional radio chatter and some muttered conference between the driver and his companion over the route they were taking. When they reached the address in Half Street, Jay spotted two agency cars already in place. They were taking no chances.

"You'd better stay here by the truck," Sam said as the other agents readied their equipment. "Insurance," he grinned.

"They're not here are they?"

"We don't think so. If she's in there I'll make sure she gets out okay."

Jay was expecting a battering ram charge. Instead, one of the agents who had been waiting for them simply rang the bell. After a minute, when no one answered, one of the team approached the door with a crowbar. He was saved the trouble by a surprised tenant returning from work. Three minutes after that Sam radioed from the apartment.

"Nothing. I'm coming down," he said.

He and Clemens stood off to one side of the small crowd that had gathered across from the apartment. News crews would be next.

"So, what happened?" Jay asked.

"To Bob? Word is it was a power-play. Enrico got Senator Aaron Starks behind him. Bob said they stormed the White House and took the President hostage, if you know what I mean."

"Have you talked to him?"

Clemens nodded. "He said he could handle this. He'll be in touch."

Jay had left Sam and walked to his apartment from Half Street to survey the ruins of the day alone. Now, he tipped the dark green bottle back and let the last of the cold beer run down his throat. He set it on the floor. The least he could do was check the answerphone. He pushed the play button and listened to the tape rewinding all the way from the end, the lower tone of the outgoing message interspersed with the higher tone of the messages. Jay walked to the kitchen, opening the refrigerator door to see if there was anything else he could plunder. The machine started to play out its recordings, a hang up, Connolly's voice telling him to call, another hang up, then a conversation not a message. Several voices, muffled, one close to the phone the others further away, the conversation cutting between Arabic and English, a television playing in the background.

"I was watching the news. I don't think they know where we are."

He couldn't believe it. It was Lis's voice. He listened transfixed, staring into the lit interior of the refrigerator as if he were seeing a re-enactment there of what he was hearing on the tape.

"Turn it off. We are leaving." A man's voice in English, accented.

Jay ran the few steps to the phone table, standing over the machine as if Lis might miraculously rise from it at any moment. "No point in asking, I guess, since I don't really know where we are. Baltimore maybe? Do you know, Nasir? Did Ali tell you?" She was incredible. Jay had no idea how she could have got the message out, how she could be calling him. He picked up the phone, thanking the phone company for pushing yet another service on him he didn't need: dial back. He punched in *69 and as he did heard a click. It was an incoming call on Call Waiting, another one of his option packages. He hit the flash button.

"Yes?"

"Turn on your TV." It was Jeff Cohen.

"Why?"

"Just turn on your TV." Cohen hung up.

The answering machine was still playing, Lis saying: "I

don't think Hussein's even his real name, do you? I've been thinking about that. I've had lots of time, you see, and Ali Hussein is like John Doe. It could be anyone . . ."

There was the sound of a slap, a hand hitting down hard, a half cry. She was with them, with Nasir, with Hussein and she was alive. Jay pressed the stop button, then *69 again.

"Jeff Cohen."

"Jeff?"

"Jay? Did you see it?"

Jay slammed the phone down, tried again. The feature would only dial back the last number that had called. It couldn't be, he thought. He had to be able to retrieve the number. He hit *69 again.

"Jeff Cohen."

"Who's our phone guy? Who knows phones?"

"Did you see?"

"See what, Jeff? For Christ's sake, who's the Bureau's phone guy? Who do I call?"

"Jesus, Jay. I don't know. Just look at the fucking TV."

It was Cohen's turn to slam the phone down. Jay dialled the operator, at the same time picking up the remote and turning on the TV in the corner. CNN came on, a night view from above. Jay recognised the Potomac, National Airport. He cut the connection, the phone still in his hand.

The shot was from a helicopter looking down on the airport. A banner flashed across the lower corner of the screen: Live. Now a reporter was speaking over the roar of the helicopter, the camera zooming in on the blur of red flashing lights round the terminal. Flights cancelled, Jay heard. No indication of numbers yet, area sealed. Then the angle changed. A live shot of another reporter on the scene but someway off, the snarl of emergency vehicles behind her, and, moving among them, the white clownish chemical suits Jay had seen earlier that afternoon, the HazMat teams, scores of them. Oh God, he thought. Oh my God. They did it.

The phone rang, startling him.

"Peterson," he said.

"Jay?" It was Clemens.

"Did you see?"

"Yes."

"How many?"

"We won't know till they start bringing out the bodies. I'm not on it. That's why I'm calling."

"What do you mean?" Jay said.

"This afternoon after we'd gone, they went over the apartment. There was a phone pushed under the cushions on the sofa. Still on, with your number on the digital display. We ran it for prints. It's her Jay. They're her prints. She was there."

CHAPTER 49

Washington D.C.

The heart of the city had stopped beating, its pulse a reflex only. Restaurants had emptied, stores closed. Flights into and out of National Airport had been shut down minutes after the attack and were not scheduled to resume. Washingtonians gathered round television sets, huddled in living rooms, sealed windows with tape, closed doors, stuffed towels underneath. Fire you could see, smell the smoke. This insidious creeping enemy was unlike anything the city had experienced and it was not reacting well.

The Situations Room at the White House was alight. No one on the President's staff had actually said it out loud but there was little more the Chief Executive could do at present than figure out what to say to America and to say it well. The Pentagon was mobilising scattered specialists with expertise in chemical and biological warfare, the networks rounding up their own teams of pundits to speculate on how, when and where the terrorists might strike next. With no responsibility claimed for the attack at National, these instant analysts were free to assign blame where they wanted. Iran, Iraq, and Syria received their share of votes as most likely sponsor. Saudi Arabia was not mentioned. Revenge was cited most often as a motive, the imprisonment of Ramze Yousef,

the World Trade bomber, the most frequently touted provo-
cation.

On the polished floor of the main concourse at Ronald
Reagan National Airport the men and women of the bio-
chemical containment teams in their outsize white chemical
suits vacuumed up every particle of moisture, every drop of
liquid, drained receptacles of standing water, emptied food
carts, cleared the shelves of surrounding stores. The great hall
echoed with the squeak of rubber soles and the hum of equipment. Forty three bodies had already been removed, men,
women and children continuing their interrupted journeys in
waterproof body-bags, labelled by relative position to the per-
petrator, the mother and her two sons who had preceded
Mahmoud to the gate, leaving separately. Senator Starks had
struggled halfway down the jetway towards the plane that
should have carried him to Atlanta, his undignified exit
recorded for posterity by the news cameras. Their random
footage after their operators had succumbed and dropped
their apparatus would play and replay Mahmoud's final dash
and its hellish consequences to the nation's viewers.
Mahmoud himself still lay protectively over his sports bag,
one arm tucked underneath his prostrate body, his head
pushed forward, chin out as if he were flying low across the
carpet. A transparent balloon tent brightly lit by a high-
intensity halogen lamp at each corner had been installed over
him, sealing off his body and the contents of his bag from the
surrounding area. He had become an exotic still life, a bizarre
exhibit, agents in protective clothing moving in slow and
cautious motion around him.

In the analysts' bull pen at a besieged FBI headquarters, a
small group was gathered round a computer screen, their

backs towards the muted televisions in the corner. They were studying a schema of North America with principal cities and major industrial conglomerations shaded in and an overlay of the sites of the transmitting libraries that Connolly had recovered from Saeed's electronic mailbox. Another graphic showed the headquarters of principal arms manufacturers, military bases and strategic planning centres in the US, many of them in and around Washington D.C.

"It's kind of crude," Cohen apologised.

"Looks fine to me," said Brian Connolly. The professor had been invited back into the fold by Marvin Frost who reckoned he needed all the help he could get. Just as long as Lorenz stayed where he was. He was seated across the aisle from Cohen's booth, his feet up on the desk idly shuffling through Jay's still unopened mail. Jay was standing, one arm draped over the wall of Cohen's booth as if this were just another day at the office. "I don't know how you stay so calm, boy," Connolly said. "Gives me the willies."

The analysts were insulated now from the escalating chaos in the corridors outside. Frenzy in SIOC, the command centre, had risen to a point that even simple communication was becoming hard. Marvin Frost was rapidly approaching paralysis and Bob Lorenz's staff, leaderless now, were cancelling out each other's efforts. The gap they had begun to narrow between themselves and their target in the course of the afternoon had stretched out to breaking.

"I got these for you." Jay turned to find Sam Clemens at his side. He passed over two sheets of paper listing the calls made from Saeed's cell-phone. "They already have units on the way to the long-distance locations. The general opinion out there," Clemens said with a backward nod of his head to the turmoil outside, "is that this could pretty much crack the case. They think the phone numbers belong to the individual cells. Kind of a straight shot."

Jay nodded then passed them onto Cohen. "Why don't you plug these into the map too." He turned back to Clemens. "Any analysis of the voice tape yet?" he asked.

"It's pretty much what we expected," Clemens said. "Timing of background, the TV program, the planes overhead all check out."

Jay had listened to the tape over and over before handing it on to the lab technicians for analysis. He tried to think about her in the abstract as a piece of the puzzle, tried to follow Ali Hussein's logic. Lis was alive and she was alive for a reason. The terrorist group had dragged her all the way from Paris, rather he had, Ali. And there was a real reason behind it, just as there was behind everything else he planned. Lis had met Khuda Bax, knew Saeed. They had tortured Khuda Bax before they had killed him. Why? What information did they need from Khuda Bax? Surely Ali Hussein knew most of what Khuda Bax knew, the route, the connections. Or didn't he? Ali himself was still an unknown, a blank. So was his plan. He had walked away from the massacre on the turnpike, from the safe-house in Anacostia, from the planned assault on Lockheed without looking back. Jay remembered the animal intensity of the look the man in the camper had given him. Was that Ali? Jay had spent time that afternoon with one of the Bureau's artists trying to recreate the face on computer. They had reached what Jay thought to be a reasonable likeness but when it was printed out it was disappointingly nondescript. It had been circulated anyway.

"Right," Cohen's voice interrupted. "Let's see what we've

got." The laser printer on the table across the aisle whirred then fed out an oversize colour print of what they could see on Cohen's monitor.

"Very nice, Jeff," Connolly said on his way back from another visit to the men's room and the packet of Marlboros in his coat pocket. "Which one's Ali?" Cohen gave Connolly a withering look.

"The red concentric circles are an arbitrary thirty-mile radius out from the location of the numbers called from the cell-phone or the library sites. The green dots are the three safe-houses, Boston, Nashua, Anacostia, the blue stars the headquarters of General Dynamics, Hughes, Raytheon and the rest – there's a key at the bottom that tells you who they are. Mahmoud was booked to Atlanta. That could be CNN, I suppose. It was one of the last calls placed. That tells us that other cells have already been armed. At least that's my reasoning."

"Why wouldn't they just air-freight the cans?"

"Could have already," Cohen answered Connolly's question. "But why send a man to the cell in Atlanta then?"

Because Ali was stepping up the program, Jay thought. The sighting at Lockheed had been both a lucky break and a trigger. Ali had dumped the attack on Lockheed just the way he had dumped the bodies at the service area in New Jersey, the way he had dumped the camper. And he had packed off his henchman, Mahmoud, to Atlanta without delay. If Mahmoud screwed up, which he did, what matter? The effect was the same. How many more Mahmouds, how many more containers, fire extinguishers, aerosol bombs? The significance of Atlanta, the headquarters of Coca Cola, was almost too obvious. It didn't fit Cohen's profile of leading arms-manufacturers as targets but it pointed up a pattern too bleak to contemplate. Ali had sleepers in businesses or organisations whose only common thread was the men employed there. Like the two employees at Patuxent Industries.

Barbara, Lorenz's assistant, appeared in the doorway of the bull pen. There was something unusual about her that Jay couldn't place for a moment. Then he got it. She wasn't wearing her telephone headset.

"He'd better not see you here," she said to Connolly as she reached them.

"Don't tell me Lorenz is back," Connolly said going back to picking through Jay's mail. Barbara turned back to Jay and Cohen. "Marv's not going to e-mail you all till the morning so I thought I'd better let you know right away since you're still here. The phone numbers? They're business centres. They're running them down now for customer receipts and eye-witness but it's going to take time. I thought you'd like to know."

"Thanks, Barbara. We really appreciate it," Jay said. "Is he okay?"

"Mr. Frost?"

"No, Bob."

"He's spending time at home with his family the way people should at this time of night." She gave the 'home' a little punch, looking right at Jay as she said it.

"What happened to the phone?" he asked.

"Who needs a phone at a time like this," she said and left.

"You want me to come with you?" Clemens asked.

"Where?"

"To see Bob."

Clemens had picked up on Barbara's cue too. "Sure."

"I'll go look for a car."

Connolly swung his feet off Jay's desk, leaning forward in the chair.

"What exactly were you lads doing in London?"

"What do you mean?" Jay asked.

Connolly read from the letter that he'd pulled out of the brown padded envelope with the hand-written address. "Dear Mr. Peterson. I had this in my pocket when we was 'interrupted.' I never know till my missus did the wash. It's worth a look. American numbers and all. I couldn't put it back so I sent it to you. My regards to Mr. Clemens. Give me a bell if there's anything needing opening here, if you know what I mean. Yours truly, Max Skinner."

Clemens took the envelope away from Connolly. It was postmarked London eleven days ago.

"What was with it?" Jay asked.

"This disk," Connolly said holding up a floppy. "Must be red-hot." The label on the disk read "'KEEP THIS' and 'U.S./M.E.!!!'" apparently in Oldham's hand-writing. A yellow Post-It was stuck to the back. "Ibrahim?" it read.

CHAPTER 50

Los Angeles

Traffic was locked on I-110 all the way up to the Willowbrook exit, three lanes stalled in either direction in a continuous, broiling stream of steel. The temperature outside had hit one hundred degrees half an hour ago and the windows of every car, truck, and bus were rolled tight against the heat, every air-conditioner blasting. Except Jammal bin Shanin's. Jammal had his windows wound down, half listening to the Imam's sermon on the tape-player, mostly savouring the afternoon. It was not unlike home: the heat, the cars, the desert. His white Chevrolet Caprice was just two years old. Everyone in Saudi drove a Caprice. Only the King, his family and advisers drove Hummers and Range Rovers. Here ordinary people owned Range Rovers and Hummers; LandCruisers and Discoveries ruled the road.

His day had been a good one. He had made Faqr, the first of the five prayer rituals, beneath the orange tree in his own backyard at dawn, smoothing out the worn rush mat, turning to the south-east, towards the black Kaaba at the centre of the Al Haram mosque beyond the curve of the earth, prostrating himself humbly. The air was cool, the traffic a hush, the scent of the green oranges an accent to his contentment.

He had been first at the employees' lot, positioning the

Caprice carefully between the yellow lines and smiling warmly to the square-jawed guard on the gate. His employer required that all its 'cast members' be clean-shaven. It was a token Jammal gave and accepted willingly. His employer was strict, demanding. There were rules one had to observe, customs. Never make fun of the characters, especially the mouse. Never talk about the company to outsiders. The rules made sense. Jammal understood rules. He had been raised to be obedient. His heart was in the east, his head in the west. His beard had been on his head.

His supervisor had slapped his hand high when they had fixed the faulty air-conditioning plant in the headquarters building. It wasn't really in Jammal's area but he had offered his help. It was machinery he knew well. Saudi Arabia was the world's leading consumer of cold air. He and two others had quickly fixed the problem. It felt good working with the other men. They had been friendly, joshing Jammal about Saudi Arabia, giving him a little grief they said. He belonged here. This was his life now, his job, this car, his little home in Willowbrook, the orange tree.

The traffic on his side of the freeway began to move. Ten minutes later he was turning onto El Segundo Street. He pulled the Caprice into the carport alongside the small white bungalow. It bothered him a little that he was coming back to an empty house. His wife and son were back in the home country on a visit leaving the man of the house alone. He got out and walked round to the side door then changed direction when he saw the yellow slip tucked into the grillwork over the front door. A delivery.

It took him fifteen minutes to locate the package service's office in the industrial estate twelve blocks from his house.

Jammal signed for the package, carefully noting the label: Warning, Contents Under Pressure and the sender: A. Hussein. No return address. He placed the package in the trunk and drove home.

It was nearly six by the time Jammal finally let himself into the house. He set the package down on the kitchen table and walked through the archway into the living room. He picked up the remote from on top of the television, next to the glowing portrait of his wife and his beautiful son, clicked the TV on, flicked through the channels, pausing for a few moments on a daytime drama and the image of a dark-haired man teasing the edge of a flimsy blouse from the bared shoulder of a blonde woman, then continued until he came to the Disney Channel, his channel. A movie was in progress, a golden retriever running through a cornfield to the sound of urgently sweet music. Jammal watched for a few moments then, leaving the set on with the volume down, went back to the kitchen. It was time for the Maghrib, the evening prayer ritual. An inner clock urged him to his knees. Another voice guided him to the package on the table.

He used a knife to cut away the tape, careful not to puncture the cardboard of the box. He opened the lid, pressing the tongues back on all four sides and exposing an air-sealed transparent bubble pack. An envelope was taped to the outside, WARNING printed on its front. The object inside gleamed red in the late afternoon sun. It was a fire extinguisher. An extension nozzle was in its own packet underneath. Jammal eased the packet gingerly from its Styrofoam bed and placed it base down on the kitchen floor. He squatted, studied its smooth round shoulders, the gleaming black of its trigger assembly. It was a very fine piece of equipment.

Jammal rose to his feet and went round the table to the refrigerator, opened the freezer door and reached into the back to extract a sealed plastic envelope. He opened the envelope, taking out his passport, a thin bundle of Saudi riyals, the title to his beloved Caprice, and two sheets of white paper. He spread the two sheets on the kitchen table next to the opened package. One bore a diagram showing Jammal how to connect the extension tube to the extinguisher and screw it into the air conditioning system; how to lock the trigger of the extinguisher. He folded the diagram into fours, placed it in the garbage disposal, turned on the water and the appliance. The disposal growled for a few seconds then Jammal turned it off.

He picked up the other sheet of paper. Both had been faxed to the business centre in Compton with a cover sheet: To be collected by Jammal Shahin. No precautions had been taken to hide the contents of the fax. A casual reader would have made nothing of either paper. This one spelled out the instructions in the diagram, reiterating the caution Jammal should exercise, instructing him on the proper use of rubber gloves and protective face covering, optimum time for the operation. There was no indication of what he should do or what he might expect to happen once he had performed the tasks set out for him. The message ended with a simple exhortation: Inshallah.

It was time, Jammal thought. He would do it tomorrow morning just the way he had been told, Inshallah, God willing. He took his mat, walked into the living room and with his back to the TV, facing East, began the ritual of evening prayer.

CHAPTER 51

Spruceville, West Virginia

Night had already fallen on the hill farm in West Virginia three thousand miles to the east. The wind was lazily flapping a tattered windsock tacked to a pole. The pole stood off to one side of a grassy field, a twenty-foot wide swath newly cut down its middle and running a hundred yards or more to a wall of thickly planted fir trees. The tree farm had been in the McKenzie family for four generations but it didn't look like it would survive into a fifth. It was hard to get help anymore and John and Kelly McKenzie's only son had gone off to college the year before. This year he'd come back but only at Christmas, the selling season. He'd told them he was going west for the summer. Some girl in California.

Across from the windsock sat an ageing Piper Cub, its wings fitted with crop-dusting sprays, a large barrel-shaped tank under the fuselage. McKenzie did his own maintenance on the plane and swore the plane could fly to California and back if it had to. Kelly McKenzie had just shrugged her shoulders, a sad light in her eyes. The farmhouse was situated at the other end of the crude runway from the trees, a white clapboard building with an open-sided porch wrapping round two of its sides and a green tin roof topping it. "About as old as me," McKenzie would wisecrack. McKenzie and his wife sat in its parlour-kitchen in their usual chairs, she in the rocker, he on the old armchair by the window. They had fallen asleep in front of the television apparently. The newscast was updating the story of the terrorist attack on National Airport, wide-eyed witnesses describing where they were, how they felt when the shots were fired, the screams, the panic. John and Kelly McKenzie didn't move when the sirens sounded from the TV's speaker, didn't comment on the horror, wouldn't now.

Nasir had strapped them almost casually into their chairs using a minimum of tape to bind them. He had administered a triple dose of the morphine base that he had first given to Lis Charnay. He had applied the needle to the bared arms of the farmer and his wife in a most professional way, swabbing the insertion point with alcohol. Afterwards he had carefully broken down his equipment replacing it piece by piece in its plastic carrying case. The drug had hit the McKenzies' systems almost simultaneously and within seconds of its application, the shock reduced both John and Kelly to a state marginally this side of existence.

"Like old times don't you think?" Lis said from across the room. "All of us under one roof again. Nasir going about his usual business, Saeed glued to his computer. Right, Saeed? Dodging reality again are we? What's it this time? *Sim City*? *Castles*?"

It had been more than seven hours since Nasir had delivered the knock-out dose to Lis at the apartment in Half Street, three hours since she had forced them to pull the car over to the side of the road and stuck her finger as far down her throat as she dared, retching helplessly, her body buckled under the spasms. Saeed had helped her back into the car. Then she had drunk. Each time they passed a convenience store or a restaurant as they headed west on 66 she had begged them to stop so she could get a drink: water, soda, coffee, anything. Saeed had pleaded for her, Ali had nodded consent. Later they had stopped again, Lis racked with pain, crouched by the roadside and vomiting up all the liquid she had forced into her body, fighting to beat back the encroaching effect of the drug, inhaling the cold mountain air as if it could cleanse her.

They had arrived an hour before in Khamis' old Pontiac. Khamis, the tenant at the apartment on Half Street in Anacostia, the ex-employee of Patuxent Industries, had driven the whole way, Lis and Ali in front, Saeed and Nasir in the back. They had been met at the gate on the road by Suhail, Khamis' cousin. Suhail had turned McKenzie's crumpled Ford pick-up around and headed up the track to the farm. They had followed. Suhail had showed up on the McKenzies' farm out of nowhere six months before and the old man had been desperate enough to hire him on the spot, never questioning his apparent good fortune. Suhail was a good boy. Worked well.

At the farmhouse Nasir and Suhail had gone in first, the others waiting in the Pontiac. Nasir had reappeared five minutes later waving the rest in. They had settled into a familiar routine, Ali and Saeed unloading their equipment from the car, Saeed rigging his work station. Nasir had arranged the tools of his trade, the portable pharmacy, a battered Ingram machine gun. Only the two newcomers, Suhail and Khamis seemed uneasy, sitting uncomfortably on straight-backed chairs against the wall under a picture of the McKenzies' son at his high school graduation.

Lis crossed to where Saeed had set up his computer on the

desk where Mrs. McKenzie tallied her books. He tilted the monitor away from her as she approached, hiding the screen.

"It is no matter, Saeed," Ali said from the doorway. "She may look if she wishes. It is not of importance now." Ali was quite calm, no hint of threat in his face or manner, no indication that she had crossed some line. Saeed twisted the monitor in Lis's direction. In an upper corner was a grid containing thumbnail maps of US states. There were seven individual squares each with an outline of a state. Lis recognised California, Florida, New York, Washington and Texas immediately, had a harder time identifying Georgia and the District of Columbia. In a linked window was an informational chart giving an overview of a company, locations of headquarters and plants and a web site address. The state map highlighted in the preview window at the bottom of the screen Lis now saw was Georgia, the Atlanta address on the information panel home of either Coca-Cola or Turner Broadcasting.

"Jesus," Lis said, echoing the comment she had made when she first entered Khuda Bax's apartment in Paris. It was a different view, a similar vision.

Lis stared at the screen then at Ali. "You're crazy aren't you? You're not a victim, not a freedom fighter. You're just plain fucking crazy. It didn't matter whether Mahmoud got to Atlanta or not. In fact you probably reckoned he wouldn't. His picture was all over every TV and paper in the country. So what?"

"It did occur to me," Ali said casually as he crossed the room. "It is wise always to have many ideas in case one should not go right."

"Who else? Who are your other targets?" she asked, her

voice barely audible as if she wanted neither to hear nor be heard, the knowledge as deadly to her as to the intended victims.

"As I said, it is of no matter, Miss Charnay, not now. There is nothing I can do to interrupt this course of events. Saeed's organisation is very skilful. He has an ingenious mind."

Lis looked at the two men, one standing, the other seated. "You did this?" she said to Saeed. Saeed stared at the screen, unable to look at her. "For God's sake, why?"

"There are things that separate us, Miss Charnay, things that connect us," Ali said. He reached behind Saeed's computer to retrieve the videocassette he had offered Lis on the New Jersey Turnpike just before Nasir had killed the trooper. He presented it to her again.

"What is this?"

Ali didn't answer immediately. He looked at her instead, looked at her in a way he had not done before. Before she had been a piece in his plan; now, Ali was a man admiring a woman, looking frankly, instinctively. She was not the only one to see the change. Saeed, too, was watching Ali. "It is a confession, Miss Charnay," Ali said. "You have seen a little part of it already. It is a man, not quite a man, confessing to certain things he did. Khuda Bax bin Abdul Aziz." Lis took the cassette.

"And?" she said.

Ali looked towards Saaed for an instant then back at Lis. "A certain man came to me many months ago with a certain proposition."

"Osama bin Laden?" Lis said. Ali didn't respond but she knew she was right.

"This man," Ali continued, "said there was much honour

for a man who could complete a dangerous mission. How would such a man find money for this complicated and costly mission, I, Ali, asked this man."

"Bax," Lis said. Again, Ali did not respond. "What was the mission?"

"You know that already. If you do not it is only because Jay Peterson has not told you."

"The Truman? You were responsible for that?" Lis looked into Ali's eyes. For the first time, she saw pride there, conceit, knew that Ali was making this confession not as a boast but to impress her. "Why are you telling me this?"

"Because you will tell the American people. They will believe you. You will tell them that a certain member of the Fahd regime, this Bax, was involved in an attack on an American vessel, took American lives."

"Bax? You said he was just the banker. Why for God's sake?"

"What matter? He is of their tribe, is he not? Let Fahd answer."

"Why should I believe you? The attackers were all executed."

"Not every one as you can see," Ali said with a little smile. "Saeed here will tell you also. What did they care? Six heads were taken. The score was settled."

"And Thompson, Oldham, the others?"

"All traces were to be erased. Nasir is a professional." Nasir sitting now on the windowsill grinned agreement. "He works for whoever pays him. Now, I pay him. What matter."

Lis looked at the tape in her hand then back at Ali. "All this is on the tape?"

"That and other things. Mr. Bax's heroin, his boys. Things like that."

"And you want me to tell this story?"

"In time, yes. When we are gone. Now there is work to be done."

He motioned to the two men sitting by the wall. They left the room together. Lis watched their flashlight beams tipping up and down as they walked out over the grass to the plane. Then she turned back to Saeed. "You can't let this go on, Saeed," she said urgently in English. She leaned over him, her sudden movement bringing Nasir to his feet.

"Sit down, you asshole," she spat out in her elementary Arabic. "I'm having a conversation here." Then in English: "You have a life, Saeed. You could have a future here. You could bring your family, make a new beginning. That's what this country's all about, starting over, getting it right."

Saeed lifted his hands from the keyboard of Ali's laptop where they had rested all this time, the silhouettes of his palms outlined in perspiration on its surface.

"Can't you see what you're doing? This is not some little electronic game you're playing. This is real. We're people. You and me. We have histories and families and friends and . . ." She was going to say "lovers" but she read the look on Saeed's face and suddenly knew how to reach him, knew that Ali Hussein for all his wisdom and his carefully planned web of destruction had been unable to see into this young man's heart.

"You're jealous, Saeed; aren't you. Of Ali? Yes. Of Ali." She was very close to Saeed now, her back turned to Nasir. She had her arm over his shoulder, another hand at the hem of her blouse, fingering the top button, not trying to seduce him, knowing she already done that, just holding his attention, bending his will towards her. "And angry with him for what he allowed Nasir to do to me."

Saeed was very still, his eyes shifting from the diagrams and columns of type on the screen to her hand so close to his cheek and then back to the screen. "Just you, Saeed. And me. But first we would have to take care of the others, of this pig behind us," she whispered at his ear, her body arched over him now. "Just take care of him and then we could take care of each other, Saeed; the way a man should take care of a woman who cares for him."

She stopped talking, her hand moving from her blouse to his cheek, the fingers just touching it, no more. He was barely breathing, his mouth slightly open, hers almost beside it, the scent of her skin, its warmth, its touch filling his senses.

Nasir at the window began to chuckle softly, said more to himself than Lis: "You're in trouble now."

Saeed broke the spell, standing suddenly and breaking away from Lis towards the open door. Nasir watched him, the mocking grin creasing his face then breaking into a laugh. Lis stared at the computer not seeing the terrible history written there, seeing instead a weapon, hard edges she could drive into that grinning face again and again, settling the score.

A movement to her left made her stop. It was Saeed. He had left the room but returned, standing in the doorway, hands at his sides. She sensed another movement behind her, spun around, saw Nasir, his mouth wide but no sound coming out, standing, pushing away from the window towards the door, saw Saeed's arms coming up, the Ingram in the right, the left grabbing the magazine, his finger tightening on the trigger. She heard her own voice, far away, high, "Nooo," and the sudden, rattling voice of the gun exploding across the room, the flame spitting from its muzzle, the red globe of Nasir Abu Massoud's face, the terrible stream of blood and brain and pulped skull erupting in a fountain from the back of his shattered head through the window and out into the black night.

CHAPTER 52

Washington D.C.

An uneasy calm had settled on the bull pen and the corridors of the Bureau since Jay had left. The urgent conferences had dwindled to an occasional hushed exchange in the restroom, phones ringing unanswered in distant offices. The Bureau was under siege and waiting for what the dawn would bring.

Jay willed himself to start all over again. The hyper-activity of the last hours had spun the facts, what they knew, what they didn't, into a tornado of supposition that was swallowing everything in its path. In spite of all their efforts, they had finally admitted that their suspect, at least under the name Lis had provided, apparently had no record, no history. He had appeared out of nowhere. Connolly, now officially invited, was stretched out on the carpet. Jay stepped round his supine body and into the corridor. Then, on an impulse, he pushed through the fire exit and down the stairs to the garage. The duty policeman gave him a nod of recognition.

"Kind of cold out there," he said.

"Thought it might wake me up," Jay replied.

He climbed the ramp to the street. The cop was right; it was cold. Jay rolled down his shirt sleeves against the damp air then stuck his hands in his pockets walking briskly across a deserted Pennsylvania Avenue. The lighted Capitol kept silent vigil at its far end. He heard the whine of an engine overhead and looked up. A helicopter obliterated the sickle moon for a second with its black silhouette then continued its approach into the Anacostia Naval Base. Even the sky wasn't safe any more, ever since a pilot had overflown the White House causing a nasty scare for the First Family and another wave of finger pointing at the security agencies. Jay turned left towards the Navy Memorial, got half way down the block and stopped dead. Felicia Smith had said the most effective delivery system for nerve agents or biological weapons was a binary device. Even Saddam Hussein knew that. He'd got hold of some Polish M18 crop dusters, drones that could be guided onto their targets remotely. Could that be how Ali Hussein was intending to deliver his next attack? Ali surely couldn't lay hands on a drone here in the U.S. but he might be crazy enough to fly a plane into the building himself. Why not? Mahmoud had been a willing martyr. That would mean Ali or one of his group would have to know how to fly. Had they covered that?

When Jay got back upstairs, Connolly was still stretched out, his head propped on a stack of agents' reports. Cohen was slumped over his desk too. Only Judy Barron was still plugging away. "Hey, Judy?" Jay called. Her head appeared over the partition of her cubicle.

"Yeah?"

"Did you cross-reference incidents involving flights, planes, stuff like that?"

"The only thing I got was the clip on Saeed's brother. The air crash. We already went over that. Why?"

"Just a thought." Jay walked over to her desk. She shuffled

through the piles of documents on the floor beside her and resurfaced with a clipping.

"This is it. Peshawar Times," she said. "November, 1988. Brave fighters die in crash. It's just an abstract, not the full text." Jay took the yellowing fragment from her. The paper's brief account named Ibrahim bin Sayyaf as the pilot of a reconnaissance plane brought down by automatic fire. Both pilot and passenger were killed on the ground, though the account did not say whether their deaths were caused by the crash or an ensuing skirmish that took place between Russian forces and the mujahedeen. Ibrahim had been a prime candidate on their list for the "seventh man" but Judy's discovery that he been killed had knocked him off, quite literally. Jay went back to his desk, pulling up on his computer the first of the news archive services the Bureau subscribed to and keying in Ibrahim's full name, Ibrahim bin Sayyaf, along with the location and date of the crash of his plane.

The full text of the 1988 report he had read in the clipping came up. Not much more than the abstract. No information on other flyers or training sites. A dead-end. Then he heard Lis's voice. "Like John Doe." He keyed in Saif this time, changing the spelling of the last name but keeping the first name and other parameters in place. The tiny "busy" disk spun on his screen while the system scoured its database for the combination finally offering fourteen choices. Jay scrolled down through the index and stopped half way down on a New York Times report. He hit the "Display Article" key and waited.

The headline and source came up followed by the by-line. "Peshawar, November 1988." The account of the crash of the Afghan reconnaissance plane formed part of a longer background piece by a reporter travelling with the mujahedeen. Jay found the name Ibrahim Saif half way into the article. He scrolled down a few more lines and stopped. To give his piece the maximum effect the reporter had meticulously described the site of the crash, a rocky hillside just across the Afghani border, and cited the names and backgrounds of both pilot and passenger. It was the name of the second victim that got Jay's attention: Ali Fatta Hussein.

"What?" Connolly's speech was slurred, his body trying to deny the shaking it was getting. "What time is it?"

"I need your help," Jay said; "now."

Connolly eyes were still half closed as he shuffled over to the phone to dial Riyadh. "We've done this before," he said.

"We'll do it again."

Jay started his own hunt calling information in Manhattan then the three numbers they gave him. A man's voice answered the first number.

"Mr. Karlson?"

"Who's this?" The man sounded barely awake.

Jay identified himself, began his questions. Yes, Karlson had written the article and he did still work for the Times. No, he hadn't seen the crash site but he had interviewed the survivor.

"The survivor?"

"The pilot, at the 'martyrs' house' in Pakistan. He had one eye covered up, got glass in it when they crashed. They didn't know if they were going to save it. I do remember that."

Ali Fatta Hussein had died that day, Jay had no doubt of that. But Ali Hussein had been reborn and Jay had seen him in Bethesda that afternoon. Jay apologised for waking Karlson and told him he'd be getting a visit from one of his colleagues within the hour.

Connolly was still on the phone, putting one call on hold while he dialled another number. "Like I said, they'd be nuts to say a thing."

"Keep trying," Jay said.

"Okay boss," Connolly said. "Meanwhile you'll be doing what?"

"Looking for a plane." Without any other explanation Jay headed out the door, Clemens at his heels.

CHAPTER 53

Los Angeles

Small rituals are the architecture of small lives. It was Jammal's ritual to begin each day by hosing down the Caprice then polishing up its paintwork. At sunrise, the air already heavy with the scent of eucalyptus, Jammal stepped outside and looked up and down the street. He had overslept and got up later than he intended. He would have to skip washing the Caprice, skip prayers too. He felt a twinge of guilt.

The sun's orange rays touched the pocketsize lawns each side of his house. His own lawn looked brown. He would water it tonight after work. He opened the driver's door of the Caprice and released the trunk. He paused there for a moment to look at the windows of the houses opposite. Then he went back into his own house and into the kitchen. He picked up the fire extinguisher. He had taken it out of its wrapping but had put it back in the box so that it wouldn't roll around in the trunk.

He went outside again, carrying the box, and placed it carefully in the trunk. He walked round to the front of the car, got in and started the engine. Then, just in time, he remembered the nozzle and the safety equipment. He left the engine running, unlocked the house, gathered up the objects and got back into the car placing the nozzle, gloves, and mask on the seat beside him. It was five thirty. He would still be in time. He knew others would be carrying out their own assignments soon, perhaps even this very day. That gave him comfort. He had got a hint of that in his last contact with Ali Hussein when Ali told him the date had been moved up. Ali for all his mild manner was a very persuasive man. Would there be rewards? There was no need even to ask. Jammal took a secret pride in doing well by Ali. As the Caprice took off down the street Mrs. Petrocelli in the house opposite craned her neck a little further to follow its progress. She had observed the family with distaste ever since their arrival in the neighbourhood, their peculiar rituals and habits. "That Arab", as she referred to him when she spoke to the desk sergeant at the precinct several minutes later, was up to no good. She had been watching him carefully since his wife left him. Took his son she did, left "that Arab" on his own. Now he was up to something, receiving packages, leaving at all hours carrying gloves and some kind of mask. Wouldn't be surprised if he was off to rob the Seven Eleven in Compton. The desk sergeant dutifully noted the call, said he would look into it.

The sun was high, heating up the Caprice's trunk and the two and three quarter pounds of lethal VX agent in the hand-held fire extinguisher inside. The car crawled up the ridge that separated Jammal's home from the valley where he worked. Traffic was unusually heavy for this time in the morning, a convoy of tractor-trailers riding the two right hand lanes. An eighteen-wheeler blocked his way in front, another obscured his vision behind. At this rate he might even be late for work regardless of whether or not he was able to hook the cylinder in the back into the system. As his car crested the ridge the truck ahead, a flat bed carrying a protruding girder, an orange flag attached to its end, pulled out suddenly into the outside lane. Jammal followed, pushing his foot down a little harder and at the same time adjusting the mirror, trying to get a better angle on the traffic coming up behind him. As his line of vision cleared, the sun hit the mirror square on, momentarily blinding him. His foot instinctively came off the gas pedal.

From behind, so loud it seemed to come from inside the car, a Lincoln Navigator travelling at over seventy miles an hour blasted an angry warning. Jammal pushed his accelerator to the floor in response. He gave no thought to the contents of the trunk. His primary fear was for his car. The white Caprice inched forward, the Navigator riding the rear bumper, Jammal's attention now riveted to its progress in the rear-view mirror. It would be the last thing he saw.

Two miles ahead a State Police cruiser had pulled over onto the grass verge between the east- and westbound lanes. The single trooper on board had brought the car to a halt under the span of an overpass. His car wasn't hidden but, parked next to the central pillar of the bridge, it wasn't exactly obvious either. The effect on the passing traffic was immediate. The first cars and trucks to come up to the cruiser lost no more than five miles an hour but by the time the wave had washed two miles back down the highway, brake lights were coming on hard, trucks and cars squeezing out the space between them like air out of a concertina. The eighteen-wheeler in front of Jammal's Caprice heard the warning from his buddy up ahead at the same moment that the van ahead of him suddenly hit its brakes. The trucker hit his own brakes but too hard, locking them. The rig began to jack-knife. As the cab jerked left the trailer behind it continued forward but not fast enough. The opposite end of the I-beam smashed into the

Caprice at over sixty miles an hour, exploding through the windshield in a spray of glass, the vivid orange of its warning flag filling Jammal's vision in the split-second before the enormous metal projectile separated his head from his neck. In the same instant, the Navigator behind closed the final inches that separated it from the Caprice, the solid mass of its engine block cutting a swathe through the white sheet-metal and into the car's trunk and its deadly contents.

As the sound of collision was replaced by a weird chorus of sounding horns, car alarms and human wailing, the first vapours of VX leaked from the pierced tank into the hot California air.

CHAPTER 54

Virginia

In the parlour of the McKenzies' farmhouse time had stopped. Minuscule sounds that might not have registered otherwise rang out clear. Nasir's lifeless body slithered down the wall collapsing to the floor with a slight bump, the ring on his left hand clinking on the heating pipe at the base of the wall. The vibration caused a triangle of glass still hanging in the pane to fall outwards and clatter on the debris beneath. The echoes of the gunshots from the Ingram in Saeed's hand echoed and re-echoed around the hills, carrying the report of the assassin's death from one valley to another. It might have taken a second, maybe two for the man's body to come to rest and for Lis to start moving. She ripped the laptop from its phone connection and power cord, then charged for the doorway. She caught the paralysed Saeed square in the chest, knocking him aside. As she crashed through the outside door into the dirt circle in front of the farmhouse, she saw far across the landing strip the beams of flashlights yawing into the night as the men holding them began to run back towards the house. Saeed was beside her now and for a second they watched the approach of Ali and his two companions together.

Then Saeed broke for the pick-up, pulling open the driver's side door and clambering in. Lis was right behind him, shoving him along the bench-seat and pitching the laptop at his feet.

She stamped down on the clutch and turned the key. The starter motor whined once, twice then miraculously the engine fired. She pushed the gear lever hard into first, let out the clutch and the truck shuddered forward. "Put on your belt." Saeed looked at her stupidly. "Your seat-belt." At the same moment she hit the brake pedal sending Saeed pitching forward. She wrenched the lever into reverse and again let out the clutch with a jerk. The truck's tailgate smashed into the driver's side door of Khamis' Pontiac. Again, Lis shifted into first as Saeed fumbled with his seatbelt groping for the buckle beside him. She ran the truck forward thirty feet this time, stopped and reversed, her head twisted round, one arm holding on hard to the top of the bench seat behind Saeed's head. This time the crumpled tailgate hit the Pontiac harder, pushing in the door and buckling the steering column.

The three men were now visible in the light spilling from the house, slowing as they approached. She saw Ali grabbing an automatic from Suhail. She punched in the cigarette lighter in the truck's dash then pushed the gear lever back into first, grunting with determination, her hand tight on the wheel. As the truck began to roll forward she grabbed the gun from the floor at Saeed's feet and, upright again, yanked the wheel hard over to the left, the truck twenty yards from the Pontiac. She rolled the window down and pointed the blunt barrel of the gun at the vehicle. She didn't know whether to hold the barrel or the magazine, just squeezed the trigger and sprayed an untidy line of bullets into the rear of the Pontiac as the gun bucked upward. The noise of the shots was deafening in the enclosed cabin of the truck, the cordite sour in her mouth, her eyes smarting. She threw the gun back at Saeed, catching sight of the three men pressed close to the ground beyond the battered car. She pulled the glowing cigarette lighter from the dash, paused a moment to aim at the rear of the Pontiac where the first trickle of gas from the rear tank was beginning to blacken the sand, then threw it. The lighter arced into the night, rotating end over end, the red-hot tip appearing and disappearing from their view. Lis was already pushing the truck into first again. As she pulled the wheel viciously over to the right, the front wheels of the truck spinning wildly, the cigarette lighter bounced on the dirt and rolled up against the rear wheel of the other vehicle.

She didn't count, didn't look back, just instinctively lowered her head below the level of the back window, plunging the truck down the dirt track towards the road half a mile away. Saeed had recovered himself, leaned forward and retrieved the Ingram, inspecting the magazine. It was empty. "It is no good," he said, the pitch of his voice unnaturally high, the volume too loud from the recent deafening they had received. Lis didn't know if he meant the gun or their chances of escape. She didn't care. For too long she had been a part of this weird family, an unwilling relation but a still functioning part, a factor. Now it was her turn.

The truck drifted left as she took the turn round the barn at the bottom of the track. At the same time there was a flash then a wave of heat pushing them forward and, right behind them, the crump of gasoline igniting, the Pontiac lifting inches off the dirt before settling back, its windows gone, its interior blazing.

Lis pulled up hard at the farm gate letting the engine idle, realising suddenly that she was shaking, her whole body trembling with release. The natural world outside washed over her, the smell of the night, the tree frogs piping their invitations, a firefly blinking. She rammed the gear lever forward, slipped the clutch viciously and swung the truck out onto the road heading for what she hoped would be a town.

The night exuded peace. Lis leaned her head out of the window, breathing in the dampness of the coming dawn. It felt very good. They drove for a couple of minutes, neither of them speaking. At last Lis said: "What will you do?" She realised she was already thinking in a future tense, something she had not done for days.

Saeed stared ahead at the descending spiral of blacktop between the tightly ranked pines. "Will you say good words for me?" he said at last.

"What?"

"Will you speak for me?"

She shot him a look, taking in the sharp profile, the moist eyes. "What do you want me to say?" She sounded hard, didn't mean to but couldn't help it. "I'll say what happened. No more no less. I don't care whose God was offended, whose rights infringed. You've taken lives, threatened mine. My body has been abused, tortured. You tortured me, Saeed; you, Nasir, your whole dirty clan."

"Nasir was an animal," he said vehemently. "Ibrahim should never have allowed him, never. He was an animal not fit to walk the earth."

"Ibrahim?" She was honestly puzzled.

Saeed looked surprised. He'd caught himself out. Then he realised it didn't matter anymore. "Ali, Ibrahim" he said.

"What?"

"Ali Hussein is not his real name. His name is Ibrahim, Ibrahim bin Sayyaf. He is my brother. I believed him, believed his lies. But he is like all the rest. It is good he will die along with your President, with your Jay Peterson."

Somehow she had known, known all along that she had only a small piece of this story, the part that touched her. The night retreated back beyond the wash of the headlights, the scents and sounds, the remembered pain and fear flooding in. A flush of anger rose in her, bringing her foot down a little harder on the gas pedal, pushing the truck up above the sixty-mile-an-hour mark. The tyres were squealing slightly now as she threw the pick-up into the bends, the wheels holding but the body swinging out a little more with each turn.

"You and your fucking brother. Was that what all this was about? You pretended you were holy warriors on some jihad. But you're just a couple of dirty little punks, a couple of thugs." Saeed tried to interject but Lis cut him off. "Shut up. Listen to me. You used me, you and your brother. And even if you didn't, Saeed, you stood around and you watched. I'll tell whoever wants to know exactly what happened. I'll tell the story, Saeed. You'd better believe it." The road ahead suddenly flattened out, straightening for half a mile, the close forest withdrawing and giving way to marsh.

Lis let her foot lift off the gas again, her anger dissipating. At the same moment Saeed lifted his own foot and without pause brought the heel of his shoe down hard on the laptop. "Fuck you," he said in English, his eyes smarting with tears.

"Fuck you. Fuck all you people." His knee lifted to strike again hovering for a moment above the black box.

"Saeed," she yelled at him. "Don't. That's the whole plan, the whole thing." The truck slewed as her right hand grabbed at the man beside her. "Don't." Curiously, he obeyed. His right foot hung over the closed computer, his hand gripping his thigh to give it extra leverage. But Saeed wasn't looking down at the object on the floor of the truck anymore. His attention was taken by the oncoming light. A truck, a big one, the headlights spread wide, was taking up the crown of the road and bearing down on them fast.

"Go round," he shouted at her in Arabic not taking his eyes off the approaching lights. "Go round!"

She stared ahead, the lights closing too fast for her to judge, too close now for her to act. Then abruptly he commanded: "Close the window, close the window." She followed his instruction, winding furiously at the lever while he snapped all the vents. The lights swung directly onto their faces, the beams level with their eyes blinding them. The truck was on top of them, its front end about to crash through the window. At the last instant the beams lifted, pointing up into the night sky and for a fraction of a second driver and passenger saw the black silhouette of the Piper Cub lift over the cab.

"It's Ibrahim. He is crazy." Saeed's head whipped round to view the retreating aeroplane through the back window.

"He certainly is," Lis said watching the ghostly mist descending on the road, the cream-like vapour settling on the windshield. She reached her hand out for the window crank. "Don't," Saeed screamed. "Don't touch it. It is poison. Very bad."

She tried to think. Had there been a turn off, a side road? Nothing back there. "How far are we from the town?"

"What town?"

"Town, Saeed. Any town."

He stared at her stupidly and she knew it was her call. She pushed her foot as hard against the accelerator pedal as she could, the effort almost bringing her to her feet. The truck hesitated, bucked, then squealed forward along the road in front of them. She had felt sullied before, used, now she felt cold fear. Whatever Ali or Ibrahim and his cohorts had charged the Piper Cub's belly-tank with, whatever he had sprayed out of either wing was some lethal chemical. She flicked off the truck's headlights, the road ahead immediately pitch black.

"Where is he, Saeed? Where is he?" Lis yelled. Saeed ducked and bobbed trying to spot the plane, at the same time peering into the blackness down the road ahead undecided which he should fear more. "Look for him, Saeed. Find him." The darkness was beginning to thin ahead of her, the light from the sickle moon and the shadows it cast restoring minimal vision. The luminous dial of the speedometer gave their faces a demonic glow. It read eighty miles an hour. Suddenly it was Saeed's turn to scream.

"Behind, he's coming from behind!"

She glanced at the rear-view mirror, picked up the twin lights then turned back to the road, her night vision so recently acquired now lost. The flare of the lights through the back window illuminated the dashboard for an instant then just as suddenly disappeared, the plane pulling up and banking away to the left of the road. Lis's attention slipped briefly, catching the silhouette of the plane again out of the corner of her eye. Then the reason for the plane's sudden manoeuvre was directly in front of them.

"The lights. Where are the lights?" she yelled grappling for the switch. As the headlights came back on she just caught the yellow rectangle at the roadside with its writhing black arrow, the sheer wall of the cliff climbing away to their right. The road spiralled sideways to the left, falling away from the mountain. Lis pulled down on the wheel, feeling the truck beginning to slide, knowing she wasn't going to make the turn. As the back offside wheel hit the jumble of rocks along the road's edge, the truck's front end lifted. The back kicked and the pick-up somersaulted, end over end, dropping then sliding like a heavy toboggan through the mountain laurel, the lights leading the way, the bodies inside whipping and arching as the chassis bucked over the boulders in its path.

Hours later, maybe no more than a minute, she awoke. She was curled on top of Saeed. He was motionless, squashed underneath her against the passenger door, the truck at rest on its side in the middle of the lower road. She wedged herself upwards between the wheel and the now vertical bench seat, knowing there was danger but forgetting where she should look for it. Her foot kicked to give her lift, her upper body emerging through the opening of the shattered window, pulling herself up and through, one foot on the window ledge, falling forwards into the road, regaining her balance, staggering slightly then wiping her moist hand against her brow and through her hair. So quiet. The night was so quiet. And bright. The beams from the pick-up's headlights shone out across the valley catching the first wisps of fog on the river below. She stood still, knowing this wasn't over, knowing she had forgotten something. Not Saeed. He was in the cab. Alive?

Dead? Not the plane. There was no noise. Almost no noise. A car engine. It was climbing the hill. Not that, not the screeching of its tyres as it turned through the bends. Not that. She looked at her hand, at the upturned palm red with blood and the whitish liquid she had picked up from the truck's bodywork. Her mouth gaped wide. She began to scream silently, bent double in the middle of the narrow, twisting road in the hills of West Virginia, screaming from deep inside, her whole body twisted with the effort, the air round her beginning to glow with light, her voice ringing in the blackness.

"Lis?" A voice saying her name. Arms wrapping around the shell of her body. "Lis?" Pulling her off balance. Then again and very quietly: "Lis." Sam Clemens stood by the car, one hand on the top of the driver's side door the other still on the wheel, staying discretely back while Jay gathered Lis Charnay in his arms.

CHAPTER 55

Washington D.C.

"Where the fuck is everybody?" It wasn't "Good morning" but it was as close as Bob Lorenz would get on this day.

It was not quite five in the morning and Lorenz had been on his feet all night in the situations room at the White House. Starks' death at the airport had changed the political climate. No one had time for Enrico's plots and counterplots anymore. The country was at war and needed generals not schemers. Lorenz was back in favour as suddenly as he had been out. Bob Lorenz stood now in the doorway of the analysts' bull pen glaring out across the maze of hutches where "Rodin's thinkers" as he had recently nicknamed them "hid out."

"There's nobody here. We've got a national fucking crisis and they've all gone home."

The witnesses to this particular reading of Lorenz's gospel were the long-suffering Barbara and Lorenz's new wünderkind, the boy who was finally going to set the world right, Mitch Carrollton, a computer whiz from CIRTAC.

"Want me to call someone?" Carrollton offered. Barbara gave him a long-suffering look.

"Right," Lorenz barked. "I want all response-team leaders in my office in five minutes. And find someone in this shit-hole who knows where Peterson is."

"That would be me." The lazy Irish drawl of Brian Connolly preceded the professor's head as it stuck above the partition. For a second Barbara thought Lorenz might pop his last remaining fuse. It came as a surprise then, perhaps not least to Bob Lorenz himself, that the Director's reaction was as subdued as it was. "Brian! What are you doing here?"

"The work of the Lord, Robert, the work of the Lord."

"Don't push me, Connolly."

"Well, Bob, a few hours back your certified genius, Mr. Jay Peterson, analyst extraordinaire, figured out that our friend Mr. Ali Hussein was in fact a certain Mr. Ibrahim bin Sayyaf, older brother of Saeed bin Sayyaf. Both are very much alive. I confirmed this through calls placed to various parties in Saudi. I had to use subterfuges and pretexts that involved the use of this agency's name. I hope you'll forgive me under the circumstances." Connolly's manner was quite restrained, scholarly almost. His audience was too stunned to do anything else but listen.

"Given our man Ibrahim's – how shall I put this – our man's predilection, Jay calculated that there was a good chance his next move was going to involve a plane of some sort, probably a plane with some kind of spraying device given the group's preference for chemicals. The plane, he figured, would be employed agriculturally more likely than not. It was stretching the odds but again, under the circumstances, he had to narrow the search somehow. He also guessed that Ibrahim's most likely target was situated here in the capital. The cell wasn't moving south. Mahmoud had already been dispatched in that direction with disastrous effect. That only left west. That could put him about an hour, maybe two away by plane, about two hundred miles at the outer limit. Much more wouldn't really be manageable under the circumstances. At least that's what we, what he figured. I believe he gathered up what resources he could find in this office so early in the morning, given that you, Robert, were engaged elsewhere and your esteemed deputy, who invited me in here by the way, was having shall we say some difficulty in deciding the best option to pursue. Anyhow. He managed to narrow the number of registered and operable craft to five after calling the rather irate farmers who were prepared to co-operate so early in the morning. They sleep too, apparently. Mr. Peterson is quite the executive, you know. Dispatched two teams to the Eastern shore, another into Maryland, a fourth up towards Middletown and he and Mr. Clemens took off for the hills of West Virginia."

Lorenz stared at Connolly in stupefaction. "And?" he said, his voice dangerously low, knowing Connolly had more.

"And he called just, what, ten minutes ago. Seems he hit the jackpot. He and Mr. Clemens picked up two of the group at a farm in the Blue Ridge, found a third on the road apparently. He said I should track you down and bring you up to date. They think they may have come up with another problem." Lorenz said nothing, waiting for Connolly, the rest of the staffers in the room surfacing now from their cubicles. "They believe Ibrahim is already in the air."

"Where is this place?"

"Spruceville. Out by Spruce Knob. About two hours by road, maybe three."

"So?" Lorenz addressed the room; "let's go."

The farm seemed unexceptional in the full light of day. The green tin roof and dilapidated porch were no different from scores of other farmhouses in the area. From the rear seat of the Bureau helicopter Connolly looked down on the house and its adjacent buildings and thought guiltily: At least we're upwind of this lunatic. The helicopter bumped down on the grass strip beside three other aircraft, two of them bearing Air National Guard markings. A random array of trucks, cars and assorted emergency vehicles were parked on the driveway leading to the house. Figures in white, looking like snowmen from above and about as out of place in the bright sunlight, were clustered round the outbuildings. Three local fire-trucks and as many ambulances filled the road up to the farm. At the gate to the road a barricade of blue-and-white cruisers kept the first wave of press at bay.

Connolly followed Lorenz out of the helicopter. Carrollton and the communications specialists who had accompanied them brought up the rear.

"Where's Peterson?" Lorenz yelled over the din of the rotors to the agent acting as flight control.

"The farmhouse, sir."

Lorenz led his party across the grass at a jog. The air was hot and Connolly's brow was glistening with sweat by the time they got to the porch and slipped in between the helmeted agents at the door. The body brigade had removed Massoud's corpse but forensic specialists were picking over the area where he had died, collecting fragments of bloodstained glass. The McKenzies presided over the scene from their chairs. At first Connolly thought they might have passed out from the shock of seeing their house and lives so disrupted but then a fly crawled across Mrs. McKenzie's unblinking eye and he realised with a shock that they were both dead, asphyxiated by the tightly wound tape or massive doses of morphine. In the back room Jay and Sam Clemens were bent over a battered laptop. The two men turned as Lorenz's contingent entered.

"Don't touch that thing," Lorenz ordered. "Probably rigged. Carrollton, do your thing." Lorenz's new boy took over.

"What's the story?" Lorenz continued without a break.

Jay brought the new arrivals up to date. He figured they might have thirty minutes, maybe less. If Ibrahim had targeted the capital then Lorenz's helicopter could have passed him on the way in. Some irony there. The McKenzies' Piper Cub was not on the premises. The police had apprehended two of Ibrahim's foot-soldiers, Khamis and Suhail. They were under guard in the back of one of the police wagons. Outside were indications that the farm had been used as a site for the manufacture of a virus compound, a conclusion confirmed by the two Arabs. Karen Golding's specialists were still working on it but all the signs pointed to botulin.

"And he's headed for D.C.?"

"Probably," Jay said. "He didn't charge the tank here according to our friends outside. Probably didn't have time between returning here after trying to catch up with Lis." Jay paused. "Seems he sprayed the truck. She thought it was hazardous. Turned out to be detergent. It's used as an organic deterrent to keep the deer from eating the Christmas trees."

"Soap?"

"Something like."

"So where is he now?"

"I figure he came back here, loaded one or two drums of whatever they had been mixing up out there, then took off before we arrived."

"And he couldn't take his friends with him because he was already at the weight limit," Lorenz added.

"Exactly," Jay said. "There are several small abandoned strips like this one in the area. Our best guess is he used one of them as a reloading point. One of the guys here said it would take maybe thirty minutes to empty and recharge the plane's belly tank. That's why I reckon we still have thirty minutes. Unless he just takes a runner."

"And he's not going to do that?"

"Not his style," Jay said. "He'll let everything else go to hell, walk away from everything he planned and just keep going. I figure this is his last shot."

"So what are we waiting for?" Lorenz said, now conscious that he was missing something the others had already seized.

"That's the problem," Jay said.

"Tell me," Lorenz said.

"If he's up in that plane and its full of botulin or anthrax, you can't shoot it down. The HazMat team have turned up forty-four-gallon cans out there, standard size. If he's loaded just one container of that on board, blowing up the plane would be the same as triggering a binary device, a biological bomb. In the right conditions it could scatter the virus over ten or more square miles. If it's in concentrate, we're looking at a thousand plus casualties. If he drops it on a residential area – who knows."

"So scare him to the ground. Get a couple of F-16s on his wing." The set of Jay's face told Lorenz that wasn't an option either. Ibrahim would go down with the plane. Pursuit aircraft of some kind might be able to force Ibrahim to land but they couldn't prevent him from crashing. "Look, Jay," Lorenz said. "There are four million people in and around D.C. who need to know what the hell's going to happen in thirty minutes. One of them's the President. What do we say?"

"You'd better tell him we've got a full chemical alert."

For the first time in the years Connolly had known him, Lorenz seemed at a loss. He was rooted to the spot, unable to act. Then he said: "What makes you sure he's headed for D.C.?"

"Because his brother told me."

The woman's voice came from the kitchen door. It was Lis. Lorenz hadn't seen her since their meeting in Paris. He was appalled at the change. Her face was pinched and lined, dark circles under her eyes. A yellowish welt covered one side where Massoud had struck her two days before in the Anacostia apartment. She had lost a lot of weight.

Lorenz looked chastened. "You'll tell me later why he's got it in for us. Now you're going to tell me, one of you, how we head this maniac off."

CHAPTER 56

Washington D.C.

The bio-chemical alert had yet to be declared official. The coded news was still on the wires but Washington was a city tuned to secret channels. It lived for the inside rumour. Nothing had been forthcoming from the White House, nothing from the lower rungs in the chain of command. The Federal Emergency Management Agency, the Pentagon, the FBI's Domestic Emergency Support team and Crisis Management were all tight-lipped, keeping rank. It took an enterprising reporter a few phone calls to discover that Spruce Knob was experiencing a four-alarm fire and no smoke. The first live reports from the site were being aired in the capital by ten a.m. in tandem with the chaos breaking on the California freeway. By eleven what should have been a resounding public relations coup for the FBI had turned into a rout.

The first wave of cars evacuating the city hit the major roads that led to the Beltway right after the Weather Channel displayed a map of the Spruceville site. It showed prevailing winds would dump anything emanating from the Blue Ridge right over the Washington-Baltimore metroplex. The bio-chemical pundits, familiar faces since the catastrophe at National Airport two nights before, began speculating on just what had been found at the farm and the words "the deadly biological agent anthrax" quickly became an overworked item in every newscaster's lexicon. It didn't matter if the compound manufactured at the site was indeed anthrax or the deadlier poison, Botox, botulinim toxin. Everyone with a subscription to Time or Newsweek knew Saddam Hussein had stockpiled 8,000 litres of anthrax spores and 20,000 litres of Botox, the seed for both bacteria acquired originally from the US, knew that was enough to kill every human on the planet. As far as Washington was concerned the planet extended no further than the Capital Beltway. Twenty minutes after the first exodus, the circular artery was jammed solid in both directions. Fights broke out in the stalled traffic. Police attempts to restore order by overflying the major routes out of the city by helicopter, operators frantically haranguing the locked traffic below by loud-speaker, only added to the chaos.

The media's fixation with the spreading panic fanned citizens' fears like a hot wind. Images of children slipping dust-masks over their mouths and outsize plastic bags over their heads were intercut with aerial views of the city in flight. Interviews with EMS crews on the ground told it as they saw it, revealing that antidotes and vaccines, penicillin, horse serum, were non-existent. Botox was known to be 15,000 times more powerful than the VX agent that had ravaged National Airport. What was the government doing about that? The President appealed for calm.

He made his live broadcast from outside the White House, his family in attendance, to show he wasn't scared of anything blowing in the wind. Stay inside, he urged his fellow citizens; seal the windows, the air-conditioning vents, the doors. Within minutes of his broadcast those citizens sanguine enough to stay put or those without means of transport were cramming the aisles of every hardware store, convenience market, and grocery chain in search of any duct tape, masking tape, draft excluder, or all-purpose sealant they could find. More fights broke out, looting spread from poor neighbourhoods to rich neighbourhoods. One man was filmed leaving an uptown liquor store with two carts of alcohol, respectably dressed women were stripping grocery shelves of any preserved goods they could find. Pharmacies turned to battlegrounds, paint stores were looted for coveralls and plastic floor coverings, bottled water was being sold on the street by doomsday entrepreneurs for $10 the half-gallon. Most of these extraordinary occurrences went unbroadcast. The media was beginning to bunker down itself, pulling all but essential personnel off the streets and compounding the problem they had so actively contributed to by strangling the supply of accurate news just when it was most needed. Routine emergencies were pre-empted by panic calls of outbreaks of infection where there were none. Suddenly the whole city and surrounding suburbs seemed to echo with the hoot, whirr, scream and whoop of sirens. The last trumpets were blowing for the capital and its citizens.

Southwest of the city, the McKenzies' simple farmyard had taken on the appearance of a solitary carcass on an African plain. Helicopters hovered over it. Bulky communications vehicles hunched around the modest white building, their satellite communications dishes pointed at the horizon. In the darkened communications truck that had become the unified command centre for the effort to contain Ibrahim's end-run, Lorenz was getting a crash course in anthrax and Clostridium botulinum and trying to educate the White House situations staff at the same time. Felicia Smith was on videolink with Lorenz while he handled two other calls. He was back at the eye of the storm.

"That's right, Director," Smith said, her face blinking in and out of the screen as the satellite fed her image to the communications centre in Spruceville. "Early symptoms include fever, weakness and coughing for anthrax, paralysis for botulinum. Botulinum doesn't cause infection, you see. It blocks nerve transmission . . ." Professor Smith continued with her gruesome litany while Lorenz detailed off one of the special agents who had flown in with him.

"Get anything you can on this plane: fuel capacity, range, maximum speed and altitude, and get the specs on the sprayer. They have anything on traffic control yet?" he queried the specialist seated at his side. The girl, Tracy, shook her head, never taking her eyes off the screen in front of her. "It's up there," Lorenz said. "How hard can it be? What the hell do we pay the Airforce for anyway?"

"Death occurs from respiratory problems within three to nine days depending on the level of exposure," Smith went on, "two to twelve hours with botulinum. But that's not the real problem."

Her comment grabbed Lorenz's attention. "Excuse me?"

"Anthrax spores are very persistent and remain in the soil indefinitely. They could poison a water supply for weeks. You'll know what you've got, though. Anthrax can be manufactured in open air. Botulinum has to be created in an oxygen-free environment."

"Right, Felicia. Thanks. Stick around. We'll need you . . .and some more of your good news when we can get it," he added under his breath. "Karen. Where's Karen?"

"We have her on the uplink from D.C., sir," Tracy said.

"Karen?"

"Yeah, Bob."

"What's happening with prophylaxis? My expert tells me we can dope the population."

"Not enough to go round, Bob, and no time. We don't even have enough tetracycline for anthrax treatment let alone enough vaccine. If its Botox, I'm afraid we're right out of luck. The best we can hope for is distributing protective clothing and keeping as many people as we can off the streets. It's a mess out there."

"I can imagine."

"You've confirmed the target?"

"Yes. We're not wasting your time, Karen."

"Okay," Karen Golding said. "Thought I'd ask. Sorry, Bob. Got to go now."

"Sir?" A youthful Emergency Response agent stuck his head in the door of the air-conditioned truck letting in light and heat.

"Yes."

"Carrollton cracked the code on the laptop. There's an Arab phone directory in there. Every Mohammed from here to San Diego. And the targets, sir! Disneyland they got, McDonald's, Boeing. You name it." The young man's enthusiasm was getting the better of him. A glare from Lorenz shut down his report.

"Transmit the list to central command and post it to every SAC and operative centre. I want the names and sites covered now. Danson, go with him," Lorenz dispatched one of his sidemen out of the truck. "And give Carrollton a stick of candy and a pat on the head." There was no hiding his triumph. The confidence was beginning to build in Lorenz, the bullish certainty that superior force and persistence could solve any problem including this one. A babble of incoming signal on the speaker by Tracy's screen interrupted Lorenz's train of thought. "What the hell is that?"

"Don't know, sir," the girl said. "Sounds like . . ."

"Arabic. My God, it's him! Where's Peterson? Get Connolly in here. Are you rolling tape? Put him on the squawk box."

Jay was already in the truck listening intently. "He's saying you've got to get the escort off him or he'll take the plane down."

"Escort? What escort?" Lorenz exploded.

"They've got two gunships on him."

"Tell them to get the fuck away from him. They shoot that thing down we'll all be dead." Tracy punched in a secondary code on the keyboard in front of her then looked at Lorenz helplessly. He seized the intercom from her. "Who's this? You're at Andrews? Flight Deck? Right. This is Lorenz, FBI command centre. The target must not be approached. Repeat: do not approach him. Get off his back. Now. You hear me?" Grudging acquiescence came from the other end of the connection. Then: "Patch me through to the situations room at the White House."

The voice on the squawk box continued in Arabic, Peterson translating. "He says there must be no interference or he will begin dispersal. He's not afraid to go down with the plane."

"Tell him fine."

The man seated at the console next to Tracy, Ray Rodriguez, turned in his seat: "The President, sir." Lorenz took Rodriguez's headset, his hand over the microphone. "We're not transmitting to that bastard up there are we? He can't hear what I'm saying?" Rodriguez shook his head. "Mr. President?" Lorenz straightened imperceptibly. "Yes, sir. We are in contact. Yes, sir. He's headed north-east at about 155 knots holding steady at 4,000 feet. We can't confirm his probable destination as yet but we have him at about twenty five minutes out from you. No, sir. Under no circumstances must that aeroplane be brought down. Shoot him down and you've got a binary, a bio-chemical weapon, an unguided missile if you like. Right. Yes, sir. I certainly will." Lorenz handed the receiver back to Rodriguez and was suddenly aware of the voice on the squawk box. Ibrahim was speaking in English now.

"You are a fortunate man, Jay Peterson, a persistent man also."

"Fortunate?"

"You hold the heart of the woman in your hand. That is good fortune but it is a small spring only at the side of the road. You understand? Our lives are a struggle. There are many of us here in this country, many hands. When one is stilled another will pick up the sword. The struggle will continue. You will not find us all."

"We can talk this out Ibrahim; in English or in Arabic if you prefer. There is another way, a peaceful way."

The background noise came up on the squawk box, Ibrahim's voice more strident, competing with the increased interference. At the same moment Lis and Connolly entered the room with Danson behind them. The static cleared.

"You are a man of faith in your way, Jay Peterson. Now you will do something for me."

"Tell me, Ibrahim."

"I wish to speak with the woman."

"With Lis?"

"With Miss Charnay."

Jay looked at Lorenz for an instant then passed the headset and microphone to Lis. "Keep him up there," he whispered. "Any way."

"Ali? Ibrahim?" she said. There was silence from the other end. "This is Lis, Lis Charnay." The background level continued to rise and Rodriguez fingered the scanner, trying to override the automatic channel locator. "Don't lose him, Rodriguez," Lorenz hissed.

"I talked with Saeed," Lis went on. "I know what you are feeling. We can meet again. We can talk. Ibrahim?" She thought she heard the Arabic farewell, *Fee Aman Illah*, but it could just have been the roar of static. "I'm having trouble hearing you, Ibrahim."

"Ground pursuit, sir," Tracy said from her post.

"What?" Lorenz said taking the receiver. "Jesus, you're kidding." Lorenz handed back the receiver. "He jumped. Our man jumped!"

CHAPTER 57

Spruceville

Ibrahim bin Sayyaf dropped from the Piper Cub at just below four thousand feet, the plane's wing dipping for a moment then righting itself again as he jumped. As soon as the officers and agents in the pursuit team saw the tiny figure detach itself from the aircraft and cartwheel towards the ground they pulled to a halt, waiting for the parachute to open. Five seconds passed, ten, before they realised there was no parachute. They watched the spinning body drift towards them at a terminal velocity of one hundred and twenty miles per hour and seconds later drop behind the heavy line of trees that border the upper reaches of the River Potomac.

In the dimly lit truck Lorenz and his team were scrambling to reset parameters. A Marine colonel who had joined the panel of experts now hooked up to the command centre offered the suggestion that they might be able to hook the plane out of the sky with a Chinook heavy-lift helicopter. The command team considered the proposal for a minute. They all knew instinctively the risk involved was huge and the idea was abandoned. Lorenz, never shy to ask the dumb question, was the first to break the ensuing silence.

"How the hell is it staying up?"

Danson, the agent Lorenz had sent on a quest for information about the Piper Cub supplied the answer. "These models are equipped with basic autopilot, sir. It's like cruise control. The pilot can lock it on, on long flights."

Lorenz stared at Danson unseeing, still trying to get a handle on this new development. "And?"

"We've got another wrinkle. We found a faxed order to a marine supply company in Alexandria billed to Khuda Bax's credit card and shipped here. A GPS, a Global Positioning System. $285. A Magellan 3000 XL. Tracks twelve satellites, carries two hundred and fifty way points."

"You called the company?" Jay asked. Danson nodded. Lorenz waited for an explanation, his eyes shifting from Peterson to Danson then back as if he suspected some conspiracy between them. Danson went on.

"Ibrahim may have hooked the GPS up to the autopilot. Carrollton's checking the laptop for the co-ordinates to tell us exactly where the plane is headed."

"You mean it's not headed for D.C.?" Lorenz could contain himself no longer. "I'm not getting any of this. Are we looking at a disaster about to happen or some nutcase Arab prank? What's going on?"

"If you wire the GPS into the autopilot, the GPS will technically fly the plane to within three hundred feet of the selected target, maybe less" Danson answered.

"What about the sprayer? I thought he was going to spray the stuff," Lorenz said exasperated.

"Maybe he is," Jay said. "I guess you could set up a crude timer that would trip the switch on the sprayer at the right moment. Or he's just rigged up some kind of explosive to detonate on impact. Either way it's a pretty effective device. They must've had plenty of time out here to fix it up."

"Get Carrollton in here," Lorenz said. "Find out what the boy has to say. And get me that Navy weapons specialist again, Rodriguez; the one we had on from the Pentagon. He may still be on the line. And someone get Carrollton, for Christ's sake."

"I'll get him," Connolly said backing out the door.

The videolink lit up. A man's face was displayed on the screen. "Bob?" The specialist sounded quite at ease as if the final minutes before the crude biological bomb reached the capital were leisure time.

"Here."

"This is Chris Chen, satellite guidance."

Lorenz looked helplessly at Jay. He came in range of the miniature camera sited over the monitor. "Hi. This is Jay Peterson. We've reason to believe that our man has hooked up the autopilot to a differential Magellan GPS. Can it be over-ridden?"

"Possibly. It could take a while."

All eyes went to the digital clock at the far end of the room. The aeroplane had been in flight for close to forty-seven minutes and was at best now twelve to thirteen minutes out from the capital. The nose could pitch forward at any moment sending the plane and its cargo to the ground.

"We've got ten minutes tops, Mr. Chen," Lorenz said. "It had better be good."

The weapons specialist at the other end was silent then directed a question they couldn't hear to a colleague seated beside him out of range of the camera. "If the GPS is a differential, that's good. It's probably getting its orders from any one of four or five satellites. You just can't screw around with those babies, but . . ." There was more discussion at the other end. "See, we – the military that is – build an error message into the system that only the differential systems can descramble. Standard GPS is only accurate to about 150 meters. Fixed ground stations compute this error and broadcast it to your GPS that then modifies its reading accordingly. Technically, you might be able to transmit a false error signal that would tell the GPS to guide the aircraft one way or the other."

"Could it be done from a radio station?" Peterson said.

"I guess. They'd have to transmit a "known error" message in their sub-signal, basically sending a correction to what the GPS is getting off the satellites. We're not going to be able to extend the flight path. It'll still run its course. We can only change the aircraft's direction so it comes down in a different sector of the perimeter. See what I mean?"

Jay picked up the map. He drew a circle with the McKenzies' farm as the centre, Washington D.C. at one point on the circle around it, then an "X" at a point further along. He flashed it at Lorenz. "How long's this going to take?" Lorenz said

"Give us the go and we'll get right onto it."

"You've got it. Keep us posted. Nine minutes."

The small blue screen went blank. "Keep him on the audio, Rodriguez. Don't lose him. Where are the choppers we waved off? Tracy get Andrews on. Rodriguez; the President still there?"

The Flight Deck at Andrews Airforce Base was back first. "I'm here, Bob. We're scrambled."

"Put 'em back alongside," Lorenz said. "Just an escort, okay? Don't touch him."

"Yes, sir," the Air Colonel said.

Then the President's voice filled the room. "Bob?"

"Mr. President, sir. Did you get all that?"

"Yes. Sounds like the right thing to do now," the Chief Executive said. "Where are we going to put this thing down?"

"Where's it coming down?" Lorenz asked the others in the room.

"Has to be water," Peterson said. "When it breaks up there's a better chance of the tank remaining intact."

"Anyone got a better idea?" the President's voice again. No one in the command truck or any of the others on the hook-up said anything. If the plane's under-fuselage tank did crack on landing and the bacteria inside were released, the surrounding area and anywhere downstream of the crash site could be contaminated for years, the bacteria seeping into the soil and forcing evacuation for miles around.

"Seven minutes," Tracy read off the clock.

"Are you going to be able to change the direction?" the President asked.

"Can't really tell till we try," Chen chimed in from the Pentagon. "I mean we may only be able to drop it."

"How about keeping it up?"

"Same thing, sir. Don't know till we try."

A wave of heat from outside washed into the room as the outside door opened and closed. They all turned. Carrollton was standing inside the room, his eyes screwed up to adjust to the light. Connolly was beside him. Even in the dim light of the interior, it was clear that Carrollton was shaken. Connolly spoke for him. "Mr. Carrollton discovered the co-ordinates." He looked at a scrap of paper in the palm of his hand. "Thirty eight degrees fifty three point six eight four minutes north,

seventy seven degrees one minute point five zero one west."
Connolly handed it to Jay.

The Pentagon's Chen was the first to respond.
"Pennsylvania Avenue and Ninth," Chen said. "The FBI building."

"Son of a bitch," said Lorenz.

The President of Georgetown University stood on the lawn of
his riverside house in Great Falls, Virginia, looking up. Aircraft
followed the Potomac to National Airport to comply with
noise abatement restrictions, passing his house and the
University a little further downstream. You got used to it
eventually. Now he was getting used to the absence of noise.
All flights into and out of National Airport had been closed for
the last fourteen hours. The sky was unnaturally quiet.

A sudden rumble from upstream broke the spell. Two
SkyHawk helicopters shepherding a lone single-engine crop-
sprayer and the dark silhouette of an F-16 riding herd over all
three aircraft, blocked out the morning sun. The aircraft
looked awfully low. A season of wonder and unnatural acts,
he thought as the aircraft passed and the roar began to dimin-
ish.

"This is Red Leader. We are on station."

"Who's this?" Lorenz queried.

"Lieutenant Flynn, sir. We have the Piper alongside." The
woman's voice was quite calm.

"Any way we can see what you see, Lieutenant Flynn?"
There was a moment's pause then suddenly in the Spruceville

command truck they had a visual on the videolink of the Piper Cub's empty cockpit thirty feet away, could see the accompanying helicopter beyond, the broad silver ribbon of the Potomac below. There was a burst of static, then: "This is Red Leader. Target descending through 2,700 feet, air speed one hundred twenty three knots."

"It's starting its descent," Jay said.

In the basement of <u>WROX</u>, the Oldies station, Todd Carradine and two of the station's executives were trying to follow the instructions being read to them over the phone. In the streets above them they had been assured, a car was headed towards the station with a specialist on board. He would help them out when he got there. For now, the three men were just going to have to do their best.

The call to the station hadn't gone through right away. When Lorenz had finally got Ben Frankel, the station manager, on the line the man thought it was a prank. The appearance of a Washington Police Sergeant in his doorway as if by magic thirty seconds later quickly changed his mind. The contact and the explanation had absorbed another three, almost four precious minutes as Chris Chen at the Pentagon talked Carradine through the operation and agreed on the commands.

Carradine put Chen on speakerphone and read back the frequency on which he was to transmit the error signal.

"Sounds good. Go for it, Todd." Carradine punched in the transmit button. Back in Spruceville Lorenz leaned in towards the videolink to get a better look, his shoulder at a level with the operator's face. The others, Jay, Lis, crowded in behind him.

Out on the Potomac, Billy Robinson had the engine of his 90-horsepower Mako shut down, two lines out, one over the bow, the other over the stern and the Four Tops cranked up on the headphones. He didn't see the convoy above him until they were directly overhead. "Damn," he said as he watched the Piper and its three escorts, the two SkyHawks either side, the F-16 still above suddenly edge left, all four aircraft apparently turning in unison.

"Ten degrees port." It was Flynn's voice, the pilot of the first helicopter.

"Wrong way," Lorenz yelled. "Back up."

"Cease transmission. Reverse the order, Todd." Chen's voice, still unruffled.

"Two minutes," Tracy called off.

In the command centre they watched the angle tilt as the helicopter continued its bank to the left, its port escort beyond no longer visible, the ground seeming impossibly close. The tower and nave of the Washington National Cathedral entered the frame.

"It's headed right downtown," Lorenz said in a deadpan voice. His was the only comment.

"Did you get it in, Todd?" Chen asked coolly. Todd read the reverse co-ordinates into the speakerphone, his voice shaky. "Good," Chen said. "Hit the transmit again."

The viewers in the command centre watched the plane yawing in the other direction, their view swinging through the horizon off the port wing and into the blue sky as the Piper's escort mimicked its moves.

"This is Red Leader. Descending through one thousand feet, pitch twenty three degrees, new heading one hundred sixty nine degrees south and east."

"Copy Red Leader," Chen acknowledged over the background. "Cut transmission, Todd." The screen cleared and Jay and the others saw the Mall and the capital's eastern suburbs as the crop-sprayer corrected.

"Seven hundred feet," the helicopter called. "Permission to disengage."

"Permission granted. Go ahead, Red Leader. Maintain visual."

Their image yawed upwards again then suddenly switched to the belly camera of the other helicopter. They were looking down on top of the Piper as it sank towards the river. It looked insubstantial, like a paper aeroplane. Jay could see cars on the parkways either side of the river headed out of the city but not moving, tiny figures at the sides of the road. The image zoomed in then out again slightly. It was hard to tell how high the plane was without a shadow underneath it, tracking along the river's surface. For a moment it seemed as if it would slam directly into the Woodrow Wilson Bridge but it glided over. The digital read out from the satellite track, linked to the command centre's computer, showed two hundred feet above sea level. The Piper tilted suddenly to port then just as abruptly corrected as its electrical systems shut down and it lost all power. The plane was in level flight but pitching sharply. As it fell through the remaining one hundred feet it began to roll, the nose and weight underneath pulling it forward.

"It's going in," Connolly said. "God help us all."

The cockpit led, the Plexiglas shattering as the weight of the plane behind it thrust it into the brown water of the Potomac. The violent shock of impact brought up the tail, the plane somersaulting, its roof smacking onto the water. This second shock separated the rusted anchor points that held the plane's belly tank in place. With a sudden crack the galvanised cylinder with one hundred ten pounds of anthrax inside separated from the fuselage and arced over the water towards the bank, the plane that had carried it beginning to sink rapidly. The cylinder skipped once, slapping the water, then cartwheeled as it rose again. It flew another one hundred feet then fell sharply, burying itself deep into the mud along the Potomac's shore, only the upper end visible with the small nozzle that had connected it to the sprayer unit showing above the surface. A snowy egret lifted off the marsh, winging away to the south, and the cylinder slipped a couple more inches, a brown bubble pushing itself out of the surface and bursting with a faint pop. As the cylinder came to rest a milk-like liquid began to ooze from a hairline crack across the cylinder's top end and trickle down the exterior towards the mud flat.

CHAPTER 58

Nantucket

The horde was in full flight, scrambling up the bank. The minute animals climbed over each other in their panic to escape. The ground seemed to be moving.

Jay said: "You know why they're called fiddler crabs?" Lis shook her head. "Because the males have one oversize claw. See? It can weigh as much as half their weight. When they want the female's attention they wave the claw, then rub their body parts together and dance."

"Sounds irresistible."

He and Lis had left Washington behind, driven the nine hours to Hyannis then taken the slow ferry to Nantucket, twenty five miles off the coast of Massachusetts. "I want to feel like I'm getting there, not just arriving," she'd said. "I want to know how long it takes."

The city was still picking up the pieces, the clean-up crews working over the shores of the Potomac. The anthrax, it had been anthrax and not the more lethal agent botulin, that had leaked from the plane's tank had not been contained and was seeping into the Potomac. Prognosis for the area was not good. Patching up the social consequences of Ibrahim's attack was going to take as long, sorting out where to lay the blame – there was plenty to go round – and who to bill.

Connolly had insisted that Lis and Jay attend a celebration barbecue before they left. He had quit smoking but seemed to be compensating by charring the burgers on the grill even more than usual and inhaling the black fumes.

The next afternoon there had been an embarrassing function at the White House, the Presidential family and the rank and file of the Bureau's Counterterrorism section in attendance. There had been no medals as Lorenz had predicted, only some handshakes, a lot of back-slapping and as many platitudes served up as hors-d'oeuvres. That was when Connolly offered his house on Nantucket as a get-away giving Jay and Lis no time to re-consider. They had left that same afternoon in Jay's car.

They had motored up Nantucket Harbour in Connolly's ancient Boston Whaler, the engine smoking predictably. It had got them up to the head of the inlet and Coskata, a miniature estuary. There had been few people in town this early in the year. There was no one on the beach.

Jay and Lis walked along the tidal flat. The fiddler crabs fled into their holes at their approach. They found a spot on a dune where they could watch the tiny creatures go about their business without interrupting them. A heron fished at the water's edge, the sunlight catching the blue on its back, a light breeze ruffling its feathers.

"Are you always this serious?"

"I'm only serious when you're around," he said. "Mostly I have a one-track mind." He reached one arm over her, rolling in towards her body as if to embrace her.

"Not yet, Jay," she said quietly, checking his advance. It

was her turn to be serious. "Not just yet." She looked out across the water of the harbour separated from them by a low sand bar. "Do you know why he jumped?"

"Ibrahim? I guess because he knew he'd blown all his options. Why?"

"It think it was because of me."

Jay looked at her, watching her eyes, his hand reaching out to hers and taking it. His long slim fingers slid over hers, stroking her palm.

"I know this will sound strange but I think Ibrahim had lived so long alone in the wilderness, was so married to his cause that when he realised that I was more than just a means of getting his message out, when he started to show his emotions again, he couldn't take it." She turned to Jay now. "I think he couldn't live with the idea that there was some force greater than his anger, greater than his faith. Is that possible?"

Jay watched her admiringly. Then he said: "There could be no other reason."

"You!" Lis scrambled up, kicking sand over him then walked over the low dune to the sea beyond. He followed, catching up to her at the water's edge and wrapping his arms round her.

She looked at Jay, her hand lifting his glasses carefully off his nose, her mouth moving towards his. Her hand dropped, letting the glasses fall to the sand, the wide horizon of the Atlantic now rounded in their lenses.

WIND OF WRATH